NIGHT OF THE
LOVING DEAD . . .

And there, under the bridge, swathed in darkness, she leaned against him again and took his thick head between her slim, pale hands and put her mouth against his and let the sweet smell of her wash over him. She kissed him for a long moment, nipping at his lips with her teeth, and he made a small sound, like a tiny animal being stroked. But she was ahead of him. Her passion was already aroused.

And now Claire went away, to be replaced by something else.

A child of the night.

With the last flickering awareness of her departing humanity, she perceived the instant he knew he was in the love embrace of something else.

It was the instant she changed.

But that instant was too short for him to free himself. . . .

—from "Footsteps" by Harlan Ellison

Hot Blood

TALES OF PROVOCATIVE HORROR

Edited by
JEFF GELB
AND
LONN FRIEND

POCKET BOOKS
New York   London   Toronto   Sydney   Tokyo

An *Original* Publication of POCKET BOOKS

POCKET BOOKS, a division of Simon & Schuster Inc.
1230 Avenue of the Americas, New York, NY 10020

ISBN: 0-671-66424-7

First Pocket Books printing May 1989

10 9 8 7 6 5 4 3 2 1

POCKET and colophon are trademarks of
Simon & Schuster Inc.

Printed in the U.S.A.

PERMISSIONS

This book is dedicated to Joyce and Terry,
who put up with our sexual idiosyncracies.

Special thanks to . . . Dennis Etchison, David Schow, Richard Lange, Michael Garrett, Claire Zion, and Kurt Busiek.

CONTENTS

INTRODUCTION   *xiii*

CHANGELING   *1*
   Graham Masterton
THE LIKENESS OF JULIE   *27*
   Richard Matheson
THE THANG   *37*
   Robert R. McCammon
MÉNAGE À TROIS   *53*
   F. Paul Wilson
MR. RIGHT   *83*
   Richard Christian Matheson
BLOOD NIGHT   *86*
   Chet Williamson
CHOCOLATE   *102*
   Mick Garris
AGAIN   *113*
   Ramsey Campbell
BUG HOUSE   *125*
   Lisa Tuttle
VENGEANCE IS.   *146*
   Theodore Sturgeon
THE UNKINDEST CUT   *154*
   J. N. Williamson
REUNION   *160*
   Michael Garrett

FOOTSTEPS 173
 Harlan Ellison
PRETTY IS . . . 185
 Mike Newton
AUNT EDITH 196
 Gary Brandner
DAUGHTER OF THE GOLDEN WEST 205
 Dennis Etchison
MEAT MARKET 217
 John Skipp and Craig Spector
THE VOICE 224
 Rex Miller
THE MODEL 229
 Robert Bloch
CARNAL HOUSE 238
 Steve Rasnic Tem
THEY'RE COMING FOR YOU 249
 Les Daniels
SUZIE SUCKS 255
 Jeff Gelb
PUNISHMENTS 263
 Ray Garton
RED LIGHT 276
 David J. Schow

AUTHOR BIOGRAPHIES 297

INTRODUCTION

*Only two topics can be of least interest to a
serious and studious mind—sex and the
dead.*

—W. B. Yeats

Readers of fiction have long been drawn to a mix of the
taboo topics sex and horror. Experienced vicariously from
armchairs (or, more appropriately, beds), generations of
readers and film lovers have found sex and horror a marriage made in Heaven . . . or perhaps Hell. In such literary
classics as *Dracula* and *The Hunchback of Notre Dame,* and
box-office smashes like *Psycho* and *Halloween,* sex and
horror have made for perfect, if strange, bedfellows.

Hot Blood is the first major anthology to ask the world's
premier horror writers to share their secret sexual nightmares. The masters are here: Robert Bloch, Richard
Matheson, Harlan Ellison, even a contribution from Theodore Sturgeon, whose 1979 story *Vengeance Is.* is a prophet-
ic tale of perversion that hints of a disease similar to the
modern plague of AIDS. In addition, *Hot Blood* features a
collection of '80s visionaries, from Ramsey Campbell,
Robert R. McCammon, F. Paul Wilson, and Graham
Masterton, to sizzling new talents like David J. Schow,
Skipp and Spector, and Rex Miller.

Sexual attraction is, perhaps, one of the most powerful
and mysterious forces of nature, an element carefully inter-
woven between these pages. Those readers who happen to
be in the market for a new lover are urged, upon completion

of this book, to reevaluate qualities most often sought in the opposite sex and to consider adding "human" to the top of the list. In fact, these days, reading *Hot Blood* may be one of the few remaining forms of "safe sex" available.

And isn't *that* a scary thought?

Jeff Gelb
Lonn Friend
April 1989

Hot Blood

CHANGELING

Graham Masterton

The elevator door opened and there she was, looking directly into his eyes as if she had known that he was standing on the other side. Tall, beautiful, dressed utterly in white. He hesitated for a moment and then stepped back one half-shuffle to allow her to pass.

"Pardon mivrouw," he acknowledged. She smiled briefly but didn't reply. She passed him in a pungent swirl of Calvin Klein's Obsession, and he turned around and watched her walk across the marble lobby and out through the revolving door. Out on the hotel steps her long brunette hair was lifted for a moment by the April wind. Then the doorman came forward to salute her and she was gone.

"You're going up?" asked an irritated American who was waiting for him in the elevator, his finger pressed on the Doors Open button.

"I'm sorry? Oh, no. I've changed my mind."

He heard the man say, "For Chrissake, some people . . ." and then he found himself hurrying across the lobby and out through the door, just in time to see her climbing into the back of a taxi.

The doorman approached him and touched his cap. "Taxi, sir?"

"No, no, thank you." He stood holding his briefcase, the skirts of his raincoat flapping, watching the woman's taxi turn into Sarphatistraat, feeling abandoned and grainy and

1

weird, like a character in a black-and-white art movie. The doorman stood beside him, smiling uneasily.

"Do you happen to know that lady's name?" he asked. His voice sounded blurry in the wind. The doorman shook his head.

"Is she a guest here?"

"I'm sorry, sir. It is not permissible for me to say."

Gil reached into his inside pocket and for one moment considered bribery; but there was something in the doorman's smile that warned him against it. He said, "Oh, okay, sure," and retreated awkwardly back through the revolving door. The two elderly hall porters beamed and nodded at him as he returned to the elevator. Stan and Ollie, one thin and one fat. They were obviously quite accustomed to eccentric behavior.

Gil stood in the oak-paneled elevator as it took him up to the third floor and scrutinized himself in the brass-framed mirror with as much intensity as if he were a business partner whom he suspected of cracking up. He had never done anything in years as spontaneous as chasing after that woman. What the hell had come over him? He was married, with two children, he was right on top of his job. He had a six-bedroom house in Woking, a new Granada Scorpio, and he had been profiled in *Business Week* as one of the new breed of "totally committed" young entrepreneurs.

And yet he had hurried after that unknown woman as gauche and panicky as an adolescent autograph hunter.

He closed the door of his suite behind him and stood for a long time in the middle of the room with his briefcase still in his hand, thinking. Then he set the briefcase down and slowly took off his coat. *"Pity about Gil, he's thrown a wobbly."* He could almost hear them talking about him in the office. *"He was absolutely fine until that Amsterdam business. Probably suffering from overwork."*

He went to the window and opened it. The hotel room overlooked the Amstel River, wide and gray, where it was crossed by the wide elevating bridge called the Hogesluis. Trams rumbled noisily over the sluice, their bells ringing, on their way to the suburbs. The wind blew so coldly through the window that the net curtains were lifted, shuddering, and Gil found that there were tears in his eyes.

He checked his pulse. It was slightly too fast, but nothing to take to the doctor. He didn't feel feverish, either. He had been working for four days, Tuesday to Friday, sixteen to eighteen hours a day, but he had been careful not to drink too much and to rest whenever he could. Of course, it was impossible to judge what effect this round of negotiations might have had on his brain. But he *felt* normal.

But he thought of her face and he thought of her hair and he thought of the way in which she had smiled at him; a smile that had dissolved as quickly as soluble aspirin; and then was gone. And against all the psychological and anthropological logic in the world, he knew that he had fallen in love with her. Well, maybe not in *love*, maybe not actually in *love*, not the way he loved Margaret. But she had looked into his eyes and smiled at him and wafted past in beguiling currents of Obsession, and in ten seconds he had experienced more excitement, more curiosity, more plain straightforward *desire* than he had in the last ten years of marriage.

It's ridiculous, he said to himself. It's just a moment of weakness. I'm tired, I'm suffering from stress. I'm lonely, too. Nobody ever understands how lonely it can be, traveling abroad on business. No wonder so many businessmen stay in their hotel rooms, drinking too much whiskey and watching television programs they can't understand. There is no experience so friendless as walking the streets of a strange city with nobody to talk to.

He closed the window and went to the mini-bar to find himself a beer. He switched on the television and watched the news in Dutch. Tomorrow morning, after he had collected the signed papers from the Gemeentevervoerbedrijf, he would take a taxi straight to Schiphol and fly back to London. Against ferocious competition from Volvo and M.A.N. Diesel, he had won an order for twenty-eight new buses for Amsterdam's municipal transport system, all to be built in Oxford.

On the phone Brian Taylor had called him "a bloody marvel." Margaret had squealed in delight, like she always did.

But the way the wind had lifted up that woman's hair kept running and rerunning in his mind like a tiny scrap of film

3

that had been looped to play over and over. The revolving door had turned, her hair had lifted. Shining and dark, the kind of hair that should be spread out over silk pillows.

It began to grow dark and the lights began to dip and sparkle in the river and the trams began to grind their way out to Oosterpark and the farther suburbs. Gil consulted the room-service menu to see what he could have for supper, but after he had called up to order the smoked eel and the veal schnitzel, with a half-bottle of white wine, he was taken with a sudden surge of panic about eating alone, and he called back and canceled his order.

"You don't *want* the dinner, sir?" The voice was flat, Dutch-accented, polite but curiously hostile.

"No, thank you. I've . . . changed my mind."

He went to the bathroom and washed his face and hands. Then he straightened his necktie, shrugged on his coat, picked up his key, and went down to the hotel's riverside bar for a drink. The bar was crowded with Japanese and American businessmen. Only two women, and both of them were quite obviously senior executives, one lopsidedly beautiful, the other as hard-faced as a man. He sat up on a barstool and ordered a whiskey and soda.

"Cold wind today, hmh?" the barman asked him.

He drank his whiskey too quickly, and he was about to order another one when the woman came and sat just one stool away from him, still dressed in white, still fragrant with Obsession. She smiled to the barman and asked for a Bacardi, in English.

Gil felt as if he were unable to breathe. He had never experienced anything like it. It was a kind of panic, like claustrophobia, and yet it had an extraordinary quality of erotic compulsion, too. He could understand why people half-strangled themselves to intensify their sexual arousal, because as he sat there breathless he could feel himself stiffening inside his pants. He stared at himself glassy-eyed in the mirror behind the Genever gin bottles, trying to detect any signs of emotional breakdown. But did it show, when you finally cracked? Did your face fall apart like a broken jug? Or was it all kept tightly inside of you? Did it snap in the back of your brain where nobody could see?

He glanced covertly sideways, first at the woman's thigh,

then more boldly at her face. She was looking straight ahead, at the mirror. Her nose was classically straight, her eyes were cobalt-blue, slightly slanted, very European. Her lips were glossed with crimson. He noticed a bracelet of yellow and white gold, intertwined, that must have cost the equivalent of three months of his salary, including expenses, and a gold Ebel wristwatch. Her nails were long and crimson and perfect. She moved slightly sideways on her stool and he noticed the narrowness of her waist and the full sway of her breasts. She's naked underneath that dress, he thought to himself, or practically naked. She's just too incredibly sexy to be true.

What could he say to her? Should he say anything? *Could* he say anything? He thought dutifully for a moment about Margaret, but he knew that he was only being dutiful. This woman existed on a different planet from Margaret, she was one of a different species. She was feminine, sexual, undomesticated, elegant, and probably dangerous, too.

The barman approached him. "Can I fix you another drink, sir?"

"I—unh—"

"Oh, go ahead"—the woman smiled—"I can't bear to drink alone."

Gil flushed, and grinned, and shrugged, and said, "All right, then. Yes." He turned to the woman and asked, "How about you?"

"Thank you," she acknowledged, passing her glass to the barman, although there was a curious intonation in her voice which made it sound as if she were saying thank you for something else altogether.

The barman set up the drinks. They raised their glasses to each other and said, *"Prost!"*

"Are you staying here?" Gil asked the woman. He wished his words didn't sound so tight and high-pitched.

"In Amsterdam?"

"I mean here, at the Amstel Hotel."

"No, no," she said. "I live by the sea, in Zandvoort. I only came here to meet a friend of mine."

"You speak perfect English," he told her.

"Yes," she replied. Gil waited, expecting her to tell him what she did for a living, but she remained silent.

"I'm in transportation," he volunteered. "Well, buses, actually."

She focused her eyes on him narrowly, but still she said nothing. Gil said, "I go back to London tomorrow. Job's over."

"Why did you come running after me?" she asked. "You know when—this afternoon, when I was leaving the hotel. You came running after me, and you stood outside the hotel and watched me go."

Gil opened and closed his mouth. Then he lifted both hands helplessly and said, "I don't know. I really don't know. It was—I don't know. I just did it."

She kept her eyes focused on him as sharply as a camera. "You desire me," she said.

Gil didn't reply, but uncomfortably sat back on his bar stool.

Without hesitation the woman leaned forward and laid her open hand directly between his legs. She was very close now. Her lips were parted and he could see the tips of her front teeth. He could smell the Bacardi on her breath. Warm, soft, even breath.

"You desire me," she repeated.

She gave him one quick, hard squeeze, and then sat back. Her face was filled with silent triumph. Gil looked at her with a mixture of excitement and embarrassment and disbelief. She had actually reached over and squeezed him between the legs, this beautiful woman in the white dress, this beautiful woman whom every businessman in the bar would have given his Christmas bonus just to sit with.

"I don't even know your name," said Gil, growing bolder.

"Is that necessary?"

"I don't really suppose it is. But I'd like to. My name's Gil Batchelor."

"Anna."

"Is that all, just Anna?"

"It's a palindrome," she smiled. "That means that it's the same backward as it is forward. I try to live up to it."

"Could I buy you some dinner?"

"Is *that* necessary?"

Gil took three long heartbeats to reply. "Necessary in what sense?" he asked her.

"In the sense that you feel it necessary to court me somehow. To buy me dinner; to impress me with your taste in wine; to make witty small talk. To tell me all those humorous anecdotes which I am sure your colleagues have heard one hundred times at least. Is all that necessary?"

Gil licked his lips. Then he said, "Maybe we should take a bottle of champagne upstairs."

Anna smiled. "I'm not a prostitute, you know. The barman thinks I'm a prostitute, but of course prostitutes are good for business, provided they are suitably dressed and behave according to the standards expected by the hotel. If you take me up to your room now, let me tell you truthfully that you will be only the second man I have ever slept with."

Gil gave Anna a complicated shrug with which he intended to convey the feeling that he was flattered by what she had said, but couldn't take her seriously. A woman with Anna's style and Anna's body and Anna's sexual directness had slept in the whole of her life with only one man?

Anna said, "You don't believe me."

"I don't have to believe you, do I? That's part of the game." Gil thought that response was quite clever and sophisticated.

But Anna reached out toward him and gently picked a single hair from the shoulder of his coat and said very quietly, "It's not a game, my love."

She undressed in silence, close to the window, so that her body was outlined by the cold glow of the streetlights outside, but her face remained in a shadow. Her dress slipped to the floor with a sigh. Underneath, she was naked except for a tiny *cache-sex* of white embroidered cotton. Her breasts were large, almost too large for a woman with such a narrow back, and her nipples were wide and pale as sugarfrosting.

Gil watched her, unbuttoning his shirt. He could sense her smiling. She came over and buried the fingers of one hand into the curly brown hair on his chest, and tugged at it. She kissed his cheeks, then his lips. Then she reached down and started to unfasten his belt.

Gil thought: *This is morally wrong, dammit. I'm cheating the woman who gave me my children; the woman who's waiting for me to come home tomorrow. But how often does a man run into a sexual dream like this? Supposing I tell her to get dressed and leave. I'll spend the rest of my life wondering what it could have been like.*

Anna slid her hands into the back of his trousers. Her sharp fingernails traced the line of his buttocks, and he couldn't help shivering. "Lie down on the bed," she whispered. "Let me make love to you."

Gil sat on the edge of the bed and struggled out of his trousers. Then Anna pushed him gently backward. He heard the softest plucking of elastic as she took off her *cache-sex*. She climbed astride his chest and sat in the semidarkness smiling at him, her hair like a soft and mysterious veil. "Do you like to be kissed?" she asked him. "There are so many ways to be kissed."

She lifted herself up and teasingly lowered her vulva so that it kissed his lips. Her pubic hair was silky and long, and rose up in a plume. Gil kissed her, hesitantly at first, then deeper, holding her open with his fingers.

She gave a deep, soft murmur of pleasure and ran her fingers through his hair.

They made love four times that night. Anna seemed to be insatiable. When the first slate-gray light of morning began to strain into the room, and the trams began to boom over Hogesluis again, Gil lay back in bed watching her sleep, her hair tangled on the pillow. He cupped her breast in his hand, and then ran his fingers gently all the way down the flatness of her stomach to her dark-haired sex. She was more than a dream, she was irresistible. She was everything that anybody could desire. Gil kissed her lightly on the forehead, and when she opened her eyes and looked up at him and smiled, he knew that he was already falling in love with her.

"You have to go back to England today," she said softly.

"I don't know. Maybe."

"You mean you could stay a little longer?"

Gil looked at her, but at the same time he made a conscious effort to picture Margaret, as if he were watching a movie with a split screen. He could imagine Margaret sitting on the sofa sewing and glancing at the clock every few minutes to see if it was time for him to be landing at

Gatwick Airport. He could see her opening the front door and smiling and kissing him and telling him what Alan had been doing at playschool.

"Maybe another day," Gil heard himself saying, as if there were somebody else in the room who spoke just like him.

Anna drew his head down and kissed him. Her tongue slipped in between his teeth. Then she lay back and whispered, "What about two days? I could take you to Zandvoort. We could go to my house, and then we could spend all day and all night and all the next day making love."

"I'm not sure that I can manage two days."

"Call your office. Tell them you may be able to sell the good burghers of Amsterdam a few more of your buses. A day and a night and a day. You can go home on Sunday night. The plane won't be so crowded then."

Gil hesitated, and then kissed her. "All right, then. What the hell. I'll call the airline after breakfast."

"And your wife? You have to call your wife."

"I'll call her."

Anna stretched out like a beautiful sleek animal. "You are a very special gentleman, Mr. Gil Batchelor," she told him.

"Well, you're a very special lady."

Margaret had sniffled: that had made him feel so guilty that he had nearly agreed to come back to England straight away. She missed him, everything was ready for him at home, Alan kept saying, "Where's daddy?" And *why* did he have to stay in Holland for another two days? Surely the Dutch people could telephone him, or send him a telex? And why *him?* George Kendall should have been selling those extra buses, not him.

In the end, it was her whining that gave him the strength to say, "I have to, that's all. I don't like it any more than you do, darling, believe me. I miss you, too, and Alan. But it's only two more days. And then we'll all go to Brighton for the day, what about that? We'll have lunch at Wheeler's."

He put down the phone. Anna was watching him from across the room. She was sitting on a large white leather sofa, wearing only thin pajama trousers of crepe silk. Between her bare breasts she held a heavy crystal glass of Bacardi. The coldness of the glass had made her nipples tighten. She was smiling at him in a way that he found oddly disturbing. She looked almost triumphant, as if by persuading him to lie to Margaret, she had somehow captured a little part of his soul.

Behind her, through the picture window that was framed with cheese-plants and ivy, he could see the concrete promenade, the wide gray beach, the gray overhanging clouds, and the restless horizon of the North Sea.

He came and sat down beside her. He touched her lips with his fingertip, and she kissed it. His hand followed the warm heavy curve of her breast, and then he gently rolled her nipple between finger and thumb. She watched him, still smiling.

"Do you think you could ever fall in love with somebody like me?" she asked him, in a whisper.

"I don't think there is anybody like you. Only you."

"So could you fall in love with me?"

He dared to say it. "I think I already have."

She set her drink down on the glass and stainless-steel table next to her and knelt up on the sofa. She tugged down her pajama trousers so that she was naked. She pushed Gil on to his back and climbed on top of him. "You like kissing me, don't you?" she murmured. He didn't answer, but lifted his head slightly, and licked all the way down that liquid crevice from top to bottom, and swallowed.

The house was always silent, except when they spoke, or when they played music. Anna liked Mozart symphonies, but she always played them in another room. The walls were white and bare, the carpets were gray. The inside of the house seemed to be a continuation of the bleak coastal scenery that Gil could see through the windows. Apart from the houseplants there were no ornaments. The few pictures on the walls were lean, spare drawings of naked men and women, faceless most of them. Gil had the feeling that the house didn't actually belong to Anna, that it had been occupied by dozens of different people, none of whom had left their mark on it. It was a house of no individuality whatsoever. An anxious house, at the very end of a cul-de-sac that fronted the beach. The gray brick sidewalks were always swirled with gritty gray sand. The wind blew like a constant headache.

They made love over and over again. They went for walks on the beach, the collars of their coats raised up against the stinging sand. They ate silent meals of cold meat and bread and cold white wine. They listened to Mozart in other rooms. On the third morning Gil woke up and saw that Anna was awake already, and watching him. He reached out and stroked her hair.

"This is the day I have to go home," he told her, his voice still thick from sleeping.

She took hold of his hand and squeezed it. "Can't you manage one more day? One more day and one more night?"

"I have to go home. I promised Margaret. And I have to be back behind my desk on Monday morning."

She lowered her head so that he couldn't see her face. "You know that—if you go—we will never be able to see each other any more."

Gil said nothing. It hurt too much to think that he might never sleep with Anna again in the whole of his life. He eased himself out from under the quilt and walked through to the bathroom. He switched on the light over the basin and inspected himself. He looked tired. Well, anybody would be, after two days and three nights of orgiastic sex with a woman like Anna. But there was something else about his face which made him frown, a different look about it. He stared at himself for a long time, but he couldn't decide what it was. He filled the basin with hot water and squirted a handful of shaving-foam into his hand.

It was only when he lifted his hand toward his face that he realized he didn't need a shave.

He hesitated, then he rinsed off the foam and emptied the basin. He must have shaved last night, before he went to bed, and forgotten about it. After all, they had drunk quite a lot of wine. He went to the toilet, and sat down, and urinated in quick fits and starts. It was only when he got up and wiped himself by passing a piece of toilet paper between his legs that he realized what he had done. *I never sit down to pee. I'm not a woman.*

Anna was standing in the bathroom doorway watching him. He laughed. "I must be getting old, sitting down to pee."

She came up to him and put her arms around his neck and kissed him. It was a long, complicated, yearning kiss. When he opened his eyes again she was staring at him very close up. "Don't go," she whispered. "Not yet, I couldn't bear it. Give me one more day. Give me one more night."

"Anna . . . I can't. I have a family; a job."

With the same directness she had exhibited in the bar of the Amstel Hotel, she took hold of his penis and clasped it in her hand. His reaction was immediate. "Don't go," she repeated, massaging him slowly up and down. "I've been waiting so long for somebody like you . . . I can't bear to lose you just yet. One more day, one more night. You can catch the evening flight on Monday and be back in England before nine."

He kissed her. He knew that he was going to give in.

That day they walked right down to the edge of the ocean. A dog with wet bedraggled fur circled around and around, yapping at them. The wind from the North Sea was relentless. When they returned to the house, Gil felt inexplicably exhausted. Anna undressed him and helped him up to the bedroom. "I think I'm feeling the strain," he said, smiling at her. She leaned over and kissed him. He lay with his eyes open, listening to Mozart playing in another room and looking at the way the gray afternoon light crossed the ceiling and illuminated the pen-and-ink drawing of a man and a woman entwined together. The drawing was like a puzzle. It was impossible to tell where the man ended and where the woman began.

He fell asleep. It started to rain, salty rain from the sea. He slept all afternoon and all evening, and the wind rose and the rain lashed furiously against the windows.

He was still asleep at two o'clock in the morning, when the bedroom door opened and Anna came in and softly slipped into bed beside him. "My darling," Anna murmured, and touched the smoothness of his cheek.

He dreamed that Anna was shaking him awake, and lifting his head so that he could sip a glass of water. He dreamed that she was caressing him and murmuring to him. He dreamed that he was trying to run across the beach, across the wide gray sands, but the sands turned to glue and clung around his ankles. He heard music, voices.

He opened his eyes. It was twilight. The house was silent. He turned to look at his watch on the bedside table. It was 7:17 in the evening. His head felt congested, as if he had a hangover, and when he licked his lips they felt swollen and dry. He lay back for a long time staring at the ceiling, his arms by his sides. He must have been ill, or maybe he had drunk too much. He had never felt like this in his life before.

It was only when he raised his hand to rub his eyes that he understood that something extraordinary had happened to him. His arm was obstructed by a huge soft growth on his chest. He felt a cold thrill of complete terror and instantly yanked down the quilt. When he saw his naked body, he let out a high-pitched shout of fright.

He had breasts. Two heavy, well-rounded breasts, with fully developed nipples. He grasped them in his hands and realized they weren't tumorous growths, they weren't cancers, they were actual female breasts, and very big breasts, too. Just like Anna's.

Trembling, he ran his right hand down his sides, and felt a narrow waist, a flat stomach, and then silky pubic hair. He knew what he was going to feel between his legs, but he held himself back for minute after minute, his eyes closed, not daring to believe that it had gone, that he had been emasculated. At last, however, he slipped his fingers down between his hairless thighs, and felt the moist lips of his vulva. He hesitated, swallowed, and then slipped one finger into his vagina.

There was no question about it. His body was completely female, inside and out. In appearance, at least, he was a woman.

"None of this is real," he told himself, but even his voice was feminine. He climbed slowly out of bed and his breasts swayed, just the way that Anna's had swayed. He walked across the room and confronted the full-length mirror beside the dressing table. There was a woman looking back at him, a beautiful naked woman, and the woman was him.

"This isn't real," he repeated, cupping his breasts in his hands and staring intently at the face in the mirror. The eyes were his, the expression was his. He could see himself inside that face, his own personality, Gil Batchelor the bus salesman from Woking. But who else was going to be able to see what he saw? What was Brian Taylor going to see, if he tried to turn up for work? And, God Almighty, what was Margaret going to say, if he came back home looking like this?

Without a sound, he collapsed to the floor, and lay with his face against the gray carpet, in total shock. He lay there until it grew dark, feeling chilled, but unwilling or unable to move. He wasn't sure which and he wasn't going to find out.

At last, when the room was completely dark, the door opened, and a dim light fell across the floor. Gil heard a voice saying, "You're awake. I'm sorry. I should have come in earlier."

Gil lifted his head. Unconsciously, he drew his long tangled hair out of his eyes, and looked up. A man was silhouetted in the doorway, a man wearing a business suit and polished shoes.

"Who are you?" he asked hoarsely. "What the hell has happened to me?"

The man said, "You've changed, that's all."

"For Christ's sake, look at me. What the hell is going on here? Did you do this with hormones, or what? I'm a man! I'm a *man,* for Christ's sake!" Gil began to weep, and the tears slid down his cheeks and tasted salty on his lips.

The man came forward and knelt down beside him and laid a comforting hand on his shoulder. "It wasn't hormones. If I knew how it happened, believe me, I'd tell you. But all I know is, it happens. One man to the next. The man who was Anna before me—the man who took the body that used to be mine—he told me everything about it, just as I'm telling you—and just as *you'll* tell the next man that you pick."

At that moment the bedroom door swung a little wider, and the man's face was illuminated by the light from the hallway. With a surge of paralyzing fright, Gil saw that the man was him. His own face, his own hair, his own smile. His own wristwatch, his own suit. And outside in the hallway, his own suitcase, already packed.

"I don't understand," he whispered. He wiped the tears away from his face with his fingers.

"I don't think any of us ever will," the man told him. "There seems to be some kind of pattern to it; some kind of reason why it happens; but there's no way of finding out what it is."

"But you knew this was going to happen all along," said Gil. "Right from the very beginning. You *knew.*"

The man nodded. Gil should have been violent with rage. He should have seized the man by the throat and beaten his head against the wall. But the man was him, and for some inexplicable reason he was terrified of touching him.

The man said, quietly, "I'm sorry for you. Please believe me. But I'm just as sorry for myself. I used to be a man like you. My name was David Chilton. I was thirty-two years old, and I used to lease executive aircraft. I had a family, a wife and two daughters, and a house in Darien, Connecticut."

He paused, and then he said, "Four months ago I came to Amsterdam and met Anna. One thing led to another, and she took me back here. She used to make me go down on her, night after night. Then one morning I woke up and *I* was Anna, and Anna was gone."

Gil said, "I can't believe any of this. This is madness. I'm having a nightmare."

The man shook his head. "It's true; and it's been happening to one man after another, for years probably."

"How do you know that?"

"Because Anna took my passport and my luggage, and it seemed to me that there was only one place that she could go—*he* could go. Only one place where he could survive in my body and with my identity."

Gil stared at him. "You mean—your own home? He took your body and went to live in your own home?"

The man nodded. His face was grim. Gil had never seen himself look so grim before.

"I found Anna's passport and Anna's bank books—don't worry, I've left them all for you. I flew to New York and then rented a car and drove up to Connecticut. I parked outside my own house and watched myself mowing my own lawn, playing with my own daughters, kissing my own wife."

He lowered his head, and then he said, "I could have killed him, I guess. Me, I mean—or at least the person who looked like me. But what would that have achieved? I would have made a widow out of my own wife, and orphans out of my own children. I loved them too much for that. I love them still."

"You left them alone?" Gil whispered.

"What else could I do? I flew back to Holland and here I am."

Gil said, "Couldn't you have *stayed* like Anna? Why couldn't you stay the way you were? Why did you have to take *my* body?"

"Because I'm a man," David Chilton told him. "Because I was brought up a man, and because I think like a man, and because it doesn't matter how beautiful a woman you are, how rich a woman you are . . . well, you're going to find out what it's like, believe me. Not even the poorest most downtrodden guy in the whole wide world has to endure what women have to endure. Supposing every time that a woman came up to a man, she stared at his crotch instead of his face, even when they were supposed to be having a serious conversation? You don't think that happens? You did it to me, when we met at the hotel. Eighty percent of the time your eyes were ogling my tits, and I know what you were thinking. Well, now it's going to happen to you. And, believe me, after a couple of months, you're going to go pick up some guy not because you want to live like a man again but because you want your revenge on all those jerkoffs who treat you like a sex object instead of a human being."

Gil knelt on the floor and said nothing. David Chilton checked Gil's wristwatch—the one that Margaret had given him on their last anniversary—and said, "I'd better go. I've booked a flight at eleven."

"You're not—" Gil began.

David Chilton made a face. "What else can I do? Your wife's expecting me home. A straight ordinary-looking man like me. Not a voluptuous brunette like you."

"But Margaret's going to know you straight away. You

may *look* like me, but you're not me, are you? She'll know you're not me the minute you walk into the house. So will my dog."

"Bondy?"

Gil felt a prickle of deep apprehension. He had never told Anna that his dog was called Bondy.

David Chilton said, "I've taken more than your shape, Gil. I've taken your memory, too. In the middle left-hand drawer of your desk at home, you have a flashlight, most of your credit card statements, a stapler, and the souvenir issue of *Playboy* when they stopped putting staples through the centerfold. Your father used to play the bassoon on Sunday afternoons, even though your mother tried to persuade him not to."

"Oh, Jesus," said Gil, shivering.

"You want more?" asked David Chilton.

"You can't do this," Gil told him. "It's theft!"

"Theft? How can a man steal something that everybody in the whole world will agree is his?"

"Then it's murder, for God's sake! You've effectively killed me!"

"Murder?" David Chilton shook his head. "Come on, now, Anna, I really have to go."

"I'll kill you," Gil warned him.

"I don't think so," said David Chilton. "Maybe you'll think about it, the way that I thought about killing the guy who took my body. But there's a diary in the living room, a diary kept by most of the men who have changed into Anna. Read it before you think of doing anything drastic."

He reached out and touched Gil's hair, almost regretfully. "You'll survive. You have clothes, you have a car, you have money in the bank. You even have an investment portfolio. You're not a poor woman. Fantasy women never are. If you want to stay as Anna, you can live quite comfortably for the rest of your life. Or . . . if you get tired of it, you know what to do."

Gil sat on the floor incapable of doing anything at all to prevent David Chilton from leaving. He was too traumatized; too drained of feeling. David Chilton went to the end of the hallway and picked up his suitcase. He turned and smiled at Gil one last time, and then blew him a kiss.

"So long, honey. Be good."

Gil was still sitting staring at the carpet when the front door closed, and the body he had been born with walked out of his life.

He slept for the rest of the night. He had no dreams that he could remember. When he woke up, he lay in bed for almost an hour, feeling his body with his hands. It was frightening but peculiarly erotic, to have the body of a woman, and yet to retain the mind of a man. Gil massaged his breasts, rolling his nipples between finger and thumb the way he had done with "Anna." Then he reached down between his legs and gently stroked himself, exploring his sex with tension and curiosity.

He wondered what it would be like to have a man actually inside him; a man on top of him, thrusting into him.

He stopped himself from thinking that thought. *For God's sake, you're not a queer.*

He showered and washed his hair. He found the length of his hair difficult to manage, especially when it was wet, and it took four attempts before he was able to wind a towel around it in a satisfactory turban. Yet Margaret always did it without even looking in the mirror. He decided that at the first opportunity he got, he would have it cut short.

He went to the closet and inspected Anna's wardrobe. He had liked her in her navy-blue skirt and white loose-knit sweater. He found the sweater folded neatly in one of the drawers. He struggled awkwardly into it, but realized when he looked at himself in the mirror that he was going to need a bra. He didn't want to attract *that* much attention, not to begin with, anyway. He located a drawerful of bras, lacy and mysterious, and tried one on. His breasts kept dropping out of the cups before he could fasten it up at the back, but in the end he knelt down beside the bed and propped his breasts on the quilt. He stepped into one of Anna's lacy little G-strings. He found it irritating, the way the elastic went right up between the cheeks of his bottom, but he supposed he would get used to it.

Get used to it. The words stopped him like a cold bullet in the brain. He stared at himself in the mirror, that beautiful face, those eyes that were still his. He began to weep with rage. *You've started to accept it already. You've started to cope. You're fussing around in your bra and your panties and you're worrying which skirt to wear and you've already forgotten that you're not Anna, you're Gil. You're a husband. You're a father. You're a man, dammit!*

He began to hyperventilate, his anger rising up unstoppably like the scarlet line of alcohol rising up a thermometer. He picked up the dressing stool and heaved it at the mirror. The glass shattered explosively, all over the carpet. A thousand tiny Annas stared up at him in uncontrollable fury and frustration.

He stormed blindly through the house, yanking open drawers, strewing papers everywhere, clearing ornaments off tabletops with a sweep of his arm. He wrenched open the doors of the cocktail cabinet, and hurled the bottles of liquor one by one across the room, so that they smashed against the wall. Whiskey, gin, Campari, broken glass.

Eventually, exhausted, he sat down on the floor and sobbed. Then he was too tired even to cry.

In front of him, lying on the rug, were Anna's identity card, her social security papers, her passport, her credit cards. *Anna Huysmans.* The name that was now his.

On the far side of the room, halfway under the leather sofa, Gil saw a large diary bound in brown Morocco leather. He crept across the floor on his hands and knees and picked it up. This must be the diary that David Chilton had been talking about. He opened it up to the last page.

He read, through eyes blurry with tears, *Gil has been marvelous . . . he has an enthusiastic, uncluttered personality. . . . It won't be difficult to adapt to being him. . . . I just hope that I like his wife Margaret. . . . She sounds a little immature, from what Gil says . . . and he complains that she needs a lot of persuading when it comes to sex. . . . Still, that's probably Gil's fault . . . you couldn't call him the world's greatest lover.*

Gil flicked back through the diary's pages until he came to the very first entry. To his astonishment it was dated July 16, 1942. It was written in German, by a Reichswehr officer who appeared to have met Anna while driving out to Edam on military business. *Her bicycle tire was punctured. . . . She was so pretty that I told my driver to stop and to help her. . . .*

There was no way of telling, however, whether this German Samaritan had been the first of Anna's victims, or simply the first to keep a diary. The entries went on page after page, year after year. There must have been more than seven hundred of them; and each one told a different story of temptation and tragedy. Some of the men had even essayed explanations of what Anna was, and why she took men's bodies.

She has been sent to punish us by God Himself for thinking lustful thoughts about women and betraying the Holy Sacrament of marriage. . . .

She does not actually exist. There is no "Anna," because she is always one of us. The only "Anna" that exists is in the mind of the man who is seducing her, and that perhaps is the greatest condemnation of them all. We fall in love with our own illusions, rather than a real woman.

To me, Anna is a collector of weak souls. She gathers us up and hangs us on her charm bracelet, little dangling victims of our own vicissitudes.

Anna is a ghost . . .

Anna is a vampire . . .

If I killed myself, would it break the chain? Would Anna die if I died? Supposing I tried to seduce the man who was Anna before me . . . could I reverse the changing process?

Gil sat on the floor and read the diary from cover to cover. It was an extraordinary chorus of voices—real men who had been seduced into taking on the body of a beautiful woman, one after the other—and in their turn had desperately tried to escape. Business executives, policemen, soldiers, scientists, philosophers—even priests. Some had stayed as Anna for fewer than two days; others had managed to endure it for months. But to every single one of them, the body even of the plainest man had been preferable to Anna's body, regardless of how desirable she was.

By two o'clock Gil was feeling hungry. The icebox was almost empty, so he drove into Amsterdam for lunch. The day was bright but chilly, and so he wore Anna's black belted raincoat, and a black beret to cover his head. He tried her high heels, but he twisted his ankle in the hallway, and sat against the wall with tears in his eyes saying, "Shit, shit," over and over, as if he *ought* to have been able to walk in them quite naturally. He limped back to the bedroom and changed into black flat shoes.

He managed to find a parking space for Anna's BMW on the edge of the Singel Canal, close to the Muntplein, where the old mint building stood, with its clock and its onion dome. There was an Indonesian restaurant on the first floor of the building on the corner: one of the executives of the Gemeentevervoerbedrijf had pointed it out to him. He went upstairs and a smiling Indonesian waiter showed him to a table for one, overlooking the square. He ordered rijstafel for one and a beer. The waiter stared at him, and so he changed his order to a vodka and tonic.

The large restaurant was empty, except for a party of American businessmen over on the far side. As he ate his meal, Gil gradually became aware that one of the businessmen was watching him. Not only watching him, but every time he glanced up, *winking* at him.

Oh, shit, he thought. *Just let me eat my lunch in peace.*

He ignored the winks and the unrelenting stares; but after the business lunch broke up, the man came across the restaurant, buttoning up his coat, and smiling. He was big and red-faced and sweaty, with wavy blond hair and three heavy gold rings on each hand.

"You'll pardon my boldness," he said. "My name's Fred Oscay. I'm in aluminum tubing, Pennsylvania Tubes. I just couldn't take my eyes off you all during lunch."

Gil looked up at him challengingly. "So?" he replied.

"Well," said Fred Oscay, grinning, "maybe you could take that as a compliment. You're some looker, I've got to tell you. I was wondering if you had any plans for dinner tonight. You know—maybe a show, maybe a meal."

Gil was trembling. Why the hell was he trembling? He was both angry and frightened. Angry at being stared at and winked at and chatted up by this crimson-faced idiot; frightened because social convention prevented him from being as rude as he really wanted to be—that, and his weaker physique.

21

It was a new insight—and to Gil it was hair-raising—that men used the threat of their greater physical strength against women not just in times of argument and stress—but *all the time.*

"Mr. Oscay," he said, and he was still trembling. "I'd really prefer it if you went back to your party and left me alone."

"Aw, come along, now," said Fred Oscay, still grinning. "You can't mean that."

Gil's mouth felt dry. "Will you please just leave me alone?"

Fred Oscay leaned over Gil's table. "There's a fine concert at the Kleine Zaal, if it's culture you're after."

Gil hesitated for a moment, and then picked up a small metal dish of Indonesian curried chicken and turned it upside-down over Fred Oscay's left sleeve. Fred Oscay stared down at it for a very long time without saying anything, then stared at Gil with a hostility in his eyes that Gil had never seen from anybody before. Fred Oscay looked quite capable of killing him, then and there.

"You tramp," he said. "You stupid bitch."

"Go away," Gil told him. "All I'm asking you to do is go away."

Now Fred Oscay's voice became booming and theatrical, intended for all his business colleagues to hear. "You were coming on, lady. You were coming on. All through lunch you were giving me the glad-eye. So don't you start getting all tight-assed now. What is it, you want money? Is that it? You're a professional? Well, I'm sorry. I'm really truly sorry. But old Fred Oscay never paid for a woman in his life, and he ain't about to start just for some sorry old hooker like you."

He picked up a napkin and wiped the curry off his sleeve with a flourish, throwing the soiled napkin directly into Gil's plate. The other businessmen laughed and stared. One of them said, "Come on, Fred, we can't trust you for a minute."

Gil sat where he was and couldn't think what to do; how to retaliate; how to get his revenge. He felt so frustrated that in spite of himself he burst into tears. The Indonesian waiter came over and offered him a glass of water. "Aroo okay?" he kept asking. "Aroo okay?"

"I'm all right," Gil insisted. "Please—I'm all right."

He was standing on the corner of the street as patient as a shadow as David Chilton emerged from his front door right on time and began walking his cocker spaniel along the grass verge. It was 10:35 at night. David and Margaret would have been watching *News at Ten* and then *South East News* just as Gil and Margaret had always done. Then David would have taken down Bondy's leash and whistled, "Come on, boy! Twice round the park!" while Margaret went into the kitchen to tidy up and make them some cocoa.

He was wearing the same black belted raincoat and the same black beret that he had worn in Amsterdam; only now he had mastered Anna's high heels. His hair was curly and well-brushed and he wore makeup now, carefully copied from an article in a Dutch magazine.

Under his raincoat he carried a stainless-steel butcher knife with a twelve-inch blade. He was quite calm. He was breathing evenly and his pulse was no faster than it had been when he first met Anna.

Bondy insisted on sniffing at every bush and every garden gatepost, so it took a long time for David to come within earshot. He had his hands in his pockets and he was whistling under his breath, a tune that Gil had never known. At last Gil stepped out and said, "David?"

David Chilton stood stock-still. "Anna?" he asked, hoarsely.

Gil took another step forward, into the flat orange illumination of the streetlight. "Yes, David, it's Anna."

David Chilton took his hands out of his pockets. "I guess you had to come and take a look, didn't you? Well, I was the same."

Gil glanced toward the house. "Is he happy? Alan, I mean."

"Alan's fine. He's a fine boy. He looks just like you. I mean me."

"And Margaret?"

"Oh, Margaret's fine, too. Just fine."

"She doesn't notice any difference?" said Gil bitterly. "In bed, perhaps? I know I wasn't the world's greatest lover."

"Margaret's fine, really."

Gil was silent for a while. Then he said, "The job? How do you like the job?"

"Well, not too bad," David Chilton said with a grin. "But I have to admit that I'm looking around for something a little more demanding."

"But, apart from that, you've settled in well?"

"You could say that, yes. It's not Darien, but it's not Zandvoort, either."

Bondy had already disappeared into the darkness. David Chilton whistled a couple of times and called, "Bondy! Bondy!" He turned to Gil and said, "Look—you know, I understand why you came. I really do. I sympathize. But I have to get after Bondy or Moo's going to give me hell."

For the very first time Gil felt a sharp pang of genuine jealousy for Margaret. "You call her Moo?"

"Didn't you?" David Chilton asked him.

Gil remained where he was while David Chilton went jogging off after his dog. His eyes were wide with indecision. But David had only managed to run twenty or thirty yards before Gil suddenly drew out the butcher knife and went after him.

"David!" he called out, in his high, feminine voice. "David! Wait!"

David Chilton stopped and turned. Gil had been walking quickly so that he had almost reached him. Gil's arm went up. David Chilton obviously didn't understand what was happening at first, not until Gil stabbed him a second time, close to his neck.

David Chilton dropped, rolled away, then bobbed up on to his feet again. He looked as if he had been trained to fight. Gil came after him, his knife upraised, silent and angry beyond belief. *If I can't have my body, then nobody's going to. And perhaps if the man who took my body—if his spirit dies—perhaps I'll get my body back. There's no other hope, no other way. Not unless Anna goes on for generation after generation, taking one man after another.*

Gil screamed at David and stabbed at his face. But David seized Gil's wrist and twisted it around, skin tearing, so that

Gil dropped the knife on to the pavement. Gil's high heel snapped. He lost his balance and they both fell. Their hands scrabbled for the knife. David touched it, missed it, then managed to take hold of it.

The long triangular blade rose and fell five times. There was a sound of muscle chopping. The two rolled away from each other, and lay side by side, flat on their backs, panting.

Gil could feel the blood soaking his cotton blouse. The inside of his stomach felt cold and very liquid, as if his stomach had poured its contents into his whole abdominal cavity. He knew that he couldn't move. He had felt the knife slice sharply against his spine.

David knelt up on one elbow. His hands and his face were smeared in blood. *"Anna . . ."* he said unsteadily. *"Anna . . ."*

Gil looked up at him. Already, he was finding it difficult to focus. "You've killed me," Gil said. "You've killed me. Don't you understand what you've done?"

David looked desperate, "You *know,* don't you? You *know."*

Gil attempted to smile. "I don't know, not for sure. But I can feel it. I can feel you—you and all the rest of them—right inside my head. I can hear your voices. I can feel your pain. I took your souls. I took your spirits. That's what you gave me, in exchange for your lust."

He coughed blood, and then he said, "My God . . . I wish I'd understood this before. Because you know what's going to happen now, don't you? You know what's going to happen now?"

David stared at him in dread. "Anna, listen, you're not going to die. Anna, listen, you can't. Just hold on, I'll call for an ambulance. But hold on!"

But Gil could see nothing but darkness. Gil could hear nothing but the gray sea. Gil was gone; and Anna was gone, too.

David Chilton made it as far as the garden gate. He grasped the post, gripped at the privet hedge. He cried out, "Moo! Help me! For Christ's sake, help me!" He grasped at his throat as if he were choking. Then he collapsed into the freshly dug flowerbed, and lay there shuddering, the way an insect shudders when it is mortally hurt. The way any creature shudders, when it has no soul.

All over the world that night, men quaked and died. Over seven hundred of them: in hotels, in houses, in restaurants, in the back of taxis. A one-time German officer collapsed during dinner, his face blue, his head lying in his salad plate, as if it were about to be served up with an apple in his mouth. An airline pilot flying over Nebraska clung to his collar and managed to gargle out the name *Anna!* before he pitched forward on to his controls.

A sixty-year-old member of Parliament, making his way down the aisle in the House of Commons for the resumption of a late-night sitting, abruptly tumbled forward and lay between the Government and the Opposition benches, shuddering helplessly at the gradual onset of death.

On I-5 just south of San Clemente, California, a fifty-five-year-old executive for a swimming pool maintenance company died at the wheel of his Lincoln sedan. The car swerved from one side of the highway to the other before colliding into the side of a 7-Eleven truck, overturning, and fiercely catching fire.

Helplessly, four or five Mexicans who had been clearing the verges stood beside the highway and watched the man burn inside his car, not realizing that he was already dead.

The civic authorities buried Anna Huysmans at Zandvoort, not far from the sea. Her will had specified a polished black-marble headstone, without decoration. It reflected the slowly moving clouds as if it were a mirror. There were no relatives, no friends, no flowers. Only a single woman, dressed in black, watching from the cemetery boundary as if she had nothing to do with the funeral at all. She was very beautiful, this woman, even in black, with a veil over her face. A man who had come to lay flowers on the grave of his grandfather saw her standing alone, and watched her for a while.

She turned. He smiled.

She smiled back.

THE LIKENESS
OF JULIE

Richard Matheson

October

Eddy Foster had never noticed the girl in his English class until that day.

It wasn't because she sat behind him. Any number of times, he'd glanced around while Professor Euston was writing on the blackboard or reading to them from *College Literature*. Any number of times, he'd seen her as he left or entered the classroom. Occasionally, he'd passed her in the hallways or on the campus. Once, she'd even touched him on the shoulder during class and handed him a pencil which had fallen from his pocket.

Still, he'd never noticed her the way he noticed other girls. First of all, she had no figure—or if she did she kept it hidden under loose-fitting clothes. Second, she wasn't pretty and she looked too young. Third, her voice was faint and high-pitched.

Which made it curious that he should notice her that day. All through class, he'd been thinking about the redhead in the first row. In the theatre of his mind he'd staged her—and himself—through an endless carnal play. He was just raining the curtain on another act when he heard the voice behind him.

27

"Professor?" it asked.

"Yes, Miss Eldridge."

Eddy glanced across his shoulder as Miss Eldridge asked a question about *Beowulf.* He saw the plainness of her little girl's face, heard her faltering voice, noticed the loose yellow sweater she was wearing. And, as he watched, the thought came suddenly to him.

Take her.

Eddy turned back quickly, his heartbeat jolting as if he'd spoken the words aloud. He repressed a grin. What a screwy idea that was. Take *her?* With no figure? With that kid's face of hers?

That was when he realized it was her face which had given him the idea. The very childishness of it seemed to needle him perversely.

There was a noise behind him. Eddy glanced back. The girl had dropped her pen and was bending down to get it. Eddy felt a crawling tingle in his flesh as he saw the strain of her bust against the tautening sweater. Maybe she had a figure after all. That was more exciting yet. A child afraid to show her ripening body. The notion struck dark fire in Eddy's mind.

Eldridge, Julie, read the yearbook. *St. Louis, Arts & Sciences.*

As he'd expected, she belonged to no sorority or organizations. He looked at her photograph and she seemed to spring alive in his imagination—shy, withdrawn, existing in a shell of warped repressions.

He had to have her.

Why? He asked himself the question endlessly but no logical answer ever came. Still, visions of her were never long out of his mind—the two of them locked in a cabin at the Hiway Motel, the wall heater crowding their lungs with oven air while they rioted in each other's flesh; he and this degraded innocent.

The bell had rung and, as the students left the classroom, Julie dropped her books.

"Here, let me pick them up," said Eddy.

"Oh." She stood motionless while he collected them. From the corners of his eyes, he saw the ivory smoothness of her legs. He shuddered and stood with the books.

"Here," he said.

"Thank you." Her eyes lowered and the faintest of color touched her cheeks. She wasn't so bad-looking, Eddy thought. And she did have a figure. Not much of one, but a figure.

"What is it we're supposed to read for tomorrow?" he heard himself asking.

"The—'Wife of Bath's Tale,' isn't it?" she asked.

"Oh, is that it?" Ask her for a date, he thought.

"Yes, I think so."

He nodded. Ask her now, he thought.

"Well," said Julie. She began to turn away.

Eddy smiled remotely at her and felt his stomach muscles trembling.

"Be seeing you," he said.

He stood in the darkness staring at her window. Inside the room, the light went on as Julie came back from the bathroom. She wore a terrycloth robe and was carrying a towel, a washcloth, and a plastic soap box. Eddy watched her put the washcloth and soap box on her bureau and sit down on the bed. He stood there rigidly, watching her with eyes that did not blink. What was he doing here? he thought. If anybody caught him, he'd be arrested. He had to leave.

Julie stood. She undid the sash at her waist and the bathrobe slipped to the floor. Eddy froze. He parted his lips, sucking at the damp air. She had the body of a woman— full-hipped with breasts that both jutted and hung. And with that pretty child's face—

Eddy felt hot breath forcing out between his lips. He muttered, *"Julie, Julie, Julie—"*

Julie turned away to dress.

The idea was insane. He knew it, but he couldn't get away from it. No matter how he tried to think of something else, it kept returning.

He'd invite her to a drive-in movie, drug her Coke there, take her to the Hiway Motel. To guarantee his safety afterward, he'd take photographs of her and threaten to send them to her parents if she said anything.

The idea was insane. He knew it, but he couldn't fight it. He had to do it now—now when she was still a stranger to him; an unknown female with a child's face and a woman's body. That was what he wanted; not an individual.

No! It was insane! He cut his English class twice in succession. He drove home for the weekend. He saw a lot of movies. He read magazines and took long walks. He could beat this thing.

"Miss Eldridge?"

Julie stopped. As she turned to face him, the sun made ripples on her hair. She looked very pretty, Eddy thought.

"Can I walk with you?" he asked.

"All right," she said.

They walked along the campus path.

"I was wondering," said Eddy, "if you'd like to go to the drive-in movie Friday night." He was startled at the calmness of his voice.

"Oh," said Julie. She glanced at him shyly. "What's playing?" she asked.

He told her.

"That sounds very nice," she said.

Eddy swallowed. "Good," he answered. "What time shall I pick you up?"

He wondered later if it made her curious that he didn't ask her where she lived.

There was a light burning on the porch of the house she roomed in. Eddy pushed the bell and waited, watching two moths flutter around the light. After several moments, Julie opened the door. She looked almost beautiful, he thought. He'd never seen her dressed so well.

"Hello," she said.

"Hi," he answered. "Ready to go?"

"I'll get my coat." She went down the hall and into her room. In there, she'd stood naked that night, her body glowing in the light. Eddy pressed his teeth together. He'd be all right. She'd never tell anyone when she saw the photographs he was going to take.

Julie came back down the hallway and they went out to the car. Eddy opened the door for her.

"Thank you," she murmured. As she sat down, Eddy caught a glimpse of stockinged knees before she pulled her skirt down. He slammed the door and walked around the car. His throat felt parched.

Ten minutes later, he nosed the car onto an empty ramp in the last row of the drive-in theatre and cut the engine. He reached outside and lifted the speaker off its pole and hooked it over the window. There was a cartoon playing.

"You want some popcorn and Coke?" he asked, feeling a sudden bolt of dread that she might say no.

"Yes. Thank you," Julie said.

"I'll be right back." Eddy pushed out of the car and started for the snack bar. His legs were shaking.

He waited in the milling crowd of students, seeing only his thoughts. Again and again, he shut the cabin door and locked it, pulled the shades down, turned on all the lights, switched on the wall heater. Again and again, he walked over to where Julie lay stupefied and helpless on the bed.

"Yours?" said the attendant.

Eddy started. "Uh—two popcorns and a large and a small Coke," he said.

He felt himself begin to shiver convulsively. He couldn't do it. He might go to jail the rest of his life. He paid the man mechanically and moved off with the cardboard tray. The photographs, you idiot, he thought. They're your protection. He felt angry desire shudder through his body. Nothing was going to stop him. On the way back to the car, he emptied the contents of the packet into the small Coke.

Julie was sitting quietly when he opened the door and slid back in. The feature had begun.

"Here's your Coke," he said. He handed her the small cup with her box of popcorn.

"Thank you," said Julie.

Eddy sat watching the picture. He felt his heart thud slowly like a beaten drum. He felt bugs of perspiration running down his back and sides. The popcorn was dry and tasteless. He kept drinking Coke to wet his throat. Soon

31

now, he thought. He pressed his lips together and stared at the screen. He heard Julie eating popcorn, he heard her drinking Coke.

The thoughts were coming faster now: the door locked, the shades drawn, the room a bright-lit oven as they twisted on the bed together. Now they were doing things that Eddy almost never thought; that damned angel's face of hers. It made the mind seek out every black avenue it could find.

Eddy glanced over at Julie. He felt his hands retract so suddenly that he spilled Coke on his trousers. Her empty cup had fallen to the floor, the box of popcorn turned over on her lap. Her head was lying on the seat back and, for one hideous moment, Eddy thought she was dead.

Then she inhaled raspingly and turned her head toward him. He saw her tongue move, dark and sluggish on her lips.

Suddenly, he was deadly calm again. He picked the speaker off the window and hung it up outside. He threw out the cups and boxes. He started the engine and backed out into the aisle. He turned on his parking lights and drove out of the theatre.

Hiway Motel. The sign blinked off and on a quarter of a mile away. For a second, Eddy thought he read *No Vacancy* and he made a frightened sound. Then he saw that he was wrong. He was still trembling as he circled the car around the drive and parked to one side of the office.

Bracing himself, he went inside and rang the bell. He was very calm and the man didn't say a word to him. He had Eddy fill out the registration card and gave him the key.

Eddy pulled his car in to the breezeway beside the cabin. He put his camera in the room, then went out and looked around. There was no one in sight. He ran to the car and opened the door. He carried Julie to the cabin door, his shoes crunching quickly on the gravel. He carried her into the dark room and dropped her on the bed.

Then it was his dream coming true. The door was locked. He moved around the room on quivering legs, pulling down the shades. He turned on the wall heater. He found the light switch by the door and pushed it up. He turned on all the lamps and pulled their shades off. He dropped one of them and it rolled across the rug. He left it there. He went over to where Julie lay.

In falling to the bed, her skirt had pulled up to her thighs. He could see the tops of her stockings and the garter buttons fastened to them. Swallowing, Eddy sat down and drew her up into a sitting position. He took her sweater off. Shakily, he reached around her and unhooked her bra; her breasts slipped free. Quickly, he unzipped her skirt and pulled it down.

In seconds, she was naked. Eddy propped her against the pillows, posing her. *Dear God, the body on her.* Eddy closed his eyes and shuddered. *No,* he thought, this is the important part. First get the photographs and you'll be safe. She can't do anything to you then, she'll be too scared. He stood up, tensely, and got his camera. He set the dials. He got her centered on the viewer. Then he spoke.

"Open your eyes," he said.

Julie did.

He was at her house before six the next morning, moving up the alley cautiously and into the yard outside her window. He hadn't slept all night. His eyes felt dry and hot.

Julie was on her bed exactly as he'd placed her. He looked at her a moment, his heartbeat slow and heavy. Then he raked a nail across the screen. "Julie," he said.

She murmured indistinctly and turned onto her side. She faced him now.

"Julie."

Her eyes fluttered open. She stared at him dazedly.

"Who's that?" she asked.

"Eddy. Let me in."

"Eddy?"

Suddenly, she caught her breath and shrank back and he knew that she remembered.

"Let me in or you're in trouble," he muttered. He could feel his legs begin to shake.

Julie lay motionless a few seconds, eyes fixed on his. Then she pushed to her feet and weaved unsteadily toward the door. Eddy turned for the alley. He strode down it nervously and started up the porch steps as she came outside.

"What do you want?" she whispered. She looked exciting, half asleep, her clothes and hair all mussed. "Inside," he said.

Julie stiffened. "No."

"All right, come on," he said, taking her hand roughly. "We'll talk in my car."

She walked with him to the car and, as he slid in beside her, he saw that she was shivering.

"I'll turn on the heater," he said. It sounded stupidly inane. He was here to threaten her, not comfort. Angrily, he started the engine and drove away from the curb.

"Where are we going?" Julie asked.

He didn't know at first. Then, suddenly, he thought of the place outside of town where dating students always parked. It would be deserted at this hour. Eddy felt a swollen tingling in his body and he pressed down on the accelerator. Sixteen minutes later, the car was standing in the silent woods. A pale mist hung across the ground and seemed to lap at the doors.

Julie wasn't shivering now; the inside of the car was hot.

"What is it?" she asked, faintly.

Impulsively, Eddy reached into his inside coat pocket and pulled out the photographs. He threw them on her lap.

Julie didn't make a sound. She just stared down at the photographs with frozen eyes, her fingers twitching as she held them.

"Just in case you're thinking of calling the police," Eddy faltered. He clenched his teeth. *Tell her!* he thought savagely. In a dull, harsh voice, he told her everything he'd done the night before. Julie's face grew pale and rigid as she listened. Her hands pressed tautly at each other. Outside, the mist appeared to rise around the windows like a chalky fluid. It surrounded them.

"You want money?" Julie whispered.

"Take off your clothes," he said. It wasn't his voice, it occurred to him. The sound of it was too malignant, too inhuman.

Then Julie whimpered and Eddy felt a surge of blinding fury boil upward in him. He jerked his hand back, saw it flail out in a blur of movement, heard the sound of it striking her on the mouth, felt the sting across his knuckles.

"Take them off!" His voice was deafening in the stifling closeness of the car. Eddy blinked and gasped for breath. He stared dizzily at Julie as, sobbing, she began to take her clothes off. There was a thread of blood trickling from a corner of her mouth. *No, don't,* he heard a voice beg in his mind. *Don't do this.* It faded quickly as he reached for her with alien hands.

When he got home at ten that morning there was blood and skin under his nails. The sight of it made him violently ill. He lay trembling on his bed, lips quivering, eyes staring at the ceiling. I'm through, he thought. He had the photographs. He didn't have to see her any more. It would destroy him if he saw her any more. Already, his brain felt like rotting sponge, so bloated with corruption that the pressure of his skull caused endless overflow into his thoughts. Trying to sleep, he thought, instead, about the bruises on her lovely body, the ragged scratches, and the bite marks. He heard her screaming in his mind.

He would not see her any more.

December

Julie opened her eyes and saw tiny falling shadows on the wall. She turned her head and looked out through the window. It was beginning to snow. The whiteness of it reminded her of the morning Eddy had first shown her the photographs.

The photographs. That was what had woken her. She closed her eyes and concentrated. They were burning. She could see the prints and negatives scattered on the bottom of a large enamel pan—the kind used for developing film. Bright flames crackled on them and enamel was smudging.

Julie held her breath. She pushed her mental gaze further —to scan the room that was lit by the flaming enamel pan—until it came to rest upon the broken thing that dangled and swayed, suspended from the closet hook.

She sighed. It hadn't lasted very long. That was the trouble with a mind like Eddy's. The very weakness which made it vulnerable to her soon broke it down. Julie opened her eyes, her ugly child's face puckered in a smile. Well, there were others.

She stretched her scrawny body languidly. Posing at the window, the drugged Coke, the motel photographs—these were getting dull by now although that place in the woods was wonderful. Especially in the early morning with the mist outside, the car like an oven. That she'd keep for a while; and the violence of course. The rest would have to go. She'd think of something better next time.

Philip Harrison had never noticed the girl in his Physics class until that day—

THE THANG

Robert R. McCammon

*I*t was nothing like what he'd expected. No skulls on the walls, no dried bats, no shrunken heads. Not even any of those glass vials with smoke bubbling out of them, which is what he'd looked forward to seeing. It was just a little room that looked like a grocery store, with faded green linoleum tiles on the floor and a ceiling fan that groaned as it turned. Needs oil, he thought. Ceiling fan'll burn itself up without oil. Heating and cooling was his business, and right now he was sweating under the collar and there were wet rings beneath his arms. I've come over seven hundred miles to a grocery store with a creaking fan, he thought. God Almighty, what a fool I am!

"Help ya?" There was a young black man behind the counter. He wore dark glasses with white music notes on the frames, and his hair was cropped short and dyed with blue lightning bolts. He had a razor blade hanging from his left earlobe.

"No. Just looking," Dave Neilson said, in his flat Oklahoman accent. The dude behind the counter went back to reading his copy of *Interview* magazine. Dave wandered among the shelves, his heart pounding. He had never in his life felt so far from home. He picked up a bottle full of red, oily liquid: King John's Blood, the label said. Near it were bags full of white dirt that bore the labels Aunt Esther's Graveyard Dirt This Is The Real Stuff.

I'll bet it is, Dave thought. If that was graveyard dirt, his pecker was as big as Moby Dick. And that, of course, was the crux of the problem.

He'd never been to New Orleans before. Had never been to Louisiana, even. Of that he was glad; the wet August heat down here was enough to roast toadfrogs. But he liked the French Quarter all right, with its racy nightclubs and strippers who watched themselves in full-length mirrors. A man could get in trouble down here, if he had the right equipment. If he had the devil-may-care attitude. If he *dared*.

"Anythin' you lookin' for in particular, cousin?" the young black man inquired, staring at him over a photograph of Cornelia Guest.

"No. Looking, that's all." Dave scanned the shelves with frantic intensity, saw Lover's Tears, Hopping Fever, Uncle Teddy's Holy Bricks, Friendship Cream, and Intelligence Powder.

"Tourist," the young man said with a grunt.

Dave continued along the shelves, passing bottles and jars of such items as Lizard Gusto, Know-It-All Root, and Manpleaser Drops. His eyes didn't know where to go, and neither did his feet. And then he came, abruptly, to the end of the shelves—and face-to-face with an octoroon woman who had eyes like polished copper coins.

"What may I sell you?" she asked, her voice like velvet smoke.

"I'm . . . I'm just—"

"Tourist is lookin', Miss Fallon," the young man said. "Lookin' and lookin' and lookin'."

"I see that, Malcolm," she answered. Her gaze remained steady, and Dave had a dumb, nervous grin on his face. "What interests you?" Miss Fallon asked him. Her hair was long and black, streaked with gray at the temples, and she wore not a robe or cloak or a voodoo costume but a pair of Guess? jeans and a bright purple African-print blouse. "Long life?" She picked up a vial and shook it before his face. "Harmony?" Another jar. "Success in business? Love secrets?" Two more vials, filled with clouds.

"Uh . . . love secrets," he managed to say. "Right. Love secrets." He felt a fine sheen of sweat on his face. "Kind of."

"Kind of? What's that mean?"

Dave shrugged. He'd come a long way for this moment, but his nerve failed him. He stared at the green linoleum. Miss Fallon wore red Reeboks. "I . . . I'd like to talk in private," he said. Still couldn't look at her. "It's important."

"Is it? How important?"

He fumbled for his wallet. Showed her a glimpse of fifty-dollar bills. "I've come a long way. From Oklahoma. I've . . . got to talk to somebody who knows . . ." Go on, he told himself. Get it out, once and for all. "Who knows voodoo," he said.

Miss Fallon stared at him, and he felt like a lizard that had just crawled from beneath a rock. "Tourist wants to talk to somebody who knows voodoo," she said to Malcolm.

"Lord have mercy," Malcolm said, not looking up from his magazine.

"This is my place." Miss Fallon gestured around at the shelves. "My stuff. You want to talk to me, I'll take your money."

"You don't look like . . . I mean, you don't look . . ." His tongue twisted.

"I only wear my warts at Mardi Gras," she said. "You want to talk, or you want to walk?"

This was the tricky part. "It's . . . kind of a sensitive problem. I mean . . . it's a personal matter."

"They all are." She crooked a finger at him. "Follow me." She went through a doorway over which hung the kind of purple beaded curtain Dave hadn't seen since he was a Hendrix freak in college. That seemed like a hundred years ago, and the world seemed a lot older. Meaner, too. He went through the curtain of beads, and heard memories in their soft clicking. Miss Fallon sat down, not at a round table on which were spread various potions and dried mysteries, but behind a regular wooden desk that looked as if it belonged to a banker. A little sign said: Today Is the First Day of the Rest of Your Life. "Okay," she said, and laced her fingers together. Just your everyday friendly neighborhood voodoo doctor, Dave thought. "What's your problem?"

He unzipped his pants, and showed her.

There was a long moment of silence.

Miss Fallon cleared her throat. She slid a drawer open and

39

laid a knife atop her desk. "The last fella who tried this with me," she said calmly, "wound up shorter. By a head."

"No! That's not what I'm here for!" His face reddened, and he pushed himself back in and hurriedly zipped up—and caught a piece of skin in the zipper. He made a face and hopped around a few times, trying to shake loose without ripping skin. God knows he didn't need to lose any precious flesh from down there!

"You a maniac," she asked, "or you always show your doodle to ladies and jump around like a one-legged grasshopper on a hot skillet?"

"Wait. One minute. Please. Ouch . . . ouch . . . ouch!" He got himself unzipped, and everything back in its proper place. "Sorry." Sweat was dripping under his arms, and he thought he might just pass out and give up the ghost right here and now. Miss Fallon was still watching him with those burning copper eyes. "My problem is . . . you know. You saw it."

"I saw a man's thang." Miss Fallon said it with a Southern drawl. "So what?"

And here, he felt sure, was the turning point of his life. "That's what I mean!" Dave leaned over her desk, and Miss Fallon's chair *skreeked* back. "I'm not . . . you know . . . I'm not *big* enough!"

"Big enough," she repeated carefully, as if listening to a retarded fool.

"Right! I want to be bigger than I am. I want to be . . . really big. I mean *big!* Like ten, eleven . . . twelve inches, even! I want to be so big it makes my pants bulge! You see what I'm talking about?"

"I see. I don't care for it, but I see."

"All my life," Dave said, his face flushed with the excitement of finding a confidant, "I've been little down there. These things matter to a guy! If you don't feel you measure up, then everything's lousy! I've tried all those things in the magazines—"

"What thangs?" she interrupted.

"The enlargers." He shrugged, and his face flamed anew. "I ordered a pecker stretcher once. From Los Angeles. Know what they sent me? A stretcher with a red cross on it, and a letter that said they hoped my sick bird got better."

"Oh, that's wicked," Miss Fallon agreed.

"Yeah, and it was twenty dollars down the tubes! I've tried everything I can think of! And I'm still just the same as I was, only smaller in the wallet. That's why I came here. I figure . . . you people ought to know how to do it, if anybody does."

"We *people?*" she asked, her eyebrows arching.

"Yeah. Voodoo people. I've read about you folks, and all those potions and spells and stuff. I figured surely you had a spell that would help me out."

"I knew this was gonna be one of those days," Miss Fallon said, and raised her eyes to the ceiling.

"I can pay you!" Dave showed her his money again. "I've been saving up! You don't know how important this is to me."

Miss Fallon regarded him warily. "You married?" He shook his head. "Got a girlfriend?"

"No. But I hope to have a lot of girlfriends. After I get what I need, I mean. See, it's always held me back. I . . . always felt like I wasn't up to par, so . . ." He shrugged. "I just stopped trying to get dates."

"That's the thang up here workin'." She tapped her skull. "You haven't got a problem. You just think you do."

"You ought to be on this end of it!" he said, a little testily. "Please. I really need help. If I can get just maybe two or three more inches, I'll go back to Oklahoma a mighty happy man."

"Oh, Marie Laveau is gonna roll over in her grave." Miss Fallon shook her head. Then paused, reconsidering. Her eyes glinted. "Hell, Marie Laveau probably would've done it herself! I believe in pleasin' my customers, just like she did." Miss Fallon sighed, getting it straight in her mind. "Do you have three hundred dollars?" she asked him.

"Sure." Three hundred pinched him a little, but it would be worth it. "Right here." He counted out the money, then held it back as Miss Fallon reached for it. "Hold on. I wasn't born this morning. How do I know I'll get what I want?"

"Because I'm good at what I do. If I say it'll happen, it will. You pay me half now and half when you see the . . . uh . . . results. That suit you?"

"Fair enough." His hand was trembling as he gave her the money. "I *knew* you people could help me out!"

Miss Fallon left him in the office while she went out to the store. Dave heard the clink of bottles coming off the shelves. She told Malcolm to go see somebody named Aunt Flavia and bring back some of "the gunk." Then Miss Fallon took a cardboard boxload of bottles and bags into another little room next to the office, and Dave heard her pouring, mashing, and stirring. She began to sing as she worked: "Love Potion Number Nine." Malcolm returned in about thirty minutes, and Dave heard him say "Sheeeyit!" in an unbelieving voice as Miss Fallon used whatever "the gunk" was in her mixture. Dave paced the room. An hour went past. The high, sweet smell of something cooking began to leak into the office. It reeked of burning horseflesh. *Stallion balls,* Dave thought. And then, abruptly, the door opened and Miss Fallon came in carrying a steaming, dark, and muddy liquid in a Mason jar.

"Drink it down," she said, and put it in his hands.

Dave smelled it, and instantly wished he hadn't. "My God!" he said, after his fit of coughing had ceased. "What's *in* it?"

She gave him a faint smile. "You don't want to know. Trust me on this."

He brought it near his lips. His heart was hammering. He paused, weak-blooded at the crucial moment. "Are you sure this is going to work?"

"If you can keep that shit down," she said, "you'll be a man, my son."

Dave lifted the warm Mason jar, took a breath, and drank.

Oh, there are times when a human being reaches beyond the mortal coil and grips the fist of a power beyond the earthly realm. This, however, was not one of those moments. Dave spewed up black liquid, and it went all over the walls.

"Drink it down!" Miss Fallon shouted. "You paid for it, you drink it!"

"I didn't pay to be poisoned!" he shouted back. But she grasped his wrist and shoved the Mason jar toward his face, and Dave Neilson opened his mouth and the elixir flowed in like cesspool sludge. He swallowed it. Images of polluted rivers rioted in his brain. He smelled overflowing garbage cans and thought of the black crud that slides out of drainpipes when the plumber breaks them open. A mist of sweat seemed to leap from his face, and hung like humid haze in the air. But he got all the stuff down his throat without puking, and then Miss Fallon took the Mason jar and said, "Good boy. One more jarful to go."

He did it. He never would've believed he could, but he did it. And then the mess lay in the pit of his stomach, gurgling noisily and as heavy as three hundred thousand pennies.

"Now listen to me." Miss Fallon took the drained Mason jar from him. The whites of his eyes looked tinged with brown. "You're to let this settle for forty-eight hours. You throw it up, and that's the end of it."

"Oh, Lord." Dave pressed his hand to his face. He felt feverish and unsteady. "What am I supposed to do now?"

"You stay in your hotel over the weekend. See me Monday mornin', nine o'clock sharp. No cigarettes, no alcohol, no nothin'. 'Cept gumbo, and I guess some raw oysters'll be okay." She was already herding him toward the door. His legs moved like pillars of lead. Dave staggered out amid the shelves, and Malcolm looked up with a grin. "Ya'll come again real soon!" he chirped merrily as Dave went out the front door onto sunbaked Prince Conti Street.

Night fell, fast as a crash of cymbals. Dave slept like a swamp log, in a Bourbon Street hotel room with a chattering fan and humidity fit for alligators. The damp sheets had a way of coiling around him, and he had to fight himself free on several occasions. And then, as the music of a jazz trumpet curled like steam from a nearby bar and a bass drum beat in a strip joint, Dave sat up in bed, his pulse racing and sweat on his face.

I feel different, he thought. Somehow different. Stronger, maybe. Was that it? He wasn't sure, but his heart was pumping hard and he could almost hear the blood racing in his veins.

He pulled aside the sinewy sheet and looked at the thang.

His euphoria burst like a soda bubble. It was still shrimpy. The damned thang even appeared to be smaller than when he'd gone to Miss Fallon's. My God! he thought, panic-stricken. What if . . . what if she screwed up the spell and gave me a *reverse* potion?

No, no, he told himself. Steady, boy. Give it time. He found his wristwatch and peered at the luminous hands. It was twenty minutes after eleven, only eight hours since he'd drunk the gunk. The room was as hot as a bayou prison, and Dave got up with the sludge sliding in his belly. He walked to the window, overlooking the gaudy neon signs and flesh parade of Bourbon Street, and stared down at the throng of sinners. The bass drumbeat pounded at his attention. His gaze found the red neon that said Kitt's House. Beneath that sign was painted Lovely Belles Totally Nude. He watched as a couple of college boys went in, and three Japanese men came out grinning.

Go back to bed, he thought. Sleep. Wait for Monday morning.

He stared at Kitt's House, and sleep was far from his mind.

What would it hurt to go over there? he asked himself. What would it hurt, if I just sit down and watch a few dancers strut their stuff? I don't have to order a drink. What would it hurt?

It took him maybe fifteen minutes to decide for sure. Then he got dressed, and he went down to where the action throbbed.

Kitt's House needed a fumigator. The smoke hung in heavy layers, the red lights pulsed with the jukebox music, and a ham-handed palm demanded five dollars cover charge. Dave found a table and sat where he could watch a brunette girl gyrate in the red glare, her body gleaming with a faint sheen of oil. The place wasn't crowded, but there was enough hollering and laughter to let you know it was almost midnight. And then Dave smelled musky perfume, and a blond girl with very large, very firm-looking breasts came close to his face.

"Uh . . . I'll . . . uh . . . nothing, thanks," he managed.

"Dude, honey, it's a one-drink minimum. 'Kay?" She popped bubble gum, her lips red and moist. Dave stared at her breasts, his eyes almost crossing. They didn't have anything like this in Oklahoma.

"Beer," he said, without thinking. His voice trembled. "Just beer."

"You got it." She put a napkin in front of him, and smiled. "I'm Scarlett. I dance, too. Be back real soon." She walked away, and he watched her go. The music was thunderous. He took a deep breath to clear his head, but it just got cloudier. It occurred to him that he was inhaling the smoke from twenty or so cigarettes. He began to cough, and it came upon him to get up and get out, but blond Scarlett appeared with a Miller on her tray. She smiled again, a smile that nailed him to his seat. "Here y'go, dude," she said, and plunked it down in front of him. "Three-fifty." She held the tray down for him to put the money on, and as he stared at her breasts she looked up into his face and said, "You like what you see, dude?"

"Oh . . . I . . . don't mean to . . ."

She laughed, blew a bubble, and popped it. Then she went on to entice the college boys.

Dave started to drink the beer. Quickly put it down again. No! Miss Fallon had said no alcohol! But all that seemed so unreal now, though there was an unreality to Kitt's House, too; it was as if he'd traded one unreality for another. I threw away one hundred and fifty bucks, he thought. Plus swilled some of the foulest stuff I ever—

"Hi again," Scarlett said, all blond hair, red lips and bared breasts. "Want me to dance for you?"

"Dance? For me? I . . . don't . . ."

"Table dance. Right here." She stroked the tabletop. "Five dollars. You like this music?"

"Yeah, I guess," he said, and Scarlett climbed up onto the table and he stared at her red G-string that had So Many Men So Little Time stitched across the front in purple.

Dave didn't know what the music was. He only knew it was rock'n'roll, and he liked it. Scarlett stood above him, her eyes locked with his, and she began to circle her hips round and round as she teased her fingertips in swirls around her nipples. I'm a long, long way from Oklahoma, Dave thought, and he took a deep swig of beer before he knew what he was doing. Scarlett's flat belly writhed. She turned around, clenching and relaxing the muscles of her behind. Dave drank more beer and watched wide-eyed as

Scarlett hooked her thumbs in her G-string and began to work it down, inch-by-inch, over her oil-glistening thighs. And then Scarlett whirled around, in time with the beat, and there it was. There it was, right over his face. There it was, there it was, there it . . .

He felt a pulsebeat between his legs. His mouth was dry and open in an astonished O. Scarlett's hips went around, and he followed their progress. Another pulse, startlingly strong, between his legs. He thought: What the hell is—

Something surged in his crotch. Something twitched and pounded, burning with heat.

He gasped as his pants bulged. And bulged. And . . .

His zipper exploded. Something huge and freakish burst out of it, still expanding. Scarlett danced and blew a bubble, unaware, as the thang grew beneath the table and thunked against the table's bottom like a flesh-covered baseball bat. Dave's eyes were wide, and he couldn't speak. The thang was still growing, veins blue and huge. Scarlett felt the table shake, and then the entire table began to rise up off the floor.

"Hey!" Scarlett shouted. The bubble burst over her lips. "What're you do—"

The thang, totally out of control, overturned the table on its rigid ascent. Scarlett went over, too, and as Dave stood up he saw with a mixture of horror and fascination that the thang protruded at least fifteen inches from his burst zipper. Scarlett started to get up, furious and beautiful, and she saw it. Her face blanched, going fish-belly white under the red glare. She made a soft moaning sound, and fell backward to the carpet in a dead faint.

The brunette dancer screamed and pointed. Dave was trying to grasp hold of the thang, but it was writhing back and forth like a cobra, and he realized with fresh terror that his testicles had swollen to the size of small cannonballs. Somebody hit the jukebox, the needle skidding screechingly across the tracks. There was a moment of dead silence as Dave grappled with the thang. It had grown two more inches, and was still pistoning itself outward bound.

"Good God A'mighty!" a hoarse male voice yelled. "The sumbitch is *possessed!*"

People rushed for the doors, overturning tables and chairs. Dave's thang was monstrously thick, the size of a small artillery piece. Its weight careened him around the room in crazed circles, and behind the bar a Latin-looking guy held up a Crucifix and dived for cover. Dave caught the thrashing head; he ran for Bourbon Street, turning the thang like a rudder before him.

He was sure that in all the generations of its existence, Bourbon Street had seen many sights. He doubted, though, that any of those sights had caused such commotion: shouting, laughter, shrieks, and screams, fainting from some of the women. The thang's head could've fit in a combat helmet, its twenty-two-inch length throbbing with menacing intent. The French Quarter revelers parted before him, and Dave saw a red-eyed drunk salute him and keel to the concrete. A carriage horse reared up, pawing the air, its own equipment puny in comparison to the thang.

Shouts and screams followed him down Bourbon Street. Two tall, big-boned women in glittery dresses yelled, "Glory be!" and "Lord I'm havin' a heart attack!" Dave had staggered several paces beyond them when he realized they were men dressed as women. A group of people who wore white makeup and frightwigs began to chase him along the street, and whether they were men or women Dave didn't know. He gripped the thang, ruddering it in the direction he needed to go, and he prayed he could get to his hotel before . . . well, just before.

He ran through the dimly lit lobby, leaving the guy behind the counter gawking and frantically wiping his glasses. Then Dave hoisted himself up the stairs, the thang's head banging on the risers before him. He fled to his room, slammed the door shut, and threw the latch.

He pressed his back against the door, gasping for breath.

The thang began to shrink. It rapidly deflated, along with the bulging blue testicles. Dave felt his center of balance shifting, and he staggered around a bit before he could find his equilibrium again. The thang went down through seventeen inches, fifteen, thirteen, eleven, nine, six, four . . . *choke!* . . . three. And then the devilish thang hung like a boiled shrimp again, the testicles the size of small river stones. The pounding of his pulse had subsided, and all that blood had been re-routed to the main currents once more.

Dave laughed. It had a crazy note in it, because Dave had

realized Miss Fallon's elixir certainly worked—but if every erection was gargantuan, what woman would welcome such a monster? His head spun; he got to the telephone, tore open the phone book, and turned to "Fallon." There was a baker's dozen. Feverishly he began to dial the first number. A man answered and immediately slammed the phone down when Dave asked, "Does the woman who has the voodoo shop live there?"

And so it went, hang-up after hang-up. One woman scorched his ears with salty Cajun expletives. Dave sat with the phone in his lap after he'd called the last Fallon and an elderly man had told him to go to hell. It was going to be an eternity before dawn.

Dave took a cold shower. The thang slept, deceptively small. Dave got in bed, pulled the sheet up to his neck, closed his eyes in the steamy room, and counted sheep. He found himself counting moist-lipped strippers, dancing on tabletops. The thang gave a little twitch that made the hair stand up on the back of Dave's neck. He thought desperately of having a tax audit, and the thang settled down once more. Dave turned over on his stomach and finally went to sleep.

He opened his eyes. It was still dark. The noise of Bourbon Street had quieted, but his heart hammered. What had wakened him? He lay still, listening.

From the street came a woman's shout, a voice that was sultry and perhaps more than a little intoxicated: "Hey, anybody want a freebie? Last call, fellas! Ginger's givin' it away!"

Oh, my God, Dave had time to think, before his body began to rise on a fleshy, throbbing pole.

"Hey, you studs!" Ginger called. "Come on! I *need* a man, baby!"

Dave grabbed hold of the iron bedframe, locking his fingers. The thang wriggled out from under him, already seventeen inches long and rapidly expanding in girth. The huge head twisted toward the room's door, and it began thrusting with a strength that wrenched his grip from the bedframe. The thang pulled him with it, onto the floor, and as Dave landed on his belly the cannonball-sized testicles quivered and marched toward the door like alien pods. The thang was in control now, and Dave reached up, grabbing a table; it crashed over, along with a lamp. The thang strained upward, trying to grip the doorknob.

"Come on!" Ginger called impatiently. "Anybody got six inches he wants to get—"

Oh, Lord, Dave thought; if she only knew.

The thang's head rammed against the door. There was no pain, but the door cracked. Dave grabbed the thang, as if he were choking a snake. The thang twisted loose from his hands and battered against the door. With a single, violent thrust it smashed through the wood, a fleshy battering ram, and sent nerveshocks all the way to the top of Dave's skull.

"I want to *paaaarrrrrteeeee!*" Ginger howled, like an outcast animal.

"I'm in charge here, dammit!" Dave shouted as he grabbed the writhing thang with both arms and dragged it back in. "I'm in charge here, you dumb piece of me—"

The thang turned, reddened as if enraged, and twined itself around Dave's throat.

He could see the headline of the newspaper when they found his body. That image gave him strength; he grappled with the thang as it squeezed his throat, servant against master, and his testicles pulsed like renegade brains. He got his hand in the coils, forcing some breathing space. The thang twisted away from him, almost disdainfully, and crashed against the door. The hinges creaked, one of them tearing loose from the wall in a flurry of paint and splinters.

"Aw, ya bunch of cockless bastards!" Ginger said; her voice was fading as she drifted on along Bourbon Street.

The thang thrashed wildly back and forth, pistoning against the door. The second hinge broke, and the door crashed down into the hallway. Another door opened, an elderly man and woman peering out; they saw what appeared to be a naked man fighting a pale python, and they retreated into their room and began to drag furniture against their door.

Dave caught the thang in a strangling grip. The head turned crimson, the veined length coiling back and forth in muscular fury. "No!" Dave shouted, sweat on his face. "No! No! No!"

He thought he heard the damned thang whimper. It shrank, and the testicles almost instantly decreased. In another moment the thang had contracted to its usual tiny self, and Dave was never so glad of anything in his life.

He was about to struggle up off his stomach when he saw two shoes on the floor in front of his face. Standing in those shoes was the desk clerk, whose eyes had bulged behind his glasses. "We don't permit," he said coolly, "this kind of behavior in our establishment."

The desk clerk and a security guard stood watch while Dave dressed and packed. The door was paid for—MasterCard to the rescue—and in about ten minutes Dave was standing on deserted Bourbon Street with his suitcase in his hand and his shirttail hanging out.

The sun was rising over New Orleans, and already the heat shimmered in waves off the cobblestones.

He was sitting on the curb in front of Miss Fallon's shop when Malcolm came along to open up at nine-thirty.

"You done screwed up, didn't you?" Malcolm asked him. "Yep! I knew it. You done screwed up."

Dave went inside, sat down in a corner like a dunce, and waited for Miss Fallon.

She arrived, wearing pink jeans and a paisley-print blouse, around ten-thirty. Malcolm hooked a finger toward Dave's corner. "Tourist messed up," Malcolm said, and Miss Fallon just sighed and shook her head.

"Okay, okay! So I drank a beer!" Dave said, once they were inside Miss Fallon's office. "Nobody's perfect! I wanted two or three extra *inches,* not extra *yards!* You gave me something Frankenstein would've been proud of!"

"Is that so?" She couldn't help laughing behind her cupped hands.

"Don't laugh! It's not funny! Hell, no! I can't go through life busting doors down with this . . . this *monster!* Change me back! Hell, keep the money, just change me back!"

Miss Fallon, seated regally behind her desk, looked up at his inflamed face. "Sorry. I can't do that."

"Oh, you want more money? Right? Hell, I'm down to my last few pennies! You take Visa? MasterCard? That's all I've—"

"I can't change you back," Miss Fallon said. "There's no spell or potion for somebody who wants a *smaller* thang."

"Oh." It was a small whisper, and he felt the wind gust out of him.

"Sorry." She shrugged. "If you'd let it settle like I told you, you'd be okay. But . . ." She trailed off; there was nothing more to be said.

"I can't . . . I can't go back home like this! Lord, no! I mean . . . what if I got an erection on the *plane?*"

Miss Fallon thought about that for a moment, her brow furrowed. "Hold on," she said finally, and picked up her telephone. She dialed a number. "Hi. It's me. Come on over, and bring the works." She hung up; merry good humor sparkled in her copper eyes.

"What is it? Who'd you call?"

"My Aunt Flavia. She makes the gunk. Part of what you drank." Miss Fallon tapped her fingertips on her desk. "You want to get back to what you were, right?"

"Yes! I'll do anything! I swear to God!"

Miss Fallon leaned forward slightly. "Would you let us experiment on you?"

"Experi . . ." The word clogged in his throat. "Like how?"

"Nothin' painful. Just tryin' an elixir here, an elixir there. You'll have to grow a cast-iron stomach, but we might be able to come up with a cure. Over time, that is."

"Time?" Ants of terror crawled in his belly. "How much time?"

"A month." She flicked a bit of dust off her desk. "Two, maybe. Three at the most."

Three months, he thought. Three months of drinking sludge.

"Four months, tops," Miss Fallon said.

Dave felt light-headed, and he wavered on his feet.

"My Aunt Flavia's got a guest room at her place. I see you're already packed." She nodded toward his suitcase. "You could move in with her, if you like. Won't cost you more than a hundred a week."

Dave tried to speak; a raspy nonsense came out.

Aunt Flavia arrived, lugging a suitcase. She was a husky octoroon woman with copper eyes, her long-jawed face like a wrinkled prune. She wore a red-and-gold caftan, and she had little mouse skulls dangling from her earlobes. "Oh, he's handsome," Aunt Flavia said, showing a gold tooth as she smiled at Dave. She put the suitcase atop Miss Fallon's desk and opened it. Inside were vials of dark liquids, dirty roots, coarse powders, and a bag of Aunt Esther's Graveyard Dirt This Is The Real Stuff. "Brought the whole shootin' match," Aunt Flavia said. "We gonna start now?"

"Soon as your new boarder's ready," Miss Fallon said. Dave had turned a little green around the edges. "Oh, I forgot to tell you: my Aunt Flavia's a widow. She's always liked big men, if you understand my meanin'."

Dave saw it then, as Aunt Flavia brought out some of the bottles and bags: something loose and fleshy was brushing against the front of her caftan, down between her thighs. Something that . . . seemed very large.

"Oh, my God," Dave whispered.

"Like I say"—Miss Fallon smiled—"I believe in pleasin' my customers."

Aunt Flavia poured black liquid from one bottle to another and stirred in powder that smelled like dead bats. The liquid began to bubble and smoke. "He's the handsomest one yet," she said to Miss Fallon. "Kinda skinny, but it's the size of the thang that counts, ain't it?" She laughed and jabbed an elbow into Dave's ribs.

He stared at the little sign on Miss Fallon's desk: Today Is the First Day of the Rest of Your Life.

"Here's to a long life!" Aunt Flavia said, offering him the potion. Something rustled against her caftan.

Dave took the bottle, smiled weakly, and felt the thang give an eager little twitch.

MÉNAGE À TROIS

F. Paul Wilson

*B*urke noticed how Grimes, the youngest patrolman there, was turning a sickly shade of yellow-green. He motioned him closer. "You all right?"

Grimes nodded. "Sure. Fine." His pitiful attempt at a smile was hardly reassuring. "Awful hot in here, but I'm fine."

Burke could see that he was anything but. The kid's lips were as pale as the rest of his face and he was dripping with sweat. He was either going to puke or pass out or both in the next two minutes.

"Yeah. Hot," Burke said. It was no more than seventy in the hospital room. "Get some fresh air out in the hall."

"Okay. Sure." Now the smile was real—and grateful. Grimes gestured toward the three sheet-covered bodies. "I just never seen anything like this before, y'know?"

Burke nodded. He knew. This was a nasty one. Real nasty. He swallowed the sour-milk taste that puckered his cheeks. In his twenty-three years with homicide he had seen his share of crime scenes like this, but he never got used to them. The splattered blood and flesh, the smell from the ruptured intestines, the glazed eyes in the slack-jawed faces—who could get used to that? And three lives, over and gone for good.

"Look," he told Grimes, "why don't you check at the nurses' desk and find out where they lived. Get over there and dig up some background."

Grimes nodded enthusiastically. "Yes, sir."

Burke turned back to the room. Three lives had ended in there this morning. He was going to have to find out what those lives had been until now if he was ever going to understand this horror. And when he did get all the facts, could he ever really understand? Did he really want to?

Hot, sweaty, and gritty, Jerry Pritchard hauled himself up the cellar stairs and into the kitchen. Grabbing a beer from the fridge, he popped the top and drained half the can in one long, gullet-cooling swallow. Lord, that was *good!* He stepped over to the back door and pressed his face against the screen in search of a vagrant puff of air, anything to cool him off.

"Spring cleaning," he muttered, looking out at the greening rear acreage. "Right." It felt like August. Who ever heard of eighty degrees in April?

He could almost see the grass growing. The weeds, too. That meant he'd probably be out riding the mower around next week. Old lady Gati had kept him busy all fall getting the grounds perfectly manicured; the winter had been spent painting and patching the first and second floors; April had been designated basement clean-up time, and now the grounds needed to be whipped into shape again.

An endless cycle. Jerry smiled. But that cycle meant job security. And job security meant he could work and eat here during the day and sleep in the gatehouse at night, and never go home again.

He drained the can and gave it a behind-the-back flip into the brown paper bag sitting in the corner by the fridge.

Home . . . the thought pursued him. There had been times when he thought he'd never get out. Twenty-two years in that little house, the last six of them pure hell after Dad got killed in the cave-in of No. 8 mine. Mom went off the deep end then. She had always been super religious, herding everyone along to fire-and-brimstone Sunday prayer meetings and making them listen to Bible readings every night. Dad had kept her in check somewhat, but once he was gone, all the stops were out. She began hounding him about how her only son should join the ministry and spread the Word of God. She submerged him in a Bible-besotted life for those years, and he'd almost bought the package. She had him consulting the Book upon awakening, upon retiring, before eating, before going off to school, before buying a pair of socks, before taking a leak, until common sense got a hold of him and he realized he was going slowly mad. But he couldn't leave because he was the man of the house and there was his younger sister to think of.

But Suzie, bless her, ran off last summer at sixteen and got married. Jerry walked out a week later. Mom had the house, Dad's pension, her Bible, and an endless round of prayer meetings. Jerry stopped by once in a while and sent her a little money when he could. She seemed to be content.

Whatever makes you happy, he thought. He had taken his own personal Bible with him when he left. It was still in his suitcase in the gatehouse. Some things you just didn't throw away, even if you stopped using them.

The latest in a string of live-in maids swung through the kitchen door with old lady Gati's lunch dishes on a tray. None of the others had been bad looking, but this girl was a knockout. "Hey, Steph," he said, deciding to put off his return to the cellar just a little bit longer. "How's the Dragon Lady treating you?"

She flashed him a bright smile. "I don't know why you call her that, Jerry. She's really very sweet."

That's what they all say, he thought, and then *wham!* they're out. Stephanie Watson had been here almost six weeks—a record in Jerry's experience. Old lady Gati went through maids like someone with hayfever went through Kleenex. Maybe Steph had whatever it was old lady Gati was looking for.

Jerry hoped so. He liked her. Liked her a *lot*. Liked her short tawny hair and the slightly crooked teeth that made her easy smile seem so genuine, liked her long legs and the way she moved through this big old house with such natural grace, like she belonged here. He especially liked the way her blue flowered print shift clung to her breasts and stretched across her buttocks as she loaded the dishes into the dishwasher. She excited him, no doubt about that.

"You know," she said, turning toward him and leaning

back against the kitchen counter, "I still can't get over the size of this place. Seems every other day I find a new room."

Jerry nodded, remembering his first few weeks here last September. The sheer height of this old three-story gothic mansion had awed him as he had come through the gate to apply for the caretaker job. He had known it was big—everybody in the valley grew up within sight of the old Gati House on the hill—but had never been close enough to appreciate *how* big. The house didn't really fit with the rest of the valley. It wasn't all that difficult to imagine that a giant hand had plucked it from a faraway, more populated place and dropped it here by mistake. But the older folks in town still talked about all the trouble and expense mineowner Karl Gati went through to have it built.

"Yeah," he said, looking at his callused hands. "It's big all right."

He watched her for a moment as she turned and rinsed out the sink, watched the way her blond hair moved back and forth across the nape of her neck. He fought the urge to slip his arms around her and kiss that neck. That might be a mistake. They had been dating since she arrived here—just movies and something to eat afterward—and she had been successful so far in holding him off. Not that that was so hard to do. Growing up under Mom's watchful Pentecostal eye had prevented him from developing a smooth approach to the opposite sex. So far, his limited repertoire of moves hadn't been successful with Steph.

He was sure she wasn't a dumb innocent—she was a farm girl and certainly knew what went where and why. No, he sensed that she was as attracted to him as he to her but didn't want to be a pushover. Well, okay. Jerry wasn't sure why that didn't bother him too much. Maybe it was because there was something open and vulnerable about Steph that appealed to a protective instinct in him. He'd give her time. Plenty of it. Something inside him told him she was worth the wait. And something else told him that she was weakening, that maybe it wouldn't be too long now before . . .

"Well, it's Friday," he said, moving closer. "Want to go down to town tonight and see what's playing at the Strand?" He hated to sound like a broken record—movie-movie-movie—but what else was there to do in this county on weekends if you didn't get drunk, play pool, race cars, or watch TV?

Her face brightened with another smile. "Love it!"

Now why, he asked himself, should a little smile and a simple *yes* make me feel so damn good?

No doubt about it. She did something to him.

"Great! I'll—"

A deep, guttural woman's voice interrupted him. "Young Pritchard! I wish to see you a moment!"

Jerry shuddered. He hated what her accent did to the *r*'s in his name. Setting his teeth, he followed the sound of her voice through the ornate, cluttered dining room with its huge needlepoint carpet and bronze chandeliers and heavy furniture. Whoever had decorated this house must have been awful depressed. Everything was dark and gloomy. All the furniture and decorations seemed to end in points.

He came to the semi-circular solarium where she awaited him. Her wheelchair was in its usual position by the big bay windows where she could look out on the rolling expanse of the south lawn.

"Ah, there you are, young Pritchard," she said, looking up and smiling coyly. She closed the book in her hands and laid it on the blanket that covered what might have passed for legs in a nightmare. The blanket had slipped once and he had seen what was under there. He didn't want another look. Ever. He remembered what his mother had always said about deformed people: that they were marked by God and should be avoided.

Old lady Gati was in her mid-sixties maybe, flabby without being fat, with pinched features and graying hair stretched back into a severe little bun at the back of her head. Her eyes were a watery blue as she looked at him over the tops of her reading glasses.

Jerry halted about a dozen feet away but she motioned him closer. He pretended not to notice. She was going to want to touch him again. God, he couldn't stand this.

"You called, ma'am?"

"Don't stand so far away, young Pritchard." He advanced two steps in her direction and stopped again. "Closer," she said. "You don't expect me to shout, do you?"

She didn't let up until he was standing right next to her.

57

Except for these daily chats with Miss Gati, Jerry loved his job.

"There," she said. "That's better. Now we can talk more easily."

She placed a gnarled, wrinkled hand on his arm and Jerry's flesh began to crawl. Why did she always have to touch him?

"The basement—it is coming along well?"

"Fine," he said, looking at the floor, out the window, anywhere but at her hungry, smiling face. "Just fine."

"Good." She began stroking his arm, gently, possessively. "I hope this heat wave isn't too much for you." As she spoke she used her free hand to adjust the blanket over what there was of her lower body. "I really should have Stephanie get me a lighter blanket."

Jerry fought the urge to jump away from her. He had become adept at masking the revulsion that rippled through his body every time she touched him. And it seemed she *had* to touch him whenever he was in reach. When he first got the caretaker job, he took a lot of ribbing from the guys in town down at the Dewkum Inn. (Lord, what Mom would say if she ever saw him standing at a bar!) Everybody knew that a lot of older, more experienced men had been passed over for him. His buddies had said that the old lady really wanted him for stud service. The thought nauseated him. Who knew if she even had—

No, that would never happen. He needed this job, but there was nothing he needed *that* badly. And so far, all she had ever done was stroke his arm when she spoke to him. Even that was hard to take.

As casually as he could, he moved out of reach and gazed out the window as if something on the lawn had attracted his attention. "What did you want me to—"

Stephanie walked into the room and interrupted him.

"Yes, Miss Gati?"

"Get me a summer blanket, will you, dear?"

"Yes, ma'am." She flashed a little smile at Jerry as she turned, and he watched her until she was out of sight. Now if only it were Steph who couldn't keep her hands off him, he wouldn't—

"She appeals to you, young Pritchard?" Miss Gati said, her eyes dancing.

He didn't like her tone, so he kept his neutral. "She's a good kid."

"But does she *appeal* to you?"

He felt his anger rising, felt like telling her it was none of her damn business, but he hauled it back and said, "Why is that so important to you?"

"Now, now, young Pritchard, I'm only concerned that the two of you get along well. But not *too* well. I don't want you taking little Stephie away from me. I have special needs, and as you know, it took me a long time to find a live-in maid with Stephie's special qualities."

Jerry couldn't quite buy that explanation. There had been something in her eyes when she spoke of Steph "appealing" to him, a hint that her interest went beyond mere household harmony.

"But the reason I called you here," she said, shifting the subject, "is to tell you that I want you to tend to the roof in the next few days."

"The new shingles came in?"

"Yes. Delivered this morning while you were in the basement. I want you to replace the worn ones over my room tomorrow. I fear this heat wave might bring us a storm out of season. I don't want my good furniture ruined by leaking water."

He guessed he could handle that. "Okay. I'll finish up today and be up on the roof tomorrow. How's that?"

She wheeled over and cut him off as he tried to make his getaway. "Whatever you think best, young Pritchard."

Jerry pulled free and hurried off, shuddering.

Marta Gati watched young Pritchard's swift exit.

I repulse him.

There was no sorrow, no self-pity attached to the thought. When you were born with twig-like vestigial appendages for legs and only half a pelvis, you quickly became used to rejection—you learned to read it in the posture, to sense it behind the eyes. Your feelings soon became as callused as a miner's hands.

59

He's sensitive about my little Stephie, she thought. Almost protective. He likes her. He's attracted to her. *Very* attracted.

That was good. She wanted young Pritchard to have genuine feelings for Stephie. That would make it so much better.

Yes, her little household was just the way she wanted it now. It had taken her almost a year to set it up this way. Month after month of trial and error until she found the right combination. And now she had it.

Such an arrangement would have been impossible while Karl was alive. Her brother would never have hired someone with as little experience as young Pritchard as caretaker, and he would have thought Stephie too young and too frail to be a good live-in maid. But Karl was dead now. The heart attack had taken him quickly and without warning last June. He had gone to bed early one night complaining of what he thought was indigestion, and never awoke. Marta Gati missed her brother and mourned his loss, yet she was reveling in the freedom his passing had left her.

Karl had been a good brother. Tyrannically good. He had looked after her as a devoted husband would an ailing wife. He had never married, for he knew that congenital defects ran high in their family. Out of their parents' four children, two—Marta and Gabor—had been horribly deformed. When they had come to America from Hungary, Karl invested the smuggled family fortune in the mines here and, against all odds, had done well. He saw to it that Lazlo, the younger brother, received the finest education. Lazlo now lived in New York where he tended to Gabor.

And Marta? Marta he had kept hidden away in this remote mansion in rural West Virginia where she had often thought she would go insane with boredom. At least she had been able to persuade him to decorate the place. If she had to stay here, she had a right to be caged in surroundings to her taste. And her taste was Gothic Revival.

Marta loved this house, loved the heavy wood of the tables, the carved deer legs of the chairs, the elaborate finials atop the cabinets, the ornate valances and radiator covers, the trefoil arches on her canopy bed.

But the decor could only carry one so far. And there were

only so many books one could read, television shows and rented movies one could watch. Karl's conversational capacity had been limited in the extreme, and when he had spoken, it was on business and finance and little else. Marta had wanted to be out in the world, but Karl said the world would turn away from her, so he'd kept her here to protect her from hurt.

But Marta had found a way to sneak out from under his overprotective thumb. And now with Karl gone, she no longer had to sneak out to the world. She could bring some of the world into the house.

Yes, it was going to be so nice here.

"Tell me something," Steph said as she rested her head on Jerry's shoulder. She was warm against him in the front seat of his old Fairlane 500 convertible and his desire for her was a throbbing ache. After the movie—a Burt Reynolds type car chase flick, but without Burt Reynolds—he had driven them back here and parked outside the gatehouse. The top was down and they were snuggled together in the front seat watching the little stars that city people never see, even on the clearest of nights.

"Anything," he whispered into her hair.

"How did Miss Gati get along here before she had me?"

"A lady from town used to come in to clean and cook, but she never stayed over. You're the first live-in who's lasted more than a week since I've been working here. The old lady's been real choosy about finding someone after the last live-in . . . left."

Jerry decided that now was not the time to bring up the last maid's suicide. Steph was from the farmlands on the other side of the ridge and wouldn't know about her. Constance Granger had been her name, a quiet girl who went crazy wild. She had come from a decent, church-going family, but all of a sudden she became a regular at the roadside taverns, taking up with a different man every night. Then one night she became hysterical in a motel room—with two men, if the whispers could be believed—and began screaming at the top of her lungs. She ran out of the room jaybird naked and got hit by a truck.

Jerry didn't want to frighten Steph with that kind of story, not now while they were snug and close like this. He steered the talk elsewhere.

"Now you tell me something. What do you think of working for old lady Gati?"

"She's sweet. She's not a slave driver and the pay is good. This is my first job since leaving home and I guess I'm kinda lucky it's working out so well."

"You miss home?"

He felt her tense beside him. She never talked about her home. "No. I . . . didn't get along with my father. But I get along just fine with Miss Gati. The only bad thing about the job is the house. It gives me the creeps. I get nightmares every night."

"What about?"

She snuggled closer, as if chilled despite the warmth of the night. "I don't remember much by morning, all I know is that they're no fun. I don't know how Miss Gati lived here alone after the last maid left. Especially her without any legs. I'd be frightened to death!"

"She's not. She tried out girl after girl. No one satisfied her till you came along. She's a tough one."

"But she's not. She's nice. A real lady. You know, I make her hot chocolate every night, and she insists I sit down and have a cup with her while she tells me about her family and how they lived in the 'Old Country.' Isn't that nice?"

"Just super," Jerry said.

He lifted her chin and kissed her. He felt her respond, felt her catch some of the fervor running through him like fire. He let his hand slip off her shoulder and come to rest over her right breast. She made no move to push him away as his fingers began caressing her.

"Want to come inside?" he said, glancing toward the door of the gatehouse.

Steph sighed. "Yes." She kissed him again, then pulled away. "But no. I don't think that would be such a good idea, Jerry. Not just yet. I mean, I just met you six weeks ago."

"You know all there is to know. I'm not hiding anything. Come on."

"I want to . . . you know I do, but not tonight. It's time for Miss Gati's hot chocolate. And if I want to keep this job,

hands. In the thousand times he had mentally bedded Steph since her arrival, he had always been the initiator, the aggressor. Last night had been nothing at all like the fantasies. Steph had been in complete control—demanding, voracious, insatiable, a wild woman who had left him drained and exhausted. And hardly a word had passed between them. Throughout their lovemaking she had cooed, she had whimpered, she had moaned, but she had barely spoken to him. It left him feeling sort of . . . used.

Still trying to figure out this new, unexpected side to Steph, he walked up to the house for breakfast. The sun was barely up and already the air was starting to cook. It was going to be another hot one.

He saw Steph heading out of the kitchen toward the dining room with old lady Gati's tray as he came in the back door.

"Be with you in a minute," she called over her shoulder.

He waited by the swinging door and caught her as she came through. He slipped his arms around her waist and kissed her.

"Jerry, no!" she snapped. "Not here—not while I'm working!"

He released her. "Not your cheerful old self this morning, are you?"

"Just tired I guess." She turned toward the stove.

"I guess you should be."

"And what's that supposed to mean?"

"Well, you had an unusually active night. At least I hope it was unusual."

Steph had been about to crack an egg on the edge of the frying pan. She stopped in mid motion and turned to face him.

"Jerry . . . what on earth are you talking about?"

She looked genuinely puzzled, and that threw him. "Last night . . . at the gatehouse . . . it was after three when you left."

Her cranky scowl dissolved into an easy smile. "You must really be in a bad way!" She laughed. "Now you're believing your own dreams!"

Jerry was struck by the clear innocence of her laughter.

For a moment, he actually doubted his memory—but only for a moment. Last night had been real. Hadn't it?

"Steph . . ." he began, but dropped it. What could he say to those guileless blue eyes? She was either playing some sort of game, and playing it very well, or she really didn't remember. Or it really never happened. None of those choices was the least bit reassuring.

He wolfed his food as Steph moved in and out of the kitchen, attending to old lady Gati's breakfast wants. She kept glancing at him out of the corner of her eye, as if checking up on him. Was this a game? Or had he really dreamed it all last night?

Jerry skipped his usual second cup of coffee and was almost relieved to find himself back in the confines of the cellar. He threw himself into the job, partly because he wanted to finish it, and partly because he didn't want too much time to think about last night. By lunchtime he was sweeping up the last of the debris when he heard the sound.

It came from above. The floorboards were squeaking. And something else as well—the light sound of feet moving back and forth, rhythmically. It continued as he filled a cardboard box with the last of the dirt, dust, and scraps of rotten wood from the cellar. He decided to walk around the south side of the house on his way to the trash bins. The sound seemed to be coming from there.

As he passed the solarium, he glanced in and almost dropped the box. Steph was waltzing around the room with an invisible partner in her arms. Swirling and dipping and curtsying, she was not the most graceful dancer he had ever seen, but the look of pure joy on her face made up for whatever she lacked in skill.

Her expression changed abruptly to a mixture of surprise and something like anger when she caught sight of him gaping through the window. She ran toward the stairs, leaving Miss Gati alone. The old lady neither turned to watch her go, nor looked out the window to see what had spooked her. She just sat slumped in her wheelchair, her head hanging forward. For a second, Jerry was jolted by the sight: She looked dead! He pressed his face against the solarium glass for a closer look, and was relieved to see the gentle rise and fall of her chest. Only asleep. But what had

Steph been doing waltzing around like that while the old lady napped?

Shaking his head at the weirdness of it all, he dumped the box in the trash area and returned to the house through the back door. The kitchen was empty, so he made his way as quietly as possible to the solarium to see if Steph had returned. He found all quiet—the music off and old lady Gati bright and alert, reading a book. He immediately turned back toward the kitchen, hoping she wouldn't spot him. But it was too late.

"Yes, young Pritchard?" she said, rolling that *r* and looking up from her book. "You are looking for something?"

Jerry fumbled for words. "I was looking for Steph to see if she could fix me a sandwich. Thought I saw her in here when I passed by before."

"No, dear boy," she said with a smile. "I sent her up to her room for a nap almost an hour ago. Seems you tired her out last night."

"Last night?" He tensed. What did she know about last night?

Her smile broadened. "Come now! You two didn't think you could fool me, did you? I know she sneaked out to see you." Something about the way she looked at him sent a sick chill through Jerry. "Surely you can fix something yourself and let the poor girl rest."

Then it hadn't been a dream! But then why had Steph pretended—?

He couldn't figure it. "Yeah. Sure," he said dully, his thoughts jumbled. "I can make a sandwich." He turned to go.

"You should be about through with the basement by now," she said. "But even if you're not, get up to the roof this afternoon. The weatherman says there's a sixty percent chance of a thunderstorm tonight."

"Basement's done. Roof is next."

"Excellent! But don't work *too* hard, young Pritchard. Save something for Stephie."

She returned to her book.

Jerry felt numb as he walked back to the kitchen. The old lady hadn't touched him once! She seemed more relaxed and at ease with herself than he could ever remember—a cat-that-had-swallowed-the-canary sort of self-satisfaction. And she hadn't tried to lay a single finger on him!

The day was getting weirder and weirder.

Replacing the shingles on the sloping dormer surface outside old lady Gati's bedroom had looked like an easy job from the ground. But the shingles were odd, scalloped affairs that she had ordered special from San Francisco to match the originals on the house, and Jerry had trouble keeping them aligned on the curved surface. He could have used a third hand, too. What would have been an hour's work for two men had already taken Jerry three in the broiling sun, and he wasn't quite finished yet.

While he was working, he noted that the wood trim on the upper levels was going to need painting soon. That was going to be a hellish job, what with the oculus windows, the ornate friezes, cornices, brackets, and keystones. Some crazed woodcarver had had a field day with this stuff—probably thought it was "art." But Jerry was going to be the one to paint it. He'd put that off as long as he could, and definitely wouldn't do it in summer.

He pulled an insulated wire free of the outside wall to fit in the final shingles by the old lady's window. It ran from somewhere on the roof down to the ground—directly *into* the ground. Jerry pulled himself up onto the parapet above the dormer to see where the wire originated. He followed it up until it linked into the lightning rod on the peak of the attic garret. *Everything* connected with this house was ornate—even the lightning rods had designs on them!

He climbed back down, pulled the ground wire free of the dormer, and tacked the final shingles into place. When he reached the ground, he slumped on the bottom rung of the ladder and rested a moment. The heat from the roof was getting to him. His teeshirt was drenched with perspiration and he was reeling with fatigue.

Enough for today. He'd done the bulk of the work. A hurricane could hit the area and that dormer would not leak. He could put the finishing touches on tomorrow. He lowered the ladder to the ground, then checked the kitchen for Steph. She wasn't there. Just as well. He didn't have the energy to pry an explanation out of her. Something was cooking in the oven, but he was too bushed to eat. He grabbed half a six pack of beer from the fridge and stumbled down to the gatehouse. Hell with dinner. A shower, a few beers, a good night's sleep, and he'd be just fine in the morning.

It was a long ways into dark, but Jerry was still awake. Tired as he was, he couldn't get to sleep. As thunder rumbled in the distance, charging in from the west, and slivers of ever-brightening light flashed between the blinds, thoughts of last night tumbled through his mind, arousing him anew. Something strange going on up at that house. Old lady Gati was acting weird, and so was Steph.

Steph . . . he couldn't stop thinking about her. He didn't care what kind of game she was playing, she still meant something to him. He'd never felt this way before. He—

There was a noise at the door. It opened and Steph stepped inside. She said nothing as she came forward, but in the glow of the lightning flashes from outside, Jerry could see her removing her nightgown as she crossed the room. He saw it flutter to the floor and then she was beside him, bringing the dreamlike memories of last night into the sharp focus of the real and now. He tried to talk to her but she would only answer in a soft, breathless "uh-huh" or "uh-uh" as she tugged off his shorts. And then her wandering lips and tongue moved down his belly. When she knelt at the side of the bed and took him in her mouth, he wiped all questions from his mind, because if she answered him, she'd have to stop what she was doing, and he didn't want her to stop. Ever.

When it was finally over and the two of them lay in a gasping tangle of limbs and sheets, Jerry decided that now was the time to find out what was going on between her and old lady Gati, and what kind of game she was playing with him. He would ask her in a few seconds . . . or maybe in a minute . . . soon . . . thunder was louder than ever outside but that wasn't going to bother him . . . all he wanted to do right now was close his eyes and enjoy the delicious exhaustion of this afterglow a little longer . . . only a little . . . just close his eyes for a few seconds . . . no more . . .

"Sleep well, my love."

Jerry forced his eyes open. Steph's face hovered over him in the flashing dimness as he teetered on the brink of unconsciousness. She kissed him lightly on the forehead and whispered, "Goodnight, young Pritchard. And thank you."

It was as if someone had tossed a bucket of icy water on him. Suddenly Jerry was wide awake. *Young Pritchard?* Why had she said that? Why had she imitated old lady Gati's voice that way? The accent, with its roll of the *r,* had been chillingly perfect.

Steph had slipped her nightgown over her head and was on her way out. Jerry jumped out of bed and caught her at the door.

"I don't think that was funny, Steph!" She ignored him and pushed the screen door open. He grabbed her arm. "Hey, look! What kind of game are you playing? What's it gonna be tomorrow morning? Same as today? Pretend that nothing happened tonight?" She tried to pull away but he held on. "Talk to me, Steph! What's going on?"

A picture suddenly formed in his mind of Steph going back to the house and having hot chocolate with old lady Gati and telling her every intimate detail of their lovemaking, and the old lady getting excited, *feeding* off it.

"What's going *on!"* Involuntarily, his grip tightened on her arm.

"You're hurting me!" The words cut like an icy knife. The voice was Steph's, but the tone, the accent, the roll of the *r*'s, the inflection—all were perfect mimicry of old lady Gati, down to the last nuance. But she had been in pain. It couldn't have been rehearsed!

Jerry flipped the light switch and spun her around. It was Steph, all right, as achingly beautiful as ever, but something was wrong. The Steph he knew should have been frightened. The Steph before him was changed. She held herself differently. Her stance was haughty, almost imperious. And there was something in her eyes—a strange light.

"Oh, sweet Jesus! What's happened to you?"

He could see indecision flickering through her eyes as she

regarded him with a level stare. Outside, it began to rain. A few scattered forerunner drops escalated to a full-scale torrent in a matter of seconds as their eyes remained locked, their bodies frozen amid day-bright flashes of lightning and the roar of thunder and wind-driven rain. Then she smiled. It was like Steph's smile, but it wasn't.

"Nothing," she said in that crazy mixed voice.

And then he thought he knew. For a blazing instant, it was clear to him: "You're not Steph!" In the very instant he said it he disbelieved it, but then her smile broadened and her words turned his blood to ice:

"Yes, I am . . . for the moment." The voice was thick with old lady Gati's accent, and it carried a triumphant note. "What Stephie sees, *I* see! What Stephie feels, *I* feel!" She lifted the hem of her nightgown. "Look at my legs! Beautiful, aren't they?"

Jerry released her arm as if he had been burned. She moved closer but Jerry found himself backing away. Steph was crazy! Her mind had snapped. She thought she was old lady Gati! He had never been faced with such blatant madness before, and it terrified him. He felt exposed, vulnerable before it. With a trembling hand, he grabbed his jeans from the back of the chair.

Marta Gati looked out of Stephie's eyes at young Pritchard as he struggled into his trousers, and she wondered what to do next. She had thought him asleep when she had kissed him good night and made the slip of calling him "young Pritchard." She had known she couldn't keep her nightly possession of Stephie from him for too long, but she had not been prepared for a confrontation tonight. She would try for sympathy first.

"Do you have any idea, young Pritchard," she said, trying to make Stephie's voice sound as American as she could, "what it is like to be trapped all your life in a body as deformed as mine? To be repulsive to other children as a child, to grow up watching other girls find young men and go dancing and get married and know that at night they are holding their man in their arms and feeling all the things a woman should feel? You have no idea what my life has been like, young Pritchard. But through the years I found a way to remedy the situation. Tonight I am a complete woman—*your* woman!"

"Stephanie!" young Pritchard shouted, fear and disbelief mingling in the strained pallor of his face. "Listen to yourself! You sound crazy! What you're saying is impossible!"

"No! Not impossible!" she said, although she could understand his reaction. A few years ago, she too would have called it impossible. Her brother Karl had devoted himself to her and his business. He never married, but he would bring women back to the house now and then when he thought she was asleep. It would have been wonderful if he could have brought a man home for her, but that was impossible. Yet it hadn't stopped her yearnings. And it was on those nights when he and a woman were in the next bedroom that Marta realized that she could sense things in Karl's women. At first she thought it was imagination, but this was more than mere fantasy. She could feel their passion, feel their skin tingling, feel them exploding within. And one night, after they both had spent themselves and fallen asleep, she found herself in the other woman's body —actually lying in Karl's bed and seeing the room through her eyes!

As time went on, she found she could enter their bodies while they slept and actually take them over. She could get up and walk! A sob built in her throat at the memory. To *walk!* That had been joy enough at first. Then she would dance by herself. She had wanted so much all her life to dance, to waltz, and now she could! She never dared more than that until Karl died and left her free. She had perfected her ability since then.

"It will be a good life for you, young Pritchard," she said. "You won't even have to work. Stephie will be my maid and housekeeper during the day and your lover at night." He shook his head, as if to stop her, but she pressed on. "And when you get tired of Stephie, I'll bring in another. And another. You'll have an endless stream of young, willing bodies in your bed. You'll have such a *good* life, young Pritchard!"

A new look was growing in his eyes: belief.

"It's really you!" he said in a hoarse whisper. "Oh, my dear sweet Lord, it's really you in Steph's body! I . . . I'm getting out of here!"

She moved to block his way and he stayed back. He could have easily overpowered her, but he seemed afraid to let her get too near. She couldn't let him go, not after all her work to set up a perfect household.

"No! You mustn't do that! You must stay here!"

"This is sick!" he cried, his voice rising in pitch as a wild light sprang into his eyes. "This is the Devil's work!"

"No, no," she said, soothingly. "Not the Devil. Just me. Just something—"

"Get away from me!" he said, backing toward his dresser. He spun and pulled open the top drawer, rummaged through it and came up with a thick book with a cross on its cover. "Get away, Satan!" he cried, thrusting the book toward her face.

Marta almost laughed. "Don't be silly, young Pritchard! I'm not evil! I'm just doing what I have to do. I'm not hurting Stephie. I'm just borrowing her body for a while!"

"Out, demon!" he said, shoving the Bible almost into her face. *"Out!"*

This was getting annoying now. She snatched the book from his grasp and hurled it across the room. "Stop acting like a fool!"

He looked from her to the book and back to her with an awed expression. At that moment there was a particularly loud crash of thunder and the lights went out. Young Pritchard cried out in horror and brushed past her. He slammed out the door and ran into the storm.

Marta ran as far as the doorway and stopped. She peered through the deluge. Even with the rapid succession of lightning strokes and sheets, she could see barely a dozen feet. He was nowhere in sight. She could see no use in running out into the storm and following him. She glanced at his keys on the bureau and smiled. How far could a half-naked man go in a storm like this?

Marta crossed the room and sat on the bed. She ran Stephie's hand over the rumpled sheets where less than half an hour ago the two of them had been locked in passion. Warmth rose within her. *So good.* So good to have a man's arms around you, wanting you, needing you, *demanding* you. She couldn't give this up. Not now, not when it was finally at her disposal after all these years.

But young Pritchard wasn't working out. She had thought any virile young man would leap at what she offered, but apparently she had misjudged him. Or was a stable relationship within her household just a fool's dream? She had so much to learn about the outside world. Karl had kept her so sheltered from it.

Perhaps her best course was the one she had taken with the last housekeeper. Take over her body when she was asleep and drive to the bars and roadhouses outside of town. Find a man—two men, if she were in the mood—and spend most of the night in a motel room. Then come back to the house, clean her up, and leave her asleep in her bed. It was anonymous, it was exciting, but it was somehow . . . empty.

She would be more careful with Stephie than with the last housekeeper. Marta had been ill one night but had moved into the other body anyway. She had lost control when a stomach spasm had gripped her own body. The pain had drawn her back to the house, leaving the woman to awaken between two strangers. She had panicked and run out into the road.

Yes, she had to be very careful with this one. Stephie was so sensitive to her power, whatever it was. She only had to become drowsy and Marta could slip in and take complete control, keeping Stephie's mind unconscious while she controlled her body. A few milligrams of a sedative in her cocoa before bedtime and Stephie's body was Marta's for the night.

But young Pritchard wasn't working out. At least not so far. There was perhaps a slim chance she could reason with him when he came back. She had to try. She found him terribly attractive. But where could he be?

Sparks of alarm flashed through her as she realized that her own body was upstairs in the house, lying in bed, helpless, defenseless. What if that crazy boy—?

Quickly, she slid onto the bed and closed her eyes. She shut out her senses one by one, blocking off the sound of the rain and thunder, the taste of the saliva in her mouth, the feel of the bedclothes against her back . . .

. . . and opened her eyes in her own bedroom in the house. She looked around, alert for any sign that her room had been entered. Her bedroom door was still closed, and there was no moisture anywhere on the floor.

Good! He hasn't been in here!

Marta pushed herself up in bed and transferred to the wheelchair. She wheeled herself out to the hall and down to the elevator, cursing its slow descent as it took her to the first floor. When it finally stopped, she propelled herself at top speed to the foyer where she immediately turned the dead bolt on the front door. She noted with satisfaction that the slate floor under her chair was as dry as when she had walked out earlier as Stephie. She was satisfied that she was alone in the house.

Safe!

She rolled herself into the solarium at a more leisurely pace. She knew the rest of the doors and windows were secure—Stephie always locked up before she made the bedtime chocolate. She stopped before the big bay windows and watched the storm for a minute. It was a fierce one. She gazed out at the blue-white, water-blurred lightning flashes and wondered what she was going to do about young Pritchard. If she couldn't convince him to stay, then surely he would be in town tomorrow, telling a wild tale. No one would believe him, of course, but it would start talk, fuel rumors, and that would make it almost impossible to get help in the future. It might even make Stephie quit, and Marta didn't know how far her power could reach. She'd be left totally alone out here.

Her fingers tightened on the arm rests of her wheelchair. She couldn't let that happen.

She closed her eyes and blocked out the storm, blocked out her senses . . .

. . . and awoke in Stephie's body again.

She leapt to the kitchenette and pulled out the drawers until she found the one she wanted. It held three forks, a couple of spoons, a spatula, and a knife—a six-inch carving knife.

It would have to do.

She hurried out into the rain and ran the hundred yards uphill to the house.

Jerry rammed his shoulder against the big oak front door again but only added to bruises the door had already put there. He screamed at it.

"In God's name—open!"

The door ignored him. What was he going to do? He had to get inside! Had to get to that old lady! Had to wring the Devil out of her! Had to find a way in! Make her give Steph back!

His mother had warned him about this sort of thing. He could almost hear her voice between the claps of thunder: *Satan walks the earth, Jerome, searching for those who forsake the Word. Beware—he's waiting for you!*

Jerry knew the Devil had found him—in the guise of old lady Gati! What was happening to Steph was all his fault!

He ran back into the downpour and headed around toward the rear. Maybe the kitchen door was unlocked. He glanced through the solarium windows as he passed. His bare feet slid to a halt on the wet grass as he stopped and took a better look.

There she was: old lady Gati, the Devil herself, zonked out in her wheelchair.

The sight of her sitting there as if asleep while her spirit was down the hill controlling Steph's body was more than Jerry could stand. He looked around for something to hurl through the window, and in the next lightning flash he spotted the ladder next to the house on the lawn. He picked it up and charged the solarium like a jousting knight. Putting all his weight behind the ladder, he rammed it through the center bay window. The sound of shattering glass broke the last vestige of Jerry's control. Howling like a madman, he drove the ladder against the window glass again and again until every pane and every muntin was smashed and battered out of the way.

Then he climbed in.

The shards of glass cut his bare hands and feet but Jerry barely noticed. His eyes were on old lady Gati. Throughout all the racket, she hadn't budged.

Merciful Lord, it's true! Her spirit's left her body!

He stumbled over to her inert form and stood behind her, hesitating. He didn't want to touch her—his skin crawled at the thought—but he had to put an end to this. Now. Swallowing the bile that sloshed up from his stomach, Jerry wrapped his fingers around old lady Gati's throat. He flinched at the feel of her wrinkles against his palms, but he clenched his teeth and began to squeeze. He put all his strength into it and then let go.

He couldn't do it.

"God, give me strength!" he cried, but he couldn't bring himself to do it. Not while she was like this. It was like strangling a corpse! She was barely breathing as it was!

Something tapped against the intact bay window to the right. Jerry spun to look—a flash from outside outlined the grounding wire from the lightning rods as it swayed in the wind and slapped against the window. It reminded him of a snake—

A snake! And suddenly he knew: *It's a sign! A sign from God!*

He ran to the window and threw it open. He reached out, wrapped the wire around his hands, and pulled. It wouldn't budge from the ground. He braced a foot against the window sill, putting his back and all his weight into the effort. Suddenly the metal grounding stake pulled free and he staggered back, the insulated wire thrashing about in his hands . . . just like a snake.

He remembered that snake handlers' church back in the hills his mother had dragged him to one Sunday a few years ago. He had watched in awe as the men and women would grab water moccasins and cottonmouths and hold them up, trusting in the Lord to protect them. Some were bitten, some were not. Ma had told him it was all God's will.

God's will!

He pulled the old lady's wheelchair closer to the window and wrapped the wire tightly around her, tying it snugly behind the backrest of the chair, and jamming the grounding post into the metal spokes of one of the wheels.

"This is your snake, Miss Gati," he told her unconscious form. "It's God's will if it bites you!"

He backed away from her until he was at the entrance to the solarium. Lightning flashed as violently as ever, but none came down the wire. He couldn't wait any longer. He had to find Steph. As he turned to head for the front door, he saw someone standing on the south lawn, staring into the solarium. It was old Lady Gati, wearing Steph's body. When she looked through the broken bay window and saw him there, she screamed and slumped to the ground.

"Steph!" What was happening to her?

Jerry sprinted across the room and dove through the shattered window onto the south lawn.

Marta awoke in her own body, panicked.

What has he done to me?

She felt all right. There was no pain, no—

My arms! Her hands were free but she couldn't move her upper arms! She looked down and saw the black insulated wire coiled tightly around her upper body, binding her to the chair. She tried to twist, to slide down on the chair and slip free, but the wire wouldn't give an inch. She tried to see where it was tied. If she could get her hands on the knot . . .

She saw the wire trailing away from her chair, across the floor and out the window and up into the darkness.

Up! To the roof! The lightning rods!

Jerry cradled Steph's head in his arm and slapped her wet face as hard as he dared. He'd hoped the cold pounding rain and the noise of the storm would have brought her around, but she was still out. He didn't want to hurt her, but she had to wake up.

"Steph! C'mon, Steph! You've got to wake up! Got to fight her!"

As she stirred, he heard old lady Gati howl from the solarium. Steph's eyes fluttered, then closed again. He shook her. "Steph! Please!"

She opened her eyes and stared at him. His spirits leaped.

"That's it, Steph! Wake up! It's me—Jerry! You've got to stay awake!"

She moaned and closed her eyes, so he shook her again.

"Steph! Don't let her take you over again!"

As she opened her eyes again, Jerry dragged her to her feet.

"Come on! Walk it off! Let's go! You've *got* to stay awake!"

Suddenly her face contorted and she swung on him. Something gleamed in her right hand as she plunged it toward his throat. Jerry got his forearm up just in time to block it. Pain seared through his arm and he cried out.

"Oh, God! It's you!"

"Yes!" She slashed at him again and he backpedaled to avoid the knife. His bare feet slipped on the grass and he went down on his back. He rolled frantically, fearing she would be upon him, but when he looked up, she was running toward the house, toward the smashed bay window.

"No!"

He couldn't let her get inside and untie the old lady's body. Steph's only hope was a lightning strike.

Please, God, he prayed. *Now! Let it be now!*

But though bolts crackled through the sky almost continuously, none of them hit the house. Groaning with fear and frustration, Jerry scrambled to his feet and sprinted after her. He had to stop her!

He caught her from behind and brought her down about two dozen feet from the house. She screamed and thrashed like an enraged animal, twisting and slashing at him again and again with the knife. She cut him along the ribs as he tried to pin her arms and was rearing back for a better angle on his chest when the night turned blue white. He saw the rage on Steph's face turn to wide-eyed horror. Her body arched convulsively as she opened her mouth and let out a high-pitched shriek of agony that rose and cut off like a circuit being broken—

—only to be taken up by another voice from within the solarium. Jerry glanced up and saw old lady Gati's body jittering in her chair like a hooked fish while blue fire played all about her. Her hoarse cry was swallowed and drowned as her body exploded in a roiling ball of flame. Fire was everywhere in the solarium. The very air seemed to burn.

He removed the knife from Steph's now limp hand and dragged her to a safer distance from the house. He shook her. "Steph?"

He could see her eyes rolling back and forth under the lids. Finally they opened and stared at him uncomprehendingly.

"Jerry?" She bolted up to a sitting position. "Jerry! What's going on?"

His grip on the knife tightened as he listened to her voice, searching carefully for the slightest hint of an accent, the slightest roll of an *r*. There wasn't any he could detect, but there was only one test that could completely convince him.

"My name," he said. "What's my last name, Steph?"

"It's Pritchard, of course. But—" She must have seen the flames flickering in his eyes because she twisted around and cried out. "The house! It's on fire! Miss Gati—!"

She had said it perfectly! The real Steph was back! Jerry threw away the knife and lifted her to her feet. "She's gone," he told her. "Burnt up. I saw her."

"But how?"

He had to think fast—couldn't tell her the truth. Not yet. "Lightning. It's my fault. I must have messed up the rods when I was up on the roof today!"

"Oh, God, Jerry!" She clung to him and suddenly the storm seemed far away. "What'll we do?"

Over her shoulder, he watched the flames spreading throughout the first floor and lapping up at the second through the broken bay window. "Got to get out of here, Steph. They're gonna blame me for it, and God knows what'll happen."

"It was an accident! They can't blame you for that!"

"Oh, yes they will!" Jerry was thinking about the ground wire wrapped around the old lady's corpse. No way anyone would think that was an accident. "I hear she's got family in New York. They'll see me hang if they can, I just know it! I've got to get out of here." He pushed her to arm's length and stared at her. "Come with me?"

She shook her head. "I can't! How—?"

"We'll make a new life far from here. We'll head west and won't stop till we reach the ocean." He could see her wavering. "Please, Steph! I don't think I can make it without you!"

Finally, she nodded.

He took her hand and pulled her along behind him as he raced down the slope for the gatehouse. He glanced back at the old house and saw flames dancing in the second floor windows. Somebody down in town would see the light from the fire soon and then half the town would be up here to either fight it or watch it being fought. They had to be out of here before that.

It's gonna be okay, he told himself. They'd start a new life out in California. And someday, when he had the nerve and he thought she was ready for it, he'd tell her the truth. But for now, as long as Steph was at his side, he could handle anything. Everything was going to be all right.

Patrolman Grimes looked better now. He was back from the couple's apartment and stood in the hospital corridor with an open notebook, ready to recite.

"All right," Burke said. "What've we got?"

"We've got a twenty-three-year-old named Jerome Pritchard. Came out here from West Virginia nine months ago."

"I mean drugs—crack, Angel Dust, needles, fixings."

"No, sir. The apartment was clean. The neighbors are in absolute shock. Everybody loved the Pritchards and they all seem to think he was a pretty straight guy. A real churchgoer —carried his own Bible and never missed a Sunday, they said. Had an assembly line job and talked about starting night courses at UCLA as soon as he made the residency requirement. He and his wife appeared to be real excited about the baby, going to Lamaze classes and all that sort of stuff."

"Crack, I tell you!" Burke said. "Got to be!"

"As far as we can trace his movements, sir, it seems that after the baby was delivered at 10:06 this morning, he ran out of here like a bat out of hell, came back about an hour later carrying his Bible and a big oblong package, waited until the baby was brought to the mother for feeding, then . . . well, you know."

"Yeah. I know." The new father had pulled a 10 gauge shotgun from that package and blown the mother and kid *away, then put the barrel against his own throat and completed the job. "But why, dammit!"*

"Well . . . the baby did have a birth defect."

"I know. I saw. But there are a helluva lot of birth defects a damn sight worse. Hell, I mean, her legs were only withered a little!"

MR. RIGHT

Richard Christian Matheson

The young woman wept, "He's such an absolute bastard, doctor. He does the most horrible things."

The doctor shifted in the chair and continued to take notes. "What made you decide to come in and talk?"

The woman hesitated.

"Because he's gotten worse," she said. "Last night he asked me to fix him something to eat." Her mouth pulled downward. "He had me heat the stew until it was burning hot, then suddenly got angry about something."

The woman's voice began to shudder.

"Before I could protect myself, he grabbed my hands and held them over the stove." She held up raw palms, covered with salve.

The doctor cringed a little. "Did you call the police?"

"No. He yanked the phone out of the wall, then he beat me with his belt." She rubbed at her arms. "My whole body is covered with welts."

"How long has this been going on?" the doctor asked.

The woman gestured shakily.

"I can't remember. Three years. Maybe more."

"Have you tried to leave him?"

"Every day," the woman answered, trying to steady herself, "But he finds me. I try to turn him away but what he does to me in bed . . ."

The doctor looked up from the notes. "Can you be more

specific? It's important that I understand what you're going through. It's the first step in a successful treatment."

The woman looked at the doctor uneasily.

"Last night . . ."

"Yes . . . ?"

". . . last night, after he beat me up, he tied me to the bedposts in the bedroom." She drew shallow breath. "Then he raped me."

The doctor swallowed.

"It was horrible but at the same time it was wonderful. He does things like I've never had any man do." For the first time, the woman showed signs of a smile. "Incredible things. Like a fantasy come true."

The doctor jotted notes. "Can you describe the things he does?"

The woman fell into uncomfortable silence.

"I couldn't, it's so intimate. I just couldn't."

The doctor nodded. "When you're ready."

Unexpectedly, the woman's face tensed.

"Doctor, I'm so scared. He's so crazy and I can't make myself pull away."

The doctor made a sympathetic sound and continued to listen.

"He's killed two of my dogs and last week he killed an entire litter of my cat's kittens with a knife." The woman's eyes shut tightly. "When he was a boy, he battered a rabbit to death with a hammer. And he's done even more horrible things. He's told me."

Was there no *end?* thought the doctor.

"He tried to poison a friend of mine because she kept begging him to sleep with her and bothering him." The woman's cheekbones quivered. "He sent her candies and signed the card from her children. They were filled with arsenic. She's dying right now." The woman held her head. "Nerve damage."

The doctor set the note pad on the desk.

"Listen to me. You must leave this man, immediately. *Today.*"

"But he makes me feel things that no man has. Maybe if I compromise. Maybe you could talk to him."

"No. I'll call him for you," the doctor said, "but I'll lie. I'll tell him that I've had you moved to a hospital in another part of the country. I want you on a plane today."

The doctor touched the woman's hand.

"You *must* escape him. There's no room for compromise. This man is sick. He shouldn't be allowed around sane people."

The woman tightened her grasp on the doctor's hand like a child seeking protection. "You don't think that what he makes me feel in bed is the truth?" she asked. "Maybe he really does love me?"

The doctor shook the woman's hand, insistently.

"No! You must believe me. Your time may be running out."

"Other women have responded in the same way," the woman continued, as if to justify her plight. "He brings them all to ecstasy."

The doctor pressed a buzzer on the desk and interrupted the woman, who was beginning to cry again. "I want you to make a one-way reservation to Honolulu," the doctor told the secretary. "In Miss Shubert's name . . . for today."

The doctor took hold of the woman's shoulders.

"Now listen to me. I want you to go home and pack, take a cab to the airport and leave today. Call me when you get there. It's the only way you'll survive this maniac."

The woman looked up at the doctor with defenseless eyes and nodded.

"Good," said the doctor.

Fifteen minutes after Miss Shubert's flight had taken off, the doctor sat overlooking the city, completing notes. The buzzer sounded on one of the phone extensions and the doctor pushed down the lit button.

"Yes? This is Miss Shubert's psychiatrist," said the doctor. "No, I don't know where she is. She left today without a word. But I'm glad I reached you. I think you're somebody I'd really like to get to know."

The doctor trembled, running hands through her own hair, imagining the first thing he'd do to her.

BLOOD NIGHT

Chet Williamson

She was fire and flesh and motion. Her body coiled and released beneath his, returning thrust for thrust, the candle-light caught and held in the thin sheen of sweat that filmed her skin. He tasted the salt as his mouth searched her neck and shoulders. His orgasm was dangerously close, and he pulled his head away and looked at the oak headboard, trying to regain control, to hold back the torrent that threatened to spill out of him, a sensation too demanding to be restrained by mere flesh.

And then she moaned differently than before, and stiffened, and he knew she was there and he let himself pour into her. The moan became a low scream, and his pleasure was seasoned with bright pain as her nails sketched crimson tracks across his shoulders, down his back.

He winced, but the pain heightened the flaring in his groin, and he began to jet again, even more forcefully. He closed his eyes and let the feeling wash over him, let the sensation take him deeper into his dream until he was utterly lost in it, and the cool and unrumpled sheets of the bed where he slept alone were not even a dim, vestigial memory.

When he awoke the next morning, he became aware of sticky moisture on the sheet beneath him. His pajama bottoms were damp as well, and had turned starch-stiff at the edge of the stain.

Jesus, a wet dream, he thought. And no wonder. He couldn't remember having an erotic dream that seemed so real. He recalled in vivid detail the feel of the woman's body, her face aglow with ecstasy on the white pillow. And he could swear that the scent of her still hung in the air, a cloying, heavy, musky aroma that perfectly complemented her wildness in lovemaking.

Richard Bell tossed back the sheet, put his feet on the floor, and wished that he didn't have to go to the office, wished that the girl had been real and was still there in the bed, waiting, begging for another bout.

To Bell, making love was just that—a bout. A fight to be fought, a game of dominator and dominated, not in the sense of sadomasochism, but of a contest between two adversaries. If Bell made the girl come, he won, he had done it again—kicked the winning field goal, hit the homer in the bottom of the ninth, scored a knockout that left his opponent breathless on her back.

But there were the other times—few, thankfully—when the ball was blocked, when he swung too soon, and when the blow missed completely, leaving *him* weak and lifeless, while unsatisfied and appraising eyes busted what was left of his balls, one at a humiliatingly slow time.

He didn't like that feeling one bit, and that was why last night had been so good. They had been perfect together. He had made her come with an intensity he had not known women were capable of. It had been *damned* good, and he felt himself grow hard at the memory of it.

Enough. He hadn't had a wet dream since he was in college, and he didn't want to start pulling on it before he went to work.

Bell hopped up and walked into the bathroom, pausing to take off his stained pajamas and drop them into the hamper. He shaved and showered, but as he toweled himself dry he became aware of an irritation on his back. Wiping the steam from the mirror with a few swipes of his wet towel, he turned his back to it and looked over his shoulder.

There, starting at the top of his spine and trailing downward to where they disappeared in the thick curly hair just above his coccyx, were four thin, red welts, parallel to each other. He studied them with narrowed eyes and reached awkwardly around to touch them.

They were real. He could feel the narrow mounds like taut cords under the skin. A thought occurred to him, and he walked quickly back to the bedroom and examined the bed. There were blood stains on the bottom sheet, mere traceries of light red that he would never have noticed had he not been looking for them.

What the hell's going on here? he wondered. Did a girl sneak into his bed last night and ball him silly? Or had he been out and gotten so drunk that he didn't remember picking her up? No, there was no hangover, and the book by his bed reminded him that he had read himself to sleep. He turned the volume around and looked at the naked girl on the cover, the good-looking man with the gun pulling back a lilac sheet to expose her to the prospective buyer.

Typical paperback crap, he thought, with lots of violence, lots of action, lots of sex. For a moment his mind clicked into overdrive, and he asked himself, could that have been it? Could he have dreamed about a scene in the book and . . .

But where the hell did the marks come from?

Weird. Really weird. Maybe he had done it to himself— put his arms around his shoulders like that goofy high school gag where you muss your own hair and from behind it looks like someone else is doing it.

He looked at the clock and started to hustle. Maybe he'd tell Perry about it. Maybe Perry would know something.

Monday

"Stigmata," suggested Perry.

"Stigmata? Like the wounds of Christ that show up on people at Easter?"

Perry chuckled. "Kind of. Some people can will themselves, consciously or subconsciously, to bleed, produce scars, wounds, you name it." He put his size thirteens on his desktop and smiled benignly at Bell, who shook his head.

"Doesn't seem possible."

"Why not? You made yourself come subconsciously by what you dreamed."

Bell put a finger to his lips. "You mind? I'd rather not have everyone in the office know I still have . . ." He hesitated.

"Nocturnal emissions?" Perry grinned. "Sounds like something Captain Midnight would go on, doesn't it? But don't worry, my lips are sealed. No one will hear about your adolescent sex life from me."

"Smartass. You're married, you don't need an adolescent sex life."

Perry's face got serious for a moment, almost dreamy. "I sort of envy you the ability," he said, and sighed.

"What do you mean?"

"Well, if your dreams are *that* realistic," he said, pointing to Bell's back, "they must be beauts. Hell, you could fuck anybody, living or dead—Cybill, Cher, Madonna, Eleanor . . ."

"Eleanor?"

"Roosevelt. Looks aren't everything."

"Asshole!" Bell laughed. Then he started to think. "How could I do that?"

Perry shrugged. "Just go to sleep thinking about them, maybe."

Bell thought about what Perry had said. He thought about it at his desk, he thought about it driving home, and he thought about it as he ate his dinner. Maybe Perry was right. Maybe he *could* control his dreams, make them the next best thing to reality.

But when he thought about the women he could dream himself into bed with, Bell got scared. Movie stars, models, celebrities—in all likelihood they had two things in common. One, they were beautiful, and two, they were ballbusters.

And why not? They could call their shots, ask for the results of the AIDS tests, then bed whom they please. And if Mr. Wednesday Night turns out to be a washout in the rod department, there's always Mr. Thursday Night. Even the famous lays of the past—Messalina, Catherine the Great, Cleopatra—flop with them and you could lose your head, after they took God only knew what else first.

But what if the tables were turned? What if he, Richard Bell, became someone else in his dreams, someone who *couldn't* flop, like Don Juan, or Casanova, or even Errol f'crissake Flynn? He swallowed the last bite of TV dinner and grinned. Goddammit, it just might work.

He dumped the aluminum tray in the trash and tossed the silverware in the sink, then went into the spare bedroom and slid open the closet door. Inside were a dozen large cardboard boxes, one of which was marked "Books." He pulled it out, undid the flaps, and looked inside at the erotic souvenirs of his college days.

There was *The Pearl* (a frat house favorite for oral reading), the *Kama-sutra* (great if you liked to yell "Phut!" during sex), *My Secret Life* (he paused for a moment at that one, but kept rummaging), and there, all the way at the bottom, a dog-eared, one-volume *Memoirs of Casanova.*

What could it hurt? he thought. A little bedtime reading, that's all. He looked at his watch. 8:00. A far cry from bedtime. Yet . . .

He showered and shaved, knowing full well that he'd have to shave again the following morning. Then he turned on the bedside lamp and slid naked beneath the covers. Opening the book at random, he began to read. Soon the comfortable bed, the coolness of the sheets, and the antiquated prose soothed and relaxed him, despite the sensual subject matter. When he felt that he could sleep, he put the book aside and turned out the light, imagining himself as Casanova wrapped in the embrace of cool, marble arms ready to fling away reputation for his love. His erection grew until, in his half-waking state, he felt as if it filled the very bed, then the whole room, and finally the entire earth. And that world opened to him, becoming a vagina that hugged him tightly and impaled itself on him so deeply that he could feel the molten core of it.

Then the fantasy was over, and he was in the dream.

Tuesday

The first thing he saw when his eyes creaked painfully open the next morning was the alarm clock's stubby hands pointing to eleven. He felt panic rush from stomach to chest to throat, and he tried to push himself up. Pain shot through him, as if every muscle in his body had been stretched to the point of tearing, held there for hours, and then been snapped back without warning. He fell back moaning, and looked down the length of his body.

The sheets and blankets rolled haphazardly onto the floor like a wool and cotton river. The bottom sheet was soaked with sweat and was stiff in many places, sticky in others. Two spots were still damp with a rust-brown stain that he knew was blood.

His body was marked with bruises at elbows and knees. The pubic hair was set into hard curls by dried fluids, and powdery bloodstains ran the length of his shaft and speckled his thighs. His testicles ached miserably, and the ridge of soft skin around the head of his penis was rubbed open in several places.

Trembling from both fear and pain, he examined himself gingerly to find the source of the blood. Then he remembered the virgins.

There had been two of them, twin sisters about fourteen years of age. Their mother, a duchess he had seduced months before, had brought them to him, begging him to initiate them into womanhood before they could be rudely skewered by brothers or servants. He had done so gladly, breaking both hymens with care and dexterity so that neither flinched nor cried, then probing them both to multiple climaxes until each in turn swooned in exhaustion. He then turned his attention to the duchess, who had responded like a starved animal. He served her well and left her breathless. They were only the first.

Lying in the bed as the sun tried unsuccessfully to push through the drawn curtains, Bell remembered the women he had loved the night before—noblewomen, sluts, maids, young girls, grandmothers ripe both in years and juices; all had bowed beneath his phallic might and worshipped the great thick god he carried. All had melted like the candles that flanked the myriad beds to which he bore them. Not one had been unsatisfied.

Not one.

Bell smiled.

After the sheets were safely soaking in a prewash liquid, he called his secretary and told her that he had been throwing up all night and had slept through the morning. He assured her that he felt better and would be in the following day. After he hung up, he showered, made a light lunch, and took a nap that lasted until six o'clock. He treated himself to dinner out, and then went to a movie, careful to avoid anything with an R rating. It would be best, he thought, to get a good night's sleep.

Wednesday

The next morning he awoke refreshed, having passed a dreamless night. The bruises had faded to a pale gray, the minor abrasions had healed, and his muscles, though still stiff, were not as sore as before. He pressed his scrotum delicately, but whatever cords or muscles had been swollen had once again receded to normality, and he felt only a slight, infrequent ache.

When he arrived at the office, Perry was waiting for him, coffee in hand. "Well?" he said. "Who'd you sleep with that wiped you out for a day? King Kong?"

Bell laughed in spite of himself. "Flu. A little touch of flu, that's all."

Perry nodded knowingly. "Sure. The French flu. Come on, Rick, who was it? Mata Hari? Marilyn Monroe? The Trapp Family Singers?"

"Look, I told you. Flu. Plain old diarrhea-throw-up-dizzy-sweaty flu. No dreams, no women, no nothing. Flu."

"Oh-*kay!*" Perry stood up and walked to the door. "I'd tell *you*, Rick. But if you want to pretend it's flu, when I *know* you're playing Don Giovanni, it's oh-*kay.*" He walked out, then popped his head back into the office, whispered, "I hope you catch dream-crabs," and disappeared.

That night Bell took Perry's suggestion. He couldn't find anything on Don Juan in the Waldenbooks he visited after work, so he went to the library and took out Byron's poem and the libretto of Mozart's opera.

They were enough.

In a way he was surprised at Bell/Don Juan's performance. He was not nearly as gifted as Bell/Casanova, having an instrument of less length than Bell's own, but it was the technique that made Bell proud and made the ladies unutterably happy. In his dream Bell did more with hands, mouth, and feet than he had ever thought possible. And he was satisfied, too, many times over, for what Don Juan had lacked in size, he made up for in staying power. It was a case of parry as opposed to thrust, and Bell could not decide which he, or the whimpering receptacles of his art, preferred.

When he awoke he felt drained but happy. There were no cuts, no blood, no large bruises as there had been when he had played the insatiable Casanova. The bed, as before, looked like a battlefield, but he no longer felt like a war casualty.

Thursday

At work that day he ignored Perry's winks and innuendos, and thought about who would be the next subject in his nocturnal rogues' gallery. He finally decided, after some hesitation, on the Marquis de Sade. Except for tying a stewardess to the bed one night (at her request), Bell had never indulged in pleasure-through-pain sex. Rough stuff had always put him off, for, although he felt he could have gotten a buzz from a little gentle sadism, he was not willing to be victimized reciprocally.

But a dream was different. He could be the complete master there, totally in control, and there were no real victims in a dream, only the willing and eager masochists his imagination could create. Nothing could harm him. Nothing could harm de Sade.

That night, a worn, green paperback of *The 120 Days of Sodom* provided the inspiration, and he fell into a dream of blood and screams and pain that glowed redly in the night. Skin ripped like paper, bones broke with muffled snaps, and through it all came the groans of the tortured and the slow drip of blood on the stone floor. That night flesh was made to be broken, orifices to be filled, and fill them he did, until his tool became the most awful torturer's instrument of all, a red hot club to tear and rend and draw the shrieks that made it swell even more prodigiously and spew its seed in jets of liquid fire. And Bell/de Sade laughed at the shrieks and loved the night and knew that at last *here* was truth.

Friday

He awoke slowly, unwilling to leave the dream. But daylight was unrelenting, and soon his eyelids twitched open, revealing his body and the bed in which he lay.

They were both drenched with blood. The stench of it hung in the room like a thick cloud, and had drawn several flies inside through holes in screens and loose window fittings. He stared as one crawled across his stomach and settled in the red, wet pit of his navel, like a tiny starling in a birdbath of blood.

Bell lurched out of the bed, but before he reached the bathroom, brown bile mixed with blood *(God! did I drink it, too?)* gushed from his mouth, and he vomited everything onto the wooden boards of the hall. Everything except the fear. The taste of that remained long after toothpaste and mouthwash had removed the sour taste of vomit from his mouth.

He called in sick, then set to work cleaning up, scraping and wiping up the mess in the hall, stripping the bed and throwing the covers in a garbage bag, sponging the blood off the bed frame and the hardwood floor of the bedroom. The mattress, sodden with blood, was ruined.

And all the time he worked he thought about the night before and how he could relate it to anything he knew of humanity. He had *enjoyed* it, had actually derived pleasure from the torment of others. And not, perhaps, only torment. All the blood. Could a person lose so much blood and live? Had he killed in his dream?

Then memory came to him—a naked girl barely in her teens, forced by taut chains to stand spread-eagled, bleeding from a hundred tiny cuts . . . and he, a knife in his hand, coming up behind her for the last time, erection pointing toward the stones of the arching vault, the knife passing from his sight and the girl slumping in her chains with a terrible finality while he laughed and then he . . .

No!

He retched at the thought, and pummeled his temples to drive out the memory by force. His body fell onto the soaking mattress like a stone onto a sponge, and he babbled to himself in a high-pitched voice, "No, no, no, no, no, I didn't, I couldn't, no, no . . ." and started to cry.

Then from inside he heard another voice, still his, that soothed and calmed. *It wasn't real,* it said. *It was a dream.*

The blood! The blood was real!

You made the blood. You created it as you created the dream, and the people in it.

But I killed them!

You killed in a dream. You killed that which never existed.

But if I killed in a dream . . . I would kill in real life. If I enjoyed it then, I would enjoy it . . . in reality!

No. There is no punishment in a dream. No real pain, no real death. In reality, circumstances are different.

Circumstances?

There was no answer. Suddenly Bell felt very sad, very tired. He finished cleaning the bedroom, using scissors and a carving knife to cut the mattress into sections small enough to put into garbage bags. He could not have put it out intact with the trash. There would have been unpleasant questions about the blood.

It was late afternoon when he finished. After a supper of scrambled eggs and toast, he fell asleep on the couch and did not wake up until sunrise. He had no dreams.

Saturday

Lying there on the couch in the early morning, the horrors of two nights before seemed farther away. It was Saturday, he thought. No responsibilities, no appointments. A day to rest, to think.

When the shopping mall near his apartment opened, he went to a furniture store and ordered a new mattress to be delivered that afternoon. It felt good to get out. The past few days had stifled him, and the sensation of being among people again was intoxicating. He bought four new rock albums at Sam Goody's, a coffee table book on football at B. Dalton's, and two new sweaters. Around noon his stomach reminded him that he had had nothing since the eggs the night before, so he went into a quiet restaurant far from the mall's central hub.

Halfway through his burger, fries, and beer, Karen walked in, arms loaded with packages. She was a secretary in Sales, a divorcée with whom Bell had chatted once or twice at the coffee machine. One time he asked her out, but she had plans to go away for the weekend and asked for a rain check. He had not asked her out again.

But now he smiled and waved, beckoning her to his booth. He craved normality, someone to talk to. She smiled in response and joined him.

"Hi," she said, out of breath. "Wow, what a morning. What are you up to?"

"Same as you—shopping." It was nice to sit there with her, just talking and comparing purchases. She ordered a BLT and a beer, and as the conversation wound on, he felt himself happy to be with her. The dreams became just that—dreams. Nothing but harmless and unharmed phantoms, despite their physical manifestations. He almost forgot about the blood.

When the check came he picked it up despite her protests. "Look," he said, "one time you asked me for a rain check, so this is it, okay? In fact, let's go the whole way. How about a movie?"

She giggled like a schoolgirl. "Now?" He nodded. "I haven't been to a matinee in ages. Okay. What'll we see?"

There was a new Steve Martin comedy at one of the theaters in the mall's multiplex, and they just made the two o'clock show. They ate popcorn and laughed together, and before long his arm was around her shoulders and she was nestling contentedly into his warmth. He remembered the new mattress as they were walking out of the theater.

"Oh, Christ," he said. "I just remembered I've got a furniture delivery at my place."

She smiled. "That's a new excuse."

He took her hand and squeezed it. "No excuse. I'm serious. I'd better get over there before I miss them."

"Well," she said, "this was fun. Thank you."

It *was* fun, he thought. He liked Karen and wanted to see her again. Soon. "What about dinner?"

"Tonight?"

"Tied up?"

She hesitated, then shook her head. "I'd like that. Want to pick me up?"

The truck was just pulling out of the parking lot as he drove in. He waved frantically at the driver, who stopped and backed up over the sidewalk to unload. When the mattress was safely on the box spring and the truck was gone, Bell showered, shaved, dressed, and tried to read a magazine until six-thirty came.

It was difficult. The smell of blood was still in the air, even though he had opened all the windows and turned on the exhaust fans in the kitchen and bathroom. The early autumn breeze blowing past the curtains chilled him, and in the oncoming darkness he thought once more about his ability, his power—his curse, as he was now beginning to think of it. And the more he thought, the more he knew that there was great danger in it, if not physically, then mentally.

Being with Karen had made him realize how much the past few days (rather, *nights*) had changed him. He had always been a loner, but on those nights when he had been Don Juan and Casanova, and yes, de Sade, too, sex was better than it had ever been before. That was what frightened him, for he knew those nights were only masturbatory fantasies that pulled him inward, toward the self, barring the rest of humanity from his life. And he knew that if it continued, it would be harder and harder to return, and ultimately he would want to stay in the dreams forever.

He would not let that happen. He would be with people, not dream-haunts, and when he dreamed, he would dream as other people did, of things that become dim shadows by daylight, and left no trace of their momentary and nebulous existence in his sleeping mind.

It would be easy, he thought. The dreams, those horrid and wonderful dreams that had crossed the line of reality, had not come unbidden. He had wanted them, and as they had come as subjects before a king, so he could banish them from his dreamland and awake in peace, without blood and guilt and reflections on the fragility of circumstance.

Bell and Karen had dinner at a small restaurant that served excellent fresh seafood. They talked and laughed like old friends and held hands across the table over after-dinner drinks. The suggestion that they go to Bell's place was greeted with a sly enthusiasm, and he couldn't help but think that she both suspected and desired his intended ending to the evening.

He held his breath as he opened his apartment door, expecting the sweet blood smell. But the fans and the night air had removed all but a trace of the odor, and it seemed now only as if a rare steak had been grilled there recently. It was not offensive, Bell thought. Not offensive at all. On the contrary.

They sat on the couch, sipping sherry and talking softly, Karen's eyes becoming liquid, melting under his gaze. Then he was holding her, they were kissing, and his hands were sliding over her back, up to the nape of her neck where the soft hair grew in wispy curls, then over her shoulder, cupping her breast, while her tongue pressed against his, and little grunting sounds came from somewhere inside her.

He whispered something about being more comfortable in the bedroom, and they stood up, holding the embrace as tightly as possible, and moved down the short hall. She made a comment about breaking in a new mattress, and he laughed, heartily enough to be appreciative, but not enough to break the mood.

Despite the buildup, despite her readiness, despite his all-consuming desire, it was terrible. When they drew together naked for the first time, the only thing Bell could think of was a dream, was Don Juan and how he could compare to him; Casanova and his phallic power next to Richard Bell's. Foreplay was interminable, and Karen moaned with the need of him long after he could have entered.

But he could not get hard, no matter what Karen did, and the more impassioned her efforts grew, the more flaccid he became, until, in desperation, he entered her roughly with his hand, kneading and prodding until at last she suffered a small, quivering climax.

Bell rolled off of her and switched off the dim bedside light so that he wouldn't have to see her face, unsatisfied and accusing. He felt her hand on his shoulder, but was too full of despair to pull away. Her voice muttered softly, sympathetically, "S'okay. It happens."

Not to me! Never to me, bitch! The thoughts burst out wildly, uncontrolled, and their strength frightened him. He made a noncommittal noise translatable as agreement, chagrin, despondence, whatever she wanted to hear.

She spoke again. "Sleepy?" She was rubbing his chest now, making unseen whorls in the dark hair around his nipples.

"Mmm." He turned on his side, his back to her. She ran her finger down his spine, sighed, and lay still, her hand resting in the saddle of his waist. In less than two minutes she was asleep.

Blood was in his face; he could feel it. The red warmth of shame coated his body as he lay there, his penis a dead lump between his thighs. *Bitch,* he thought, and the word repeated in his mind like a litany. *Bitch Bitch Bitch Bitch Bitch*—a mantra of rage that dragged him down into sleep with claws that shredded sanity.

And in his dreams that spongy slab of flesh that had betrayed him *(No—that had been betrayed!)* grew firm at last, its ovoid head flaring upward like an uncaged beast's, the tumescent rondure of it shrieking with the demand to once more pierce the world. But instead of that universal vagina, it saw Karen bound, legs spread, on an altar of marble. The head of the phallus tensed, then drew back, paused, and shot forward like a battering ram as Bell, strangely detached from the penis-thing that grew out of him, screamed *BITCH* at a volume whose intensity masked all other sound. And as the thick cord of tissue tore into her with shattering force, he started to laugh, and laugh, and laugh again as the blood spouted, until the dream and the world itself were nothing but a red joke in the darkness.

Sunday

She was dead when he awoke. What was left reminded him not so much of a human being as a watermelon he had blown up with a cherry bomb when he was a boy. The sight sickened him, but did not surprise him. The knowledge that he had caused her death, had taken the final step, was strangely comforting, like a cool hand on his brow, and a voice that whispered soothingly, "It's over now. It's all right. The worst is over." He remembered his mother, gently talking him out of a bad dream.

It *was* over. Only one thing remained. Payment. Retribution, fitting and just. And he knew how he could receive it. It was so simple.

He found the book quickly, as if it had been waiting for him. He looked up the name in the index, turned to the listed pages, and started to read. When the chapter was over, he turned off the light and lay beside the dead woman there in the darkness, letting no alien thought impinge upon his meditation on what he had read.

Sleep pressed down upon him, and he slipped into the dream like a fish into water. He first became aware of the shape above him, moving rhythmically over his body. Then came the pain down below, in the unfamiliar cave of dry tissue between his legs. When he bent his neck and looked down at his body, he saw the man's hands, coarse and grimy, rubbing the small breasts that protruded from the gap in the rough woolen sweater Bell wore. The man's upper garments were on, but his trousers were down around his ankles as he plunged grunting into Bell's body, into the leathery vagina that refused to moisten. Finally the man collapsed on top of Bell's body, lay still for a moment, then pushed upward and drew himself out with an abruptness that brought a sharp whine from the lips of the dream-woman Bell had become.

The man pulled up his trousers and took a coin from his pocket. With a cross between a laugh and a snarl, he threw it onto the bed, aiming at the recess he had just vacated.

Bell giggled, half in delight at payment, half in fear, and sat up, wiping the coin on the hem of his dirty gray skirt until it was free of spilled semen and sweat. Then he put it into a small purse that hung on a drawstring from a waist button, and called a thank you after the man, who had just shut the door behind him.

The red soreness diminished to a dull ache, and Bell held himself, used long, light strokes to try and dispel the last of the pain. He rose from the bed and hobbled to a worn and rickety nightstand, where he dipped a yellowed handkerchief in cold, filmy water and pressed it between his thighs. Soon the coolness relaxed and strengthened him. He sighed heavily and adjusted his sweater and long skirts. A look in the dulled and hazy mirror told him that he was ready to go out once again, and he crossed to the door.

He was about to open it when he hesitated, as if a voice had called to him from far away in warning. But it lasted only a second, and was easily dismissed. The woman's head shook in both negation and acceptance, the hand turned the knob and opened the door, and Richard Bell walked down the weathered steps and into the dark streets of Whitechapel to meet his destiny.

When the manager of the apartment complex unlocked Bell's door a few days later, he immediately noticed the smell the neighbors had complained of. He expected to find something dreadful as he came nearer the closed bedroom door from behind which the odor was emanating. He was not disappointed. The woman's body was barely recognizable as human.

But what gave the manager bad dreams for a year afterward was the man who lay beside her, ears and nose cut away, but his peacefully smiling mouth untouched. His lower torso had been slashed open, the organs methodically removed and lined up on the bloody sheets. It was the same way that Mary Kelly, a penniless prostitute, had been dissected by Jack the Ripper a century before.

CHOCOLATE

Mick Garris

I woke up wearing someone else's smile.

It was chocolate. The smell, the flavor, the unmistakable texture of the good stuff . . . creamy, dreamy, and dark, so rich that it woke me up. As it dissipated, it left in its place an overwhelming rush of disappointment, bordering on depression.

Now, I'm not a guy who salivates at the mention of a Hershey bar—I've always prided myself of my clear thinking and level-headedness—but in my dream state that morning, I'd have killed for a hollow Easter bunny.

I never dream . . . not so I remember, anyway. On the rare occasion that I *do* dream, I never remember the dream, merely the dreaming. I'll wake up, my head filled with the most amazing bubbles and shadows of boundless nocturnal thought, only to have it vanish as I dredge myself into the waking world. Dreamland and I remain perfect strangers.

But this chocolate heaven stayed with me into the light of the morning sun. The purity of its taste, the milky calm of it melting down my throat, the gentle caffeine rush flowed through me with such sensual pleasure that I immediately understood why our great-grandparents considered the stuff a powerful aphrodisiac.

Since the divorce led me into the gym and a macrobiotic

diet all those months ago, this was wish fulfillment I never knew I desired. I can take sweets or leave them. I *thought*. But if I take them, I can hire out to Macy's on Thanksgiving Day.

But the diet isn't so tough. Nothing ever used to be much of a problem. Sure, the marriage was less than successful, but we handled it in a civilized manner. We didn't hit each other, or scream all night, or fight endlessly. It just didn't work, so we ended it. It was a passionless affair, immediately after the vows were said, and we're better off now apart than together. And Babette and I are still friends.

The day The Dream woke me, I had to go shopping. Since the Schick Center aversion therapy, it's no big deal. I could guide my cart past the beckoning candy and cookies with considerable ease. But today the lingering taste made life more difficult. With fierce determination I loaded the basket with the required rabbit food: sprouts, spinach, pao darko tea—you know the stuff. But it was when I headed to the meat counter for the ground turkey that I heard their little voices.

A Nestle's Crunch called me by name; the Cadbury with hazelnuts was trying to crawl into my cart; the M&Ms— plain and peanut—were trying to melt in my mouth, not in my hands. I turned away from the meat counter and went looking for Mr. Goodbar.

I raced home with my bounty and tore into the candy with a voracious desire. Stuffing it into my mouth, where there should have been a surge of sensual satisfaction, a chocolate itch scratched by Godiva, there was only letdown.

It was creamy, rich and sweet . . . but *meaningless*. I could take it or leave it. Even though alone, I went pink with embarrassment; it really wasn't worth the hypoglycemic rush I knew I would have to endure. I didn't crave that shit.

I gagged down a salad and washed it down with unfiltered carrot juice.

Yum.

Senses are important to me. I create artificial flavors for the food industry, and my first fear was that the olfactory was acting up, and my career might be jeopardized. But the Chocolate Experience was an isolated one, and it was soon forgotten.

It must have been two weeks later when the sneezes blasted me from slumber at about four in the morning. It was the damned cat. In my sleep it hummed and sputtered in my lap, as I stroked it, loved it, cuddled it as if it were my closest life-long chum.

But I'm allergic to cats.

Okay, I love animals, am a member of Defenders of Wildlife and the Cousteau Society, but I just hate cats. They're sneaky, annoying, leave their hair all over the furniture—which they've clawed to shreds—and make my eyes go red and teary. My deviated septum packs up and explodes when one of the little darlings is near.

So what in the hell am I doing cuddling and cooing Puff in my sleep? And with all deference to the wisdom of my allergies, since when does *dreaming* of a cat make me sneeze?

Something was going on here that I didn't understand. It struck me that perhaps I was dreaming someone else's dreams.

But it turned out to be more than the purloining of slumber fantasy. What was happening to me was much more than a dream.

One night, while driving home from a particularly tiresome day at the lab, the dream spilled into my waking hours. I was overwhelmed with affection and warmth, overflowing with a rush of romance that would have made the Brontë sisters blush. Somehow, I was a human radio tower, receiving emotions of such depth that I nearly crashed the Mazda.

Here I am on the way home from Consolidated Flavor Enhancement, looking forward to choosing from a variety of at least half a dozen boxes of Lean Cuisine in the freezer, a light beer, and a stroke magazine I hid in the evening *Examiner,* and I was nearly knocked senseless by this rush of true love so inestimably foreign to me.

I thought I'd been in love a hundred times—I know I told a hundred women I loved them, and I sure meant it at the time—but I'd never known true love. And compared to this experience, I'd never known even a reasonable facsimile. With a crescendo of sudden shame and embarrassment, I realized I didn't know shit about love. I was hit in the face with my shallowness, so incapable of emotional depth that I never knew such feelings existed.

When the transmission ended, it left me drained, and unbelievably sad.

Supposedly you never miss what you've never had, but now that I'd felt this exhilaration, I was left deflated and so depressed that I actually cried on my way home.

Even as a child, I never cried. I used to lie in bed at night, trying to summon up the image of my dead grandfather to make myself feel enough to spill tears, usually without success.

And now, caught in the valley-bound gridlock of rush hour traffic, my anticipation of Pritikin bread and Cookin' Bag chicken was trespassed by the swelling and spilling of heretofore arid tear ducts.

To a newcomer, feeling is pain.

But it was a glorious pain, and once felt, I needed to experience it again. What was happening to me? And why?

Over the ensuing weeks the transmissions were random. Somehow, I was a psychic burglar, stealing someone else's senses. Without warning, I would see through someone else's eyes, taste with their mouth, or—by far the best of all—feel what they were feeling.

But nothing I could do could will the transmissions on. They struck at random, and always alone: smell without sight, touch without hearing, emotions without sight.

However, now that I seemed to understand what was happening, and looked forward to receiving the signals, they were denied me. I *wanted* to feel the emotions of a *true* human being, someone who felt deeply and passionately, and seemed to take a proper place on the planet. I felt like a welfare tenant in Hearst Castle, that I deserved to be evicted from the planet for impersonating a human being. I wanted to be allowed to grow.

But days passed, and the only emotions to roll about in my head were, disappointingly, my own. I kept occupied at the lab, made myself so busy that it kept me from wishing for an empathy rush.

Just an ingredient or two from perfecting an imitation honeydew flavor for Jelly Bellies, it struck again. No longer confined to dream infiltrations, the transpositions chose to attack in my waking hours, and usually at the most inopportune of moments.

Like the first time, it began with a smell. It was almost roses. In my business, I knew immediately that it wasn't real roses, but a very good simulation. I've since identified it: tea rose perfume. And then the feeling. I covered myself with my arms, suddenly standing naked in the middle of the lab, toweling myself dry, powdering my body, softly, luxuriously, sensually pampering myself.

It was a *woman!*

And as swiftly as she was there, she was gone, and the heavenly scent of almost-rose on her skin gave way to the syrupy stink of near-honeydew. A bad bargain, but it left me with a raging erection.

Though I hadn't seen her, I knew she was beautiful, judging her from the inside out. She was filled with love and goodwill, and her abrupt departure was painful. I needed to know her better. I needed to know her at all.

That was the day. From that point on it was all I could do to live my own life. I thought about her endlessly, wondering who she was, where she lived, what could be the sonnet that was her name. What did she look like?

The next phase was paranoia.

Was she receiving me? Was this sensual exchange a two-way circuit, or merely a party line on which I was invited to listen in? And if she were receiving me, she could see how relentlessly superficially my life had been lived. Before finding her, my deepest thought was the perfection of imitation top sirloin, and I was sure she'd found me out. She *must* know about the men's magazines that littered my bedroom and bathroom . . . and in turn be aware of the inordinate amount of time spent with my left hand. Even *before* the divorce. I suddenly felt very lonely, in the most literal sense of the word, knowing that she deserved better than me.

And so did I.

For the most part, what I received from her were the most beautiful and pure thoughts and feelings that I had ever experienced. They were so good, so generous, so giving that I could but envy her. I threw out the beaver books, dusted and vacuumed the house, and even scrubbed the toilet. I even began to make the bed every morning. You never know . . .

Perhaps my attempts to impress her through the two-way mirror I imagined existed between us were a little overboard, but I had to be my best for her, and thereby for myself. I wrote checks to wildlife organizations; I began to compose hopelessly romantic poems; I had fresh roses around me at all times; I even went so far as to buy a cat. If she knows, it is worth the sneezing and the watery eyes.

I tried not to consider the more likely possibility: that she was blissfully unaware of my existence. I needed to find her, to see her, to talk to her, to make her a living, breathing soul mate, who would no doubt find me her ideal companion for the rest of our lives. I knew that it had become obsession; I needed her to know it, too. My most fervent hope was that she would transmit while writing the return address on an envelope, or while giving out her phone number. Was that too much to ask? After all, didn't there have to be a reason for our psyches to become entwined in the ether?

She just kept doing little things that drove me more and more madly in love with her. She *sang* in the mornings! Can you imagine a soul so bright and cheerful that it could start the morning with a song? She laughed a lot. And when she cried, it was for joy. But it broke my heart to feel the wet of her tears. She needed my shoulder.

You'd have fallen in love with her, too. But I was there first.

In bed one night I drifted off to sleep in her bubble bath. The water in her tub was so bubbly and relaxing that I just couldn't keep my eyes open. I hoped she slept as easily as I.

It was only a couple hours later that I bolted awake.

There were hands on my chest. Rough-hewn and horny, they gripped and kneaded our breasts, twisting, massaging, pinching extended nipples, and I felt overpowering heat in my loins. I realized in aroused horror that she was sending again, and this time . . . it still embarrasses me to even think about it.

I felt our breasts get hard with the rough handling. I felt a hot, wet mouth circle the nipple, the tongue tickling the hardened teat into a miniature tower of flesh. My heart thudded with fear, confusion . . . and excitement that I hoped I could attribute to her. I didn't know how to react; he was playing rough, but it felt . . . *good.*

I could feel wet heat working its way down my body, and before I knew it, I felt penetration! My body had by now completely given way to hers, and I felt things I'd never felt before—nor wanted to! The first stroke was absolutely the most shocking experience I'd ever known. And it kept going.

And then, before taking leave of me, the experience reached its apex, and I experienced my first vaginal and clitoral orgasms. And to complete the set, my rocket launched, making a mess of the newly washed sheets.

After the physical devastation, I just lay there in bed, sweating, feeling guilt and shame, and a curious sense of empathy that no other man can know. I was nauseated with postcoital confusion and didn't sleep the rest of the night.

Sleeping never got any easier. She was constantly on my mind, the thought of her gnawing at me. I needed her as much as I wanted her, and I'd never wanted anything so much in my life. Even though I only received flashes of her for a few minutes total during the course of a week, I felt that I knew her better than any man has known any woman. And for some time, there was no reason to believe that it wasn't true.

Who chooses their soul mate?

Would that it were so simple. To meet all of the available potential partners, and using mind and body, making the most intelligent decision for a life partner. No, love chooses us, not the other way around. And once hooked, there is little turning back. I was in love with a nameless woman I'd never seen, who quite probably had no idea I even existed. Had I known it was hopeless, I might have been able to stop it. And I might not. But I didn't, and I didn't want to. And neither would you.

A few days later she was sending again. I looked down, and we were painting our nails. Her hands were long and tapered, and the polish was a wet, blood red. The polish was applied slowly, gracefully, peacefully, and her thoughts, as ever, were loving and calm. When she finished, my view followed her hand as it grabbed the door of the bathroom medicine cabinet and pulled it open.

That her image whooshing by in the cabinet mirror was so casual and inevitable, it took me a moment to realize that I had actually *seen* her! Instantly, the transmission fled, freeing my own senses to realize what just happened. The vision settled in, the lightning flash of memory permanently embedded on my cerebellum, and my fury with the brevity of the vision gave way to tides of joy. In my mind, at least, I had grasped the holy grail, if only for a fraction of a second.

She was breathtaking!

That was no surprise, having known her as I did. But she was nothing short of a goddess. Her hair, still damp from the shower, was brown, and fell to her bare, milky shoulders. Her pale green eyes were huge and innocent. And she was naked. Her firm, small breasts acted as proud hosts for her attentive, brown, eraserlike nipples.

She was truly all that a human being could be. And then, she was gone.

It was fully three weeks before I heard from her again: three weeks of the most intense loneliness I'd ever felt. I wanted her so badly that I couldn't eat, which suited my waistline if not my heart. It was the cruelest form of impotence I could imagine; I needed her to know that she was the most important thing in my life.

I kept putting in the hours at work, but my heart and mind were far away. I managed to bring the Honeydew Project to a reasonable end, and the Jelly Belly people were happy, but I knew it wasn't perfect. I didn't care; that shit didn't mean anything to me now. I wanted to share my good fortune with *her*.

I found myself riding an emotional roller coaster, and I was never sure if it was hers, mine, or ours. My spirits would soar to the heights of ecstasy, and in moments plummet to the depths of gut-churning despair. In one moment I'd share a smile with everyone I'd pass, and in another be screaming at the slightest misdemeanor that encountered me. I'd gone from a man whom few had ever seen angry, to a veritable amusement park of emotional frayed ends.

The next time she visited me was embarrassing, but at least it was a visit.

As a child, did you ever dream of going to the bathroom, only to wake up and find that you'd wet the bed? I did it a couple of times when I was little, lying in the top bunk over my older brother. Boy was he pissed!

Well, that's what happened. But it wasn't a dream; it was her! She must have gotten up in the middle of the night, and I woke up peeing in my bed. It was the weirdest eliminatory experience I've ever had; I was pissing for her, and it felt like it was coming from someplace it wasn't.

When she went back to bed, we couldn't sleep. Something was bringing us pain, and I couldn't bear her hurt. She deserved only joy, and there was nothing I could do about it. And, with random rancor that too often typifies those things over which we have no control, this transmission lasted longer than any previous one.

But I didn't mind; it was time together. And perhaps she was reaching out to me for help. I would have died to keep her from hurting, and I hope somehow she knew that.

I felt tears splash down on my naked chest, but when I looked down, my skin was dry. I ached for her, and she was gone.

All I could do was worry about the woman I loved. I wanted nothing more than to block out all of her pain, to bring the boundless joy back into that beautiful, uncluttered, loving intelligence. I called in sick the next day, for even though I was no longer receiving, I was nauseated with her anguish.

Later that day it came in a brief flash of incredible anger, and was gone. It was a shock getting this unannounced flash of temper stabbing through me in the middle of my Weight Watchers whole wheat pizza like that. The strength and nastiness of the emotion was devastating; it was something of which I thought she was incapable. Something must have pushed her to the brink to ignite such horrible fury, and I wanted to destroy it for her.

By night, however, it appeared that all was well. I was watching a heart operation on PBS, when suddenly I broke into a gale of her melodious laughter. It was a joyous, cleansing experience for us, and I knew that she must have crossed that bridge over troubled water. I actually cried with the joy of relief that the gorilla on her back had been banished. God, I never wanted her to hurt like that again!

She was gone quickly, but I went to sleep happy. I probably dreamed about her.

A few days later I knew she was still happy. Her next transmission was uncluttered and clear. She must have been lying in a meadow somewhere beautiful. I could feel the prickling of the grass and took deep breaths of the cool, fresh air, scented with just the faintest touch of real carnations. We were completely at peace, and I happily wore her smile again. Now that my fear for her happiness was put to rest, I could go back to needing and wanting her again. If only we could meet, I thought, I'd give her anything she wanted: all the love and support she could stand, and then some. But I wouldn't smother her, I promised aloud.

Though I ached to be with her, I was sleeping better. I knew she was untroubled, and that made my life better as well. I knew that someday soon, somehow I would find her. That's all there was to it.

And then, several days went by without so much as a smell from her, and I worried anew. I would freak out on those occasions, *certain* I'd lost her, that I'd never hear from her again. Hurt and crestfallen, I never allowed the feelings to become anger or resentment. That was beneath me and the purity of my love. I would try to convince myself that I was lucky to have had as much of her as I did, that she had made my life better and more complete just by existing.

But that didn't cheer me. I missed her terribly.

Then came Saturday. I was lying on the couch watching the *Seventh Voyage of Sinbad* for the first time since I was about twelve. Trust me, it doesn't hold up. In fact, it lulled me into a sleep so deep it was as if somebody had flipped a switch and turned off the world.

Then came the rush, and I slept so soundly that nothing made any sense. My hands gripped something tightly, and I was completely confused. I was lashing out, poking, slashing. The blanket began to lift, and I felt like filth.

We were killing.

I felt the long, phallic blade in our hands hit flesh. It slowed at impact, then ripped through the living meat in sickening penetration. We hacked repeatedly through the squirming, helpless flesh, hitting bone with jarring abruptness, then tearing through. The vibrations of flesh being rent moved through my hands and into my body, settling in the acid pit of my stomach, and I shivered with the hideousness of it. I felt the warm, wet spray of blood like tears on my face, felt it run down my arm in pulsing hot rivers.

Then, the slashing stopped, and she was gone. The next emotions were my own. I felt indescribably dirty and savage, with a sense of degradation I had never known. I wore a bloody sheath of sickness and depravity I'm certain will never come off. If you haven't felt it, you can't know it . . . and I never did before this. I was red with shame and humiliation, sweating a foul stench of guilt. I retched repeatedly over the side of the couch until I went limp, my stomach empty. And then I couldn't stop the tears that splashed into the puddle.

That was months ago. I haven't heard from her since. This is the longest time by far between transmissions, and I'm resigned to the likelihood that there will be no more. She lied to me, cheated on me, used me. I want to hate her, flush her from my mind.

But I can't. Love chooses us. And I can't stop thinking about her. So I'm still waiting, just in case.

I need someone to tell me how to feel.

AGAIN

Ramsey Campbell

Before long Bryant tired of the Wirral Way. He'd come to the nature trail because he'd exhausted the Liverpool parks, only to find that nature was too relentless for him. No doubt the trail would mean more to a botanist, but to Bryant it looked exactly like what it was: an overgrown railway divested of its line. Sometimes it led beneath bridges hollow as whistles, and then it seemed to trap him between the banks for miles. When it rose to ground level it was only to show him fields too lush for comfort, hedges, trees, green so unrelieved that its shades blurred into a single oppressive mass.

He wasn't sure what eventually made the miniature valley intolerable. Children went hooting like derailed trains across his path, huge dogs came snuffling out of the undergrowth to leap on him and smear his face, but the worst annoyances were the flies, brought out all at once by the late June day, the first hot day of the year. They blotched his vision like eyestrain, their incessant buzzing seemed to muffle all his senses. When he heard lorries somewhere above him he scrambled up the first break he could find in the brambles, without waiting for the next official exit from the trail.

By the time he realized that the path led nowhere in particular, he had already crossed three fields. It seemed best to go on, even though the sound he'd taken for lorries proved, now that he was in the open, to be distant tractors. He didn't think he could find his way back even if he wanted to. Surely he would reach a road eventually.

Once he'd trudged around several more fields he wasn't so sure. He felt sticky, hemmed in by buzzing and green—a fly in a fly-trap. There was nothing else beneath the unrelenting cloudless sky except a bungalow, three fields and a copse away to his left. Perhaps he could get a drink there while asking the way to the road.

The bungalow was difficult to reach. Once he had to retrace his journey around three sides of a field, when he'd approached close enough to see that the garden which surrounded the house looked at least as overgrown as the railway had been.

Nevertheless someone was standing in front of the bungalow, knee-deep in grass—a woman with white shoulders, standing quite still. He hurried round the maze of fences and hedges, looking for his way to her. He'd come quite close before he saw how old and pale she was. She was supporting herself with one hand on a disused bird-table, and for a moment he thought the shoulders of her ankle-length caftan were white with droppings, as the table was. He shook his head vigorously, to clear it of the heat, and saw at once that it was long white hair that trailed raggedly over her shoulders, for it stirred a little as she beckoned to him.

At least, he assumed she was beckoning. When he reached her, after he'd lifted the gate clear of the weedy path, she was still flapping her hands, but not to brush away flies, which seemed even fonder of her than they had been of him. Her eyes looked glazed and empty; for a moment he was tempted to sneak away. They gazed at him, and they were so pleading that he had to go to her, to see what was wrong.

She must have been pretty when she was younger. Now her long arms and heart-shaped face were bony, the skin withered tight on them, but she might still be attractive if her complexion weren't so gray. Perhaps the heat was affecting her—she was clutching the bird-table as though she would fall if she released her grip—but then why didn't she go in the house? Then he realized that must be why she needed him, for she was pointing shakily with her free hand at the bungalow. Her nails were very long. "Can you get in?" she said.

Her voice was disconcerting: little more than a breath, hardly there at all. No doubt that was also the fault of the heat. "I'll try," he said, and she made for the house at once, past a tangle of roses and a rockery so overgrown it looked like a distant mountain in a jungle.

She had to stop breathlessly before she reached the bungalow. He carried on, since she was pointing feebly at the open kitchen window. As he passed her he found she was doused in perfume, so heavily that even in the open it was cloying. Surely she was in her seventies? He felt shocked, though he knew that was narrow-minded. Perhaps it was the perfume that attracted the flies to her.

The kitchen window was too high for him to reach unaided. Presumably she felt it was safe to leave open while she was away from the house. He went round the far side of the bungalow to the open garage, where a dusty car was baking amid the stink of hot metal and oil. There he found a toolbox, which he dragged round to the window.

When he stood the rectangular box on end and levered himself up, he wasn't sure he could squeeze through. He unhooked the transom and managed to wriggle his shoulders through the opening. He thrust himself forward, the unhooked bar bumping along his spine, until his hips wedged in the frame. He was stuck in midair, above a grayish kitchen that smelled stale, dangling like the string of plastic onions on the far wall. He was unable to drag himself forward or back.

All at once her hands grabbed his thighs, thrusting up toward his buttocks. She must have clambered on the toolbox. No doubt she was anxious to get him into the house, but her sudden desperate strength made him uneasy, not least because he felt almost assaulted. Nevertheless she'd given him the chance to squirm his hips, and he was through. He lowered himself awkwardly, head first clinging to the window frame while he swung his feet down before letting himself drop.

He made for the door at once. Though the kitchen was

almost bare, it smelled worse than stale. In the sink a couple of plates protruded from water the color of lard, where several dead flies were floating. Flies crawled over smeary milk bottles on the window sill or bumbled at the window, as eager to find the way out as he was. He thought he'd found it, but the door was mortise-locked, with a broken key that was jammed in the hole.

He tried to turn the key, until he was sure it was no use. Not only was its stem snapped close to the lock, the key was wedged in the mechanism. He hurried out of the kitchen to the front door, which was in the wall at right angles to the jammed door. The front door was mortise-locked as well.

As he returned to the kitchen window he bumped into the refrigerator. It mustn't have been quite shut, for it swung wide open—not that it mattered, since the refrigerator was empty except for a torpid fly. She must have gone out to buy provisions—presumably her shopping was somewhere in the undergrowth. "Can you tell me where the key is?" he said patiently.

She was clinging to the outer sill, and seemed to be trying to save her breath. From the movements of her lips he gathered she was saying, "Look around."

There was nothing in the kitchen cupboards except a few cans of baked beans and meat, their labels peeling. He went back to the front hall, which was cramped, hot, almost airless. Even here he wasn't free of the buzzing of flies, though he couldn't see them. Opposite the front door was a cupboard hiding mops and brushes senile with dust. He opened the fourth door off the hall, into the living room.

The long room smelled as if it hadn't been opened for months, and looked like a parody of middle-class taste. Silver-plated cannon challenged each other across the length of the pebble-dashed mantelpiece, on either side of which were portraits of the royal family. Here was a cabinet full of dolls of all nations, here was a bookcase of *Readers Digest* Condensed Books. A personalized bullfight poster was pinned to one wall, a ten-gallon hat to another. With so much in it, it seemed odd that the room felt disused.

He began to search, trying to ignore the noise of flies—it was somewhere further into the house, and sounded disconcertingly like someone groaning. The key wasn't on the obese purple suite or down the sides of the cushions; it wasn't on the small table piled with copies of *Contact,* which for a moment, giggling, he took to be a sexual contact magazine. The key wasn't under the bright green rug, nor on any of the shelves. The dolls gazed unhelpfully at him.

He was holding his breath, both because the unpleasant smell he'd associated with the kitchen seemed even stronger in here and because every one of his movements stirred up dust. The entire room was pale with it; no wonder the dolls' eyelashes were so thick. She must no longer have the energy to clean the house. Now he had finished searching, and it looked as if he would have to venture deeper into the house, where the flies seemed to be so abundant. He was at the far door when he glanced back. Was that the key beneath the pile of magazines?

He had only begun to tug the metal object free when he saw it was a pen, but the magazines were already toppling. As they spilled over the floor, some of them opened at photographs: people tied up tortuously, a plump woman wearing a suspender belt and flourishing a whip.

He suppressed his outrage before it could take hold of him. So much for first impressions! After all, the old lady must have been young once. Really, that thought was rather patronizing too—and then he saw it was more than that. One issue of the magazine was no more than a few months old.

He was shrugging to himself, trying to pretend that it didn't matter to him, when a movement made him glance up at the window. The old lady was staring in at him. He leapt away from the table as if she'd caught him stealing, and hurried to the window displaying his empty hands. Perhaps she hadn't had time to see him at the magazines—it must have taken her a while to struggle through the undergrowth around the house—for she only pointed at the far door and said, "Look in there."

Just now he felt uneasy about visiting the bedrooms, however absurd that was. Perhaps he could open the window outside which she was standing, and lift her up—but the window was locked, and no doubt the key was with the one he was searching for. Suppose he didn't find them? Suppose he couldn't get out of the kitchen window? Then she would have to pass the tools up to him, and he would open the house that way. He made himself go to the far door while he was feeling confident. At least he would be away from her gaze, wouldn't have to wonder what she was thinking about him.

Unlike the rest he had seen of the bungalow, the hall beyond the door was dark. He could see the glimmer of three doors and several framed photographs lined up along the walls. The sound of flies was louder, though they didn't seem to be in the hall itself. Now that he was closer they sounded even more like someone groaning feebly, and the rotten smell was stronger too. He held his breath and hoped that he would have to search only the nearest room.

When he shoved its door open, he was relieved to find it was the bathroom—but the state of it was less of a relief. Bath and washbowl were bleached with dust; spiders had caught flies between the taps. Did she wash herself in the kitchen? But then how long had the stagnant water been there? He was searching among the jars of ointments and lotions on the window ledge, all of which were swollen with a fur of talcum powder; he shuddered when it squeaked beneath his fingers. There was no sign of a key.

He hurried out, but halted in the doorway. Opening the door had lightened the hall, so that he could see the photographs. They were wedding photographs, all seven of them. Though the bridegrooms were different—here an airman with a thin mustache, there a portly man who could have been a tycoon or a chef—the bride was the same in every one. It was the woman who owned the house, growing older as the photographs progressed, until in the most recent, where she was holding onto a man with a large nose and a fierce beard, she looked almost as old as she was now.

Bryant found himself smirking uneasily, as if at a joke he didn't quite see but which he felt he should. He glanced quickly at the two remaining doors. One was heavily bolted on the outside—the one beyond which he could hear the intermittent sound like groaning. He chose the other door at once.

It led to the old lady's bedroom. He felt acutely embarrassed even before he saw the brief transparent nightdress on the double bed. Nevertheless he had to brave the room, for the dressing table was a tangle of bracelets and necklaces, the perfect place to lose a key; the mirror doubled the confusion. Yet as soon as he saw the photographs that were leaning against the mirror, some instinct made him look elsewhere first.

There wasn't much to delay him. He peered under the bed, lifting both sides of the counterpane to be sure. It wasn't until he saw how gray his fingers had become that he realized the bed was thick with dust. Despite the indentation in the middle of the bed he could only assume that she slept in the bolted room.

He hurried to the dressing table and began to sort through the jewelry, but as soon as he saw the photographs his fingers grew shaky and awkward. It wasn't simply that the photographs were so sexually explicit—it was that in all of them she was very little younger, if at all, than she was now. Apparently she and her bearded husband both liked to be tied up, and that was only the mildest of their practices. Where was her husband now? Had his predecessors found her too much for them? Bryant had finished searching through the jewelry by now, but he couldn't look away from the photographs, though he found them appalling. He was still staring morbidly when she peered in at him, through the window that was reflected in the mirror.

This time he was sure she knew what he was looking at. More, he was sure he'd been meant to find the photographs. That must be why she'd hurried round the outside of the house to watch. Was she regaining her strength? Certainly she must have had to struggle through a good deal of undergrowth to reach the window in time.

He made for the door without looking at her, and prayed that the key would be in the one remaining room, so that he could get out of the house. He strode across the hall and tugged at the rusty bolt, trying to open the door before his fears grew worse. His struggle with the bolt set off the sound like groaning with the room, but that was no reason for him to expect a torture chamber. Nevertheless, when the bolt slammed all at once out of the socket and the door swung inward, he staggered back into the hall.

The room didn't contain much: just a bed and the worst of the smell. It was the only room where the curtains were drawn, so that he had to strain his eyes to see that someone was lying on the bed, covered from head to foot with a blanket. A spoon protruded from an open can of meat beside the bed. Apart from a chair and a fitted wardrobe, there was nothing else to see—except that, as far as Bryant could make out in the dusty dimness, the shape on the bed was moving feebly.

All at once he was no longer sure that the groaning had been the sound of flies. Even so, if the old lady had been watching him he might never have been able to step forward. But she couldn't see him, and he had to know. Though he couldn't help tiptoeing, he forced himself to go to the head of the bed.

He wasn't sure if he could lift the blanket, until he looked in the can of meat. At least it seemed to explain the smell, for the can must have been opened months ago. Rather than think about that—indeed, to give himself no time to think—he snatched the blanket away from the head of the figure at once.

Perhaps the groaning had been the sound of flies after all, for they came swarming out, off the body of the bearded man. He had clearly been dead for at least as long as the meat had been opened. Bryant thought sickly that if the sheet had really been moving, it must have been the flies. But there was something worse than that: the scratches on the shoulders of the corpse, the teeth marks on its neck—for although there was no way of being sure, he had an appalled suspicion that the marks were quite new.

He was stumbling away from the bed—he felt he was drowning in the air that was thick with dust and flies— when the sound recommenced. For a moment he had the thought, so grotesque he was afraid he might both laugh wildly and be sick, that flies were swarming in the corpse's beard. But the sound was groaning after all, for the bearded head was lolling feebly back and forth on the pillow, the tongue was twitching about the grayish lips, the blind eyes were rolling. As the lower half of the body began to jerk weakly but rhythmically, the long-nailed hands tried to reach for whoever was in the room.

Somehow Bryant was outside the door and shoving the bolt home with both hands. His teeth were grinding from the effort to keep his mouth closed, for he didn't know if he was going to vomit or scream. He reeled along the hall, so dizzy he was almost incapable, into the living room. He was terrified of seeing her at the window, on her way to cut off his escape. He felt so weak he wasn't sure of reaching the kitchen window before she did.

Although he couldn't focus on the living room, as if it wasn't really there, it seemed to take him minutes to cross. He'd stumbled at last into the front hall when he realized that he needed something on which to stand to reach the transom. He seized the small table, hurling the last of the *Contact* magazines to the floor, and staggered toward the kitchen with it, almost wedging it in the doorway. As he struggled with it, he was almost paralyzed by the fear that she would be waiting at the kitchen window.

She wasn't there. She must still be on her way around the outside of the house. As he dropped the table beneath the window, Bryant saw the broken key in the mortise lock. Had someone else—perhaps the bearded man—broken it while trying to escape? It didn't matter, he mustn't start thinking of escapes that had failed. But it looked as if he would have to, for he could see at once that he couldn't reach the transom.

He tried once, desperately, to be sure. The table was too low, the narrow sill was too high. Though he could wedge one foot on the sill, the angle was wrong for him to squeeze his shoulders through the window. He would certainly be stuck when she came to find him. Perhaps if he dragged a chair through from the living room—but he had only just stepped down, almost falling to his knees, when he heard her opening the front door with the key she had had all the time.

His fury at being trapped was so intense that it nearly blotted out his panic. She had only wanted to trick him into the house. By God, he'd fight her for the key if he had to, especially now that she was relocking the front door. All at once he was stumbling wildly toward the hall, for he was terrified that she would unbolt the bedroom and let out the thing in the bed. But when he threw open the kitchen door, what confronted him was far worse.

She stood in the living room doorway, waiting for him. Her caftan lay crumpled on the hall floor. She was naked, and at last he could see how gray and shriveled she was— just like the bearded man. She was no longer troubling to brush off the flies, a couple of which were crawling in and out of her mouth. At last, too late, he realized that her perfume had not been attracting the flies at all. It had been meant to conceal the smell that was attracting them—the smell of death.

She flung the key behind her, a new move in her game. He would have died rather than try to retrieve it, for then he would have had to touch her. He backed into the kitchen, looking frantically for something he could use to smash the window. Perhaps he was incapable of seeing it, for his mind seemed paralyzed by the sight of her. Now she was moving as fast as he was, coming after him with her long arms outstretched, her gray breasts flapping. She was licking her lips as best she could, relishing his terror. Of course, that was why she'd made him go through the entire house. He knew that her energy came from her hunger for him.

It was a fly—the only one in the kitchen that hadn't alighted on her—which drew his gaze to the empty bottles on the window sill. He'd known all the time they were there, but panic was dulling his mind. He grabbed the nearest bottle, though his sweat and the slime of milk made it almost too slippery to hold. At least it felt reassuringly solid, if anything could be reassuring now. He swung it with all his force at the center of the window. But it was the bottle which broke.

He could hear himself screaming—he didn't know if it was with rage or terror—as he rushed toward her, brandishing the remains of the bottle to keep her away until he reached the door. Her smile, distorted but gleeful, had robbed him of the last traces of restraint, and there was only the instinct to survive. But her smile widened as she saw the jagged glass—indeed, her smile looked quite capable of collapsing her face. She lurched straight into his path, her arms wide.

He closed his eyes and stabbed. Though her skin was tougher than he'd expected, he felt it puncture dryly, again and again. She was thrusting herself onto the glass, panting and squealing like a pig. He was slashing desperately now, for the smell was growing worse.

All at once she fell, rattling on the linoleum. For a moment he was terrified that she would seize his legs and drag him down on her. He fled, kicking out blindly, before he dared open his eyes. The key—where was the key? He hadn't seen where she had thrown it. He was almost weeping as he dodged about the living room, for he could hear her moving feebly in the kitchen. But there was the key, almost concealed down the side of a chair.

As he reached the front door he had a last terrible thought. Suppose this key broke too? Suppose that was part of her game? He forced himself to insert it carefully, though his fingers were shaking so badly he could hardly keep hold of it at all. It wouldn't turn. It would—he had been trying to turn it the wrong way. One easy turn, and the door swung open. He was so insanely grateful that he almost neglected to lock it behind him.

He flung the key as far as he could and stood in the overgrown garden, retching for breath. He'd forgotten that there were such things as trees, flowers, fields, the open sky. Yet just now the scent of flowers was sickening, and he couldn't bear the sound of flies. He had to get away from the bungalow and then from the countryside—but there wasn't a road in sight, and the only path he knew led back toward the Wirral Way. He wasn't concerned about returning to the nature trail, but the route back would lead him past the kitchen window. It took him a long time to move, and then it was because he was more afraid to linger near the house.

When he reached the window, he tried to run while tiptoeing. If only he dared turn his face away! He was almost past before he heard a scrabbling beyond the window. The remains of her hands appeared on the sill, and then her head lolled into view. Her eyes gleamed brightly as the shards of glass that protruded from her face. She gazed up at him, smiling raggedly and pleading. As he backed away, floundering through the undergrowth, he saw that she was mouthing jerkily. "Again," she said.

BUG HOUSE

Lisa Tuttle

The house was a wreck, resting like some storm-shattered ship on a weedy headland overlooking the ocean. Ellen felt her heart sink at the sight of it.

"This it?" asked the taxi driver dubiously, squinting through his windshield and slowing the car.

"It must be," Ellen said without conviction. She couldn't believe her aunt—or anyone else—lived in this house.

The house had been built, after the local custom, out of wood, and then set upon cement blocks that raised it three or four feet off the ground. But floods seemed far less dangerous to the house now than the winds, or simply time. The house was crumbling on its blocks. The boards were weatherbeaten and scabbed with flecks of ancient grey paint. Uncurtained windows glared blankly, and one shutter hung at a crazy angle. Between the boards of the sagging, second-story balcony, Ellen could see daylight.

"I'll wait for you," the driver said, pulling up at the end of an overgrown driveway. "In case there's nobody here."

"Thanks," Ellen said, getting out of the back seat and tugging her suitcase after her. She counted the fare out into his hand and glanced up at the house. No sign of life. Her shoulders slumped. "Just wait to be sure someone answers the door," she told the driver.

Trudging up the broken cement path to the front door,

Ellen was startled by a glimpse of something moving beneath the house. She stopped short and peered ahead at the dark space. Had it been a dog? A child playing? Something large and dark, moving quickly—but it was gone now or in hiding. Behind her, Ellen could hear the taxi idling. For a brief moment she considered going back. Back to Danny. Back to all their problems. Back to his lies and promises.

She walked forward again, and when she reached the porch she set her knuckles against the warped, grey door and rapped sharply, twice.

An old, old woman, stick-thin and obviously ailing, opened the door. Ellen and the woman gazed at each other in silence.

"Aunt May?"

The old woman's eyes cleared with recognition, and she nodded slightly. "Ellen, of course!"

But when had her aunt grown so old?

"Come in, dear." The old woman stretched out a parchment claw. At her back, Ellen felt the wind. The house creaked, and for a moment Ellen thought she felt the porch floor give beneath her feet. She stumbled forward, into the house. The old woman—her aunt, she reminded herself—closed the door behind her.

"Surely you don't live here all alone," Ellen began. "If I'd known—if Dad had known—we would have . . ."

"If I'd needed help I would've asked for it," Aunt May said with a sharpness that reminded Ellen of her father.

"But this house," Ellen said. "It's too much for one person. It looks like it might fall down at any minute, and if something should happen to you here, all alone . . ."

The old woman laughed, a dry, papery rustle. "Nonsense. This house will outlast me. And appearances can be deceiving. Look around you—I'm quite cozy here."

Ellen saw the hall for the first time. A wide, high-ceilinged room with a brass chandelier and a rich oriental carpet. The walls were painted cream, and the grand staircase looked in no danger of collapse.

"It does look a lot better inside," Ellen said. "It looked deserted from the road. The taxi driver couldn't believe anyone lived here."

"The inside is all that matters to me," said the old woman. "I have let it all go rather badly. The house is honeycombed with dry rot and eaten by insects, but even so it's in nowhere near as bad shape as I am. It will still be standing when I'm underground, and that's enough for me."

"But, Aunt May . . ." Ellen took hold of her aunt's bony shoulders. "Don't talk like that. You're not dying."

That laugh again. "My dear, look at me. I am. I'm long past saving. I'm all eaten up inside. There's barely enough of me left to welcome you here."

Ellen looked into her aunt's eyes, and what she saw there made her vision blur with tears.

"But doctors . . ."

"Doctors don't know everything. There comes a time, my dear, for everyone. A time to leave this life for another one. Let's go in and sit down. Would you like some lunch? You must be hungry after that long trip."

Feeling dazed, Ellen followed her aunt into the kitchen, a narrow room decorated in greens and gold. She sat at the table and stared at the wallpaper, a pattern of fish and frying pans.

Her aunt was dying. It was totally unexpected. Her father's older sister—but only eight years older, Ellen remembered. And her father was a vigorously healthy man, a man still in the prime of life. She looked at her aunt, saw her moving with painful slowness from cupboard to counter to shelf, preparing a lunch.

Ellen rose. "Let me do it, Aunt May."

"No, no, dear. I know where everything is, you see. You don't. I can still get around all right."

"Does Dad know about you? When was the last time you saw him?"

"Oh, dear me, I didn't want to burden him with my problems. We haven't been close for years, you know. I suppose I last saw him—why, it was at your wedding, dear."

Ellen remembered. That had been the last time she had seen Aunt May. She could hardly believe that woman and the one speaking to her now were the same. What had happened to age her so in only three years?

May set a plate on the table before Ellen. A pile of tuna and mayonnaise was surrounded by sesame crackers.

"I don't keep much fresh food on hand," she said. "Mostly canned goods. I find it difficult to get out shopping much anymore, but then I haven't much appetite lately, either. So it doesn't much matter what I eat. Would you like some coffee? Or tea?"

"Tea, please. Aunt May, shouldn't you be in a hospital? Where someone would care for you?"

"I can care for myself right here."

"I'm sure Dad and Mom would love to have you visit . . ."

May shook her head firmly.

"In a hospital they might be able to find a cure."

"There's no cure for dying except death, Ellen."

The kettle began to whistle, and May poured boiling water over a teabag in a cup.

Ellen leaned back in her chair, resting the right side of her head against the wall. She could hear a tiny, persistent crunching sound from within the wall—termites?

"Sugar in your tea?"

"Please," Ellen responded automatically. She had not touched her food, and felt no desire for anything to eat or drink.

"Oh, dear," sighed Aunt May. "I'm afraid you'll just have to drink it plain. It must have been a very long time since I used this—there are more ants here than sugar grains."

Ellen watched her aunt drop the whole canister into the garbage can.

"Aunt May, is money a problem? I mean, if you're staying here because you can't afford—"

"Bless you, no." May sat down at the table beside her niece. "I have some investments and enough money in the bank for my own needs. And this house is my own, too. I bought it when Victor retired, but he didn't stay long enough to help me enjoy it."

In a sudden rush of sympathy, Ellen leaned over and would have taken her frail aunt in her arms, but May fluttered her hand in a go-away motion, and Ellen drew back.

"With Victor dead, some of the joy went out of fixing it up. Which is why it still looks much the same old wreck it was when I bought it. This property was a real steal, because nobody wanted the house. Nobody but me and Victor." May cocked her head suddenly and smiled. "And maybe you? What would you say if I left this house to you when I die?"

"Aunt May, please don't—"

"Nonsense. Who better? Unless you can't stand the sight of it, but I'm telling you the property is worth something at least. If the house is too far gone with bugs and rot you can pull it down and put up something you and Danny like better."

"It's very generous of you, Aunt May. I just don't like to hear you talk about dying."

"No? It doesn't bother me. But if it disturbs you, then we'll say no more about it. Shall I show you your room?"

Leading the way slowly up the stairs, leaning heavily on the banister and pausing often in her climb, May explained, "I don't go upstairs anymore. I moved my bedroom downstairs because the climb was too much trouble."

The second floor smelled strongly of sea-damp and mold.

"This room has a nice view of the sea," May said. "I thought you might like it." She paused in the doorway, gesturing to Ellen to follow. "There are clean linens in the hall closet."

Ellen looked into the room. It was sparely furnished with bed, dressing table and straight-backed chair. The walls were an institutional green and without decoration. The mattress was bare, and there were no curtains at the french doors.

"Don't go out on the balcony—I'm afraid parts of it have quite rotted away," May cautioned.

"I noticed," Ellen said.

"Well, some parts go first, you know. I'll leave you alone now, dear. I'm feeling a bit tired myself. Why don't we both just nap until dinner time?"

Ellen looked at her aunt and felt her heart twist with sorrow at the weariness on that pale, wrinkled face. The small exertion of climbing upstairs had told on her. Her arms trembled slightly, and she looked grey with weariness.

Ellen hugged her. "Oh, Aunt May," she said softly. "I'm going to be a help to you, I promise. You just take it easy. I'll look after you."

May pulled away from her niece's arms, nodding. "Yes, dear, it's very nice to have you here. We welcome you." She turned and walked away down the hall.

Alone, Ellen suddenly realized her own exhaustion. She sank down on the bare mattress and surveyed her bleak little room, her mind a jumble of problems old and new.

She had never known her Aunt May well enough to become close to her—this sudden visit was a move born of desperation. Wanting to get away from her husband for a while, wanting to punish him for a recently discovered infidelity, she had cast about for a place she could escape to—a place she could afford, and a place where Danny would not be able to find her. Aunt May's lonely house on the coast had seemed the best possibility for a week's hiding. She had expected peace, boredom, regret—but she had never expected to find a dying woman. It was a whole new problem that almost cast her problems with Danny into insignificance.

Suddenly she felt very lonely. She wished Danny were with her, to comfort her. She wished she had not sworn to herself not to call him for at least a week.

But she would call her father, she decided. Should she warn him against telling Danny? She wasn't sure—she hated letting her parents know her marriage was in trouble. Still, if Danny tried to find her by calling them, they would know something was wrong.

She'd call her father tonight. Definitely. He'd come out here to see his sister—he'd take charge, get her to a hospital, find a doctor with a miracle cure. She was certain of it.

But right now she was suddenly, paralyzingly tired. She stretched out on the bare mattress. She would get the sheets and make it up properly later, but right now she would just close her eyes, just close her eyes and rest for a moment . . .

It was dark when Ellen woke, and she was hungry.

She sat on the edge of the bed, feeling stiff and disoriented. The room was chilly and smelled of mildew. She wondered how long she had slept.

Nothing happened when she hit the light switch on the wall. So she groped her way out of the room and along the dark hall towards the dimly perceived stairs. The steps creaked loudly beneath her feet. She could see a light at the bottom of the stairs, from the kitchen.

"Aunt May?"

The kitchen was empty, except for the light of a fluorescent tube above the stove. Ellen had the feeling that she was not alone. Someone was watching. Yet when she turned, there was nothing behind her but the undisturbed darkness of the hall.

She listened for a moment to the creakings and moanings of the old house, and to the muffled sounds of sea and wind from outside. No human sound in all of that, yet the feeling persisted that if she listened hard enough, she would catch a voice . . .

She could make out another dim light from the other end of the hall, behind the stairs, and she walked toward it. Her shoes clacked loudly on the bare wooden floor of the back hall.

It was a night-light that had attracted her attention, and near it she saw that a door stood ajar. She reached out and pushed it further open. She heard May's voice, and she stepped into the room.

"I can't feel my legs at all," May said. "No pain in them, no feeling at all. But they still work for me, somehow. I was afraid that once the feeling went they'd be useless to me. But it's not like that at all. But you knew that; you told me it would be like this." She coughed, and there was the sound in the dark room of a bed creaking. "Come here, there's room."

"Aunt May?"

Silence—Ellen could not even hear her aunt breathing. Finally May said, "Ellen? Is that you?"

"Yes, of course. Who did you think it was?"

"What? Oh, I expect I was dreaming." The bed creaked again.

"What was that you were saying about your legs?"

More creaking sounds. "Hmmm? What's that, dear?" The voice of a sleeper struggling to stay awake.

"Never mind," Ellen said. "I didn't realize you'd gone to bed. I'll talk to you in the morning. Good night."

"Good night, dear."

Ellen backed out of the dark, stifling bedroom, feeling confused.

Aunt May must have been talking in her sleep. Or perhaps, sick and confused, she was hallucinating. But it made no sense to think—as Ellen, despite herself, was thinking—that Aunt May had been awake and had mistaken Ellen for someone else, someone she expected a visit from, someone else in the house.

The sound of footsteps on the stairs, not far above her head, sent Ellen running forward. But the stairs were dark and empty, and straining her eyes towards the top, Ellen could see nothing. The sound must have been just another product of this dying house, she thought.

Frowning, unsatisfied with her own explanation, Ellen went back into the kitchen. She found the pantry well stocked with canned goods and made herself some soup. It was while she was eating it that she heard the footsteps again—this time seemingly from the room above her head.

Ellen stared up at the ceiling. If someone was really walking around up there, he was making no attempt to be cautious. But she couldn't believe that the sound was anything but footsteps: someone was upstairs.

Ellen set her spoon down, feeling cold. The weighty creaking continued.

Suddenly the sounds overhead stopped. The silence was unnerving, giving Ellen a vision of a man crouched down, his head pressed against the floor as he listened for some response from her.

Ellen stood up, rewarding her listener with the sound of a chair scraping across the floor. She went to the cabinet on the wall beside the telephone—and there, on a shelf with the phone book, Band-Aids and lightbulbs was a flashlight, just as in her father's house.

The flashlight worked, and the steady beam of light cheered her. Remembering the darkness of her room, Ellen also took a lightbulb before closing the cabinet and starting upstairs.

Opening each door as she came to it, Ellen found a series of unfurnished rooms, bathrooms and closets. She heard no more footsteps and found no sign of anyone or anything that could have made them. Gradually the tension drained out of her, and she returned to her own room after taking some sheets from the linen closet.

After installing the lightbulb and finding that it worked, Ellen closed the door and turned to make up the bed. Something on the pillow drew her attention: examining it more closely, she saw that it seemed to be a small pile of sawdust. Looking up the wall, she saw that a strip of wooden molding was riddled with tiny holes, leaking the dust. She wrinkled her nose in distaste: termites. She shook the pillow vigorously and stuffed it into a case, resolving to call her father first thing in the morning. May could not go on living in a place like this.

Sun streaming through the uncurtained window woke her early. She drifted towards consciousness to the cries of seagulls and the all-pervasive smell of the sea.

She got up, shivering from the dampness which seemed to have crept into her bones, and dressed quickly. She found her aunt in the kitchen, sitting at the table and sipping a cup of tea.

"There's hot water on the stove," May said by way of greeting.

Ellen poured herself a cup of tea and joined her aunt at the table.

"I've ordered some groceries," May said. "They should be here soon, and we can have toast and eggs for breakfast."

Ellen looked at her aunt and saw that a dying woman shared the room with her. In the face of that solemn, inarguable fact, she could think of nothing to say. So they sat in a silence broken only by the sipping of tea, until the doorbell rang.

"Would you let him in, dear?" May asked.

"Shall I pay him?"

"Oh, no, he doesn't ask for that. Just let him in."

Wondering, Ellen opened the door on a strongly built young man holding a brown paper grocery bag in his arms. She put out her arms rather hesitantly to receive it, but he ignored her and walked into the house. He set the bag down in the kitchen and began to unload it. Ellen stood in the doorway watching, noticing that he knew where everything went.

He said nothing to May, who seemed scarcely aware of his

presence, but when everything had been put away, he sat down at the table in Ellen's place. He tilted his head on one side and eyed her. "You must be the niece," he said.

Ellen said nothing. She didn't like the way he looked at her. His dark, nearly black eyes seemed to be without pupils—hard eyes, without depths. And he ran those eyes up and down her body, judging her. He smiled now at her silence and turned to May. "A quiet one," he said.

May stood up, holding her empty cup.

"Let me," Ellen said quickly, stepping forward. May handed her the cup and sat down again, still without acknowledging the young man's presence. "Would you like some breakfast?" Ellen asked.

May shook her head. "You eat what you like, dear. I don't feel much like eating . . . there doesn't seem to be much point."

"Oh, Aunt May, you really should have something."

"A piece of toast, then."

"I'd like some eggs," said the stranger. He stretched lazily in his chair. "I haven't had my breakfast yet."

Ellen looked at May, wanting some clue. Was this presumptuous stranger her friend? A hired man? She didn't want to be rude to him if May didn't wish it. But May was looking into the middle distance, indifferent.

Ellen looked at the man. "Are you waiting to be paid for the groceries?"

The stranger smiled, a hard smile that revealed a set of even teeth. "I bring food to your aunt as a favor. So she won't have to go to the trouble of getting it for herself, in her condition."

Ellen stared at him a moment longer, waiting in vain for a sign from her aunt, and then turned her back on them and went to the stove. She wondered why this man was helping her aunt—was she really not paying him? He didn't strike her as the sort for disinterested favors.

"Now that I'm here," Ellen said, getting eggs and butter out of the refrigerator, "you don't have to worry about my aunt. I can run errands for her."

"I'll have two fried eggs," he said. "I like the yolks runny."

Ellen glared at him, but realized he wasn't likely to leave just because she refused to cook his eggs—he'd probably cook them himself. And he *had* bought the food.

But—her small revenge—she overcooked the eggs and gave him the slightly scorched piece of toast.

When she sat down she looked at him challengingly. "I'm Ellen Morrow," she said.

He hesitated, then drawled, "You can call me Peter."

"Thanks a lot," she said sarcastically. He smiled his unpleasant smile again, and Ellen felt him watching her as she ate. As soon as she could she excused herself, telling her aunt she was going to call her father.

That drew the first response of the morning from May. She put out a hand, drawing it back just shy of touching Ellen. "Please don't. There's nothing he can do for me, and I don't want him charging down here for no good reason."

"But, Aunt May, you're his only sister—I have to tell him, and of course he'll want to do something for you."

"The only thing he can do for me now is to leave me alone."

Unhappily, Ellen thought that her aunt was right—still, her father must be told. In order to be able to speak freely, she left the kitchen and went back to her aunt's bedroom where she felt certain there would be an extension.

There was, and she dialed her parents' number. The ringing went on and on. She gave up, finally, and phoned her father's office. The secretary told her he'd gone fishing, and would be unreachable for at least two days. She promised to give him a message if he called, or when he returned.

So it had to wait. Ellen walked back towards the kitchen, her crepe-soled shoes making almost no sound on the floor.

She heard her aunt's voice: "You didn't come to me last night. I waited and waited. Why didn't you come?"

Ellen froze.

"You said you would stay with me," May continued. Her voice had a whining note that made Ellen uncomfortable. "You promised you would stay and look after me."

"The girl was in the house," Peter said. "I didn't know if I should."

"What does she matter? She doesn't matter. Not while

I'm here, she doesn't. This is still my house and I . . . I belong to you, don't I? Don't I, dearest?"

Then there was a silence. As quietly as she could, Ellen hurried away and left the house.

The sea air, damp and warm though it was, was a relief after the moldering closeness of the house. But Ellen, taking in deep breaths, still felt sick.

They were lovers, her dying aunt and that awful young man.

That muscular, hard-eyed, insolent stranger was sleeping with her frail, elderly aunt. The idea shocked and revolted her, but she had no doubt of it—the brief conversation, her aunt's voice, could not have been more plain.

Ellen ran down the sandy, weedy incline towards the narrow beach, wanting to lose her knowledge. She didn't know how she could face her aunt now, how she could stay in a house where—

She heard Danny's voice, tired, contemptuous, yet still caring: "You're so naive about sex, Ellen. You think everything's black and white. You're such a child."

Ellen started to cry, thinking of Danny, wishing she had not run away from him. What would he say to her about this? That her aunt had a right to pleasure, too, and age was just another prejudice.

But what about *him?* Ellen wondered. What about Peter —what did he get out of it? He was using her aunt in some way, she was certain of it. Perhaps he was stealing from her—she thought of all the empty rooms upstairs and wondered.

She found a piece of Kleenex in a pocket of her jeans and wiped away the tears. So much was explained by this, she thought. Now she knew why her aunt was so desperate not to leave this rotting hulk of a house, why she didn't want her brother to come.

"Hello, Ellen Morrow."

She raised her head, startled, and found him standing directly in her path, smiling his hard smile. She briefly met, then glanced away from, his dark, ungiving eyes.

"You're not very friendly," he said. "You left us so quickly. I didn't get a chance to talk to you."

She glared at him and tried to walk away, but he fell into step with her. "You shouldn't be so unfriendly," he said. "You should try to get to know me."

She stopped walking and faced him. "Why? I don't know who you are or what you're doing in my aunt's house."

"I think you have some idea. I look after your aunt. She was all alone out here before I came, with no family or friends. She was completely unprotected. *You* may find it shocking, but she's grateful to me now. She wouldn't approve of you trying to send me away."

"I'm here now," Ellen said. "I'm a part of her family. And her brother will come . . . she won't be left alone, at the mercy of strangers."

"But I'm not a stranger any more. And she doesn't want me to leave."

Ellen was silent for a moment. Then she said, "She's a sick, lonely old woman—she needs someone. But what do you get out of it? Do you think she's going to leave you her money when she dies?"

He smiled contemptuously. "Your aunt doesn't have any money. All she has is that wreck of a house—which she plans to leave to you. I give her what she needs, and she gives me what I need—which is something a lot more basic and important than money."

Afraid that she was blushing, Ellen turned and began striding across the sand, back towards the house. She could feel him keeping pace with her, but she did not acknowledge his presence.

Until he grabbed her arm—and she let out a gasp that embarrassed her as soon as she heard it. But Peter gave no sign that he had noticed. Having halted her, he directed her attention to something on the ground.

Feeling foolish but still a little frightened she let him draw her down to a crouching position. A battle had drawn his attention, a fight for survival in a small, sandy arena. A spider, pale as the sand, danced warily on pipe-cleaner legs. Circling it, chitinous body gleaming darkly in the sunlight, was a deadly black dart of a wasp.

There was something eerily fascinating in the way the tiny antagonists circled each other, feinting, freezing, drawing back and darting forward. The spider on its delicate legs seemed nervous to Ellen, while the wasp was steady and single-minded. Although she liked neither spiders nor wasps, Ellen hoped that the spider would win.

Suddenly the wasp shot forward; the spider rolled over, legs clenching and kicking like fingers from a fist, and the two seemed to wrestle for a moment.

"Ah, now she's got him," murmured Ellen's companion. Ellen saw that his face was intent, and he was absorbed by the deadly battle.

Glancing down again, she saw that the spider was lying perfectly still, while the wasp circled it warily.

"He killed him," Ellen said.

"Not he, she," Peter corrected. "And the spider isn't dead. Just paralyzed. The wasp is making sure that her sting has him completely under control before going on. She'll dig a hole and pull the spider into it, then lay her egg on his body. The spider won't be able to do a thing but lie in the home of his enemy and wait for the egg to hatch and start eating him." He smiled his unpleasant smile.

Ellen stood up.

"Of course, he can't feel a thing," Peter continued. "He's alive, but only in the most superficial sense. That paralyzing poison the wasp filled him with has effectively deadened him. A more advanced creature might torment himself with fears about the future, the inevitability of his approaching death—but this is just a spider. And what does a spider know?"

Ellen walked away, saying nothing. She expected him to follow her, but when she looked back she saw that he was still on his hands and knees, watching the wasp at her deadly work.

Once inside the house, Ellen locked the front door behind her, then went around locking the other doors and checking the windows. Although she knew it was likely that her aunt had given Peter a key to the house, she didn't want to be surprised by him again. She was locking the side door, close by her aunt's room, when the feeble voice called, "Is that you, dear?"

"It's me, Aunt May," Ellen said, wondering who that

"dear" was meant for. Pity warred briefly with disgust, and then she entered the bedroom.

From the bed, her aunt gave a weak smile. "I tire so easily now," she said. "I think I may just spend the rest of the day in bed. What else is there for me to do, except wait?"

"Aunt May, I could rent a car and take you to a doctor—or maybe we could find a doctor willing to come out here."

May turned her grey head back and forth on the pillow. "No. No. There's nothing a doctor can do, no medicine in the world that can help me now."

"Something to make you feel better . . ."

"My dear, I feel very little. No pain at all. Don't worry about me. Please."

She looked so exhausted, Ellen thought. Almost all used up. And looking down at the small figure surrounded by bedclothes, Ellen felt her eyes fill with tears. Suddenly, she flung herself down beside the bed. "Aunt May, I don't *want* you to die!"

"Now, now," the old woman said softly, making no other movement. "Now, don't you fret. I felt the same way myself, once, but I've gotten over that. I've accepted what has happened, and so must you. So must you."

"No," Ellen whispered, her face pressed against the bed. She wanted to hold her aunt, but she didn't dare—the old woman's stillness seemed to forbid it. Ellen wished her aunt would put out her hand or turn her face to be kissed: she could not make the first move herself.

At last Ellen stopped crying and raised her head. She saw that her aunt had closed her eyes and was breathing slowly and peacefully, obviously asleep. Ellen stood up and backed out of the room. She longed for her father, for someone to share this sorrow with her.

She spent the rest of the day reading and wandering aimlessly through the house, thinking now of Danny and then of her aunt and the unpleasant stranger called Peter, feeling frustrated because she could do nothing. The wind began to blow again, and the old house creaked, setting her nerves on edge. Feeling trapped in the moldering carcass of the house, Ellen walked out onto the front porch. There she leaned against the railing and stared out at the grey and white ocean. Out here she enjoyed the bite of the wind, and the creaking of the balcony above her head did not bother her.

Idly, her attention turned to the wooden railing beneath her hands, and she picked at a projecting splinter with one of her fingernails. To her surprise, more than just a splinter came away beneath her fingers: some square inches of the badly painted wood fell away, revealing an interior as soft and full of holes as a sponge. The wood seemed to be trembling, and after a moment of blankness, Ellen suddenly realized that the wood was infested with termites. With a small cry of disgust, Ellen backed away, staring at the interior world she had uncovered. Then she went back into the house, locking the door behind her.

It grew dark, and Ellen began to think longingly of food and companionship. She realized she had heard nothing from her aunt's room since she had left her sleeping there that morning. After checking the kitchen to see what sort of dinner could be made, Ellen went to wake up her aunt.

The room was dark and much too quiet. An apprehension stopped Ellen in the doorway where, listening, straining her ears for some sound, she suddenly realized the meaning of the silence: May was not breathing.

Ellen turned on the light and hurried to the bed. "Aunt May, Aunt May," she said, already hopeless. She grabbed hold of one cool hand, hoping for a pulse, and laid her head against her aunt's chest, holding her own breath to listen for the heart.

There was nothing. May was dead. Ellen drew back, crouching on her knees beside the bed, her aunt's hand still held within her own. She stared at the empty face—the eyes were closed, but the mouth hung slightly open—and felt the sorrow building slowly inside her.

At first she took it for a drop of blood. Dark and shining, it appeared on May's lower lip and slipped slowly out of the corner of her mouth. Ellen stared, stupefied, as the droplet detached itself from May's lip and moved, without leaving a trace behind, down her chin.

Then Ellen saw what it was.

It was a small, shiny black bug, no larger than the nail on

her little finger. And, as Ellen watched, a second tiny insect crawled slowly out onto the shelf of May's dead lip.

Ellen scrambled away from the bed, backwards, on her hands and knees. Her skin was crawling, her stomach churning, and there seemed to be a horrible smell in her nostrils. Somehow, she managed to get to her feet and out of the room without either vomiting or fainting.

In the hallway she leaned against the wall and tried to gather her thoughts.

May was dead.

Into her mind came the vision of a stream of black insects bubbling out of the dead woman's mouth.

Ellen moaned, and clamped her teeth together, and tried to think of something else. *It hadn't happened.* She wouldn't think about it.

But May was dead, and that had to be dealt with. Ellen's eyes filled with tears—then, suddenly impatient, she blinked them away. No time for that. Tears wouldn't do any good. She had to think. Should she call a funeral home? No, a doctor first, surely, even if she was truly past saving. A doctor would tell her what had to be done, who had to be notified.

She went into the kitchen and turned on the light, noticing as she did so how the darkness outside seemed to drop like a curtain against the window. In the cabinet near the phone she found the thin local phone book and looked up the listing for physicians. There were only a few of them. Ellen chose the first number and—hoping that a town this size had an answering service for its doctors—lifted the receiver.

There was no dial tone. Puzzled, she pressed the button and released it. Still nothing. Yet she didn't think the line was dead, because it wasn't completely silent. She could hear what might have been a gentle breathing on the other end of the line, as if someone somewhere else in the house had picked up the phone and was listening to her.

Jarred by the thought, Ellen slammed the receiver back into the cradle. There could be no one else in the house. But one of the other phones might be off the hook. She tried to remember if there were another phone upstairs, because she shrank at the thought of returning to her aunt's room without a doctor, someone in authority, to go with her.

But even if there were another phone upstairs, Ellen realized, she had not seen it or used it, and it was not likely to be causing the trouble. But the phone in her aunt's room could have been left off the hook by either her aunt or herself. She would have to go and check.

He was waiting for her in the hall.

The breath backed up in her throat to choke her, and she couldn't make a sound. She stepped back.

He stepped forward, closing the space between them.

Ellen managed to find her voice and, conquering for the moment her nearly instinctive fear of this man, said, "Peter, you must go get a doctor for my aunt."

"Your aunt has said she doesn't want a doctor," he said. His voice came almost as a relief after the ominous silence.

"It's not a matter of what my aunt wants anymore," Ellen said. "She's dead."

The silence buzzed around them. In the darkness of the hall Ellen could not be sure, but she thought that he smiled.

"Will you go and get a doctor?"

"No," he said.

Ellen backed away, and again he followed her.

"Go and see her for yourself," Ellen said.

"If she's dead," he said, "she doesn't need a doctor. And the morning will be soon enough to have her body disposed of."

Ellen kept backing away, afraid to turn her back on him. Once in the kitchen, she could try the phone again.

But he didn't let her. Before she could reach for the receiver, his hand shot out, and he wrenched the cord out of the wall. He had a peculiar smile on his face. Then he lifted the telephone, long cord dangling, into the air above his head, and as Ellen pulled nervously away, he threw the whole thing, with great force, at the floor. It crashed jarringly against the linoleum, inches from Ellen's feet.

Ellen stared at him in horror, unable to move or speak, trying frantically to think how to escape him. She thought of the darkness outside, and of the long, unpaved road with no one near, and the deserted beach. Then she thought of her aunt's room, which had a heavy wooden door and a telephone which might still work.

He watched her all this time, making no move. Ellen had the odd idea that he was trying to hypnotize her, to keep her from running, or perhaps he was simply waiting for her to make the first move, watching for the telltale tension in her muscles that would signal her intentions.

Finally, Ellen knew she had to do something—she could not keep waiting for him to act forever. Because he was so close to her, she didn't dare try to run past him. Instead, she feinted to the left, as if she would run around him and towards the front door, but instead she ran to the right.

He caught her in his powerful arms before she had taken three steps. She screamed, and his mouth came down on hers, swallowing the scream.

The feel of his mouth on hers terrified her more than anything else. Somehow, she had not thought of that—for all her fear of him, it had not occurred to her until now that he meant to rape her.

She struggled frantically, feeling his arms crush her more tightly, pinning her arms to her sides and pressing the breath out of her. She tried to kick him or to bring a knee up into his crotch, but she could not raise her leg far enough, and her kicks were feeble little blows against his legs.

He pulled his mouth away from hers and dragged her back into the darkness of the hall and pressed her to the floor, immobilizing her with the weight of his body. Ellen was grateful for her jeans, which were tight-fitting. To get them off—but she wouldn't let him take them off. As soon as he released her, even for a moment, she would go for his eyes, she decided.

This thought was firmly in her mind as he rose off her, but he held her wrists in a crushing grip. She began to kick as soon as her legs were free of his weight, but her legs thrashed about his legs, her kicks doing no harm.

Abruptly, he dropped her hands. She had scarcely become aware of it and hadn't had time to do more than think of going for his eyes, when he, in one smooth, deceptively casual motion, punched her hard in the stomach.

She couldn't breathe. Quite involuntarily, she half doubled over, knowing nothing but the agonizing pain. He, meanwhile, skinned her jeans and underpants down to her knees, flipped her unresisting body over as if it were some piece of furniture, and set her down on her knees.

While she trembled, dry-retched, and tried to draw a full breath of air, she was aware of his fumbling at her genitals as scarcely more than a minor distraction. Shortly thereafter she felt a new pain, dry and tearing, as he penetrated her.

It was the last thing she felt. One moment of pain and helplessness, and then the numbness began. She felt—or rather, she ceased to feel—a numbing tide, like intense cold, flowing from her groin into her stomach and hips and down into her legs. Her ribs were numbed, and the blow he had given her no longer pained her. There was nothing—no pain, no messages of any kind from her abused body. She could still feel her lips, and she could open and close her eyes, but from below the chin she might as well have been dead.

And besides the loss of feeling, there was loss of control. All at once she fell like a rag doll to the floor, cracking her chin painfully.

She suspected she was still being raped, but she could not even raise her head and turn to see.

Above her own labored breathing, Ellen became aware of another sound, a low, buzzing hum. From time to time her body rocked and flopped gently, presumably in response to whatever he was still doing to it.

Ellen closed her eyes and prayed to wake. Behind her shut lids, vivid images appeared. Again she saw the insect on her aunt's dead lip, a bug as black, hard and shiny as Peter's eyes. The wasp in the sand dune, circling the paralyzed spider. Aunt May's corpse covered with a glistening tide of insects, crawling over her, feasting on her.

And when they had finished with her aunt, would they come and find her here on the floor, paralyzed and ready for them?

She cried out at the thought and her eyes flew open. She saw Peter's feet in front of her. So he had finished. She began to cry.

"Don't leave me like this," she mumbled, her mind still swarming with fears.

She heard his dry chuckle. "Leave? But this is my home."

And then she understood. Of course he would not leave. He would stay here with her as he had stayed with her aunt, looking after her as she grew weaker, until finally she died and spilled out the living cargo he had planted in her.

"You won't feel a thing," he said.

VENGEANCE IS.

Theodore Sturgeon

You have a dark beer?"

"In a place like this you want dark beer?"

"Whatever, then."

The bartender drew a thick-walled stein and slid it across. "I worked in the city. I know about dark beer and Guiness and like that. These yokels around here," he added, his tone of voice finishing the sentence.

The customer was a small man with glasses and not much of a beard. He had a gentle voice. "A man called Grinny . . ."

"Grimme," the barman corrected. "So you heard. Him and his brother."

The customer didn't say anything. The bartender wiped. The customer told him to pour one for himself.

"I don't usual." But the barman poured. "Grimme and that brother Dave, the worst." He drank. "I hate it a lot out here, yokels like that is why."

"There's still the city."

"Not for me. The wife."

"Oh." And he waited.

"They lied a lot. Come in here, get drunk, tell about what they done, mostly women. Bad, what they said they done. Worse when it wasn't lies. You want another?"

"Not yet."

146

"No lie about the Fannen kid, Marcy. Fourteen, fifteen, maybe. Tooken her out behind the Johnsons' silo, what they done to her. And then they said they'd kill her, she said anything. She didn't. Not about that, not about anything, ever again, two years. Until the fever last November, she told her mom. She died. Mom came told me 'fore she moved out."

The customer waited.

"Hear them tell it, they were into every woman, wife, daughter in the valley, any time they wanted."

The customer blew through his nostrils, once, gently. A man came in for two six-packs and a hip-sized Southern Comfort and went away in a pickup truck. " 'Monday-busy,' I call this," said the barman, looking around the empty room. "And here it's Wednesday." Without being asked, he drew another beer for the customer. "To have somebody to talk to," he said in explanation. Then he said nothing at all for a long time.

The customer took some beer. "They just went after local folks, then."

"Grimme and David? Well, yes, they had the run of it, most of the men off with the lumbering, nothing grows in these rocks around here. Except maybe chickens, and who cares for chickens? Old folks, and the women. Anyway, that Grimme, shoulders *this* wide. Eyes *that* close together, and hairy. The brother, maybe you'd say a good-lookin' guy for a yokel, but, well, scary." He nodded at his choice of words and said it again. "Scary."

"Crazy eyes," said the customer.

"You got it. So the times they wasn't just lyin', the women didn't want to tell and, I got to say it, the men just as soon not know."

"But they never bothered anyone except their own valley people."

"Who else is ever around here to bother? Oh, they bragged about this one and that one they got to on the road, you know, blonde in the big convertible, give them the eye, give them whiskey, give them a good time up on the back roads. All lies and you know it. They got this big old van. Gal hitch-hiker, they say the first woman ever used 'em both up. Braggin', lyin'. Shagged a couple city people in a little hatchback, leaned on them 'til the husband begged 'em to ball the wife. I don't believe that at all."

"You don't."

"What man would say that to a couple hairy yokels, no matter what? Man got to be yellow or downright kinky."

"What happened?"

"Nothing happened, I told you I don't believe it! It's lies, brags and lies. Said they found 'em driving the quarry road, 'way yonder. Passed 'em and parked the van to let 'em by, look 'em over. Passed 'em and got ahead, when they caught up David was lying on the road and Grimme made like artificial you know, lifeguards do it."

"Respiration."

"Yeah, that. They seen that and they stopped. The couple in the hatchback got out. Grimme and David jumped 'em. Said the man's a shrimpy little guy looked like a perfessor, woman's a dish, too good for him. But that's what they said. I don't believe any of it."

"You mean they'd never do a thing like that."

"Oh, they would all right. Cutting off the woman's clo'es to see what she got with a big old skinning knife. Took a while, they said it was a lot of laughs. David holdin' both her arms behind her back one-handed, cuttin' away her clo'es and makin' jokes, Grimme holdin' the little perfessor man around the neck with the one elbow, laughin', 'til the man snatched his head clear and that's when he said it. 'Give it to him,' he told the woman. 'Go on, give it to him,' and she says 'For the love of God don't ask me to do that.' I don't believe any man ever would say a thing like that."

"You really don't."

"No way. Because listen, when the man jerked out his head and said that, and the woman said don't ask her to do that, *then* the perfessor guy tried to fight Grimme. You see what I'm saying? If Grimme breaks him up and stomps on the pieces, then you could maybe understand him beggin' the woman to quit and give in. The way Grimme told it right here standing where you are, the man said it when Grimme hadn't done nothing yet but hold his neck. That's the part Grimme told over and over, laughin'. 'Give it to him,' the man kept telling her. And Grimme never even hit him yet.

'Course when the little man tried to fight him Grimme just laughed and clobbered him once side of the neck, laid him out cold. That was when the woman turned into a wildcat, to hear them tell it. It was all David could do to hold her, let alone mess around. Grimme left him to it and went around back to see what they got in their car. Mind you, I don't know if he really done all this; I'm just telling you what he said. I heard it three, four times just that first week.

"So he opened up the back and there was a stack of pictures, you know, painting like on canvas. He hauled 'em all out and put 'em all down flat on the ground and walked up and back looking at them. He says 'David, you like these?' and David, he said 'Hell no' and Grimme walked the whole line, one big boot in the middle of each and every picture. And he says at the first step that woman screamed like it was her face he was stepping on and she hollered 'Don't, don't, they mean everything in the world to him!' She meant the perfessor, but Grimme went ahead anyway. And then she just quit, she said go ahead, and Dave tooken her into the van and Grimme sat on the perfessor till he was done, then Grimme went in and got his while Dave sat on the man, and after that they got in their van and come here to get drunk and tell about it. And if you really want to know why I don't believe any of it, those people never tried to call the law." And the barman gave a vehement nod and drank deep.

"So what happened to them?"

"Who—the city people? I told you—I don't even believe there was any."

"Grimme."

"Oh. Them." The barman gave a strange chuckle and said with sudden piety, "The Lord has strange ways of fighting evil."

The customer waited. The barman drew him another beer and poured a jigger for himself.

"Next time I see Grimme it's a week, ten days after. It's like tonight, nobody here. He comes in for a fifth of sourmash. He's walking funny, kind of bowlegged. I thought at first trying to clown he'd do that. But every step he kind of grunted, like you would if I stuck a knife in you, but every step. And the look on his face, I never saw the like before. I

149

tell you, it scared me. I went for the whiskey and outside there was a screaming."

As he talked his gaze went to the far wall and somehow through it, his eyes very round and bulging. "I said 'What in God's name is that?' and Grimme said, 'It's David, he's out in the van, he's hurting.' And I said, 'Better get him to the doctor,' and he said they just came from there, full of pain-killer but it wasn't enough, and he tooken his whiskey and left walking that way and grunting every step, and drove off. Last time I saw him."

His eyes withdrew from elsewhere, back into the room, and became more normal. "He never paid for the whiskey. I don't think he meant to stiff me, the one thing he never did. He just didn't think of it at the time. Couldn't," he added.

"What was wrong with him?"

"I don't know. The doc didn't know."

"That would be Dr. McCabe?"

"McCabe? I don't know any Dr. McCabe around here. It was Dr. Thetford over to Allersville Corners."

"Ah. And how are they now, Grimme and David?"

"Dead is how they are."

"Dead? . . . You didn't say that."

"I didn't?"

"Not until now." The customer got off his stool and put money on the bar and picked up his car keys. He said, his voice quite as gentle as it had been all along, "The man wasn't yellow and he wasn't kinky. It was something far worse." Not caring at all what this might mean to the bartender, he walked out and got into his car.

He drove until he found a telephone booth—the vanishing kind with a door that would shut. First he called Information and got a number; then he dialed it.

"Dr. Thetford? Hello . . . I want to ease your mind about something. You recently had two fatalities, brothers. . . . No, I will not tell you my name. Bear with me, please. You attended these two and you probably performed the autopsies, right? Good. I hoped you had. And you couldn't diagnose, correct? You probably certified peritonitis, with good reason. . . . No, I will *not* tell you my name. And I am not calling to question your competence. Far from it. My purpose is only to ease your mind, which presupposes that you are good at your job and you really care about a medical anomaly. Do we understand each other? Not yet? Then hear me out. . . . Good."

Less urgently, he went on: "An analogy is a disease called granuloma inguinale, which, I don't have to tell you, can destroy the whole sexual apparatus with ulcerations and necrosis, and penetrate the body to and all through the peritoneum . . . Yes, I know you considered that and I know you rejected it, and I know why . . . Right. Just too damn fast. I'm sure you looked for characteristic bacterial and viral evidence as well, and didn't find any.

". . . Yes, of course, Doctor—you're right and I'm sorry, going on about all the things it isn't without saying what it is.

"Actually, it's a hormone poison, resulting from a bio-chemical mutation in—in the carrier. It's synergistic, wildly accelerating—as you saw. One effect is something you couldn't possibly know—it affects the tactile neurones in such a way that morphine and its derivatives have an inverted effect—in much the same way that amphetamines have a calmative effect on children. In other words, the morphine aggravated and intensified their pain. . . . I know, I know; I'm sorry. I made a real effort to get to you and tell you this in time to spare them some of that agony, but—as you say, it's just too damn fast.

". . . Vectors? Ah. That's something you do not have to worry about. I mean it, Doctor—it is totally unlikely that you will ever see another case.

". . . Where did it come from? I can tell you that. The two brothers assaulted and raped a woman—very probably the only woman on earth to have this mutated hormone poison. . . . Yes, I *can* be sure. I have spent most of the last six years in researching this thing. There have been only two other cases of it—yes, just as fast, just as lethal. Both occurred before she was aware of it. She—she is a woman of great sensitivity and a profound sense of responsibility. One was a man she cared very little about, hardly knew. The other was someone she cared very much about indeed. The cost to her when she discovered what had happened was—well, you can imagine.

"She is a gentle and compassionate person with a pro-found sense of ethical responsibility. Please believe me when I tell you that at the time of the assault she would have done anything in her power to protect those—those men from the effects of that . . . contact. When her husband— yes, she has a husband, I'll come to that—when he became infuriated at the indignities they were putting on her, and begged her to give in and let them get what they deserved, she was horrified—actually hated him for a while for having given in to such a murderous suggestion. It was only when they vandalized some things that were especially precious to her husband—priceless—that she too experienced the same deadly fury and let them go ahead. The reaction has been terrible for her—first to see her husband seeking vengeance, when she was convinced he could rise above that—and in a moment find that she herself could be swept away by the same thing. . . . But I'm sorry, Dr. Thetford— I've come far afield from medical concerns. I meant only to reassure you that you are not looking at some mysterious new plague. You can be sure that every possible precaution is being taken against its recurrence. . . . I admit that total precautions against the likes of those two may not be possible, but there's little chance of its happening again. And that, sir, is all I am going to say, so good—

"What? Unfair? . . . I suppose you're right at that—to tell you so much and so little all at once. And I do owe it to you to explain what my concern is in all this. Please—give me a moment to get my thoughts together.

". . . Very well. I was commissioned by that lady to make some discreet inquiries about what happened to those two, and if possible to get to their doctor in time to inform him—you—about the inverted effect of morphine. There would be no way to save their lives, but they might have been spared the agony. Further, she found that not knowing for sure if they were indeed victims was unbearable. This news is going to be hard for her to take, but she will survive it somehow; she's done it before. Hardest of all for her— and her husband—will be to come to terms with the fact that, under pressure, they both found themselves capable of murderous vengefulness. She has always believed, and by her example he came to believe, that vengeance is unthinkable. And he failed her. And she failed herself." Without a trace of humor, he laughed. " 'Vengeance is mine, saith the

Lord.' I can't interpret that, Doctor, or vouch for it. All I can derive from this—episode—is that vengeance *is*. And that's all I intend to say to you—what?

". . . One more question? . . . Ah—the husband. Yes, you have the right to ask that. I'll say it this way: There was a wedding seven years ago. It was three years before there was a marriage, you follow? Three years of the most intensive research and the most meticulous experimentation. And you can accept as fact that she is the only woman in the world who can cause this affliction—and he is the only man who is immune.

"Dr. Thetford: good night."

He hung up and stood for a long while with his forehead against the cool glass of the booth. At length he shuddered, pulled himself together, went out and drove away in his little hatchback.

THE UNKINDEST CUT

J. N. Williamson

*E*dmunster had never before liked the feeling of other men's flesh on his, so he was perfectly miserable when Stanwall's plump hands closed round his privates. They were called that with good reason, in his view, and Edmunster suffered the older man's clammy touch only because he had decided it was finally time, and he must.

Yet for the hundredth time, perhaps, Edmunster wondered if he would really be able simply to function from day to day, once this was beyond him. It did not seem sensible or realistic to hope he would not be altered in those ways that . . . mattered. That was what Bruce Peterson and Roger Hinesley assured him, however, in voices much too loud for such delicate exchanges of confidences. But then, they would say that. It was typical of birds such as Peterson, and Hinesley; these were modern times and a man had to do what this kind of man had to do. All that. They'd had no appreciation of what such a choice, such a decision, meant to a proud man like Lawrence F. Edmunster.

Frequently sighing, trying not to tremble or to flinch away, he looked all the way down and saw that Stanwall was on the verge of beginning. It didn't help the way Miss Allair was in and out of the room, nor that the woman seemed amazingly disaffected or bored by the terrible thing Stanwall was about to do to him. With bare legs raised, he turned his face to the discreetly draped window in mortification and, a last time, contemplated how it'd been for him. Wonderful, that was how. Natural, and normal, and he had no intention of lying about it now. He'd enjoyed women as much as the next man—more—and simply because *this* was happening did not mean Larry Edmunster felt obliged to repudiate a wholly healthy, enjoyable past.

He'd blurted out—"Is it going to hurt much?"—before he could stop himself.

The serious Stanwall glanced up from between Edmunster's legs as if annoyed at being distracted. "I told you it would not. Lots of men—right this instant—are having this done. Don't forget, Larry, you came to me. Voluntarily."

I knooow, Edmunster thought, cursing his weakness.

But the truth was, the procedure was the solitary, responsible decision remaining to him after getting two of his last four lovers pregnant.

And it was true that both Bruce and Roger swore that a vasectomy would not interfere with Edmunster's free-swinging pursuit of pleasure.

"I am going to make the incision in a moment," Stanwall announced. "Don't worry. The local I gave you has dulled all sensations and you may not feel a thing."

When Edmunster squeezed his eyes shut, they popped open again at once. How ridiculous, how ludicrous he looked. It was taped back at such a definitely unnatural, sickening angle he felt utterly helpless. *May not* feel a thing also meant he *might* feel a *lot.* His sensations did feel dulled, though. All of them, actually. Perhaps that was only the vulnerability of being exposed, or the fettered humiliation of the way it was rendered entirely *hors de combat;* but now he was starting to feel torpid, enfeebled . . . prostrate . . . the whole length of his body.

"Doctor." His own voice seemed detached; distant. "How soon . . . after . . . will I dare—have relations?"

"Oh, a few days," Stanwell grunted. His silver surgical instrument suddenly flashed like a murder weapon as the window curtains ballooned with the late afternoon draft. *No feeling.* Miss Allair, observed Edmunster, had left the room now. "Basically, it depends upon you, Larry," Stanwall said. "Your own mental outlook." The scalpel stopped moving, and pricked. *God!* Edmunster's nerve ends sought to scream, but he managed merely a subdued, rather sickish whimper. "There are neurotic types who experience severe psychological trauma."

"Bruce and Rodge, they didn't mention that at all," Edmunster said hastily; "so what if—"

"Hold perfectly still!"

He was a statue, an icon; he was a mountain rooted in time, unbudgeable granite. An earthquake's rebuke.

Dr. Stanwall's head completely blocked the horrid view now. Once more, while he might have imagined it, those sensitive ganglia which had served Lawrence F. Edmunster faithfully and with passionate devotion sent shrill, psychic protestations careening through his hair-trigger brain.

"You knew my wife."

Vague, being polite, Edmunster managed a smile at the top of the physician's head. Why had Stanwall put it in the past tense? "Yes, I know Stephanie." He attempted to call up her face, but all he saw hoving into view was the shockingly naked body of another Stephanie. "Charming girl."

"Not actually charming," said the doctor. "Indescribably lovely, and sensual. Thrilling and precious, to me; she's eleven years younger. Larry, mistakes that happen during this par*tic*ular phase of surgery are rare. They do tend to be irreversible, however; I thought you should know the worst. Yet the main concern is what can go on in one's own mind. Some men—a minute percentage of those who undergo vasectomies as out-patients—are never able, quite, to achieve another orgasm. A somewhat smaller figure, generally due to their immature way of mentally coping with bodily modifications—and their own, ongoing guilt feelings —never manages an erection again." Dr. Stanwall's fingers —maybe they were sutures, it was impossible to see through his *goddamned head!*—clenched firmly on Lawrence Edmunster's member. "You knew my beautiful wife in the Biblical sense." And the member went totally numb.

He *did* mean *that* Stephanie! *I never was much good,*

remembering names, the patient admitted to himself. "Listen, Doctor, I—"

"Do not move a *muscle!*" The command was from an infinite professional remove. Again the window curtains billowed, as if something ghastly entered. "Not if you want a *chance* of ever doing it again."

"Please." He whispered it, got no reply. Frozen, Edmunster heard the word *irreversible* pound at him, echoing. He craned his neck exactingly, as painstakingly as it was possible for a human creature without using extraneous tendons and musculature. With all his heart he tried to witness the older man's last, terminal handiwork . . . and couldn't make out a damned thing. "For God's sake, Doctor—what've you *done* to me?"

Stanwell smiled and stepped back. He held his hands high as if in a gesture of innocence, or perhaps remorseful repugnance. "What you came to me to do, Larry. A vasectomy. Only what *you* sought."

When he attempted to stand, Edmunster was too weak. Staring down in absolute apprehension, handsome features a blur of terror even to himself, he saw he was still taped in place. But now he wore a tidy, white dressing. Edmunster inhaled sharply. One ruby-red drop of blood was seeping through. He had experienced no pain, he had no feeling, there. Not a bit.

"Sometimes, of course," Dr. Stanwell ruminated, "we men don't know exactly what it is we seek. Patients have been known to go to their physicians for very deep-seated, intimate reasons they can't acknowledge, even to themselves. On occasion, Larry, due to the enormous and influential power of the human mind, men go because of shame—or guilt—and want their doctor somehow to expiate their sins. Odd, isn't it, that can seem the only way?"

There was more going on beneath Edmunster's waist. Miss Allair was pulling up his shorts, then his trousers, with the brisk competence of a mother dressing her little boy. That was the first time today Edmunster observed that she was beautiful, and statuesque; and when he tried to think about her sterling physical attributes in the old, motivational way that had unfailingly elicited highly stimulating results, he felt only a sharp, disagreeable *tugging* sensation there . . . and a sense of ballooning, cosmic loss.

When Allair had zipped him up, Edmunster was shaken and relieved.

"The procedure wasn't too bad, was it?" Stanwall was energetically washing his hands, scrubbing the hell out of them, at his basin. He smiled more, now he was finished. In Edmunster's memory he couldn't recall ever seeing that smile on the doctor's homely face. "Once a man is no longer doing those nasty things that rest so heavily on his shoulders, Larry, he usually becomes a different person. Entirely. Remember, you did the right thing today." He bobbed his head, let his merry eyes watch Edmunster's expression in the mirror above the basin. "Just use that as your consolation, all right?"

Nodding, the space in his brain that retained visual images going on staring at that hearty, open smile, Lawrence Edmunster went out to the waiting room. The nurse, doubling as the doctor's secretary, was making out his bill. A physician who did that for a living wouldn't need a great many secretaries. Allair was bent over her desk and Edmunster might easily have stared down her capacious uniform blouse.

On stiff legs, moving cautiously, he crossed the carpeted floor to the window and stared, straight ahead, through the pane. Peering down, just then, did not seem advisable; prudent. Instead, Edmunster looked at the drab sky as if seeing it that way for the first time and wondered, dully, about psychological trauma, psychosomatic illnesses. Responsible decisions made too late in the game; safe sex; guilt; and little medical horror stories.

Finally Edmunster turned his gaze downward, toward the busy city streets on which he'd strode with manly confidence, then toward himself, below the waist. By comparison, the streets did not seem so distant, so out of reach. *It usually works out all right; depends upon the individual man.* Edmunster's sigh made his whole body tremor from head to toe.

And behind him, from the physician's inner office, there was the sound of chuckling and someone starting to sing. Miss Allair was smiling when Edmunster turned—smiling as if she, too, might begin to sing with satisfaction or shared amusement at any moment.

But regardless of how hard he tried, Edmunster couldn't feel a darned thing. Not anger; not even the gratification of having done the right thing. All he wanted to do was hold perfectly still, forever.

REUNION

Michael Garrett

*B*ut you don't really *love* me," Carla sighed as she pushed Jason's persistent hand from her unsnapped jeans.

Jason Strong slumped against the back seat of his '66 Mustang, then rolled down a steamy window. Cool air rushed inside, bringing with it the endless chant of night creatures from the rural darkness outside.

Jason returned his attention to Carla. Moonlight glistened from teardrops that dampened her cheeks as she sobbed quietly at his side.

"We've been *over* this," Jason complained. "I've told you a thousand times that I—"

"But not like you really meant it," she interrupted. "Not like it means *forever.*"

With a groan of frustration, Jason massaged his temples between the outstretched fingertips of his left hand. College was getting rough, and Vietnam was breathing down his neck. And now this unexpected restraint from Carla. He had hoped she would at least give in to heavier petting tonight. They had dated for weeks, both of them virgins, and Jason was determined to end that condition soon.

"Jason?" she interrupted his thoughts. "Do you promise we'll always be together?"

"Of course!" he stormed impatiently.

Moments of awkward silence numbed the stand-off until Jason squeezed between the two front bucket seats to switch on the radio. Their favorite song was playing—"Cherish" by The Association. Jason edged closer to Carla and met her lips in an extended kiss. She sighed at his embrace, at the stroking of her breasts. His right arm around her tightly, Jason dropped his left hand to her lap where her jeans remained open and inviting.

This time she offered no resistance.

At last, Jason thought. His fingers slipped inside the scratchy denim lining of the zipper, under the elastic band of her panties, then crawled spider-like through a tangled web of pubic hair. He felt himself growing unbearably aroused as he pushed his hand further to the velvet dampness between her legs. Jason exhaled to relieve the tension. God, she felt warm down there.

Her musky fragrance scented the confined quarters of the automobile. Beads of sweat bubbled across Jason's face and neck as his left hand grew warmer and warmer. He wanted to explore her secrets further but she practically sizzled at his touch. Something's wrong, he thought. Nobody can be *this* hot . . .

Jason gasped for air, sensing a sudden shift in Carla's mood. No longer tense, she moaned softly into his ear, squirming with delight as the temperature inside the car climbed steadily higher.

Jason closed his eyes. His fingers . . . they felt raw and began to sting . . . to *burn* . . .

He jerked his hand from her denims and stared with disbelief. A ribbon of smoke trailed the motion of his hand and drifted toward the fogged back windshield, his palm sweltering with a pale orange sheen. Candle-like flames flickered from his fingertips, and he began to scream—a coarse, hollow shriek barely audible above the verbal elation of his companion. Carla's eyes glowed like crimson coals as she looked on in approval.

A torch-like blaze flared from Jason's outstretched hand, consuming his shirt sleeve as it crept slowly up his arm, the stench of burning flesh tainting the air.

Frantically Jason beat his arm against the seat to extinguish the fire. He jerked and screamed as the pain grew more intense—

And then he awoke.

For the fourth consecutive night, the same dream awakened him—not entirely a product of his imagination, but instead, a flashback from twenty years past, an incident all-too-real except for the nightmarish fiery conclusion.

The illuminated numbers of the digital clock shone dimly through the darkness—3:43 A.M. Jason Strong, a family man in his late thirties, struggled through another interruption of sleep, his heart racing from both fear and sexual excitement as Kathy, his wife, slept undisturbed at his side.

Carefully Jason pushed the covers away, wiped perspiration from his face, and took another deep breath.

As before, the graphic vision left him not only frightened, but aroused and unfulfilled as well. Unfortunately, Kathy hated being awakened to make love, and would likely question his inopportune horniness. So Jason lay awake the remainder of the night, and worried for the first time that he might be losing his mind.

"Jason!" Kathy's voice shrilled. Jason's head jerked in response.

"Uh . . . yes, honey?"

Kathy stared at him across the cluttered remains of dinner at the kitchen table.

"What on earth has been wrong with you lately?" she asked. "You hardly spoke to the kids tonight, and now you're staring into space again. Are you feeling all right? Is something wrong at work?"

"Oh, no," he answered, dabbing a napkin at his lips with nervous embarrassment. "It's nothing, really. I was just thinking."

But when he looked at Kathy, he saw Carla instead. Jason remembered every inch of his first love's body, and could almost feel her youthful flesh again. In his mind, he re-experienced the sensuous cupping of her ass in his palms as he faced her naked in the shallow waters of a moonlight swim. He sensed her fingernails clawing at his back, her hot breath at his ear, her—

"Jason!" Kathy snapped. "Will you please speak to me?"

Jason swallowed hard and shook his head.

"I'm sorry, Kat," he said. "I guess I'm just exhausted. Please try to understand."

Kathy began to clear the table, wearing expressions of hurt and aggravation. "I really don't understand," she complained as the dinnerware clattered loudly into the sink. The faucet ran a stream of hot water over the dirty dishes as Jason cleared his throat and stood beside the table.

"Do you mind if I skip the shopping spree tonight?" he asked. "I'm really bushed . . ."

Kathy frowned, then reconsidered. "I know you're not feeling well, honey," she said with a semblance of a smile.

Jason hung his head, feeling a nervous twitch in his cheek, his eyes watering as if he were about to cry.

"Why don't you slip into your pajamas and watch football while we're gone?" Kathy suggested with a loving hug.

Jason exhaled and sighed. "I love you, Kat," he muttered. And with his voice breaking, he added, "And I always will. I promise."

The Dolphins were ahead by two touchdowns when the telephone jarred Jason from the doldrums of Monday Night Football. He yawned and twitched at the cold hardwood floor on his bare feet as he padded to the kitchen and grabbed the receiver.

"Hello?" he mumbled.

Silence.

"Hello?" he repeated impatiently.

The line crackled with static interference, then a favorite oldie from the sixties drifted faintly from the receiver, "Then You Can Tell Me Goodbye" by The Casinos. Carla's transparent image materialized before him, a telephone receiver pressed against a mass of matted brown hair at her ear, her free arm extended toward him. Tears streaked her eye makeup, and coagulated blood oozed from a fresh cut at her wrist. Jason's eardrums pounded, his mouth suddenly dry and cotton-like.

"Carla?" he muttered into the receiver.

There was no response.

"Carla, is that *you?*"

He remembered making love in the back seat of his car and the first time they had made it in a bed. He could almost feel the texture of her skin, the warmth and sensitivity of her touch as the past events sharpened with clarity.

But then the memories changed, as if directed by an external source. Scenes from his youth were suddenly engulfed by rising mental flames, like film transparencies curled and destroyed by fire. Jason's hand began to tremble as he reached to hang up the phone. His pajamas were soaked with perspiration—he felt dizzy and needed to sit.

At the kitchen table Jason considered what he might do next. It was early yet. Kathy would be out at least a couple more hours.

He desperately needed someone to talk to.

Jason stared across the candle-lit bar room table at Bill Reese, his best friend. The Hogs-Eye Saloon, a favorite of theirs, was quiet as usual tonight except for the sound of Monday Night Football that whispered from a big-screen television across the room.

"She's really getting the best of me," Jason groaned as he lowered a half-empty mug to the tabletop.

"I never knew Carla. What was so special about her?" Bill asked.

Jason took another sip, then continued.

"She was my first lay! That makes her pretty damn special, right?"

"Yeah, but I'm not going ape-shit over *my* first lay," Bill countered with a shake of his head.

Jason stared blankly ahead. "She was not only my first, but she was also the *best* I ever had. It's like a curse—my sex life has never been as good."

"She was just a kid, for Christ's sake, and according to you, a virgin!" Bill crowed. "How could she possibly have been such a good lay?"

Jason tried to describe the way Carla performed. "It never really occurred to me till now," he said. "Since she was my first, I had nothing to compare her with. I thought *all* girls could screw like that. But, brother, was I wrong!"

Jason slumped against the back of his hardwood chair, the alcohol beginning to loosen his nerves. "There was something unique about the way she . . . you know . . . felt inside," he blushed. "It was such a tight fit and yet, once I was inside her, it was as if she wouldn't let go, like she had complete control of her muscles down there."

Bill sipped his drink. "Maybe it was a quirk of nature, like being double-jointed or something," he said.

"It was so intense, the way she drained me, that I could seldom last longer than four or five strokes before I'd explode inside her. She was fan-*tastic.*"

Bill shook his head in apparent disbelief. "If she was so great, why did you dump her?"

"I told you," Jason countered. "She was my *first* lay. I thought *all* girls could screw like that." Growing uncomfortable, he turned his head and stared at the mirrored reflection of an attractive waitress leaning over the bar behind him.

"The strange thing about it," Jason finally went on, "I remember most of our relationship so clearly, and yet beyond a certain point it all seems different now—like my memory of her has been changed somehow. I used to get excited when I thought about her, like she was a fulfilled fantasy from the past, but since that damned phone call tonight, I feel mostly nervous . . . and afraid."

Bill drained his mug. "Why are you feeling this way *now?*" he asked. "Hell, it's been twenty years!"

"Dammit, that's just it—I don't know why!" Jason growled. "Everybody gets dumped at one time or another. Barbie Williams gave me the axe in college. She sure as hell didn't show *me* any mercy . . ."

"Hey, calm down, man," Bill said. "Don't get strung out over Barbie, too."

Jason ran his fingers across the five o'clock shadow that sandpapered his cheeks. He leaned forward across the table and lowered his voice.

"Last night, sometime after the last dream, I woke up on top of Kathy. I had been kissing her neck in my sleep, stroking her thighs. We were about to make love. But in my mind she was *Carla. I thought she was Carla, and it scared the shit out of me when I realized she wasn't!*" Jason slammed an open hand hard against the table surface, rattling the mugs and ashtrays. "I'm afraid I might be losing it," he added. "I've never been this way before." Nearby drinkers looked on in amusement as Bill leaned over to pat his friend on the shoulder.

"Hey, relax, Jase—relax," Bill whispered. "Take a deep breath and calm down."

Jason drained the rest of his beer and loosened his collar. "You know what else is so shit-kickin' strange?" he said in a voice that had turned strangely tranquil.

"What?"

"Right now, sitting here with you, I can see her in my mind more clearly than ever. It's almost as if her image was branding itself into my brain with a hot poker, and I can't get rid of it."

Jason ordered another beer and stared at Bill through eyes that began to sting and feel swollen. Either the beer was getting to him . . . or something worse.

"She loved me," he slurred. "She loved me, but I didn't really love her. I told her I did. I promised her I'd be with her forever. I lied to her, just to get into her pants."

"Hey, you were just a kid yourself," Bill countered. "And, besides, most guys do that at one time or another."

"Does that make it right?" Jason snapped. "She was a great piece of ass, so I used her. She trusted me and I took advantage of her."

Bill shifted in disgust. "Jason, you're a grown man, and this happened years ago. Why let your conscience bother you now? It's all behind you, and I doubt she's losing any sleep over it nowadays. You probably never even cross her mind anymore."

"She was more mature than me. More serious," Jason said, ignoring Bill's point. "She wanted us to be together always, and I was only interested in sex. And when I got tired of her, I dumped her."

Jason paused to wipe a sheen of sweat from his forehead. "She cried. God, how she cried," he continued, tears pooling in his eyes. "She was still in high school, and I was a freshman in college. I never saw her after we broke up. Never returned her calls. I shredded her letters without even opening them. Hell, I was a big shot. A stud. Why did I need her anymore? I was ready to move on to someone else."

Bill cleared his throat, then smiled. "You're making too much out of all this," he said. "Why don't you just call Carla? Hell, all you need is to talk to her and get this out of your system. You'll feel a hundred percent better."

Jason raised his brow. "That's not a bad idea. But Kathy wouldn't like it."

"She doesn't have to know. I mean, it's not as if you intend to ball your old girlfriend again, right?"

Jason hesitated, then slowly nodded. "Good point," he said. "But Carla won't be easy to find. She's probably been married at least once by now. Her name's changed. Hell, she might even live in another state for all I know . . ."

"Take it one step at a time," Bill suggested. "Start with the telephone book. You can check with her parents, with mutual friends. It might take awhile, but you'll track her down eventually."

Jason smiled. It was certainly worth a try.

He awoke the next morning exhausted again from loss of sleep, his eyes red and swollen, his body sluggish and unresponsive. Carla had clearly become an obsession, one he knew would have to be resolved soon.

At work he stayed secluded in his office and spent the day trying to locate her. He checked several possibilities in the telephone directory, but found nothing. Not even her parents were listed.

His efforts temporarily stalled, Jason considered how isolated his relationship with Carla had been. They had had no mutual friends. In fact, they had shared very little in common. Regardless, the difficulty of locating her seemed only to fuel his desire, and he was more determined than ever to find her. But maybe it had become more than just a passing fixation. Maybe he really wanted to fondle Carla's breasts again, to experience her extraordinary sexual prowess just one last time. At this point it was difficult to define exactly what he had in mind. He only knew that he *had* to keep searching.

After work, and an apologetic, excuse-ridden phone call to Kathy, Jason skipped dinner and drove directly to Carla's hometown in the next county. Much of the previously wooded terrain along the way had been cleared for new housing, and a country store he and Carla frequented looked long since closed, its doors and windows now boarded over.

As he rounded the final curve toward her old driveway, he almost expected her to be standing in the yard, waving her usual warm hello—but instead was shocked to find her entire neighborhood erased by a recently completed interstate highway, its asphalt surface carving directly through the hill where Carla's house once stood. Gone also was the opportunity to inquire of neighbors as to Carla's current whereabouts. It was as if all traces of her existence had been wiped away.

Jason sat in anguish behind the steering wheel and rolled down the window. He imagined her old house at the top of the hill, her Dad's new cherry-red Chevy parked in the carport, her dog Buster scampering across the yard. With his head out the window for a breath of fresh air, the whisper of the breeze against Jason's face brought memories of another special place where he and Carla had spent countless evenings long ago. Without hesitation, he stared at the purple skies of the setting sun and floored the accelerator.

The old church was still standing, but badly in need of paint, and from its side extended the same dead end road that once served as Jason and Carla's private lover's lane. Jason backed the car over loose gravel to the end of the road, killed the engine, and doused the headlights, just as he'd done almost every Friday night twenty years before. A full moon crept from behind an errant cloud, illuminating the church steeple that spired above a cluster of pines. Moon shadows danced across the empty road.

With a rush, Jason could somehow sense it all again—the sounds and scents as they made love in the cramped back seat of the car. He remembered how, when the act was done and perspiration covered their bodies, a gentle breeze would pass through the open windows, chilling their naked skin.

From the stillness of night a gust of wind swept beneath the car, rocking its frame as if in mock imitation of their lovemaking motions. Fallen leaves swirled across the road ahead, and particles of dust thickened the air. Jason stepped from the car to clear his lungs and stopped dead in his tracks, pivoting to face what he felt surely had been someone behind him. No one was there, though the familiar presence he'd longed for seemed to surround him, as if Carla were once again somewhere very near.

"Carla?" he whispered. The silence of the darkened countryside was still and lifeless, and the unusual warmth grew stronger still. The church was dark, not another person in sight. Jason pocketed both hands and followed the feverish, luring force.

He stepped from the road into dense overgrowth, pushing aside branches from obstructing trees as he made his way along a narrow path to a clearing behind the church. Across a hill before him lay the scattered tombstones of an unkempt cemetery, and it seemed odd that he'd never noticed it when he and Carla had parked nearby before. An eerie stillness broken only by intermittent blasts of wind enveloped the hillside, coaxing him forward. He paused only to wipe sweat from his neck, then continued.

Surrounding the hill was a six-foot wall with crumbling sections of brick and a rusted arch that towered above a front entrance. Nervous, but unable to turn back, Jason stepped beneath the archway, torrents of wind urging him up the weathered concrete steps. Moonlight grave markers glowed faintly in the distance as tall blades of unmown grass stirred in the wind and whipped against his ankles.

As Jason trudged across abandoned graves, his eyes darted from headstone to headstone, blood pulsing faster and harder through his veins. He noticed the heat growing more intense as he was irresistibly drawn to a simple marker near the top of the hill. Without reading its inscription, Jason knew he had finally found Carla.

He trembled with remorse. Had she taken her own life because of him?

The air was hot, humid and heavy. He shuddered and took a deep breath as a burning fear singed his skin. Abruptly, the wind died; the cemetery was still again. Jason dried his eyes, trying to regain his composure, but as he attempted to turn away, he found his feet anchored firmly to the ground above Carla's grave. Panic-stricken, Jason tried with all his strength to pull away, but he was hopelessly stuck.

The silence was broken by an unspoken voice.

I want you, the wind whispered—or had the words come from within his own mind?

A gust of wind roared up the hill, lifting rotted floral arrangements from other graves and scattering them in pieces across the grassy slope. Tiny plastic flowers pelted Jason's cheeks as he attempted in vain to break away.

Ooooooooooh.

He heard a moan—her moan, like years before, at the point of orgasm.

Jason held his breath, his collar tight against his neck as he envisioned Carla's grief-stricken teenage face the last time he'd seen her, the night they'd broken up. He remembered how her tears had suddenly ceased, how she'd stared him coldly in the eye and snarled, "You'll come back someday. Just wait and see."

Jason's eyes refocused on her polished granite headstone. He leaned over and, using both hands, pushed hard to free himself, but Carla's will remained unbroken—he had been drawn to her, trapped like an insect on flypaper.

Come, her panting voice persuaded from beneath the ground. *I want you.* Her breath came in passionate gasps, the same way she'd responded in the back seat of his car.

Abruptly, the ground softened and churned against Jason's feet. He stretched his arms in a futile attempt to catch hold of something for support, but the ground was steamy and mushy. His feet having sank several inches already, Carla's headstone was now out of reach.

Jason's thoughts whirled. What had attracted him to Carla in the days of his youth? She hadn't been especially pretty, and her personality was nothing special—but of course neither had really mattered at the time, for he had been blinded by a teenage fascination with sex.

Deeper! Deeper! Carla's voice begged as Jason's knees slipped below the surface. He could feel the loosened soil sucking past his ankles and closing around his legs. He remembered how Barbie had dumped *him* in college, and for one brief moment he sympathized with the pain Carla must have felt when he'd callously done the same to her.

Jason sank waist deep, clawing desperately at the ground above the grave, stems of weeds breaking off into his hands, his arms flailing wildly to grasp anything for support, the loose soil repacking itself around his legs as he slipped lower. Finally his shoes came to rest against something solid. Oh, my God, he thought—*the top of her coffin.* The force grew stronger, pulling him closer to hell until his shoes crashed through the lid of the time-weakened casket. Tiny shards of rusted metal pierced through his socks, jabbing into the flesh of his ankles.

From below, the heat lapped at his thighs. Jason twisted and jerked, trying to free himself as the fetid stench of his own searing flesh made him gag.

An unwanted erection strained against his pants. Jason tried to resist but instead felt his pulse quicken with involuntary sexual excitement, as if he were a mere puppet in the fondling hands of the devil himself. Waves of terror-inspired release clashed with the fiery torture at his legs.

In his mind, he could see Carla again. She was reaching for him, unzipping his pants. The heat—oh, God—*the heat* . . .

"No!" he screamed in horror. *"This can't be happening!"*

The last sound he heard was Carla's ghastly voice screeching to climax as the simmering earth closed over his head . . .

Barbie Edwards jerked a sheet of paper from her printer and crushed a cigarette butt into an ashtray atop her cluttered desk. The steady tap-tap-tap of other keyboards around the large corporate office clicked almost in unison. She exhaled a final plume of smoke and stared at a framed photo of her husband on her desk.

Roger—was their relationship in danger? she wondered. God, it seemed forever since they'd made love. Two-career marriages were plagued with pressure, she'd been warned, but somehow she'd always believed that she and Roger could withstand just about anything.

Well, it was probably nothing. She simply hadn't been in the mood for sex lately, that's all. Still, it was puzzling how memories of Jason Strong had recently returned. Gosh, it must have been at least ten or twelve years since he'd last crossed her mind.

Jason had been such a sweet guy—sometimes selfish and

a bit insecure—but they had certainly had good times together. Of course, that had been in the wild college days of the late sixties. Dropping acid, making love. And, my, could that boy get her off! In fact, Jason Strong was likely the best she'd ever had. At the time she hadn't realized how foolish it had been to let him get away. And Jason had been devastated when her interest had been drawn elsewhere.

Poor Jason. Funny how those broken promises never bothered her until now.

Barbie inserted a clean sheet of paper into her printer and glared at a seemingly endless stack of correspondence on her desk. Suddenly she stopped and stared blankly ahead.

She was feeling that untimely warmth again between her legs. There was certainly no reason to be aroused. And yet, without a doubt, she was wet. Barbie squirmed in her seat and spread her legs a bit further apart. God, she felt hot.

She shook another cigarette from a near-empty package and thumbed the ridged wheel of her cigarette lighter, momentarily hypnotized by the dancing flame that sparked forth.

It reminded her of a dream she'd had about Jason just the night before. Barbie shrugged and reached for the telephone directory.

Maybe he still lived nearby . . .

FOOTSTEPS

Harlan Ellison

*F*or her, darkness never fell in the City of Light. For her, nighttime was the time of life, the time filled with moments of light brighter than all the cheap neon sullying the Champs-Élysées.

Nor had night ever fallen in London; nor in Bucharest; nor in Stockholm; nor in any of the fifteen cities she had visited on this holiday. This gourmet tour of the capitals of Europe.

But night had come frequently in Los Angeles.

Precipitating flight, necessitating caution, producing pain and hunger, terrible hunger that could not be assuaged, pain that could not be driven from her body. Los Angeles had become dangerous. Too dangerous for one of the children of the night.

But Los Angeles was behind her, and all the headlines about the INSANE SLAUGHTER, about the RIPPER, about the TERRIBLE DEATHS. All that was behind her . . . and so were London, Bucharest, Stockholm, and a dozen other feeding grounds. Fifteen wonderful banquet halls.

Now she was in Paris for the first time, and night was coming with all its light and all its promise.

In the Hôtel des Saints Pères she bathed at great length, taking the time she always took before she went out to dine, before she went out to find passion.

She had been startled to find the hotels in France did not provide washcloths. At first she had thought the chambermaid had forgotten to leave one, but when she called down to the reception desk, the girl who answered the phone could not understand what she was asking for. The receptionist's English was not good; and French was almost incomprehensible to Claire. Claire spoke Los Angeles very well: which was of no use in Paris. It was fortunate language was no barrier for Claire when she was ordering a meal. No problem at all.

They made querulous sounds at one another for ten minutes till the receptionist *finally* understood she was asking for a washcloth.

"Ah! *Oui, mademoiselle,*" the receptionist said, *"le gant de toilette!"*

Instantly, Claire knew she had hit it. "Yes, that's right . . . *oui . . . gant,* uh . . . *gant* whatever you said . . . *oui* . . . a washcloth . . ."

And after *another* ten minutes she understood that the French thought the cloth with which one washed one's body was too personal to leave in a hotel room, that the French carried their own *gants de toilette* when they traveled.

She was amazed. And somehow mildly pleased. It bespoke a foreign way of life that promised new tastes, new thrills, possibly new highs of love. What she thought of as transports of ecstasy. In the night. In the bright light of darkness.

She lingered a long time in the bath, using the shower head on a flexible metal cord to wash her long blonde hair. The extremely hot bath water around her lower body, between her thighs, the cascade of hot water pouring down over her, eased the tension of the plane trip from Zurich, washed away the first signs of jet-lag that had been creeping up on her since London. She lay back in the tub and let the water flow over her. Rebirth. Rejuvenation.

And she was ferociously hungry.

But Paris was world-renowned for its cuisine.

She sat at a table outside Les Deux Magots, the café on the Boulevard St.-Germain where Boris Vian and Sartre and Simone de Beauvoir had sat in the Forties and Fifties, thinking their thoughts and sometimes writing their words of existential loneliness. They sat there drinking their *pastis,* their Pernod, and they were filled with a sense of the oneness of humanity with the universe. Claire sat and thought of her impending oneness with selected parts of humanity . . . And the universe was of no concern to her. For the children of the night, loneliness was born in the flesh. It lay at the core of the bones, it swam in the blood. For her, the idea of existential solitude was not an abstract theory; it was her way of life. From the first moment of awareness.

She had dressed for effect. Tonight the blue sky silk, slit high in the front. She sat at the edge of the crowd, facing the sidewalk, her legs crossed high, a simple glass of Perrier *avec citron* before her. She had not ordered *pâté* or *terrine:* never taint the palate before indulging in a gourmet repast. She had avoided snacking all day, keeping herself on the trembling edge of hunger.

And the moveable feast walked past.

He was in his early forties, stuffy-looking, holding himself erect like Marshal Foch in the guidebook history of France she had bought. This man wore a sincere gray suit, double-breasted, pompously cut to obscure the fact that the quality was not that good.

The man—whom Claire now thought of as Marshal Foch—walked past, caught a flicker of nylon as she crossed her legs for his benefit, glanced sidewise and met the stare of her green eyes, and bumped into an old woman with a string bag filled with greens and bread. They did a little dance trying to avoid each other, and the old woman elbowed him aside roughly, muttering an obscenity under her breath.

Claire laughed brightly, warmly, disarmingly.

Marshal Foch looked embarrassed.

"Old women have very sharp elbows," she said to him. "They stay at home with pumice stone and sharpen them every day." He stared at her, and the expression that passed over his face assured her she had him hooked.

"Do you speak English?"

He took a long moment to shift linguistic gears and took a step closer. He nodded. "Yes, I do." His voice was deep, but measured: the voice of a man who watched the sidewalk as he walked, watched to make certain he did not filthy his shoes with dog droppings.

"I'm sorry I don't speak French," she said, drawing a deep breath so the blue sky silk parted slightly at her bosom. Making certain he didn't miss it, she let a pale, slim hand drift to her breasts as if in apology. He followed the movement with his narrowed eyes. Hooked, oh yes, hooked.

"You are American?"

"Yes. From Los Angeles. You've been there?"

"Yes, oh of course. I have been in America many times. My business."

"What is your business?"

Now he stood before her table, his briefcase hanging from his left hand, his chest pulled up to conceal the soft opulence gravity and age had brought to his stomach.

"I could sit down perhaps?"

"Oh, yes, of course. Certainly. How rude of me. Do sit down."

He pulled out the metal chair beside her, pushed the briefcase under, and sat down. He crossed his legs very carefully, like Marshal Foch, making certain the creases were sharp and straight. He sucked in his stomach and said, "I am dealing in artists' prints. Very fine work of new painters, graphic artists, airbrush persons. I travel very much in the world."

Not by foot, Claire thought. *By 747, by Trans Europ Express, by chic tramp steamers carrying only a dozen curried passengers as supercargo. Not by foot. You haven't a stringy inch on your succulent body, Marshal Foch.*

"I think that sounds wonderful," Claire said. Enthusiasm. Heady wine. Doors standing open. Invitations on stiff cockleshell vellum, embossed with elegant script. And, as always, since the morning of the world—spiders and flies.

"Oh, yes, I think so," he said, chuckling with pride. He did not say *think;* he pronounced it *sink.*

Sink. Down and down into the green water of her fine cool eyes.

He offered her a drink, she said she had a drink, he offered her *another* drink, some other kind of drink, some *stronger* drink. But she said no, she had a drink, thank you. Thus did she let him know she was not a prostitute. It was always the same, in any great city. Strong drink.

She hoped he could not hear her stomach growling.

"Have you had dinner?" she asked.

He did not answer immediately. *Ah, you have a wife and children waiting for you, waiting to start dinner, perhaps in Neuilly,* she thought. *Why, you dirty middle-aged man.*

Then he said, "Ah, *non.* But I must make the phone call to break engagement of a business nature. You would care to have dinner with me, perhaps?"

"I think that would be lovely," she said, showing him, by a turn of her head, the precise angle that highlighted her excellent cheekbones. Before she had finished the sentence he was out of the chair and heading for the *cabines téléphoniques.*

She sat and sipped her Perrier, waiting for dinner to return.

That was quick, she thought, as he hustled back to her. *Let me guess what you said, darling: something important has come up . . . a buyer from Doubleday shops in America . . . he is interested in the Kawalerowicz and the Meynard prints . . . you know I hate staying in the city so late . . . but I must . . . ah, non, Françoise, don't be like zat . . . tell the children I bring them a tarte . . . stop! stop! I must stay longer . . . I will come as soon as I can . . . eat without me . . . I will not argue with you . . . goodbye . . . au revoir . . . salut . . . à bientôt . . . gimme a break, will you, I want to get laid . . . I can hear you saying it now, my dear Marshal Foch.*

And she thought one thing more: *I hope they don't try to keep your dinner hot for you.*

He smiled at her but there was strain in his face. It wasn't all that good a face to contain strain. But he tried valiantly not to show the effect of the phone call. "Now we go, yes?"

She stood up slowly, letting the parts assemble in the most esthetic manner, and the smile on his face grew more placid. Oh yes: hooked.

They began walking. She had already done some walking in the area. Be prepared, that's the Girl Scouts' marching song.

She steered him into the Rue St. Benoît, thinking she could have dinner there without attracting a crowd. But it was still too early in the evening. The night life of Paris flows through the streets till well after two a.m. and dining *alfresco* is next to impossible. Claire never liked to hurry through a meal.

There were two restaurants at the end of Rue St. Benoît, and he suggested both of them. She made a charming move and said, "Why don't we walk a little farther. I want someplace more . . . romantic." He did not argue. Down Rue St. Benoît.

Left into Rue Jacob. Too busy.

Right onto Rue des Saints Pères. Still too busy. But up ahead . . . the river. The dark Seine, in the evening.

"Can we walk down to the river?"

He looked confused. "You want dinner, yes?"

"Oh, sure. Of course. But first let's walk down to the river. It's so beautiful, so lovely at night; this is my first time in Paris; it's so *romantic.*" He did not argue.

On their right the bulk of a large building lay in darkness. She looked up at it, and past it, to the sky, in which the full moon shone like a waiting message.

Dining under the full moon was always nice.

He said, "This building is l'École des Beaux-Arts. Very famous." He pronounced it *fay*-moose. She laughed.

Dark. Always light. Sweet full moon riding through the heavens. Dinner warm and waiting. And then there was a bridge sweeping across the dark river. And steps leading down to the bank. Ah.

"Le Pont Royal," Marshal Foch said, indicating the bridge. "Very *fay*-moose." They walked across the quay and she led him down the steps. On the bank, two meters above the languid Seine, she turned and looked to left and right. Now she leaned against him and stood on her toes and kissed him. He sucked in his stomach, but it was not to hide the rotundity. She took him by the hand and led him toward the Pont Royal.

"Under the bridge," she said.

The sound of his breathing.

The sound of her high heels on the ancient stones.

The sound of the city above them.

The sound of the full moon glowing golden and getting larger in the sky.

And there, under the bridge, swathed in darkness, she leaned against him again and took his thick head between her slim, pale hands and put her mouth against his and let the sweet smell of her wash over him. She kissed him for a long moment, nipping at his lips with her teeth, and he made a small sound, like a tiny animal being stroked. But she was ahead of him. Her passion was already aroused.

And now Claire went away, to be replaced by something else.

A child of the night.

Child of loneliness.

With the last flickering awareness of her departing humanity she perceived the instant he knew he was in the love embrace of something else, the child of the night.

It was the instant she changed.

But that instant was too short for him to free himself. Now her spine had curved, and now her mouth had filled with fangs, and now the claws had grown, and now the body beneath the blue sky silk was matted with fur, and now she was dragging him down, and now she was on top of him, and now the claws were ripping the sincere gray suit from his flesh, and now one blackened claw sliced a line through his throat so he could not scream; and now it was dinnertime.

It had to be done carefully and quickly.

He was erect, his penis swollen with arrested lust. Now she had him naked and on his back, and she was on him, and settling down over him; and he entered her, even as he gurgled his life away. She rode him, bucking and sweating, while his mouth worked futilely and his eyes grew large and surrounded by white.

Her orgasm was accompanied by a howl that rose up over the Seine and was lost in the night sky above Paris where the golden sovereign of the full moon swallowed it, glowing just a bit brighter with passion.

And down in the dark, surfeited with passion, she dined elegantly.

The food in Berlin had been too starchy; in Bucharest the blood had run too thin and the taste had not risen; in Stockholm the dining was too bland; in London too stringy; in Zurich too rich, she had been ill. Nothing to compare with the hearty fare in Los Angeles.

Nothing to compare with home cooking . . . until Paris.

The French were justly famous for their cuisine.

And she ate out every night.

It was a very good week, her first week in Paris. An elegant older man with bristling white moustaches who spoke of the military, right up to the end. A shampoo girl from a chic shop, who wore a kind of fluorescent purple jumpsuit and red candy-apple cowboy boots. An American student from Westfield, New York, studying at the Sorbonne, who told her he was in love with her, until the end when he said nothing. And others. Quite a few others. She was afraid her figure was going to hell.

And now it was Saturday again. *Samedi.*

She had felt like dancing. She was a good dancer. All the right rhythms at just the right times. One of her meals had said the most interesting *boîte,* at the moment, was a bar and restaurant combined with a *discothèque* called Les Bains-Douches, which translated as "the bath and shower" because it had formerly been a bath and shower house since the nineteenth century.

She had come to the Rue du Bourg l'Abbé and had stood before the large glass in the heavy door. A man and a woman were behind the glass, selecting who could come in and who could not. In Paris, the more one is kept out of the club, the more one wishes to enter.

The man and the woman looked at her. Both reached to unlock the door. Claire knew what she looked like; the appeal was evident to male and female alike. She had never worried for a moment about gaining access. Inside.

And now, all around her, the excitement and the color and the firm strong young flesh of Paris moved in stately passion like underwater plants.

She danced a little, she drank a little, she waited.

But not for long.

He wore a very tight T-shirt with the words 1977 NCAA Soccer Champions on it. But he was not an American, nor an Englishman. He was French and his jeans, like his shirt, were very tight. He wore motorcycle boots with little chains banding the toe. His hair was long and waved back careless-ly, but he did not have the sloe eyes of a punk. The eyes were sharp and blue and too intelligent for the face in which they rested. He stared down at her.

For a few moments she was unaware of him standing

there, even though he was directly in front of her table. She was watching a particularly elegant couple performing lifts at the far right side of the dance floor; and he stood there, watching her without interference.

But when she looked up and he did not turn away, when his eyes did not narrow and he did not grow nervous as she turned the full power of her personality on him, she knew tonight would very likely be the best gourmet dining she had ever had.

His name was Patrick. He was a good dancer; they danced well together; and he held her tighter than a stranger had any right to hold her. She smiled at the thought because they would not be strangers for long; soon, if the night filled with light, they would be very intimate. Eternally intimate.

And when they left he suggested his apartment in Le Marais.

They went over the river to the old section, now quite fashionable. He lived on the top floor, but he was not wealthy. He told her that. She found him quite charming.

Inside, he turned on a soft blue light and another that was recessed in the wall behind a long chrome planter box filled with fat, healthy plants.

He turned to her and she reached out to take his head between her hands. He reached up and stopped her hands, and he smiled and said, in French she could understand, "You would eat some food?" She smiled. Yes, she *was* hungry.

He went into the kitchen and came back with a tray of carrots and asparagus and shredded beets and radishes.

They sat and talked. He talked, for the most part. In a French manner that posed no problems for her. She couldn't understand that. He spoke as fast and with as much complexity as all other Frenchmen, but when others spoke to her, in the hotel, in the street, in the disco, it was gibberish; when he spoke, she understood perfectly. She thought he might have learned English somewhere and was speaking partially in her native tongue. But when her mind tried to halt one of the words she thought might be in English, it was gone too fast. But after a while she stopped worrying about it and just let him talk.

And when she leaned toward him, finally, to kiss him on

the mouth, he reached across and put his hand up under her long blonde hair, up to the nape of the neck, and brought her face close.

Through the window she could see the waning moon. She smiled faintly within the kiss: it was not necessary to have a full moon. It never had been. That was where the legends were wrong. But the legend was correct about silver bullets. Silver of any kind. And therein lay the reason a vampire cast no reflection. (Except that was merely *another* legend. There were no vampires. Only children of the night who had been badly observed.) Because Jesus had been betrayed by Judas for thirty pieces of silver, the metal had been put to an evil purpose and was therefore, thereafter, invested with the power to turn away evil. So it was not the *mirror* that cast no reflection of the children of the night, it was the silver backing. Claire could be seen in a mirror of polished steel or aluminum. She could bathe in the river and see her reflection.

But never in a silver-backed mirror.

Such as the one over the fireplace just across from where she sat on the sofa with Patrick.

A *frisson* of warning went through her.

She opened her eyes. He was looking past her.

Into the mirror.

Where he sat alone, embracing nothing.

And Claire began to leave, to be replaced by the child of the night.

Fast. She moved very fast.

Spine curves, fur mats, teeth lengthen, teeth sharpen, claws grow. And her hand that was no longer a hand came up as she shoved him away from her, raking the razoring claws across his throat.

The throat opened wide.

And the green sap flowed out. For a moment. And then the wound magically puckered, drew together, formed a white line of scar, and then vanished altogether.

He watched her as she watched him heal.

For the first time in her life she was frightened.

"Would you like me to put on some music?" he asked. But he did not speak. His mouth did not move.

And she understood why his French had not been incomprehensible to her. He was speaking inside her head, without sound.

She could not answer.

"If not music, then perhaps you'd like something to eat," he said. And he smiled.

Her hands moved in vagrant ways, without purpose. Fear and total confusion commanded her. He seemed to understand. "It's a very large world," he said. "The spirit moves in many ways, in many forms. You think you're alone, and you are. There are many of us, one of each, last of our kind, perhaps, and each of us is alone. The mists part and the children emerge, and after a while the old ones die, leaving the last of the children motherless and fatherless."

She had no idea what he was saying. She had always known she was alone. That was simply the way it was. Not the foolish concept of loneliness of Sartre or Camus, but *alone,* all alone in a universe that would kill her if it knew she existed.

"Yes," he said, "and that's why I have to do something about you. If you are the last of your kind, then this life of chances, just to satisfy your needs, must end."

"You're going to kill me. Then do it quickly. I always knew that would happen. Just do it fast, you weird son of a bitch."

He had read her thoughts.

"Don't be a fool. I know it's hard not to be paranoid; what you've been all your life programs that into you. But don't be a fool if you can stop. There's nothing of survival in stupidity. That's why so many of the last of their kind are gone."

"What the hell *are* you?!?" she demanded to know.

He smiled and offered her the tray of vegetables.

"You're a carrot, a goddam carrot!" she yelled.

"Not quite," said the voice in her head. "But from a different mother and father than you; from a different mother and father than everyone else out on the streets of Paris tonight. And neither of us will die."

"Why do you want to protect *me?*"

"The last save the last. It's simple."

"For what? For what will you protect me?"

"For yourself . . . for me."

He began to remove his clothes. Now, in the blue light, she could see that he was very pale, not quite the shade that facial makeup had lent him; not quite white. Perhaps the faintest green tinge surging along under the firm, hard skin.

In all other respects, and superbly constructed, he was human; and tumescently male. She felt herself responding to his nakedness.

He came to her and carefully, slowly—because she did not resist—he removed her clothes; and she realized that she was Claire again, not the matted-fur child of the night. When had she changed back?

It was all happening without her control.

Since the time a very *long* time ago when she had gone on her own, she had controlled. Her life, the lives of those she met, her destiny. But now she was helpless, and she didn't mind giving over control to him. Fear had drained out of her, and something quicker had replaced it.

When they were both naked, he drew her down onto the carpet and began to make slow, careful love to her. In the planter box above them she thought she could detect the movement of the hearty green things trembling slightly, aching toward them and the power they released as they spasmed together in a ritual at once utterly new because theirs was the meeting of the unfamiliar, yet ancient as the moon.

And as the shadow of passion closed around her she heard him whisper, "There are many things to eat."

For the first time in her life, she could not hear the sound of footsteps following her.

PRETTY IS . . .

Mike Newton

Shelly Teasdale sat and watched the new boy as he finished off his fourth lap of the indoor pool. His name was John Assad—she knew that much—and he possessed an athlete's grace. He led the other swimmers easily.

"A penny for your thoughts," said Marcy Melcher, seated on her left.

"No deal."

"No *need*," said Karen Reinhardt, planted on her right. "I'll tell you what she's thinking."

"Go ahead, if you're so clever."

"Well, unless you're studying for midterms by osmosis," Karen said, smiling, "I'd say you're scoping *him*, and wondering how long he's good for in the sack."

Beside her, Marcy giggled. "It's the same thing, either way. She's working on biology."

Between them, Shelly feigned offense. "I swear, I don't know why I waste my time with either one of you."

"That's easy," Karen answered. "We're your Chi Omega sisters, and we've known you like forever. Which is why I've got the power to read your horny little mind."

"He's hot, I'll grant you that."

"Stop drooling, Marcy."

"Must I?"

"Is he dating anybody steady?" Shelly tried to make the question casual, but Marcy snickered all the same.

A shrug from Karen. "I don't think he's dating anybody, period."

"You think he's shy?"

"Or gay? Now, there's a waste."

"Down, girl."

"If *he* says so."

"You two are being childish." Shelly rose, but they were after her before she reached the bottom of the bleachers.

"Marcy, I believe we struck a nerve."

"I'd say so."

Karen nudged her with an elbow. "Are you gonna try him on, or what?"

She couldn't hide the smile. "I might."

Behind her, Marcy made a clucking sound. "Poor Tommy isn't going to like that."

Shelly tossed her head and set the famous amber waves in motion. "I can handle Tommy."

From her childhood, Shelly had possessed a knack for handling men. Her father had been first, supplanted over time by playmates, teachers, boyfriends, and employers. She had learned the value of a smile, a wiggle, and a glimpse of thigh. Manipulation elevated to the status of an art form. And it never failed.

She had been handling Tommy Blackmon from the start of their relationship, last spring. Both euphemistically and literally. Shelly was not virginal, by any means, but you could not have proved the opposite from Tommy's recent scorecard. He was lucky to receive a hasty handjob these days, and he had not seen her stripped for action since the frat bash back on Labor Day, when she had downed too many coolers in a hurry.

She preferred to keep him hungry, in suspense, occasionally doling out her favors as a just reward, withholding them more often as a form of punishment—or simply for her own amusement. It was a technique which she had polished to perfection, and it served her well.

Her reputation as a tease was well-deserved, but she was never short of offers. Boys surrounded her like flies on honey, conscious of her game, each hoping *he* might be the one to wear down her resistance.

With a boy—a *man*—like John Assad, she thought it

might be different. If he was strong enough to tame her, giving up the game might have its own rewards.

"I've gotta run. I'm late."

And Shelly hurried off across the commons, smiling to herself and cherishing a tingle of anticipation.

Let the games begin.

"Hey, babe, you in there?"

Shelly's eyes came into focus on a hand that waggled inches from her nose. "I'm sorry, what?"

She sat with Tommy Blackmon in the student union, facing him across a cafeteria table with textbooks and paper cups of Coke between them. He had been regaling her with tales of basketball, but she had not been listening. Her eyes and mind had been on John Assad, three tables over, seated by himself and studying.

Disgruntled, Tommy followed the direction of her gaze and saw the new boy, turning back to face her with a scowl. "You window-shopping?"

"Don't be stupid, Tommy. I'm just . . . curious."

"I'll bet."

She registered his jealousy, dismissing it. "He's interesting, don't you think?"

No idiot (despite his lousy math professor's stated views), Tom Blackmon knew where Shelly's interest lay—and *lay* would be the operative word. He kept the observation to himself and asked, instead, "What do you wanna know?"

She stared at Tommy for a moment, as if he had spoken in a foreign language. "What?"

He grinned. "I got a buddy—you know, Hardy Cox?— who works part-time in records, and he tells me things. You wanna know about the new boy?" Tommy aimed an index finger at his temple. "Well, I got it all in here."

"I'm sure."

"You don't believe me? Fine. For openers, he's not American."

"I *knew* that, Tommy."

"Yeah? I bet you didn't know he's from Iraq. Or was it Lesbia? One of those rag-head Middle Eastern countries, anyway. He transferred in from USC two months ago. They booted him."

Her eyes flicked back to Tommy's grinning face. "I don't believe it."

"Would I lie? Some kind of trouble with a girl on campus. Way I hear it, things got ugly and he had to split."

"What happened?"

"Well . . . I don't exactly have the details yet, but people talk."

"That's cheap."

"You think so? Like they say, babe, where there's smoke . . ."

"You're being juvenile."

Across the room the new boy straightened, stretched. His eyes met Shelly's, and she felt a sudden heat between her legs that made her squirm. The moment stretched into infinity, abruptly terminated as he rose to leave. She was aware of Tommy speaking to her, from a distance, but she could not understand his words.

"I'm sorry, what?"

On Thursday Shelly stood outside the new boy's final class and waited for him to appear. She had obtained his schedule by interrogating Chi Omega sisters who shared classes with him, or who knew someone that did. A few had questioned Shelly, but she had been cool, collected, even when their tone was catty. Most of them were envious that she had landed Tommy Blackmon, captain of the basketball and swimming teams. She didn't mind if they were jealous of her plan to have a little something extra, on the side.

But Shelly Teasdale didn't feel collected now. She wasn't cool. She felt all fluttery and nervous, like a schoolgirl, as she waited in the corridor outside of Physics 401. She worried that her nerve might fail her at the crucial moment.

Startled by the passing bell, she jumped and nearly dropped her books. *Not yet,* she thought, and stood aside as students started filing out. It would not do for him to see her waiting in the hall. The gambit must not seem contrived or artificial, if she hoped to make it work.

He was among the last to exit, and she caught his profile through a tiny window set into the door. Head down, pretending to be wrapped up in a bulky novel that her

English prof had recently assigned, she moved to intercept him on a hard collision course, correcting once when it appeared that she might miss him.

Impact spilled his books along with hers. They crouched together, almost knocking skulls, and Shelly murmured an apology. His boots were snakeskin, polished to a satin luster. Shelly risked a glance and found him watching her. His eyes, she saw up close, were green with shifting flecks of gold.

He helped her to her feet and said, "That really wasn't necessary."

"What?"

"I hoped that we might meet. I've seen you watching me."

Her cheeks were burning as she said, "I'm sure I don't know what you mean."

He shrugged. "Too bad. I thought . . . well, never mind."

"What did you think?"

"That you might like to join me for a cup of coffee."

Shelly smiled. "I might, at that."

The student union was not crowded as they entered. Shelly made a quick inspection for familiar faces, thankful when she came up empty. Tommy would be off at practice, but she didn't need some busybody telling tales. When she was ready to enlighten him, she would be pleased to break the news herself. *If* there was anything to tell.

John bought the coffee, waving off her bid to make it dutch. When they were seated, facing each other, Shelly found him smiling at her in amusement.

"What?"

"It just occurred to me that we have not been introduced. My name is John Assad."

"I know. I'm—"

"Shelly Teasdale, yes."

"You know my name?"

"I have been watching you, as well."

She blushed again and concentrated on her coffee, covering.

"At home," he said, "our meeting might have taken months."

"I'm glad we're not at home," she said with perfect candor. "Did you come to the United States with family?"

He frowned and shook his head. "My father is a priest. He would not leave his homeland, and my mother's place is at his side."

"Is that from the Koran?"

His barking laugh surprised her, drawing glances from the nearby tables. "I am not a Moslem."

"Oh, I'm sorry." Shelly was embarrassed. "I assumed . . ."

"The East accommodates a wide variety of sects. Ours predates Islam by perhaps a thousand years. Its doctrines are . . . unique."

"I'd like to hear about it sometime."

"Possibly you shall."

"What brings you to the West?"

"An education, as you see. I feel that our traditions may be best preserved by learning modern ways. I have been a year in London, nearly two in the United States."

"How do you like America?"

"It stimulates me. You have so much freedom here, in travel, sports, and entertainment."

"And the women?"

"Ah." His smile was shrewd. "I find them quite . . . desirable."

Green-gold eyes had strayed to Shelly's sweater as he spoke, and while they lingered there she felt another tremor. *Desirable, indeed!*

"Shelly, I was wondering . . . but, no."

"What is it, John?"

"I was about to ask if you would come with me tomorrow night, for dinner and a film."

"And now you've changed your mind?" She did not have to feign the tone of disappointment in her voice.

"It is not proper, on such short acquaintance."

Shelly laughed despite herself. "Two years, and you're still concerned about propriety?"

"If I *had* asked you . . ."

"I'd have said come by the Chi Omega house at seven-thirty."

"Ah."

"So, have we got a date?"

"It seems we do." He glanced at his expensive-looking watch and frowned. "Regrettably, there are appointments I must keep."

He rose and leaned across the table, took her hand, and raised it to his lips. Surprised for openers, she was astounded when he turned it gently over, opening her fingers, pressing lips against her palm. His tongue flicked out to tickle her, a darting feather, leaving Shelly weak and wet.

"Until tomorrow."

Desirable. After dinner and a movie, Shelly thought she just might offer him a little something in the nature of dessert.

There was a bit of trivia to deal with first, potentially unpleasant, but she wasn't worried. Shelly knew that she could handle it. No sweat.

The phone rang half a dozen times at Delta house before somebody picked it up. She asked for Tommy, settled back, and spent the down-time practicing a level tone of voice.

"Hullo?"

"Hi, Tommy."

"Babe, what's happening?"

She saw no reason to delay the worst. "I have to take a raincheck on tomorrow night."

"Oh, yeah?" Suspicion in his voice. "Why's that?"

"Well . . ." Shelly had rehearsed a lie, but now it failed her. "Something's just come up, that's all."

"I'll bet. This *something* got a name?"

"Don't be like that."

"Hey, let me guess. The new boy, right?"

"What difference does it make?"

"No difference, Shell. Not one damn bit."

Her anger flared. "You're acting like you own me, Tommy. We're no steady thing, you know."

"Don't sweat it, babe."

"I hate it when you call me that."

"Well, pardon me, Miss Tease-tail. Maybe you'll get better service from your rag-head."

"Dammit, Tommy—"

She was talking to the dial tone now, and Shelly cradled

the receiver violently, surprised to find her hands were trembling. She spent a moment working on her pulse rate, slowing it to an approximation of the norm.

No stupid jock could kiss her off like that. With perfect confidence, she knew that Tommy would be hers whenever she desired. One call, and she could have him eating from her hand, or better yet . . .

She thought of John Assad and felt the giddy rush again. She would let Tommy stew awhile. It couldn't hurt, and after Friday night she might not *want* him back.

"You like this better?"

Shelly stood before the full-length mirror, naked save for nylon panties, holding up a dress for her companions to examine.

"Too much yellow," Karen offered.

Marcy grinned. "It makes you look Chinese."

She tried another and another, casting each aside when they did not appear precisely right.

"So, how did Tommy take it?" Karen asked her.

"Like a child."

"What else is new?"

A puzzled frown from Marcy. "Let me get this straight. You want him to be *glad* you're seeing someone else?"

"Not glad, but Christ, he acts like I'm his slave or something."

She was holding up another dress, dark green, and Karen said, "That's pretty."

Marcy giggled. "Pretty is as pretty does."

"Puh-leese."

"I like it." Shelly wriggled into it, zipped up, and made a slow turn to admire herself. "That's it."

"By George, I think she's got it."

"What all's on the menu for tonight?"

"A movie and whatever."

Marcy moaned. "Oh, God, I *love* whatever."

Karen made a face. "I think you're turning nympho on us, Melcher."

"Hey, don't knock it." Marcy turned to Shelly, smiling sweetly. "If you're done with Tommy, can I borrow him?"

"Hands off. I'll have him back before you know it."

"Double-headers," Marcy snickered. "I admire your style."

The movie was a bomb, with Whoopi Goldberg striving for a happy medium between hilarity and sensuality, achieving neither. Shelly followed little of it, concentrating her attention on the man beside her, tingling when their hands made accidental contact in the tub of popcorn. She had not been this excited on a date in months—or was it years?

Assad, for his part, had not tried to take her hand or slip an arm around her shoulders, though she would have welcomed the attention. Shelly wondered if he felt intimidated by her, if her chosen outfit had offended him somehow. If so, he had a funny way of showing it, eyes gravitating to her ample cleavage over dinner, in the small French restaurant where they had stopped before proceeding to the theater.

At half-past ten, when they emerged, a biting wind had nearly cleared the streets.

"Some coffee?"

"Better not," she said. "I'd never get to sleep."

He seemed to have a sudden inspiration. "How about a swim?"

"This time of night? You're joking."

"Not at all. I know a place."

"We'll freeze."

He smiled. "Oh, ye of little faith."

She did not ask him how he had obtained a key to the gymnasium. It was deserted, dark inside, and Shelly felt a little like a burglar, excitement and fear playing tag with her nerves.

"Come this way."

For the first time Assad took her hand as he led her through dark and forbidding corridors. By daylight the halls would be commonplace, bland; in the darkness they might have been paths leading down to a medieval dungeon.

The pool was Olympic-sized, dark as an oil slick. Small lights, widely spaced in the ceiling, reflected like alien moons on its surface.

"The water is heated."

She felt herself tingling and blushing all over. "I don't have a suit."

"There is no one to see you."

"You're here."

"I won't look, if you say I must not."

It was warm in the gym, but her nipples were puckered. Her panties felt damp.

"You go first."

With his back turned, he stripped off his jacket and shirt, then stepped out of his shoes and his slacks. Shelly watched as he peeled off his Jockey shorts, stockings, admiring the musculature of his back, dimpled buttocks. His skin was a uniform olive, with no trace of tan lines.

Stepping quickly to the edge, he sliced the dark glass of the pool in a long, graceful dive, scarcely leaving a ripple behind. Shelly waited until he broke water, hair glistening, flat on his skull. His back arched, his feet kicked. He was gone.

Shelly tugged at her zipper, stepped free of the dress. She could swim in her panties, but they were confining her now, pinching tight at her crotch. She felt better without them.

The pool was as dark as a pit. Shelly looked for Assad, but he had not resurfaced. The water was warm on her skin as she pierced it, legs scissoring, driving her out of the deep end until she could stand on her own. Armpit-deep, she ran long, lacquered nails through her hair.

She was startled as Assad erupted from the water just in front of her, emerging like an elemental spirit. Shelly almost lost her footing, but she caught herself and laughed self-consciously.

"You took me by surprise."

He drifted closer, silent, leaning in to kiss her. Shelly's legs were trembling, and she let the water take her weight. His tongue slid easily between her teeth, and she responded with a rising passion of her own.

She waited for his hands to find her breasts, prepared to let him take her, but he broke the kiss instead. It was a trick of light and shadow, she supposed, which made his pupils seem eliptical.

She was reaching for him when he folded at the knees and

disappeared beneath the surface of the water. Big hands cupped her buttocks, fingers sinking in the cleft and pulling her off-balance, then his lips were *there,* his tongue a living thing, invading her. She shuddered, clutched his hair to keep herself from falling.

Jesus, just another second. Could he hold his breath that long?

She humped against his face, afraid that she might drown him, hardly caring as the spasms hit her, twisted her, destroyed her utterly.

John rose to meet her, and she braced herself with one hand on his shoulder. She was searching with the other hand, intent on giving him the pleasure he had given her, repaying him in kind. She found him, closed her fist around his shaft.

And caught her breath.

"John?"

"There is something I should tell you. *Show* you."

She could barely understand his words. His voice was thick, as if a strip of gauze was wrapped around his tongue.

And Shelly watched him rise before her, momentarily confused before she recognized the gleaming sinew of his lower body, smooth and streamlined where his legs had been a moment earlier. The reptile's knobby, double-headed penis thrust between broad ventral scales, dead-level with her face. Behind him, undulating coils disturbed the water of the pool.

Dumbstruck, Shelly watched his jaw fall open on elastic hinges, stretching backward past his small, inverted ears. A long, forked tongue flicked out between his dripping fangs.

He fell upon her as she summoned up the strength to scream.

AUNT EDITH

Gary Brandner

Skip's arms seemed bound immovably to his sides, his legs tight together, and his body braced stiff and straight. He was being propelled toward the entrance of a cave—dark and moist and unknown inside. He tried to speak, to call out, but no sound came from his constricted chest. Nothing. Nothing at all.

Some three hours earlier Skip had been sitting beside a lithe blond girl in the front seat of his BMW. His arm was around the girl's shoulders with his hand resting lightly on the upper swelling of her young breast. He nodded toward the blue-trimmed white cottage set back from the street where they were parked.

"So this is where Aunt Edith lives," he said. "I was expecting something more like Dracula's castle."

The girl swept her long hair to one side with a graceful movement of her head. "I suppose you say that because of the stories they tell in town about my aunt."

"I have heard that she's not your typical sweet old lady," Skip said. "Nobody seems to know what goes on out here, but there are some mighty interesting theories. Some people say the old girl is practicing voodoo. Or raising up the dead. Or maybe she's really a vampire and sleeps in her coffin." He grinned. "My guess is that she's building a monster out of spare parts. What's she really up to, Audrey?"

The girl gave a nervous little laugh. "You really shouldn't make fun. Aunt Edith may be a little . . . different, but she's the only family I have. I lost both my parents when I was a little girl, and she's been awfully good to me."

"From what I hear, your father left Aunt Edith a nice chunk of money to be good to you. At least until you're twenty-one and get what's coming to you."

"You know a lot about me."

He gave her the grin again. "I work in the bank, remember? I just don't like to see your aunt piss away what's rightfully yours."

"Skip, that's unkind."

"Hey, I was only kidding," he said. "Don't go all serious on me."

She regarded him with huge blue eyes. "It isn't the money, is it? That's not what attracted you to me?"

"Sweetheart, you know it isn't. I love you and I want to marry you. Do I look like the kind of a creep who would just want your money?"

"No, but tell me again why you *do* want me."

Skip pulled her close against his chest and nuzzled the top of her blond head. "I love you because you're young and cute and fun and sexy. I would want to marry you if you didn't have a nickel. At least that way we'd be starting off even."

As he spoke Skip's hand slid down and cupped the girl's ripe breast. He felt the nipple come alive under his fingers and thrust against the soft sweater.

Audrey turned in the seat and pushed herself against his hand. "My darling, I believe you. But I do hope you'll get along with Aunt Edith. You know how important it is that she approves. She has control of everything until my twenty-first birthday, and that's almost two years away."

"Believe me," Skip said, working with his hand, "I do know how important it is. And don't worry—I get along fine with old ladies. They want to mother me." He slid the hand down across the gentle mound of Audrey's belly to where the Spandex pants molded themselves to her crotch.

Audrey twisted in the seat, riding on his hand. "You make me vibrate like a violin string," she whispered.

With a show of reluctance Skip pulled away. "We'll have a

concert later. Now we'd better go on in and meet Auntie," he said. "She'll be wondering what we're doing out here."

For a long moment Audrey sat back against the seat, breathing deeply. "Lord!" she said. "One more minute with your hand down there and I wouldn't have cared if Aunt Edith and the whole darn town had come and stood around the car to watch us." She closed her eyes for a moment and opened them. "But you're right, darling. We'd better go in."

They walked together up a path of crushed seashells to the front door of the cottage. Behind a gauzy curtain a warm orange light glowed inside. Audrey opened the door with a key and they walked in.

The smell of sandalwood and some spice wrapped around the young couple as they entered. Skip gazed around at the cluttered living room. It looked like one of the so-called occult shops that were so popular these days. All around him were Zodiac symbols and other strange runes and signs he did not recognize. They were on wall plaques, plates, samplers, cushions, even sewn into the carpet. Colored bottles, ceramic figures, masks, strange pictures covered all available space. A stuffed monkey grinned at them from a trapeze.

"Do you really *live* with all this stuff?" he said. "I mean, this is *weird.*"

"You get used to it," Audrey said with a laugh. "Anyway, I did. It's the only home I've known really."

Skip continued his survey of the room until his eye fell on a row of six blunt, erect figurines that marched across the oak mantel. He frowned at them, trying to call up the source of the sense of familiarity he felt, but it eluded him for the moment. Then he laughed aloud as recognition came.

"Hey, do you know what those things look like?" he said, pointing.

Audrey blushed and lowered her eyes. "Yes, I know, but don't blame me. Aunt Edith makes them."

"She *makes* them?"

"It's sort of a hobby. Aunt Edith is really quite talented. She makes up her own special plastic for them. Do you want to feel one?"

"No, thanks," Skip said quickly. "The old girl must be

really spacy. No wonder they tell those wild stories about her in town."

"Hush, I think she's coming."

"Is that you, Audrey?"

The voice from the rear of the house was too rich and vibrant to fit the mental picture Skip had of elderly Aunt Edith. When the woman herself entered, his mouth dropped open.

Her presence seemed to fill the room. Tall and straight she stood, with hair of burnished copper flowing loose around her fine shoulders. Her cream-colored skin was without wrinkle or blemish. She wore a white and gold hostess gown. The top was cut to provide a matched pair of silken bags slung from her neck to carry the full, swaying breasts. An expanse of midriff was bared to reveal the delicious curve from rib cage to waist where the flare of her hips began.

Dimly, Skip became aware that Audrey was speaking.

"Aunt Edith, this is Skip Dial, the fellow I've told you about. Skip, my aunt, Miss Edith Calderon."

"How do you do, Mr. Dial." The woman made his name sound like music. A light smile touched her lips.

Skip had to swallow before he could get his voice working. "Hello," he said finally. "Please call me Skip."

"I'd like to." A mischievous spark danced deep in the woman's sea-green eyes. "Please come to the table. I've made some bouillabaisse. It's a specialty of mine."

"One of my favorites," Skip mumbled.

Aunt Edith stepped forward and took his hand to lead him into the dining alcove. He felt as though a jolt of electrical current had jumped from her fingers to his.

As they sat eating the savory fish stew Skip found it difficult to pay even polite attention to his fiancée, so powerful was the primitive aura of the aunt. Once when she rose from her seat and passed behind him on her way to the kitchen, a silken hip had brushed softly against his shoulder, making him flinch at the shock of physical pleasure.

During a lull in the table talk Skip said to the red-haired woman, "I was looking at the collection of things in your living room. Very, uh, interesting."

"Yes, aren't they. They mostly have to do with my

avocation. I'm a witch, you know. I imagine you have heard stories to that effect."

"They do say some outlandish things about you." Skip put on a tolerant smile to let her know that he was much too sophisticated to listen to the town bumpkins.

"Some of the things are probably quite true," Aunt Edith said.

Audrey spoke up, surprising Skip, who had almost forgotten she was there. "Please, Aunt Edith, you're not going to start on your theories of witchcraft again?"

"Not if you don't want me to, dear," the woman said.

"Hey, I'd like to hear about it," Skip put in, turning up the wattage on his smile. He looked around with a mock puzzled frown. "I don't see a broomstick anywhere."

"Flying is not my specialty," Aunt Edith said in her voice of dark velvet.

"Witches specialize?"

"Oh, indeed. Of course, there are a few general practitioners around, but there is so much to learn in the occult field that they never get really good at anything."

Skip leaned forward, his eyes caressing the expanse of golden bosom that threatened to overflow the restraining silk. "What's your specialty, Aunt Edith?"

She smiled at him. "Transferring souls."

He waited for her to go on, and when she did not, said, "Do you mean you can lift a soul right out of someone's body and put it somewhere else?"

"That is basically it."

"Sounds like a hard way to go," Skip said. "I mean for the guy who gets his soul lifted."

"Skip, you can say that again." Aunt Edith turned to her niece. "Audrey, I'm afraid we haven't a thing in the house for an after-dinner drink. Would you mind awfully running down to the store for a bottle of Hennesey? You do drink cognac, Skip?"

"Well, sure. Look, I could go and pick it up. My car's right outside."

"No no no. The store is just a short walk from here. And it will give you and me a chance to get acquainted."

"I don't mind," Audrey said. "I like the fresh air after dinner. Aunt Edith will take good care of you."

Skip mumbled something as Audrey went out the door. Aunt Edith rose and floated over to where he was sitting.

"Shall we go into the living room?"

Skip felt light-headed at the implied intimacies in her voice. The woman's sandalwood scent filled his head. As he got up, his shoulder bumped the resilient undercurve of her breast. Aunt Edith made no attempt to move away from his touch.

When he got his tongue in place Skip said, "Uh, tell me about this soul transfer business that you do. Exactly how do you go about it?"

They walked together into the living room. Skip fancied he could feel the heat of the woman's body even when they did not touch.

"It's rather a complicated business," she said, "but I can give you a general idea. There are certain specific moments when a man's soul is outside the protection of his body. It is at this precise instant that it must be stolen. You may have heard of the ancient superstition that says one of these unprotected times is when a person sneezes. Today we still say 'God bless you' when someone sneezes to ward off any nearby evil spirit that would snatch away the poor fellow's soul."

Skip smiled knowingly, but Aunt Edith's expression remained serious.

"There are," she continued, "other circumstances in which a man's soul is even more vulnerable for a second or two."

"That's really interesting," Skip mumbled, though he had been paying scant attention to what the woman was saying. She was facing him now, standing close enough that he could almost feel her heartbeat.

Struggling to maintain some shred of control, Skip drew a deep breath and pulled his eyes away from her breasts. His gaze came to rest on the half dozen rodlike figurines on the mantel that had caught his attention earlier.

"Those are strange-looking trinkets," he said.

Aunt Edith watched him. "Do you like them?"

"Not very much, to tell the truth. Something about them makes me feel creepy. Audrey tells me you make them."

"Yes. I have one in my workshop that's not quite finished. Would you like to see it?"

"Thanks all the same, but I don't think—"

"I should tell you that I use my bedroom for a workshop."

"But on second thought I might learn something."

"You might, indeed."

Beckoning to him, Aunt Edith led the way back through the dining alcove to a room in the rear corner of the cottage. Skip followed hungrily, watching the fluid motion of her buttocks under the clinging white silk.

The bedroom was a carnival of reds, yellows, oranges in swirling designs that seemed to draw Skip into them. The bed wore a soft crimson quilt. Beyond it was a low, round table. On this stood a figurine like those on the mantel, but somehow without the vibrancy of the others.

"Do you like it?" the woman asked. The tips of her breasts moved against his chest.

What little remained of Skip's self-control deserted him. He wrapped his arms about the woman, caressing her flawless back with trembling hands. He pulled her close and crushed his mouth on hers, feeling the full lips open under his and the warm tongue slide into his mouth like a small living thing.

His fingers found the single clasp at the back of her gown. He undid it clumsily, then gasped as the entire garment whispered to the floor. The tall woman stepped back for a moment, letting him enjoy her naked flesh. With numb fingers Skip fumbled at his belt.

"Let me do that," she said. "You lie back on the bed and relax."

She turned him effortlessly and steered him to the bed where he reclined with his eyes fixed on the woman's golden body. With deft movements she undid his clothing and whisked it away.

She paused with her hand resting flat on his bare stomach. "I have to ask this, Skip. What about Audrey?"

Several seconds ticked by before Skip could organize his thoughts enough to answer. "Audrey's a child," he rasped finally. "You and I . . . we're different. We're worldly. We *need* each other."

"Aren't you afraid this will hurt her?"

Skip thought fast. Never in his life had he wanted anything as much as he wanted this woman. He said, "She doesn't have to find out. We can still be married. You can live with us. You and I can still have each other, and Audrey will never have to know. With her money we can do anything we want to."

Aunt Edith sighed. "That's what I wanted to hear you say."

Her head dipped and the coppery wings of her hair whispered down across his naked chest and stomach like the touch of a shadow. His hands clawed at the scarlet quilt as he was sucked into a new world of unbearable pleasure.

Abruptly the woman's mouth released him and she let her body flow to the thick orange carpet beside the bed. She rolled onto her back and held her arms out to Skip.

"Come to me, my lover."

With his every nerve screaming, Skip rolled off the bed and onto the firm, yielding flesh of the woman's body. She guided him expertly with one hand and stroked his back with the other. Skip gave himself up to the whirling vortex. He slid in and down, deeper and ever deeper.

At the instant of crashing climax he felt a violent wrench unlike anything in his experience. It was like being yanked inside out. He had a momentary sensation of disembodied movement, then all feeling dissolved into a murky blur.

When Audrey returned, her aunt stood waiting for her in the living room.

"I got the cognac," the girl said, holding up a brown paper bag. "Where's Skip?"

Aunt Edith shook her head and smiled sadly at her niece. "I'm sorry, dear."

"Not another one?"

"I'm afraid so."

"You gave him the test?"

"Like the others, he failed."

"Oh, Aunt Edith, won't I ever find a man who will want me for myself and will be true to me?" She put her arms around the older woman and lay a cheek against the cushion of her breast.

"Of course you will, dear." Aunt Edith stroked the girl's

hair. "It's just a matter of meeting the right one." She smiled. "But in the meantime, remember that it's not a total loss."

"That's true." The girl sighed and stepped back from her aunt. She turned her eyes to the mantel where seven erect figures stood in a row at attention.

"Will you be wanting him tonight, Aunt Edith?"

"No, dear, you first. It's only fair."

Audrey crossed to the mantel and grasped the newest of the rigid figures. It was warm and pliable to her touch.

"Good night, Aunt Edith," she said.

"Good night, Audrey. Enjoy."

As his sensations gradually returned Skip realized he had no power of movement. After the first flash of panic he relaxed, stopped resisting, and let himself be thrust head first into the warm, wet orifice. The slippery walls closed around him, caressing him all over.

A hard way to go, maybe, he decided, but all things considered, not so bad.

DAUGHTER OF THE GOLDEN WEST

Dennis Etchison

A<small>t</small> the school were three boys who were best friends.
Together they edited the campus newspaper, wrote or
appeared in plays from time to time, and often could be seen
huddled together over waxed paper lunches, over micro-
scopes in the biology lab, sometimes until dark, over desks
leafed with papers most Saturdays, elbow to elbow with
their English Department advisor, and even over the same
clusters of girls gathered like small bouquets of poppies on
the steps of the cafeteria, joking and conning and in general
charming their way through the four long years.

Almost four years.

Don and Bob were on the tennis squad, Don and David
pasted-up the Buckskin Bugler feature pages, Bob and
David devised satirical skits for the annual Will & Prophecy
Class Assemblies, and together they jockeyed for second,
third and fourth positions in their graduating class—the
first place was held inexplicably by one of those painted-
smile, spray-haired secretary types (in fact she was Secretary
of the Senior Class) named Arnetta Kuhn, and neither
separately nor *en masse* could they dislodge, dissuade,
distract, deflower or dethrone that irritating young woman
from her destiny as Valedictorian, bent as she had been
upon her goal since childhood, long before the boys had

met, a target fixed in her mind as a stepping stone to a greater constellation of goals which included marrying the most promising young executive in Westside Hills, whoever he might happen to be, and furnishing him and a ranch-style home yet to be built on a South American Street with four dishwater-haired children and a parturient drawerful of Blue Chip Stamps. And so it went.

Until May, that is: the last lap of the home stretch.

Until Bob disappeared.

In the Formica and acetate interior of the mobile home in Westside Hills Court, Don of the thick black hair and high white forehead, lover of Ambrose Bierce and master of the sweeping backhand, and David, the high school's first longhair, collector of Marvel comics and articles on quantum physics, commiserated with Mrs. Witherson over cans of sugar-free cola (it was the only kind she had, now that Bob was gone), staring into their thumbnails and speaking softly in tones that were like a settling of throttled sighs over an as yet unmarked grave. It was a sad thing, surely, it was mysterious as hell, and most of all, each thought secretly, it was unfair, the most unfair thing he could have done.

The trophies, glassed certificates and commendations Bob had earned reflected around Mrs. Witherson, bending the dim, cold light into an aurora behind her drooped, nodding head.

"Maybe he ran off with a— With some kind of woman. The way his father did."

Instantly regretting it, a strange thing to say, really, Mrs. Witherson closed a shaking hand around the water glass and tipped it to her lips. The sherry wavered and clung, then evaporated, glistening, from the sides; she had taken it up again weeks ago, after the disappearance, and now the two were concerned about her as if by proxy. For Bob had told them, of course, of the way she had been for so long after the loss of his father. He had been too small to remember him, but he had remembered the fuming glasses and shaking hands, he had said, and now his friends remembered them, too, though they did not speak of these things or even look up as she drank.

"I thought—" *Bob's father was killed in the war,* David started to say, but stopped, even without Don's quick glance and furtive headshake.

"He had. So much. Going for him." Bob's mother drained the glass, gazing into it, and David saw the tip of her slow, coated tongue lap after the odor of nonexistent droplets along the lip. "You all know that." And it was a larger statement than it sounded, directed beyond the trailer to include and remind them all, whoever needed to be reminded of the essential truth of it, herself, perhaps, among them.

They jumped, all three of them. The telephone clattered with an unnatural, banshee urgency in the closed rectangle of the trailer. The Melmac dishware ceased vibrating on the plastic shelf as Mrs. Witherson picked up the receiver. She took it unwillingly, distastefully, between the circle of thumb and finger.

David pushed away from the unsteady, floor-bolted table and chewed the inside of his mouth, waiting to catch Don's eyes.

"Mm-hm. Ye-es. I see."

It might have been an invitation to a Tupperware party. A neighbor whose TV set was on the blink. A solicitation for the PTA, which could have accounted for the edge in her voice. But it was not; it was not. They both knew it without looking at each other, and were on their feet by the aluminum screen door seconds before Mrs. Witherson, white-faced, dropped the receiver. It swung from the coiled cord, dipping and brushing the chill linoleum floor.

The lieutenant at the police station wrote out the address of the county morgue and phoned ahead for them. They drove in silence, pretending absorption in traffic lights. It was really not like the movies. An official in a wrinkled white smock showed them three 8 x 10's and there was not much talk, only a lot of nods and carefully avoided eyes and papers to be signed. Don stepped into a locker room and returned so quickly that he must have turned on his heel the instant the sheet was lifted. During that brief moment and through the miles of neon interstices after David did not think of the photographs.

What was left of Bob had been found by a roadside somewhere far out of town.

And it was "just like the other two," the attendant said.

They drove and did not stop even when they were back in Westside. Don took corner after corner, lacing the town in smaller and smaller squares until each knew in his own time that there was nowhere to go and nothing to be said. David was aware of the clicking of the turn indicator and the faint green flickering of the light behind the dashboard. Until he heard the hand brake grind up. The motor still running. Without a word he got out and into his own car and they drove off in different directions.

David could not face his room. He hovered through the empty streets around his house for half an hour before his hands took over the wheel for themselves. He found himself in the parking lot of the Village Pizza Parlor. He drifted up next to Don's car and slipped inside, leaving the keys in the ignition.

Don was hunched to the wall, dialing the pay phone. David sidled over to a table in the corner and climbed onto the bench across from Craig Cobb, former star end for the Westside Bucks and Student Council football lobbyist.

"Hey, listen, Don told me about Bob and, hey, listen, I'm sorry."

David nodded and shuffled his feet in the sawdust.

Craig's lip moved over the edge of the frosted root beer. He probably wanted to pump David for details, but must have dimly perceived the nature of the moment and chose instead to turn his thick neck and scrutinize the player piano in the corner, now mercifully silent.

Don returned to the table.

"My mother's going over to stay with Mrs. Witherson tonight," he said, sliding in next to Craig. Then, meeting David's eyes for the first time in hours, "Craig here tells me we ought to talk to Cathy Sparks."

They looked at each other, saying, *All right, we're in something now, and we're in it together, and we both know it,* and Craig glanced from one to the other and sensed that they were in something together, and that it was about their best friend who was dead and no one knew why, and he said, "R'lly. He went out with her, y'know."

That was wrong. Bob hadn't been going with anybody last semester. If he had, they would have known. Still, the way Don's eyes were fixing him, David knew there was more to hear.

Craig repeated the story. "No, see, it was just that weekend. Saturday." Right, that was the last time they had seen Bob. He had been working on that damned Senior History paper. "I was washing my car, right? And Robert pulls in next to me, the next stall, and starts rollin' up the windows and so I ask him, you know, 'Who're you takin' to the Senior Party?' An' he says he doesn't know yet, and so I say, 'Goin' to any good orgies tonight?' and he says, 'What d'you know about the new girl?' I guess, yeah, I think he said he gave her a ride home or something. I got the idea he was goin' over to see her that night. Like she asked him to come over or something. You know."

The new girl. The one nobody had had time to get close to, coming in as she had the last month or six weeks of school. A junior. Nobody knew her. Something about her. Her skin was oiled, almost buttery, and her expression never changed. And her body. Dumpy—no, not exactly; it was just that she acted like she didn't care about how she looked most of the time; she wore things that covered her up, that had no shape. So you didn't try for her. Still, there was something about her. She was the kind of girl nobody ever tried for, but if somebody asked somebody if he'd ever gotten anything off her, you would stop what you were doing and listen real close for the answer.

"So maybe you'll want to talk to her. She's the last one to see him. I guess." The football player, unmoving in his felt jacket, glanced nervously between them.

David stared at Don, and Don continued to stare back. Finally they rose together, scraping the bench noisily against the floor.

"Only thing is, she'll be pretty hard to find, prob'ly."

"Why's that?" asked David.

"I heard she moved away soon as the school year was over."

Later, driving home, taking the long way, thinking, David remembered the photographs. The way the body was mangled. Cut off almost at the waist. He tried, but this time he could not get it out of his mind.

So they did a little detective work the next day.

Bob's mother had not seen him after that Saturday morning, when he left for the library to work on his research paper. No one else had seen him after that, either. Except Craig. And maybe, just maybe, the girl.

So.

So the family name was in the phone book, but when they got there the apartment was up for rent. The manager said they had moved out the 12th, right after finals.

So they stopped by the school.

The Registrar's office was open for summer school and Mrs. Greenspun greeted them, two of her three favorite pupils, with a warmth undercut by a solicitous sadness of which she seemed afraid to speak. It was like walking into a room a second after someone has finished telling a particularly unpleasant story about you behind your back.

Yes, she had received a call, she said, a call asking that Cathy's grades be sent along to an out-of-town address.

"The young lady lives with her older sister, I take it," confided Mrs. Greenspun.

David explained that he had loaned her a book which she had forgotten to return.

"Of course," said Mrs. Greenspun maternally. And gave them the address.

It was in Sunland, a good hour-and-a-half away.

David volunteered his old Ford. They had to stop once for directions and twice for water and an additive that did not keep its promise to the rusty radiator. In the heat, between low, tanned hills that resembled elephants asleep or dead on their sides under the sun, Don put down the term paper. They had picked it up from Mr. Broadbent, Bob's history teacher, and had put off turning it over to his mother. They had said they were going to read it but had not, sharing a vague unease about parting with the folder.

It was only the preliminary draft, with a lot of the details yet to be put in, but it was an unbelievable story.

"He was really into something strange," muttered Don, pulling moist hair away from the side of his face.

"I guess that means we can talk about it now."

"I guess," said Don. But his tone was flat and he kept watching the heat mirages rising up from the asphalt ahead.

"I've read something about it," pressed David. "It's pretty grim, isn't it." A statement.

"It's got to be the most horrible story I've ever read. Or the most tragic. Depending on how you look at it," said Don. "Both," he decided.

David felt subjects mixing. He was light in the head. He sucked on a bottle of Mountain Dew and tried to shift the conversation. "What did that guy at the coroner's office mean, do you think?"

"You mean—"

"I mean about the 'other two.'" Suddenly David realized he had not changed the subject at all.

"Well, you remember Ronnie Ruiz and—what was the other one's name?"

David remembered, all right. Two others had disappeared, one a couple of weeks before Bob, the first a few weeks before that. A month or six weeks before the end of school. He had known what the attendant meant but had been carrying around a peculiar need to hear it confirmed. "Patlian, I think. The younger one, Jimmy Patlian's brother. The junior. But I thought he ran off to join the Reserves."

"I don't know. It must have been him. Give me a swig of that shit, will you? Hey, how can you drink this?"

"I know, I know, my teeth'll fall out," said David, relieved to talk about something else. "But we always had it around the house when I was a kid. I guess you can be raised to like a thing, just like your parents' parents probably gave them the taste. Hard to put down."

"Sure, man, just keep telling yourself that until your stomach starts eating itself. Anyway, I know they found Ronnie Ruiz in some kind of traffic thing. Torn up pretty bad."

"The guy didn't even have a car, did he?"

"I don't—no, now that you bring it up. But they found him by some road somewhere. Maybe he got hit. The way I remember it, no one could identify him for sure for quite a while. Shit, man." He handed back the sweltering bottle. "This is shit."

"It's shit, all right," said David. "A whole lot of it."

"Cathy?"

"I remember you." The girl showed herself at the shadowed edge of the door, out of the blinding sun. "And you. I didn't think you'd bring anyone with you, when you called," she said to David, softly so that it was almost lost in the din of the freeway above the lot.

"This is Don. He—"

"I know. It's all right. My sister will be pleased."

The boys had worked out a scenario to ease her along but never got past side one. She had a quality of bored immobility which seemed to preclude manipulation, and a lack of assertiveness which made it somehow unnecessary.

They sat in three corners of the living room and made conversation.

She was not pretty. As their eyes mellowed to the heavily draped interior, her face began to reflect warm tones like the smooth skin of a lighted candle: oiled wax. She wore a loose, very old fashioned dress, high-necked, a ribboned cameo choker. As at school, though now the effect was in keeping with the close, unventilated room studded with fading, vignetted photographs and thin, polished relics of bone china. She moved without grace or style. She all but stood as she walked, all but reclined as she sat, inviting movement from others.

The afternoon passed. She drew them out, and they did not feel it happening.

Finally the ambience was broken momentarily. She left the room to refill their sweating glasses.

Don blinked. "There is something about that girl," he began measuredly, "and this place, that I do not like." He sounded nearly frightened about it, which was odd. "Does any of this remind you of anything?"

David rested his head against lace. His scalp was prickling. "Any of what? Remind me of what?"

When she reappeared with new iced teas, cooled with snowball-clumps of ice, Don had repositioned himself at the mantel. He fingered a discolored piece of an old mirror.

"How well did you know Bob Witherson, Cathy?" he asked, gazing into the glass as if for reflections of faces and events long past, something along the lines of a clue.

She paused a beat, then clinked the refreshments onto their coasters. Unruffled, noticed David, trying to get a fix on her.

"I met Bobby at the library," she explained. "I saw the paper he was writing. We talked about it, and he asked me to help him. I invited him over for dinner. At my sister's."

As simple as that.

David had been sitting one way for so long, his eyes picking over the same curios, that he was beginning to experience a false gestalt. When Cathy sat again, he almost saw her sink back into the familiar shimmering outline that was etched on his retinas, the image of her sitting/lying in the overstuffed chair as she had for—how long? Hours? But this time she remained perched on the edge, as if in anticipation. David found himself focusing on details of her face: the full, moistened lips. And her body: the light pressure of her slim belly rising and falling to flutter the thin gingham dress. How much fuller, more satisfied she had looked when he first saw her, right after she came to Westside. Than the last time he had seen her, too, a couple of weeks before graduation. Now she seemed fragile, starved. She was watching him.

"These pieces must be very old," said Don from across the airless room. He lifted a fragment of a teacup. It was decorated in the delicate handiwork of another era, blue and red and purple flowers scrolled into the pure white ground surface of the chinaware.

David, watching Cathy watching him as he waited to make a move, resented the interruption.

"Yes." She spoke easily from another level, undistractible. "My great-great grandmother brought them with her from Springfield. In Illinois."

David inched forward.

"They came West, did they?" continued Don strangely, getting at something. "Would . . . do you mind? I mean, I was wondering," he faltered, atypically, "where did they settle? I mean, where do you come from?"

"Sacramento, originally."

David rose. He crossed the room halfway. He stopped on a worn virgule in the carpet. Cathy's eyes opened wider to him. He was aware in a rush of the power assumed by someone who simply waits and asks no questions. But understanding it made it no less effective.

"Your sister has an interesting house," said David.

"You might like to see the rest," she offered coolly.

But Don was still busy formulating something and he would not let go. David had seen that expression before.

"Why," Don asked carefully, his words hanging like bright bits of dust in the air, "did Bob ask you to help him on his paper?" So he saw what was happening to David, saw it and recognized it and tried to push past it anyway. "Why *would* he?" he directed at David, as if the obvious reasons were not enough.

For once Cathy ignored a question. She got up and walked into the hallway, drawing it out as long as she could, aware of his eyes on her back. Perhaps she was smiling. She turned. Out of Don's line of sight she said, "The parts you haven't seen yet are in here." And so saying she leaned forward, grasped the hem of her long dress and lifted it to the waist. She was naked underneath. Her eyes never left David.

The moment was unreal. She seemed to tilt before his eyes.

David moved toward the hall.

Don, thinking she was far into another room, launched a volley of words in a frantic stage whisper.

"We've got to get together on this," he said. And, "Think." And, "I say her people came through Truckee in 18—what. 1846." And, "David, what about it? What does that mean to you?" And, "That's why he wanted her help on the research. It's starting to add up. Does that make sense, Davey? Does it? Does it?!" And, "I don't know, it's crazy, but there's something more. What's the matter, you think it's something that scares me? Why should it? You think I'm fucking crazy? *Do you?*"

As David entered the bedroom the roar of the freeway gained tenfold, a charge of white sound in his ears. He thought she was saying something. He could not see her at first. Then a flurry of cloth and a twisting blur of white skin. Disjointedly he remembered Don as he had left him there in the darkening living room as the sun went down outside. Here in the bedroom it was almost completely dark—the east side of the house, the drapes thicker. Gradually his ears attuned to sounds closer than the churning traffic. Words Don had spoken in that choked whisper: *What about it? What about it?* Over and over like a ticking clock inside him. He felt his body flushed, feverish. People who live like this must be afraid of the cold. His eyes began to clear. He was aware of a slow, tangled movement about the edges of the room. Probably the curtains in the breeze. *Afraid of the cold.* He saw her now faintly like a fish in dark waters, under ice, sliding horizontally beneath him on the curve of the bed. He felt himself fevered, swelling. Her cold, damp fingers raised his shirt and found the hairs on his chest. She slipped under his belt, thumbed and pulled, straining the buckle. He heard his zipper winding open. Did he? The shapes moving against the walls in the breeze. Hushed, swishing sounds. The freeway? Closer, closer. *There was no breeze.* "Are you hungry?" she asked and then laughed a kind of laugh he had never heard before. She slid back and forth under him, spreading her fishbelly-white legs wider. He moved to her, his body trembling. "No." Her voice. Of course. Of course. "First let me eat you." She said it. All right. All right? In the protracted second as she sat up, as she gripped his waist like a vise, sudden images flashed to mind: words written in the dark and illuminated from within. They came in a surge, crowded in on him. My sister will be pleased, she had said. What sister? He laughed. Almost laughed. Now he was sure of the presence of others in the room. They undulated along the walls. How many? This is crazy. She had sisters, yes, that was it, sisters, from Sacramento, descended from Truckee and the great trek to Sutter's Fort. "Oh my God," he said aloud, his voice cracking. And in the next second every-thing, all of it came at once. As he felt her mouth enfold him he saw Bob with her, and as her lips tightened he saw Bob in the photographs, and as her teeth scraped hungrily over him, drawing him deeper into her, he saw Bob's body, torn, consumed almost to the waist, and as the teeth bit down for the first time, bit down and would not be released, grinding sharply together, it all exploded like a time bomb and he heard his scream off the walls and the freeway's pulse, above her house, the road where young men were tossed afterwards like so much garbage and the sound of the sighing women as he passed into unconsciousness and Don burst confused into the room with the second draft from her desk where he had found it and before he could form an answer or even another question about Bob's paper on the Donner Party and her strange knowledge of it her sisters swooped from the corners where they had been crouched in waiting and then they were upon him, too.

MEAT MARKET

John Skipp and Craig Spector

A rustling on sheets. The sliding of flesh over flesh, softly merging. Wetness, spreading slowly from the center of the bed. All motion. All flow.

Above, always above, the clock is ticking. Ticking off seconds that turn into hours. Slicing time into measured increments with a sound that cuts like a scalpel's blade. Cutting staccato gashes across the near-perfect stillness of the room.

They try to ignore the ticking. To be lost in the motion. And the flow.

When Doreen left him, Tom Savich was in some serious pain. His chest ached. His balls ached. His spine felt as though it had been yanked out, bone by knobby bone, then sewn back in the wrong way. His guts felt mangled and ravaged from the inside. His eyes burned. His lips chapped and bled.

In his brain . . . in all the soft places where he stored his memories of her, his estimates of her worth, his plans of a future together . . . there were black, puckered holes. They bled so tangibly, so profusely, that he found himself wondering when *all* thought would be drowned and buried by the copious flow.

Once again: he was in some serious pain.

It was painfully obvious. Anyone could tell that he'd just been hit, and hard. They stayed away in droves: the women, particularly. Tom found that he really could not blame them a bit. He knew how unappetizing he looked.

So he toughed it out. He waited for the wounds to scab over and heal. He gave himself the time and the solitude he needed to recover, to get his bearings, to go out and love again.

It took about a month.

And then his friend Jerry called up to ask if he felt like hitting Dio's after work on Friday. Maybe pick up a couple of sweet little pieces.

"What can you lose?" Jerry asked.

"Everything," he replied. "My heart. My mind."

"Name of the game," Jerry said.

Moving, now. The ticking, forgotten. Nothing but the waves of passion and immersion. Rushing over them, now, with mounting fury.

As they move.

Tom Savich thought about it. He gave it some intense consideration. The idea simultaneously attracted and repelled, which was pretty much what he had come to expect, considering how much emotional baggage he was carrying around with Dio's name written all over it.

Because Dio's was *the* pickup spot in the garment district, the stretch of Manhattan that gave Fashion Avenue its name. It was the place where hawkers of overpriced clothing went after hours to find their partners for the night. It was the place where business and pleasure, predator and prey came together in an atmosphere of dim light, alcohol and smoky haze to consummate their endless affairs.

It was the place where Tom first met Doreen, in fact. And Kirsten. And Molly. And the one before that. And the one before *that*. Ad infinitum. It was the place where he had always gone when the need became too great, because it was designed to meet such needs, and it had never failed him.

The question is, he told himself, *do I really need it that badly?* It was not a question that could be answered rationally. It could only be measured in terms of scar tissue and hunger. How much of one, to appease the other? And was it really worth it?

In the end, Jerry persuaded him. It wasn't that hard. Tom Savich had gone a month without. He had pulled himself back together, admirably, from a nasty piece of circumstance. The hunt must go on. If he wanted it, all he had to do was go out and get it.

And as it turned out, he really did want it very badly.

More than that: he *needed* it.

Inside, now. Dark. Deep. Firm parts over firm parts touching soft soft parts, probing deeper. Pushing, pulling. Into each other.
While the clock. Is ticking. Ticking.
Overhead.

Inside Dio's, insanity reigned. By 6:30, there was no more room to stand. Warm bodies vying not only for attention, but for a square foot of floor space to call their own. Large color screens curled over the corners, flashing jump-cut images of perfectly undulating flesh. The big neon clock over the entrance swept round and round, reminding all players of the need for speed. From the balcony, Dio's looked like an army ant farm: a swarm of expensive suits and low-cut blouses, limbs and backs and faceless heads, swaying with the beat, crawling all over each other.

"It's a jungle down there," Tom said. "I'd forgotten what a jungle this is." His eyes flickered between the videos above and the spectacle below and the sweeping, glowing hands; his drink sat, unattended, on the table before him. He might as well have been talking to himself.

"You're just wired, Tommy." Jerry, too, was staring over the rail; but he grinned, white teeth showing under the flat gleam of his eyes. "You just need to loosen up some. Get your thumb out of your ass. This is supposed to be fun, remember?"

"Yeah, right." Down below, somebody had finally scored with the gorgeous blond by the cash register. A dozen men turned despondently to look for other prey. Tom Savich felt suddenly very tired. Of it all. He sighed deeply. The clock swept round. The bodies writhed. The music throbbed on.

"Listen. Killer." Jerry's tone was derisive, a wee bit impatient. "I'm not going to babysit you, man. If you're bound and determined to have a miserable time, there's no sign up saying you have to stick around. I just thought you had yourself patched up better than that." Tom looked over sharply, stung. "I just thought you were ready to get over that shit."

"It's just . . ." Tom knee-jerked, suddenly on the defensive. He found that he couldn't look at his friend for a moment; there was something in Jerry's expression . . . something ugly and feral . . . that made him distinctly uncomfortable. "It's just that this place is such a meat rack, man. I . . ."

"Oh. And you're *above* that sort of thing, I take it." Jerry laughed. Tom felt stupid. Jerry continued. "Come on, Savich. Cut me a break. The Virgin Mary has never been your patron saint. I've been in this bar with you more times than . . ."

"It's just been a long time," Tom countered. "And I don't see anything that really gets me going. And I just can't seem to feel it."

"Well," and now Jerry sat beaming like a Buddha, convinced that he'd finally broken through. "You might want to start by finishing your goddam drink," he said, indicating the untouched glass on the table. "A few more of those, *I'm* gonna start lookin' good to you!"

And it was true: at least halfway. Though Tom made it clear that Jerry would always be an ugly sucker, he did find that Dio's became far more appetizing about two drinks down the road. He began to loosen up. He began to have fun. He began to ignore the dull pangs that went off, deep within.

And that was, of course, when he spotted her.

Building up. Sharp breaths. Sharp movement. In. Out.
In. Out. Consuming.
The wet spot, slowly growing in the center of the bed.

Her name was Linda. She said that she worked for Murjani, International. "I wanted to be a model," she continued, "but they told me I was too short. So now, instead of modeling clothes on the cover of *Vogue,* I hustle 'em in the showroom."

"That's a damn shame," he told her. "I mean it." And he did. *She must have been tremendous as a kid,* he thought. *When she was fresh. Wish I could've been there.*

That would have been some fifteen years ago. Linda wasn't a kid anymore. Very faintly, he could see the scars that the years had left on her. She'd borne them well. She was still a looker. And there was something tough about her . . . a worldly wisdom, a sense of having learned to survive . . . that he found very appealing. With Linda, he knew, there'd be no need for bullshit and fancy dances. She wouldn't stand for it. It made him happy.

He wanted it to be with her.

Perhaps they'd find it.

In each other.

Moaning, now. Breath coming in firebursts. Backs arching. Eyes flashing. Teeth glistening. Loins pounding.

As the climax builds.

And the moment draws near.

And the clock slices holes in the night.

They spoke for a while, of a number of things. Her eyes were large and dark and penetrating. Her face had a slight flush, blood tip-toeing gingerly to the surface. When she smiled, her lips were red and full. They made themselves clear.

She wanted it as badly as he did.

After that, there was nothing left to say.

Hoarse cries in the darkness. The animals, revealed. Flesh sliding over flesh over tensed muscles, writhing.

As he nibbles at her throat.

And she digs into his back.

And the rhythm drags them forward, like the pounding of their blood. Like the ticktock scalpel slashing at the warm body of Time.

While the wet spot grows. And grows. And grows.

They went to his apartment on Riverside Drive by taxi, nuzzling each other and the hip-flask that she carried in her bag. The pain was gone now . . . the hunger firmly in its place . . . and all seemed propelled by a drunken exhilaration, pounding through him like a thousand primitive drums.

And then they were in the apartment, where they quickly dispensed with formalities, as well as their clothing. He was startled, but not surprised, by the red gash that ran the length of her soft underbelly, dwarfing the scores of other old wounds that pock-marked her flesh.

Tom Savich glanced down at his own scars for a moment: some as recent as Doreen, some dating back to his very first piece in high school, all those many years before. Some of them gleamed whitely, like bleached bones, like that fabled picket fence; others blushed red, embarrassing memories that he didn't want to think about. Not now. Not now . . .

And then he was looking at her again, as she moved toward him. Memory drowned in the sight of her body; the sagging breasts, the tightening nipples, the hips that undulated in a dance as old as the first woman, converging with the first man, on the day of the birth of human hunger.

And as they descended on the bed together, he only knew that it was all right. That the past was irrelevant, as irrelevant as the future, in the face of the moment itself.

It was only natural.

Now.
The first scream. Ten thick grooves, carving lengthwise down fleshy expanse. Jaws, clamping down. A hot spray. Muffled howl.
Taste of meat, raw and steaming. An audible tearing away. Head, whipping from side to side while its mouth bellows agony. Twists with rage. And attacks.
In the moment.
In the flow.
While the clock ticks off seconds that slice like razors into the soft parts that no claw could reach, no tooth impale, no casual glance reveal.
And the dark wet tendrils stream outward from the center of the bed . . .

Linda was gone when he awoke. It was better that way. It was hard enough to face his own wounds, in private. He didn't want to see what he had done.

She had left very few traces of herself behind. A bit of blood, on the bathroom floor. She was meticulous. He was glad. It meant that she still had her presence of mind; she would be okay; she would make it.

Of course, there was still the bed. There would always be the bed.

Later, after breakfast, he would definitely have to burn the sheets.

And put on clean ones.

For the next time.

THE VOICE

Rex Miller

I am Dallas's Ruler of the Night, the voice in the shadows, whispering of stardust and moonglow and bossa nova rhythm.

The scratchy cut be-bops through the coda and the automatic cart-light flashes a five-second cue as I wait to perform. The engineer pots me up full as the red light blinks and the final note slides under my first words to the faithful:

"Cliffie Brown. Joy Spring." The hand behind the ear, old style. I smile up at the face on the other side of the double-paned glass. My engineer McVey punches up a spot and twangs into the studio intercom:

"I never heard of the cat."

"You never heard of the cat because he's dead. He was very young. He was the Ritchie Valens of the jazz trumpet."

I open the turntable well where we keep the ice bucket. About a third of the Thermos gone. Drinking on the air seems unthinkable to a civilian. But contrary to public image, air personalities are often paranoid, quivering skin-bags of insecurities, their professionalism measured not in behavior but in air sound and ratings. Drink, smoke, attack the receptionist if you must, but just make sure you sound *great*. Total control is our brand of semi-pro ball. I take the Beefeater's Express nightly. That's my ticket out there.

"Those sloppy esses are gettin' pretty sibilant, bro,"

McVey laughs. "One more Beefy-Weefy and it's the Robert McVey show!"

"Whatever it takes, we can handle it," I assure him. The Friends-and-Groupies line, or FAG line as we call it, lights up and I stab at the glowing button.

"Yellow."

"Yellow yourself." It's my lady. The Voice.

"Heeeeeyyyyy, you're just what I need right about now."

"It's nice to be needed," she breathes. This lady Patricia has a voice that would peel a banana.

"You could say that. Yes. Can you, ahh, hang on?"

"What should I hang on to?" she breathes into the other end of the phone. I just about shove my pen through the logbook.

I turn on the intercom. "Don't give me the mic," I tell McVey. "It's your show. You wanted it. You got it. Just don't play anything weird." I kill the monitor.

"You must have McVey tonight," she purrs. She knows everything about me by now. So many long talks into the wee hours. "You miss me any?" Her VOICE—my Lord! My arms are covered with chill bumps.

"Yeah." It's all I can do to speak. She can do that to me. I suppose she could do it to any man. She has the command of a professional singer or announcer or public speaker. She knows how to use her voice.

"I've missed you so much," I say. "I can't take much more of this. You know?"

"I know, I know." She chuckles deep in her sexy throat. We'd talked for weeks yet the time had never been right to meet. There was a problem. Patricia was married. A cruel, extremely wealthy and equally possessive man several years her senior. By her account, he had kept her all but a prisoner in her own home.

I knew where she lived. I'd driven past many a time, hoping for just a glimpse of her through the windows. I knew I was playing way out of my league, but you know how it is.

"I just can't take his suspicions and his behavior," she says. "I've only stayed with him because of the children."

"Listen," I say, doodling furiously on the back of the log,

"are we going to get together or what? At least let's meet, just to say hi in person." She starts to speak and I keep going. "Please—let me at least come over and say hello—or meet me someplace for a quick drink. I'll be very discreet." There is the sound of Patricia taking a long, deep breath.

"Promise you won't stay long. You'd just—you know—come by and say hello, then you'd go. I'm willing to chance it, but you've got to promise me you'll never come over without my permission or call me or try to see me without us setting it up in advance."

"Sure."

"It isn't really fair to you. I just can't offer you much of anything in the way of a relationship."

"Let me worry about that, okay? We'll play it however you say. I just want to be with you. Okay?"

"Okay. It's not very smart of us. But I'm tired of being smart." We breathe at each other over Ma Bell's lines. "He's going to be leaving town Friday afternoon. But just for a few minutes—okay?"

"Yeah, okay, sure." I'd agree to anything. I'm starting to feel the Beefeater's. Full of the gin and the rush.

I know I never did such a pulled-together show in my life as I do the rest of that evening. The show just *cooks* for miles.

For an hour I go on like I invented radio. I suppose it's my love song to Patricia—my lady of the telephone.

The days blur and the time between now and Friday is gone and I'm off the air, driving through the city, and before I know it, I'm ringing the doorbell, and I hear a voice over another intercom, my life now one big intercom conversation.

"It's open." God, what a sexy sentence. It's open. It just knocks me down and runs over me. I want to go home and build a shrine to her. Light candles around her statue. Pray to Our Lady of the Perfect Tonsils.

I open the ornate door and step into Patricia's world of wealth and taste. I move down plushly carpeted stairs into the most beautiful room I've ever been in.

I am drawn toward that voice again, this time from a darkened corner of what appears to be a sunken conversation pit, and I look in the direction of that sexy voice and see her for the first time.

"Ummmmm, you're a big one," she says in that unmistakable, throaty contralto.

My heart is in my throat as I say, "Wow."

"Do I pass?" She is sitting in profile to me from where I am moving toward her, perched on a kind of throne chair like some actress on a movie set. A regal princess on a throne, she is shockingly beautiful. I'm talking fucking BEAUTIFUL. Movie star knockout gorgeous stone beautiful, Daddy.

Porcelain white china skin, the way I imagined it in my fantasies. Dark eyes and long brunette hair under a white shawl of the most delicate and precious lace. Her body slim and lovely and perfect, profiled in a tight white dress that might have been a wedding gown or the courting costume of an aristocrat. White high heels that must have been five or six inches tall. Legs, reed-slim and long and heart-stoppingly sexy, crossed just so. And a dainty hand, reaching out of the shadows to touch me as I move closer.

"Hi," she says, and the love I feel for her is so real and all-pervasive and staggering that I can only say "Wow" and expel the breath I've been holding since I'd first seen her.

Such a theatrical moment. The light seems planned just so, to flatter and spotlight her, yet keep her shadowy and mysterious all at the same time. A princess sitting on the darkest edge of this circle of radiant light, she pulls me into its nimbus with an urgent whisper.

"I've waited so long to kiss you." Her voice, the voice of ultimate sex, sears me with its heat. She pulls my face down to hers. Like a teenager, I close my eyes and kiss that perfection and my heart feels like it will explode. Time has no meaning and reality can not be conceptualized.

A deft hand of fine china reaches for the zipper of my trousers and she takes my masculinity in her small, delicate fingers and leans forward and it is then that the shawl pulls back just enough so that, for the first time, I see all of her face.

A harlequin face. Only half a face. The other half is a skull—a slick, desperate screaming nightmare of a thousand sweat-soaked sheets. A latex mask of a skull, of hospital crocodiles man-eating swampscream tortured skin pulled tight werewolf gladiator wounds hell in the flaming river rubbery skin pulled thing stretched awful hideous oh my God I'm sorry baby inhuman red raw bleeding oh Jesus in Heaven skull pulled tight oh Christ it's okay, darlin', really, you're going to be all right, tell Daddy all about it, and the frightening apparition of the skull mask half-woman smiles up at me as the mask must have done a time or two before and whispers those hot, icy, agonizing hurt words, words that do not belong to a voice of Velvet, a voice made to whisper words of love and sex and beauty and stiffening erection-causing lust.

"I was in a fire," she says. Yes, I can see that. Where is my pulled-together shit now when I can only back up, back-pedaling like an idiot, turning, wanting to run, wanting to scream.

Maybe she says don't leave. Or let's have a cup of Maxwell House. Or maybe she tells me how many grafts had been done before they got that tight, rubbery thing over half the skull, before they got those hideous red things stretched across the face, before they made the other half scream across the white bone.

Or maybe she says, "I'm lucky to be alive," and I'm going oh baby oh my God bless you honey I'm sorry I'm so sorry but I'm fucking LEAVING you know I can't handle it. And maybe she says something about how it's like that all down the right side or the left side and would I like to "SEE IT YOU DIRTY CHICKENSHIT SONOFABITCH!"

Her voice is slashing out at me as I run for the car. "Come on back!" she shrieks at me from the intercom. "COME BACK AND I'LL SHOW YOU ALL OF IT, YOU NO-GOOD COCKSUCKER." The words, hard-edged as bad acid, stabbing me as I run.

"WHAT A FUNNY JOKE ON BOTH OF US," she screams from her throne, because she had seen me too.

And that is how I leave her, in her state of grace, the remorseless legacy of a God who will not be questioned. I go home to pray for us, for myself, of course, and for Our Lady Patricia.

THE MODEL

Robert Bloch

*B*efore I begin this story, I must tell you that I don't believe a word of it.

If I did, I'd be just as crazy as the man who told it to me, and he's in the asylum.

There are times, though, when I wonder. But that's something you'll have to decide for yourself.

About the man in the asylum—let's call him George Milbank. Age thirty-two, according to the records, but he looked older; balding, running to fat, with a reedy voice and a facial tic that made me a little uptight watching him. But he didn't act or sound like a weirdo.

"And I'm not," he said, as we sat there in his room on the afternoon of my visit. "That's why Dr. Stern wanted you to see me, isn't it?"

"What do you mean?" I was playing it cool.

"Doc told me who you were, and I know the kind of stuff you write. If you're looking for material—"

"I didn't say that."

"Don't worry, I'm glad to talk to you. I've been wanting to talk to someone for a long time. Someone who'll do more than just put down what I say in a case history and file it away. They've got me filed away now and they're never going to let me out of here, but somebody should know the truth. I don't care if you write it up as a story, just so you don't make me out bananas. Because I'm going to tell it like it is, so help me God. If there *is* a God. That's what worries me—I mean, what kind of a God would create someone like Vilma?"

That's when I became conscious of his facial tic, and it disturbed me. He noticed my reaction and shook his head. "Don't take my word for it," he said. "Just look at the women in the magazine ads. High-fashion models, you know the type? Tall, thin, all arms and legs, with no bust. And those high cheekbones, the big eyes, the face frozen in that snotty don't-touch-me look.

"I guess that's what got to me. Just as it was supposed to. I took Vilma's look as a challenge." His face twitched again.

"You don't like women, do you?" I said.

"You're putting me on." For the first and only time he grinned. "Man, you're talking to one of the biggest womanizers in the business!" Then the grin faded. "At least I was, until I met Vilma.

"It all came together on a cruise ship—the *Morland,* one of these big new Scandinavian jobs built for the Caribbean package tours. Nine ports in two weeks, conducted shore trips to all the exotic native clipjoints.

"But I was aboard for business, not pleasure. McKay-Phipps, the ad agency I worked for, pitched Apex Camera a campaign featuring full-page color spreads in the fashion magazines. You know the setup—big, arty shots of a model posed against tropical resort backgrounds with just a few lines of snob-appeal copy below. *She travels in style. Her outfit—a Countess D'Or original. Her camera—an Apex.* That kind of crud, right?

"Okay, it was their money and who the hell am I to say how they throw it around? Besides, it wasn't even one of my accounts. But Ben Sanders, the exec who handled it, went down the tube with a heart attack just three days before sailing, and I got nailed for the assignment.

"I didn't know diddly about the high-fashion rag business or cameras either, but no problem. The D'Or people sent along Pat Grigsby, their top design consultant, to take charge of the wardrobe end. And I had Smitty Lane handling the actual shooting. He's one of the best in the business, and he got everything lined up before we left—worked out a complete schedule of what shots we'd take and where, checked out times and locations, wired ahead for clearances and firmed-up the arrangements. All I had to do was come along for the ride and see that everyone showed up at the right place at the right time.

"So on the face of it I was home free. Or away from home free. There are worse things than two weeks on a West Indies cruise in February with all expenses paid. The ship was brand new, with a dozen top-deck staterooms, and they'd booked one for each of us. None of those converted broomcloset cabins, and if we wanted we could have our meals served in and skip the first-sitting hassle in the dining room.

"But you don't give a damn about my vacation, and neither did I. Because it turned out to be a real downer.

"Like I said, the *Morland* hit nine ports in two weeks, and we were scheduled to do our thing in every one of them. Smitty wanted to shoot with natural light, so that meant we had to be on location and ready for action by 11 A.M. Since most of the spots he'd picked out were resorts halfway across the various islands, we had to haul out of the sack before seven, grab a fast continental breakfast, and drag all the wardrobe and equipment onto a chartered bus by eight. You ever ride a 1959 VW minibus over a stretch of rough back country road in steambath temperatures and humidity? It's the original bad trip.

"Then there was the business of setting up. Smitty was good but a real nitpicker, you know? And by the time Pat Grigsby was satisfied with the looks of the outfits and the way they lined up in the viewfinder and we got all those extra-protection shots, it was generally two o'clock. We had our pics but no lunch. So off we'd go, laughing and scratching, in the VW that had been baking in the sun all day, and if we boarded the ship again by four-thirty we were just in time for Afternoon Bingo.

"About the rest of the cruise, I've got good news and bad news.

"First the bad news. Smitty didn't play Afternoon Bingo. He played the bar—morning, afternoon, and night. And Pat

Grigsby was butch. She must have made her move with Vilma early on and gotten thanks-but-no-thanks, because by the third day out the two of them weren't speaking except in line of duty. So that left Vilma and me.

"This was the good news.

"I've already told you what those high-fashion models look like, and I guess I made it sound like a grunt from a male chauvinist pig, but that's because of what I know now. At the time, Vilma Loring was something else. One thing about models—they know how to dress, how to move, what to do with makeup and perfume. What it adds up to is poise. Poise, and what they used to call femininity. And Vilma was all female.

"Maybe Women's Lib is a good thing, but those intellectual types, psychology majors with the stringy hair and the blue-jeans always turned me off.

"Vilma turned me on just looking at her. And I looked at her a lot. The way she handled herself when we were shooting—a real pro. While the rest of us were frying and dying under the noon sun, she stayed calm, cool and collected. No sweat, not a hair out of place, never any complaints. The lady had it.

"She had it, and I wanted it. That's why I made the scene with her as often as I could, which wasn't very much on the days we were in port. She always sacked out after we got back from a location and I couldn't get her to eat with me; she liked to have meals in the stateroom so she wouldn't have to bother with clothes and make-up. Naturally that was my cue to go into the my-stateroom-or-yours routine, but she wasn't buying it. So during our working schedule I had to settle for evenings.

"You know the kind of fun and games they have on shipboard. Second-run movies for the old ladies with blue hair, dancing on a dime-size floor to the music of a combo that would make Lawrence Welk turn in his baton. And the floor shows—tap dancers, magic acts, overage vocalists direct from a two-year engagement at Caesar's Palace—in the men's room.

"So we did a lot of time together just walking the deck. With me suggesting my room for a nightcap and she giving me that it's-so-lovely-out-here-why-don't-we-look-at-the-dolphins routine.

"I got the message, but I wasn't about to scrub the mission. And on the days we spent at sea I stayed in there. I used to call Vilma every morning after breakfast and when she wasn't resting or doing her nails I lucked out. She was definitely the quiet type and dummied up whenever I asked a personal question, but she was a good listener. As long as I didn't pressure her she stayed happy. I picked up my cue from that and played the waiting game.

"She didn't want to swim? Okay, so we sat in deck chairs and watched the action at the pool. No shuffleboard or deck tennis because the sun was bad for her complexion? Right on, we'd hit the lounge for the cocktail hour, even though she didn't drink. I kept a low profile, but as time went on I had to admit it was getting to me.

"Maybe it was the cruise itself that wore me down. The atmosphere, with everybody making out. Not just the couples, married or otherwise; there was plenty going for singles, too. Secretaries and schoolteachers who'd saved up for the annual orgy, getting it all together with used-car salesmen and post-graduate beach bums. Divorcees with silicone implants and new dye jobs were balling the gray-sideburn types who checked out Dow-Jones every morning before they went ashore. By the second week, even the little old ladies with the blue hair had paired off with the young stewards who'd hired on for stud duty. The final leg, two days at sea from Puerto Rico to Miami, was like something out of a porno flick, with everybody getting it on. Everybody but me, sitting there watching with a newspaper over my lap.

"That's when I had a little Dear Abby talk with myself. Here I was, wasting my time with an entry who wouldn't dance, wouldn't drink, wouldn't even have dinner with me. She wasn't playing it cool, she was playing it frigid.

"Okay, she was maybe the most beautiful broad I've ever laid eyes on, but you can't look forever when you're not allowed to touch. She had this deep, husky voice that seemed to come from her chest instead of her throat, but she never used it for anything but small talk. She had a way of staring at you without blinking, but you want someone to look at you, not through you. She moved and walked like a dream, but there comes a time when you have to wake up.

"By the time I woke up it was our last night out and too late. But not too late to hit the bar. There was the usual ship's party and I'd made a date to take Vilma to the floor show. I didn't cancel it—I just stood her up.

"Maybe I was a slow learner or a sore loser. I didn't give a damn which it was, I'd just had it up to here. No more climbing the walls; I was going to tie one on, and I did.

"I went up aft to a little deck bar away from the action, and got to work. Everybody was making the party scene so I was the only customer. The bartender wanted to talk but I turned him off. I wasn't in the mood for conversation; I had too much to think about. Such as, what the hell had come over me these past two weeks? Running after a phony teaser like some goddamn kid with the hots—it made no sense. Not after the first drink, or the second. But the time I ordered the third, which was a double, I was ready to go after Vilma and hit her right in the mouth.

"But I didn't have to. Because she was there. Standing next to me, with that way-out tropical moon shining through the light blue evening gown and shimmering over her hair.

"She gave me a big smile. 'I've been looking for you everywhere,' she said. 'We've got to talk.'

"I told her to forget it, we had nothing to discuss. She just stood there looking at me, and now the moonlight was sparkling in her eyes. I told her to get lost, I never wanted to see her again. And she put her hand on my arm and said, 'You're in love with me, aren't you?'

"I didn't answer. I couldn't answer, because it all came together and it was true. I *was* in love with Vilma. That's why I wanted to hit her, to grab hold of her and tear that dress right off and—

"Vilma took my hand. 'Let's go to my room,' she said.

"Now there's a switch for you. Two weeks in the deep-freeze and now this. On the last night, too—we'd be docking in a few hours and I still had to pack and be ready to leave the ship early next morning.

"But it didn't matter. What mattered is that we went right to her stateroom and locked the door and it was all ready and waiting. The lights were low, the bed was turned down and the champagne was chilling in the ice bucket.

"Vilma poured me a glass, but none for herself. 'Go ahead,' she said. 'I don't mind.'

"But I did, and I told her so. There was something about the setup that didn't make sense. If this was what she wanted, why wait until the last minute?

"She gave me a look I've never forgotten. 'Because I had to be sure first.'

"I took a big gulp of my drink. It hit me hard on top of what I'd already had, and I was all through playing games. 'Sure of what?' I said. 'What's the matter, you think I can't get it up?'

"Vilma's expression didn't change. 'You don't understand. I had to get to know you and decide if you were suitable.'

"I put down my empty glass. 'To go to bed with?'

"Vilma shook her head. 'To be the father of my child.'

"I stared at her. 'Now wait a minute—'

"She gave me that look again. 'I have waited. For two weeks I've been waiting watching you and making up my mind. You seem to be healthy, and there's no reason why our offspring wouldn't be genetically sound.'

"I could feel that last drink but I knew I wasn't stoned. I'd heard her loud and clear. 'You can stop right there,' I told her. 'I'm not into marriage, or supporting a kid.'

"She shrugged. 'I'm not asking you to marry me, and I don't need any financial help. If I conceive tonight, you won't even know about it. Tomorrow we go our separate ways—I promise you'll never even have to see me again.'

"She moved close, too close, close enough so that I could feel the heat pouring off her in waves. Heat, and perfume, and a kind of vibration that echoed in her husky voice. 'I need a child,' she said.

"All kinds of thoughts flashed through my head. She was high on acid, she was on a freak sex-trip, some kind of a nut case. 'Look,' I said. 'I don't even know you, not really—'

"She laughed then, and her laugh was husky too. 'What does it matter? You want me.'

"I wanted her, all right. The thoughts blurred together, blended with the alcohol and the anger, and the only thing left was wanting her. Wanting this big beautiful blond babe, wanting her heat, her need.

"I reached for her and she stepped back, turning her head when I tried to kiss her. 'Get undressed first,' she said. 'Oh, hurry—please—'

"I hurried. Maybe she'd slipped something into my drink, because I had trouble unbuttoning my shirt and in the end I ripped it off, along with everything else. But whatever she'd given me I was turned on, turned on like I've never been before.

"I hit the bed, lying on my back, and everything froze; I couldn't move, my arms and legs felt numb because all the sensation was centered in one place. I was ready, so ready I couldn't turn off if I tried.

"I know because I kept watching her, and there was no change when she lifted her arms to her neck and removed her head.

"She put her head down on the table and the long blond hair hung over the side and the glassy blue eyes went dead in the rubbery face. But I couldn't stir, I was still turned on, and all I remember is thinking to myself, without a head how can she see?

"Then the dress fell and there was my answer, moving toward me. Bending over me on the bed, with her tiny breasts almost directly above my face so that I could see the hard tips budding. Budding and opening until the eyes peered out—the *real* eyes, green and glittering deep within the nipples.

"And she bent closer; I watched her belly ride and fall, felt the warm panting breath from her navel. The last thing I saw was what lay below—the pink-lipped, bearded mouth, opening to engulf me. I screamed once, and then I passed out.

"Do you understand now? Vilma had told me the truth, or part of the truth. She was a high-fashion model, all right—but a model for *what?*

"Who made her, and how many more did they make? How many hundreds or thousands are there, all over the world? Models—you ever notice how they all seem to look alike? They could be sisters, and maybe they are. A family, a race from somewhere outside, swarming across the world, breeding with men when the need is upon them, breeding in their own special way. The way she bred with me—"

I ran out then, when he lost control and started to scream. The attendants went in and I guess they quieted him down, because by the time I got to Dr. Stern's office down the hall I couldn't hear him any more.

"Well?" Stern said. "What do you make of it?"

I shook my head. "You're the doctor. Suppose you tell me."

"There isn't much. This Vilma—Vilma Loring, she called herself—really existed. She was a working professional model for about two years, registered with a New York agency, living in a leased apartment on Central Park South. Lots of people remember seeing her, talking to her—"

"You're using the past tense," I said.

Stern nodded. "That's because she disappeared. She must have left her stateroom, left the ship as soon as it docked that night in Miami. No one's managed to locate her since, though God knows they've tried, in view of what happened."

"Just what *did* happen?"

"You heard the story."

"But he's crazy—isn't he?"

"Greatly disturbed. That's why they brought him here after they found him the next morning, lying there on the bed in a pool of blood." Stern shrugged. "You see, that's the one thing nobody can explain. To this day, we don't know what became of his genitals."

CARNAL HOUSE

Steve Rasnic Tem

Gene's phone rang again, the third time that evening. "Yes?" he asked again, as if the very ring were his name.

"Are you coming over, Gene? Could you come over?"

He held back any immediate reaction. He didn't want her to hear him sigh, or groan. He didn't want her to hear the catch he knew was waiting in his throat.

"Ruth," he said.

"Who else would it be?" she said, as if in accusation.

For just a second he felt like defying her, telling her about Jennie. The impulse chilled him. She couldn't know about Jennie. Not ever. "No other woman," he finally said.

She was silent for a time, but he knew she was still there. He could hear the wind worrying at the yellowed windowshade in her bedroom. Her window would be closed, he knew, but it would leak badly. There would be a draft that went right through the skin. But none of that would bother her.

"Come over, Gene," she finally said.

"Okay. I'll be there."

"I'll wait," she said, as if there were a choice. He hung up the phone.

The house was at the end of a long back street on the west end of town. It was one of the oldest in the area, its lines ornate, archaic, and free of the various remodeling fads that had passed through this neighborhood over the years. Gene had always appreciated the dignity of the Victorian style.

But he also knew that Victorians could be extraordinarily ugly, and this house was a perfect representative of that type. The exterior color seemed to be a mix of dark blue, dark green, and gray, which resulted in a burnt stew of a shade, a rotting vegetable porridge. The paint had been thickly applied, splatters and drips of it so complicating the porch lines and filigreed braces under the roof that they looked like dark, coated spiderwebs. The windows and doors were shadowed rectangles; he couldn't make out their details from the street.

All but a few of the houses along this tree-shadowed lane were abandoned. Some were boarded up, some burned out, some so overgrown with wild bushes and vines and weeds they were virtually impenetrable. Here and there a few houses had been torn down, the lots given over to bramble gardens or refuse heaps. And in the occasional house a light burned behind a yellowed shade, its tenders hidden.

Gene stood on the porch of her house for a very long time. He could feel Ruth inside that dark place, perhaps lying quietly on stiff white sheets, perhaps sitting up, motionless, listening. He imagined her listening a great deal these days, her entire body focused on the heartbeats of the mice in the corners, the night birds outside in the crooked trees. He imagined that focus broadening to include the systemic pulse of the moths beating against the dim bulb of the lone streetlight on the corner, the roaches crawling over the linoleum next door, his own nervous tics as he stood on this porch, hesitant to go in.

He imagined Jennie in a dark house like this, at the end of some other god-forsaken street, waiting, her eyes forced open, waiting for him. And he hated himself for imagining it.

At first he had been so pleased that Jennie had kicked the habit. He'd seen it as a cleansing when she'd gone through the house in a rage, looking for needles, spoons, all that other paraphernalia she'd always carefully kept hidden. But now she'd been ill for months. She wouldn't tell him what it was; she didn't have to. She would no longer make love to him. Last night she had refused to kiss him. And cleanliness to the point of sterility had become an obsession. They didn't talk about it.

Now, standing on this darkened porch in a shunned neighborhood, he could imagine it was Jennie he was visiting, not Ruth at all.

He was staring at the brown, flaking screen door when it lightened briefly. Pale skin pressed into the mesh from the other side. The lips, endlessly bisected, were almost as pale as the rest of the flesh, but with a hint of silver in their curves. "Coming in?" the lips said, in an almost toneless question.

As Gene stepped forward the pale flesh backed away, leaving the mesh as dark and empty as before. The hinges were oddly silent when he moved them, as if perfectly greased, but that seemed so unlikely his hand shook slightly before he let go of the greenish brass knob. The door fell back against the frame without sound.

The staircase climbed out of the dark burgundy well of the entrance hall into the smoky shadows of the second story. The paneled doors to the parlor on his left and the rooms ahead of him were closed, as they had been every time he had been here.

The woman standing on the staircase was nude, her flesh pasty, her face so pale and features so blurred that in the darkness Gene didn't know if it was Ruth or one of her companions. Her breasts were high and full, catching the available light on their upper curves. The nipples were shadows, as if half-remembered and only vaguely applied. Her pubic hair was so thick, so dark, that in this dimness it looked as if someone had blown a hole through her groin, and it was a triangular window on the dark staircase behind her he was seeing instead.

Her black hair suddenly moved across the pale shoulders like a snake. "Hurry," she whispered huskily in Ruth's voice. She turned and moved up the stairs, so effortlessly that her buttocks remained smooth and firm throughout the movement. After a moment he followed, his hands ahead of him, suddenly too anxious to stay trapped in his pockets. They groped and pawed their way through the darkness. Not for the first time he wished he could tell someone about all this. Anyone. He wished he had someone here with him, to tell him whether what he was seeing was real. He thought how, after all this time, he had so few friends.

That dwindling of friendships had all started in college. There had been Ruth, but she hadn't really been a friend, just the woman he'd always been pursuing. He had known Jennie back then, but only distantly. She had dated the friend of a friend, and he remembered her as someone always desperate for fun, as if she didn't have a serious thought in her skull.

First he had pursued Ruth, then he had pursued Jennie. There had never been any time to make friends.

"Kiss me," Ruth whispered, and Gene moved his lips slowly over hers. "Now bite," she said, and his teeth gently prodded her unyielding flesh.

Making love to her was strange. Making love to her was like a cutting, a notching of her hard, white, translucent flesh. Each time required more effort on his part before she could feel anything.

"There . . . there," she said. "I felt . . . something."

He rubbed against her rhythmically, slowly at first and then faster, but it felt less like a making of love than like a sandpapering, an attempt to wear away the old, dull skin in order to expose fresh nerves, in order to feel something.

He had a sudden urge to strike her unresponsive flesh, slap and pinch it, anything to bring it awake. He knew Ruth wouldn't mind. But he would.

He could not look into Ruth's eyes when he made love to her. He could not bear that faraway stare. He continued to scrape himself against her, cut into her, and her body felt like a pair of scissors squeezing him, cutting through flesh and nerves and bone.

Her odor was sour and animal-like. Her flesh seemed to melt into the stark white sheets. He had a sudden skirmish with the thick tangle of her hair, the twisted sheets, and came up gasping for air, thinking of Jennie.

Ruth stared up at him from her resting place (Had he ever imagined her anywhere else?), looking as if she could read his mind.

When he left before dawn Ruth stayed in her bed. Not sleeping, really. And yet not fully awake. This was the usual way. In the other upstairs rooms he thought Ruth's companions must be similarly greeting the departures of their lovers.

A shadow moved suddenly into the hall, staggering. The man raised his white face, eyes dark and hooded with fatigue. The man, as if embarrassed, turned his head away again and made his way quickly down the stairs.

As Gene walked off the porch the rest of the neighborhood seemed suddenly to burn into a new life. He turned back around to look at the house. Its windows stayed dark and shaded, the sun doing little to lighten its colors.

Jennie was still in bed when he got back to the apartment, only her head outside the sheet, the flesh drawn so tightly at temples and chin that her face looked hard, carved from wood. The bedroom shade was drawn to keep the morning light out.

"Jennie . . ." he whispered, but nothing came in reply.

The apartment was a mess. He could see the nest she must have made in front of the TV the night before. A U-shaped wall of firm cushions in front of the couch, the firmer the better to hold up her back and neck, the open space filled with blankets and pillows. Like the living room castles he used to build as a kid. A phalanx of overflowing ashtrays and snack trays had been arranged around the castle, but the food had been barely nibbled. Jennie always seemed to be consumed by this aimless hunger, and yet nothing would satisfy her. At times she could hardly eat anything at all. And yet the hunger still gnawed at her, and she kept loading up on the junk food, trying to find something she would eat.

Gene could picture her sitting here wrapped up in her blankets, her small face peering out at the TV, her nervous hands grabbing for cigarettes and snacks she would not eat. She seemed smaller with each passing day, more vulnerable, more and more like a kid. Less like a woman. He hated himself for thinking that way. As if Ruth were more than that.

Jennie wasn't the kind to sit up and wait—at least she never had been before. Their relationship had never been exclusive; that had never been part of the rules. Yet he kept thinking of her sitting up all night, and maybe, just maybe waiting up for him. And he hated himself for that as well.

Suddenly he felt starved. He went to the refrigerator and

jerked the door open, the bottles and jars inside rubbing against each other musically. He reached for the quart bottle of orange juice.

When he started to open it he noticed that the lid wasn't on securely. He held the bottle up to the light from the narrow, curtainless kitchen window. As he turned it slowly he detected the faint impression of a lip print near the rim. She was just like a kid. More and more. He felt a sudden flash of anger, and poured out all the juice, discarded the bottle in the can under the sink. At first she'd been so careful, sterilizing her silverware, her cups and plates, making sure he didn't handle anything she'd had in her mouth. Like she was dirty.

They hadn't made love in some time. He couldn't even remember the last time they'd kissed.

Now he was ashamed of himself, looking at the discarded juice bottle. You can't catch it that way. He'd told all their friends that, his family who thought he should have nothing more to do with her. But he was scared. He knew better, but he was scared of Jennie.

And yet if he could love her illness away, kiss and rub it away, he would do it.

"I heard something." The voice behind him was so weak he hardly recognized it. "I didn't know you were home."

He turned around. She had the comforter wrapped tightly around her. The narrow muscles in her cheeks and throat trembled. He tried to smile at her, but couldn't quite get the idea up to his lips. "You should be in bed," he said. "You'll get cold."

"I'm always cold," she snapped.

"I know, Jennie." He went to her and put his arms around her. "I know." He squeezed her. After a moment's hesitation she squeezed back, or at least what passed as a squeeze for her.

"Hold me in bed?" she whispered.

"I'll hold you in bed," he said softly, leading her into the other room. "I'll hold you as long as you want. Forever if you want."

After an hour or so she was asleep again. Gene lay with her, massaging her back gently with his hands, feeling the lines of every muscle, every bone. And then the phone rang.

"Are you coming over?" He could hear Ruth's voice, and static, and wind.

"I was just there," he said quietly, watching Jennie stir in her sleep.

"But are you coming over? I need you to come over." Ruth's voice was steady, focused, obsessive.

"Ruth . . ."

"I need you."

He'd chased Ruth all through college. Every once in a while he would stop, and think how ridiculous he looked, what a fool he was, but those pauses for self-examination had been few and far between. She'd had the voice he heard in his dreams, gestures he could mimic in his sleep, skin that had felt like no other. He'd never wanted to think about whether his feelings for her were real, or whether this was truly a balanced, healthy relationship. Those questions simply had not applied. There had been nothing real about her, and he hadn't cared if there was a balance—he'd felt deliriously unbalanced. He'd simply had to have her.

He'd met her the first day of classes. The friend of a friend of a friend, although he could no longer remember which ones. He'd been introduced as a "math wizard."

"Then you'll have to tutor me sometime," she had said, with this simply amazing smile. And he had. If she'd asked him to, he'd have done all her work for her. There had never been "magic" before; now there was a magic he could not let go.

"I need you," she'd said, but it had meant something different back then. She'd needed his help with school, and she'd needed him to tell her how beautiful she was—so that she could be convinced that someone else might find her attractive. Even when she'd made love to him, it was to convince her that someone else—and that someone else seemed to change depending on her mood—would want to make love with her.

"You make me feel good," she'd say. "You make me feel alive." But she had never asked how she made him feel.

She should have asked. Because sometimes she had made him feel less than alive. He'd shied away from any other relationship, just in hope that she would be the one. He hadn't kept up his friendships. He'd convinced himself that his life would not work without her in it. He'd convinced himself that his relationship with her was a crucial turning point in his life, and that this was a relationship he dared not fail. Every woman he had met resembled her in some way. She'd become the measure for every female gesture, glance, or expression.

"Kiss me, Gene. There and there and there. Am I still beautiful?" He could hear noises in other parts of the house: Ruth's companions and their lovers.

"Yes," he said, with his lips urging her skin toward some vague warmth. "You've always been beautiful." He ran his fingers through her hair, and felt them go deep, too deep, into the dark waves that surrounded her depthless eyes, her pale, night-surrounding mouth.

"Good. That's good, Gene," Ruth whispered, holding him tighter and tighter within the scissors her body made. He wondered what she could possibly be thinking. It scared him that he could not even guess what she was thinking.

But then he'd never been able to guess what she was thinking. Even as she'd died, the thing that had haunted him the most was trying to figure out what she was thinking.

He'd been walking on the quadrangle at the center of campus. It had been a bright, sunny day, bright enough to burn away the haze that had accumulated the previous week. Both a haze of weather and the haze that had built up in his mind after several weeks of an unusually frenetic and unproductive pursuit of Ruth. In fact, the contrast had bothered him. The sunlight had felt just too bright, the campus setting too stark, too livid.

Suddenly there was a crash, screams. A large crowd had gathered near the stone wall that bordered South Drive. When he got there he saw a red Ford that had come up onto the sidewalk and knocked a third of the wall down.

He'd pushed his way through the crowd. Several people had been huddled over a woman on the sidewalk. Gene could see the long cuts on her legs, the nylons scraped away, the real skin scraped away below that, the shards of glass in her sides.

Then someone had shifted and Gene could see that it was Ruth lying on the sidewalk, that it was Ruth who had contained so much blood. Somehow he got through the crowd. He had said things, terrible and inarticulate things, but he could no longer remember what they were. And then it was *he* huddled over Ruth, the mask of her face *in his hands* and staring up at him, and it was a mask because the back of her head was gone, sprayed in carnival colors across the granite and marble of the rough wall.

But Gene had kept talking to her, holding the ruin of her head in his hands and sweet-talking her, kissing her open eyes and kissing her lips, passionately kissing her lips with tongue and tooth and caress as if to arouse her, then desperately rubbing at her breasts, even as her broken ribs caught on his shaking hands. Sweet-talking her, kissing and rubbing her, as if he were loving her awake after a long night asleep in his arms.

When they finally pulled him away from her Gene screamed as if they were taking him apart. But Gene could not remember that scream. What he would remember instead, and so vividly, was that sudden fantasy he'd had that his kisses had been working, that Ruth's eyes had just begun to focus.

"Gene?" And it had remained a fantasy until the evening she'd first called. "Could you come over?" Until she needed him to tell her how beautiful she was once again. "I need you, Gene." Until she needed him to put his hands, once again, into the thick waves of her dark hair. And to feel his fingers go too deeply through the hair into the space where the back of her skull should have been. Until she needed him to tell her she was still alive.

"There, there. I think I felt something. I'm sure I felt something." In desperate need to make her feel, he had bitten her left breast as hard as he could. It was like putting his teeth into leather. And still no blood would well, no bruise would form. "Don't leave now, Gene. So close. I could almost feel."

Passing the bedroom doors of Ruth's companions, he could hear their lovers softly weeping.

He'd decided that night that he would leave the phone off the hook. He'd prepare dinner, the biggest meal Jennie had had in some time if he had to cook all night. But he ended up spending more than an hour in the meat department of their local grocer, and still he wasn't able to choose anything. The chicken looked too pale, bloodless, as if it had all been dead too long. And you couldn't eat anything dead so long, could you? He was sure it would have no taste, no color.

And all the cuts of beef and pork looked somehow unreal to him. Too much red. Too much blood. He could not believe anything dead could have that much color.

Only the fatty parts looked real. The smooth, too-soft curves and hills of fat.

He rubbed each cut of meat through its sheer plastic covering. He thought he was close to knowing what they wanted from him—he could see it in the way their color changed when he pressed his living fingers into the meat through the plastic. But he couldn't quite bring himself to trust anything in that cold landscape of cut meats.

The lights were out in the apartment when he finally got back. Again, Jennie had left a mess, but he could hardly blame her for that. But she'd always been so orderly, almost obsessive about it, so he supposed this increasing laxness probably did not bode well.

"Jennie?" he whispered from the bedroom door. She said nothing, but the dim light that slipped beneath the bottom of the shade illuminated her head, the soft blond curls, the face that looked even more beautiful to him the paler it became.

She slept so soundly. He knew she would be in no mood for a meal. He could feel tears on his cheeks, running into the corners of his mouth.

Quietly he slipped out of his clothes and joined her under the covers. She did not stir, even when he pressed his cool body against her nakedness.

He began to kiss her, to taste her, and when she still did not respond he began to nip, to bite. He began to cry, massaging her breasts, probing her pubic area with his fingers, trying to kiss her, love her awake. But she remained cold and dry. The only air stirring in the room seemed to be his own, ragged breath.

Gene knocked on the dark screen door, and waited this time. This time, he knew, required a more definite invitation.

Her pale face appeared in the screen, her dark eyes taking in the bundle by his feet: the dull green blanket, the soft blond hair that still trapped the light, the pale skin with its tinge of silver.

"Is there room?" Gene whispered. "Room for her?"

Again Ruth looked at the bundle. Then her eyes floated up to hold him. "You'll still come? You'll be there when I call?"

Gene pulled his jacket closer, unable to keep warm. "Yes . . ." he said finally. "I'll be there when you call."

The screen door opened without sound, and the women inside the dark house dragged the bundle across the threshold.

It was two weeks before the next phone call. But he was there to pick up the receiver on the first ring.

"Hello," he said.

"Gene?" Jennie's voice said. "Are you coming over? I need you, Gene. I need you to come over."

248

THEY'RE COMING FOR YOU

Les Daniels

M r. Bliss came home from work early one Monday afternoon. It was a big mistake.

He'd had a headache, and his secretary, after offering him various patent medicines, complete with their manufacturers' slogans, had said, "Why don't you take the rest of the day off, Mr. Bliss."

Everyone called him Mr. Bliss. The others in the office were Dave or Dan or Charlie, but he was Mr. Bliss. He liked it that way. Sometimes he thought that even his wife should call him Mr. Bliss.

Instead, she was calling on God.

Her voice came from on high. From upstairs. In the bedroom. She didn't seem to be in pain, but Mr. Bliss could remedy that.

She wasn't alone; someone was grunting in harmony with her cries to the creator. Mr. Bliss was bitter about this.

Without even waiting to hang up his overcoat, he tiptoed into the kitchen and plucked from its magnetic rack one of the Japanese knives his wife had ordered after watching a television commercial. They were designed for cutting things into small pieces, and they were guaranteed for life, however long that happened to be. Mr. Bliss would see to it that his wife had no cause for complaint. He turned away

249

from the rack, paused for a sigh, then went back and selected another knife. The first was for the one who wanted to meet God, and the second for the one who was making those animal noises.

After a moment's reflection he decided to use the back stairs. They were more secretive, somehow, and Mr. Bliss intended to have a big secret just as soon as he could get organized.

He had an erection for the first time in weeks, and his headache was gone.

He moved as quickly and carefully as he could, sliding across the checkerboard linoleum and taking the back stairs two at a time in slow, painful, thigh-straining stretches. He knew there was a step which creaked, couldn't recall which one it was, and knew he would step on it anyway.

That hardly mattered. The groans and wails were reaching a crescendo, and Mr. Bliss suspected that not even a brass band behind him could have distracted the people above him from their business. They were about to achieve something, and he wanted very much to be there before they did.

The bedroom took up the entire top floor of the house. It had been a whim of his to flatter his young bride with as spacious a spawning ground as his salary would allow; the tastefully carpeted stairs led up to it in front as inexorably as the shabby wooden stairs crept up the back.

Mr. Bliss creaked at the appointed spot, cursed quietly, and opened the door.

His wife's eyes, rolled back in her head, were like wet marble. Her lips fluttered as she blew damp hair from her face. The beautiful breasts that had persuaded him to marry her were covered with sweat, and not all of it was hers.

Mr. Bliss didn't even recognize the man; he was nobody. The milkman? A census taker? He was plump, and he needed a haircut. It was all very discouraging. Cuckolding by an Adonis would at least have been understandable, but this was a personal affront.

Mr. Bliss dropped one knife to the floor, grasped the other

in both hands, and slammed its point into the pudgy interloper at the spot where spine meets skull.

It worked at once. The man gave one more grunt and toppled over backward, blade grinding against bone as head and handle hit the floor.

Mrs. Bliss was there, baffled and bedraggled, spread-eagled naked against sopping sheets.

Mr. Bliss picked up the other knife.

He pulled her up by the hair and stabbed her in the face. She blubbered blood. Madly but methodically, he shoved the sharp steel into every place where he thought she'd like it least.

Most of his experiments were successful.

She died unhappily.

The last expression she was able to muster was a mixture of pain, reproach, and resignation that thrilled him more than anything she'd shown him since their wedding night.

He wasn't done with her yet. She had never been so submissive.

It was late that night before he put down the knife and put on his clothes.

Mr. Bliss had made a terrible mess. Cleaning up was always a chore, as she had so frequently reminded him, but he was equal to the task. The worst part was that he had stabbed the water bed, but at least the flood had diluted some of the blood.

He buried them in separate sections of the flower garden and showed up late for work. This was an unprecedented event. The quizzical eyebrows of his colleagues got on his nerves.

For some reason he didn't feel like going home that night. He went to a motel instead. He watched television. He saw a movie about someone killing several other people, but it didn't amuse him as much as he'd hoped. He felt that it was in bad taste.

He left the "Do Not Disturb" sign on the doorknob of his room each day; he did not wish to be disturbed. Still, the unmade bed to which he returned each night began to bother him. It reminded him of home.

After a few days Mr. Bliss was ashamed to go to the office.

He was still wearing the same clothes he'd left home in, and he was convinced that his colleagues could smell him. No one had ever longed for the weekend as passionately as he did.

Then he had two days of peace in his motel room, huddling under the covers in the dark and watching people kill each other in a phosphorescent glow, but on Sunday night he looked at his socks and knew he would have to go back to the house.

He wasn't happy about this.

When he opened the front door, it reminded him of his last entrance. He felt that the stage was set. Still, all he had to do was go upstairs and get some clothes. He could be gone in a matter of minutes. He knew where everything was.

He used the front stairs. The carpeting made them quieter, and somehow he felt the need for stealth. Anyway, he didn't like the ones in the back anymore.

Halfway up the stairs, he noticed two paintings of roses that his wife had put there. He took them down. This was his house now, and the pictures had always vaguely annoyed him. Unfortunately, the blank spaces he left on the wall bothered him, too.

He didn't know what to do with the paintings, so he carried them up into the bedroom. There seemed to be no way to get rid of them. He was afraid this might be an omen, and for a second considered the idea of burying them in the garden. This made him laugh, but he didn't like the sound. He decided not to do it again.

Mr. Bliss stood in the middle of the bedroom and looked around critically. He'd made quite a neat job of it. He was just opening a dresser drawer when he heard a thump from below. He stared at his underwear.

A scrape followed the thump, and then the sound of something bumping up the back stairs.

He didn't wonder what it was, not even for an instant. He closed his underwear drawer and turned around. His left eyelid twitched; he could feel it. He was walking without thinking toward the front stairs when he heard the door below them open. Just a little sound, a bolt slipping a latch. Suddenly the inside of his head felt as big as the bedroom.

He knew they were coming for him, one from each side. What could he do? He ran around the room, slamming into each wall and finding it solid. Then he took up a post beside the bed and put a hand over his mouth. A giggle spilled between his fingers, and it made him angry, for this was a proud moment.

They were coming for him.

Whatever became of him (no more job, no more television), he had inspired a miracle. The dead had come back to life to punish him. How many men could say as much? Come clump, come thump, come slithering sounds! This was a triumph.

He stepped back against the wall to get a better view. As both doors opened, his eyes flicked back and forth. His tongue followed, licking his lips. He experienced an ecstasy of terror.

The stranger, of course, had used the back stairs.

He had tried to forget what a mess he had made of them, especially his wife. And now they were even worse.

And yet, as she dragged herself across the floor, there was something in her pale flesh, spotted with purple where the blood had settled, and striped with rust where the blood had spilled, that called to him as it rarely had before. Her skin was clumped with rich brown earth. She needs a bath, he thought, and he began to snort with laughter that would soon be uncontrollable.

Her lover, approaching from the other side, was hardly marked. There had been no wish to punish him, only to make him stop. Still, the single blow of the TV knife had severed his spine, and his head lurched unpleasantly. The odd disappointment Mr. Bliss had felt in the man's flabbiness intensified. After six days in the ground what crawled toward him was positively puffy.

Mr. Bliss tried to choke back his chuckles till his eyes watered and snot shot from his nose. Even as his end approached, he saw their impossible lust for vengeance as his ultimate vindication.

Yet his feet were not as willing to die as he was; they backed over the carpet toward the closet door.

His wife looked up at him, as well as she could. The eyes in her sockets seemed shriveled, like inquisitive prunes. A part of her where he had cut too deeply and too often dropped quietly to the floor.

Her lover shuffled forward on hands and knees, leaving some sort of a trail behind him.

Mr. Bliss pulled the gleaming brass bed around to make a barricade. He stepped back into the closet. The smell of her perfume and of her sex enveloped him. He was buried in her gowns.

His wife reached the bed first and grasped the fresh linen with the few fingers she had left. She hauled herself up. Stains smeared the sheets. This was certainly the time to slam the closet door, but he wanted to watch. He was positively fascinated.

She squirmed on the pillows, arms flailing, then collapsed on her back. There were gurgles. Could she be really dead at last?

No.

It didn't matter. Her lover crawled over the counterpane. Mr. Bliss wanted to go to the bathroom, but the way was blocked.

He cringed when his wife's lover (who was this creeping corpse, anyway?) stretched out fat fingers, but instead of clawing for revenge, they fell on what had been the breasts of the body beneath him. They began to move gently.

Mr. Bliss blushed as the ritual began. He heard sounds that had embarrassed him even when the meat was live: liquid lurchings, ghastly groans, and supernatural screams.

He shut himself in the closet. What was at work on the bed did not even deign to notice him. He was buried in silk and polyester.

It was worse than he had feared. It was unbearable.

They hadn't come for him at all.

They had come for each other.

SUZIE SUCKS

Jeff Gelb

Mike Crawford pissed about four bottles of beer into the urinals of the Red Cedar Grille. He looked around the drably-lit bathroom and noticed the lipstick scrawled above one of the mirrors. "Suzie Sucks," it read, and underneath it was a phone number. At first Mike grinned, wondering whether "Suzie" knew her name was becoming famous at one of downtown's better watering holes. Then he nearly pissed on his shoe as he jerked in surprise. The phone number listed beneath her name was his own.

He zipped himself up, rushing over to the scribbled message to stare in disbelief. How had his phone number—and worse, his girlfriend's name—come to be displayed there?

Furiously, Mike cleaned off the message as best he could with a paper towel. Shaking with anger, he re-entered the bar, where he cornered his co-worker and drinking buddy, Joey Clark. Mike slapped Clark hard across the small of his back, spilling his drink.

"Where's the lipstick, Dick-breath?" Mike yelled.

"What's with you?" Clark asked, wiping margarita stains from his shirt collar.

"Don't play dumb, asswipe. I saw the message in the men's room."

"I think you've had your fill, buddy boy. Time to go home

to your girlfriend." Clark said the word "girlfriend" as if it were something dirty.

"You don't like Susan?" Mike snapped.

"I don't even know her—how could I like her? How could you, for that matter? You've hardly known her a week and she's already moved into your place. You ask me, she's digging for gold—yours."

Mike grabbed Clark's still-moist shirt collar. "Fuck your opinions," Mike growled. "And your lipstick." He shoved his friend roughly against the edge of the bar and walked out.

The apartment was dark as Mike entered, and the phone was ringing. He ran to answer it but the answering machine picked up the call. He heard a strange man's voice.

"Suzie? This is Dick Downes, 555-4330. I saw your message and I thought maybe we could go out sometime. Give me a call."

Mike stood in the darkened living room of his suburban condo, his hands clenched into tight fists.

"That asshole Clark," he snarled, stomping over to the answering machine and rewinding it. The machine recycled itself and started playing earlier messages.

"Hey, Suzie, baby, I got ten inches waitin' for ya. How's $50 sound? Call me. Bill—555-4545."

"Hello? Hello? Is this Suzie, the one from the restaurant rest room? This is Henry. I'd like to speak with you sometime. My number's 555-2187."

Mike roared with anger, tearing the tape out of the answering machine and flinging it into a nearby waste basket.

"I'll kill the son-of-a-bitch," he muttered.

"Mike, you're not eating," Susan said. "Did I cook the fish too long?"

Mike looked at Susan's cute face, so full of midwestern innocence. How could he tell a girl who'd just moved out to the coast from her parents' farm in Indiana that his best buddy had made her the butt of a crude practical joke?

Mike shook his head. "Just not hungry tonight," he

mumbled. Susan looked at him, concern etched across her fragile features. No wonder he'd fallen for her at the church social last weekend. She looked like a lost puppie, her big blue eyes roaming the room for a friendly face.

He'd struck up a conversation with Susan, and found her to be charmingly shy. As she warmed up to him, she explained that she was fresh out of college and had recently moved out west to work for a computer manufacturer. It was her first time away from home, she'd explained, and she'd found herself lonesome for family and friends. A girlfriend at work had told her about the weekly church social, which was basically a meeting place for divorced singles. Her friend, a stringy-haired plain-jane with thick thighs, had dragged Susan along for company, then immediately ran off to talk to any men who blinked in her direction. Susan had told Mike she was about to leave and catch a bus home when he'd rescued her.

Over coffee and donuts, Susan had explained that she was being evicted from her apartment because they were suddenly going condo. The look in her eyes and an itch in Mike's crotch made him ask if she would want to stay at his place until she saved enough money for an apartment.

She'd immediately blanched and studied her hands. Mike quickly added that his condo had two bedrooms, each with locking doors.

He'd talked her into returning to his apartment that night and, after verifying that the spare bedroom did indeed have its own lock, she thanked him profusely and went to bed.

It had taken every ounce of his discipline not to use his master key to enter her bedroom and jump her bones. There was something about her that absolutely drove him wild. God knows she wasn't the best looking woman he'd ever been with. But there was something in her angelic face that just slayed him.

True to his word, he'd left her alone that night, instead lying awake, thinking of her. He'd lazily stroked his cock as he recalled her marvelously blue eyes, her tiny, turned-up nose, and the full, pouty lips that were so out of place on the otherwise innocent face.

* * *

Ten days had passed and he still hadn't touched her.

She was a constant temptation, of course, but always in the most innocent ways: like the time she'd been watering his plants and the rays of sun streaming through the window had caught her in profile, outlining the tiny, upthrust breasts under her crisp, white cotton blouse. Or when she'd been searching through his cupboards for the frying pan and he'd seen her nipples under her t-shirt top.

Innocent. She was that, but she was driving him sexually crazy. What the hell was he waiting for? Why didn't he go for it? She certainly trusted him by now; in fact, he worried that she might have become *too* comfortable with him, thinking of him more as a big brother than a boyfriend.

Just when Mike was certain he'd blown any chance of a romance with her, she'd interrupted a quiet dinner in his apartment to lean over the small table and kiss him softly with her pillowy lips. He pulled her by the back of her head into his face, crushing those lips into his and slipping his tongue deep into her mouth. It was the first time he'd tasted her; she had an odd flavor Mike couldn't place.

She gasped, pulled back, then allowed herself to surrender to his embrace as he pulled her across the table top, sending dishes and cups crashing to the tiled floor. She was spread across the table like some luscious dessert.

He fumbled at his zipper, his huge erection bounding out of his pants thankfully. He approached her but she shook her head, whispering, "No."

Embarrassed that he'd overstepped his bounds, Mike backed away from her, adjusting himself back into his pants.

"I'm sorry, Susan," he stammered. "I don't know what came over me."

To his monumental surprise, she smiled at him and tugged at his undershorts. "I just don't do . . . *that,*" she explained. "We can do something else . . . if you like."

Mike watched as she wriggled out of her dress and panties and let them fall to the floor. She resumed her spread-legged prone position on the glass table top and whispered, "I want you inside me."

The telephone rang. Mike groaned. The answering machine clicked on.

"Suzie? I saw your little message in the men's room at the Racquet Club. You want some oral action? Just give me a call . . ."

Mike ran over to the phone and picked it up, but was answered by a dial tone. He slammed down the receiver and then, as if the telephone answering machine were at fault, he picked it up and threw it against the wall.

He turned to face Susan, but she'd disappeared into the bathroom, door closed behind her. Mike could hear the muffled sound of her crying.

Fists clenched, Mike thought, "This joke's gone too far."

Mike slammed open the real estate office's door. Joey Clark was helping a middle-aged couple fill out some forms.

Brushing his way past the startled clients, Mike slammed a hammy fist into Clark's surprised face, which turned pink and then began to spurt blood from its nose.

"God, I think it's broken!" Clark screamed. "Get out of here before I call the cops!"

The middle-aged couple ran from the office as Mike shoved Clark against the wall, shouting, "Where else did you scribble your nasty little note, you perverted bastard? Tell me!"

"You're out of your mind," Clark cried, as he tried to protect his face from further blows. "You're gonna land in jail for this, I swear to God."

Mike let go of Clark's shoulders, letting him drop to the floor in a heap, and then stomped out of the office, shouldering his way past astonished employees.

He phoned home but there was no answer and, of course, the answering machine was history. His anger somewhat abated, Mike decided to cook dinner for Susan, hoping to patch things up. He tried in frustration to think of a way to explain to her the cruelty of his "friend," but it was hopeless.

He returned home with arms full of groceries, banging at the door with a foot. No one answered so he let himself in. Susan's clothing was gone. Mike searched for a message but there was none.

Mike was sucking on his fifth beer of the night when the phone rang. He stumbled over, picked it up, and before he could speak, a male voice asked, "Suzie? Just wanted you to know I'd be a little late. I'll be at Cafe Noir by 9:30. I'm the one with the biggest joint in the joint."

As Mike parked his Subaru at the darkened gas station across the street from the night club, he spotted Susan entering.

He sat in the car seat for a while, trying to sober up and collect his thoughts. It looked like Joey Clark had been right all along: Susan was hardly innocent. In fact, it was even possible that she had somehow put those obscene messages on the men's room walls herself—or had a pimp do it for her.

The smoke in the bar was thick as fog, but Mike spotted Susan against the far wall, speaking to a guy in a three-piece suit.

Mike hugged a darkened corner and watched them. The man had his arm around Susan, and she wasn't objecting. Mike saw her lean forward and whisper something to the man as one of her hands lightly brushed against the front of his polyester trousers.

"Suzie Sucks." The phrase kept repeating itself in Mike's mind like a broken record. *But she doesn't suck,* he reminded himself. *At least not for free.* The girl had been nothing but a hooker all along.

Suzie was leaving the club with Mr. Three Piece Suit in tow. Following, Mike saw them climb into a Cadillac and drive off. He then ran to his car and quickly weaved into traffic. Suzie and her John were headed north toward the Hollywood hills. Mike guessed they would park by the Hollywood reservoir and then Suzie would earn her money —and her reputation.

He turned his lights off as he approached the crest of the hill where he saw the Caddy parked. Sliding out of his car, Mike walked softly uphill till he found a hidden vantage point from which he could view the car's occupants.

Suzie's head was in the guy's lap, rising and falling slowly. Mike could hear the John's moans of ecstasy, the sound assaulting his ears like shards of flying glass. *How much?*

Mike wondered absently. *How much did it cost to have those lips make a man groan like that?*

Now there were new sounds from inside the car: gasps and even a tiny shriek. Mike's blood ran cold as his mind envisioned the John as one of those serial killer types who preyed on hookers. Maybe he was slitting Suzie's pretty throat right now. Maybe he shouldn't care, Mike thought for an instant.

He bounded out from behind the bushes and pulled the passenger car door open. The interior light came on, illuminating Suzie's shocked expression.

"Oh my God," she sputtered, blood dribbling from her mouth.

"Did this asshole hurt you?" Mike heard himself saying. *Jesus,* he thought, *I still love this slut.* "I'll kill him," he hissed, as he started to pull the John out of the car.

"Too late," Suzie whispered.

Mike pulled away from the man and watched his head flop to the dashboard, where it struck with a hollow thud. The corpse fell sideways past them onto the pavement.

"Jesus," Mike whispered. "You killed him."

"That's right," she said.

"But you had to, right? I mean, he was attacking you." Mike couldn't see any sign that the man had been armed. But he'd obviously struck her—Suzie's mouth was still bleeding. Even as he watched, she wiped her tongue along her wide upper lip, licking off the blood. She was smiling.

Mike had never noticed those oversized incisors before. *She looked like a goddamned doberman,* he thought.

"It's not your blood," he realized aloud, his voice quivering.

She smiled at him, dabbed at the bloodstains with a paper tissue, and started the car's engine. She reached over to him, patting his hand.

"That's why I couldn't . . . you know," she said. "I just didn't trust myself. The bloodlust runs strongest during sex."

As she pulled away from the curb and started back down

the hill toward the lights of Hollywood, she blew him a kiss. "I'll really miss you, Mike," she called out.

In a daze, Mike tripped over the corpse and landed in a heap by the victim's feet. As he started to rise, he saw a pool of blood forming under the corpse's crotch.

Suzie Sucks, Mike thought with a shudder.

PUNISHMENTS

Ray Garton

I arrived in Manning the day after I read of Jayne's death in the paper. It was front-page news across the country, the kind of story the press wrings dry.

TEENAGER KILLS CHURCH ORGANIST
IN BIZARRE SEX SLAYING

I wouldn't have read it if I hadn't seen Jayne's picture, her big tortoiseshell glasses perched on her small nose, dull brown hair gathered in the back, her usually timid, fleeting smile opening brightly for the camera. It was a recent picture and she'd changed little in the last ten years.

I immediately arranged to take a day off work, saw that my pet, Clarissa, had plenty of food and water, and left Los Angeles for Manning.

I was raised in Manning, a small Seventh-Day Adventist village in the Napa Valley. My parents still lived there, but when I arrived, I went straight to the boy's house. It was easy enough to find; reporters were gathered on the sidewalk waiting for a glimpse of the killer. I parked my rented car across the street and stared at the house, wondering what the boy was like, how he'd met her. And if she'd done to him what she did to me . . .

* * *

When I was sixteen, I thought of Jayne Potter only as the woman who, each week, placed a square brown cushion on the church organ bench, sat down, and played for services. I didn't find her attractive; she had fair skin, dressed plainly, and always wore her hair in a bun or braided. She didn't wear makeup, but, because that was against Seventh-Day Adventist rules, neither did any of the girls at the Adventist prep school I attended. *They,* however, were the stars of my fantasies; although restricted by dress codes, they somehow managed to dress in ways that accentuated their curves and angles to the fullest. Repression is the mother of creativity, I always say.

Miss Potter attended every church function and gave more than her share of time to its causes. At a bake sale or potluck, she was impossible to distract, so great was her concentration on her duties; she seemed driven, as if she *had* to participate in church activities, as if she were repaying an important debt. But in spite of her sizable contributions to the church, the congregation seemed to ignore her; sometimes I even thought they were *shunning* her. Most people that participatory were quite popular socially. Not Miss Potter. She smiled and nodded a lot but spoke little and was seldom if ever spoken to.

It wasn't until she came down with a summer cold and my mother had me take her some homemade cream of vegetable soup that our relationship began. I drove to her place in my mom's car. Miss Potter lived on the north side of town in a mobile home nestled by itself at the foot of a shady hill.

It was a hot summer day, but she came to the door wearing a heavy white terrycloth robe. I didn't expect to be invited in, but she did so immediately. Once inside, with the glare of sunlight out of my eyes, I could see that she wasn't wearing her glasses and her hair was down, full and wavy on her shoulders and back, and I discovered something. It wasn't an instant discovery; it took a while to sink in and wasn't fully absorbed until after I'd left her. I discovered that Miss Potter was beautiful.

She didn't seem sick. Her eyes were puffy, but that might have been from crying. I would later realize that she had been. I lost count of the times I found her crying when I came over for my visits. In fact, I lost count of the visits.

Inside, her trailer was dimly lighted; only one small lamp was on by the sofa, but its dark gray shade shed little light. It was sparsely furnished and the walls were bare except for the most hideous portrait of the crucifixion I've ever seen; blood, dark and viscous, poured from Christ's head, hands and feet, and from the gaping hole in his side. His face was a long, cadaverous nightmare.

She thanked me for the soup, took it to the kitchen, then sat on the sofa with a smile, gracefully folding her legs beneath the robe. She patted the cushion beside her and I sat, but there was nothing graceful about *my* movements. I was a clumsy and shy teenager, particularly in the presence of females. Especially ones wearing robes. Miss Potter managed to put me at ease, though; we made small talk about school and the upcoming church picnic. As she spoke, she frequently patted my shoulder, hand, and knee— innocuous conversational gestures, but ones I'd never noticed in her before. She was somehow . . . different.

After insisting I call her Jayne, she discovered my interest in reptiles and softly said, "Ah, then, I have a book you'll enjoy." She scooted forward and leaned across my lap toward a small bookcase against the wall.

My heart quivered like Jell-O. A shadowed valley plunged between the lapels of her robe and flesh shifted slightly; her skin was white as summer clouds and a faint green-blue vein meandered over the curve of her left breast, disappearing in the shadows. I wanted so badly to follow that vein down her robe that my fingers actually twitched to reach out and pull the lapel aside. I blushed furiously and stood when she moved, preparing to leave.

At the door she gave me the book, gently touched a cool hand to the back of my neck, and said, "This will give you an excuse to come back and see me." As I stepped out, something brushed my behind; it could have been a shifting wrinkle in my jeans or the corner of the end table by the door . . . or her fingers.

Of course, it *was* her fingers, but I couldn't bring myself to believe it then. I did, however, masturbate my way through variations of that fantasy for the next few nights in the secrecy of my bedroom. Masturbation is, of course, another no-no among Adventists, but I've often attributed any stability I may now possess to my refusal to stop masturbating even after my biology teacher told the class it could cause a nervous breakdown.

I wanted to talk about this fantasy, as boys do, with my best—and nearly *only*—friend, Gary Sigman, but Gary wasn't saying much to anyone that summer. The previous fall his parents had divorced; both were teachers at the Adventist grammar school in Manning, and lost their jobs because of it. (The church cannot prevent divorces, but it does punish those involved for allowing their marriages to fail.) Gary became pale and withdrawn. Everyone attributed his subsequent sullenness and weight loss to the upset of the divorce. Everyone but me. I knew something *else* had happened to Gary; he looked older and didn't laugh much anymore. But it was out of my reach, so I decided to let him make the first move to open up. If he had, we might have spent those summer evenings on my back porch whispering about Miss Potter. But he didn't.

When I returned the book three days later, Jayne met me at the door wearing that same robe. I thought that was odd; it was midafternoon and surely she was no longer ill. She greeted me pleasantly and led me to the sofa where she presented me with another book. It was huge and full of color photographs of rare and exotic reptiles.

"I don't want to loan it out," she said, sitting close to me and opening the book on our laps, "but you're welcome to look at it here if you want. Anytime."

As we paged through the book, her leg rubbed slightly against mine; beneath the book, my crotch began to bulge. I realized I had imagined nothing three days before but didn't know what to do; dry-mouthed and trembling, I stared blindly at the book, aware only of the burning friction between her leg and mine. When she unexpectedly pulled the book away, I found myself staring down at my erection. Jayne was staring at it, too. Smirking. She *slowly* reached over and touched it. Caressed it. Squeezed it slightly. My lungs convulsively sucked in a breath.

"Do you like hot fudge sundaes, Paul?" she whispered, leaving the room to clatter around in the kitchen a moment. "I do. Would you like one?"

I think I shook my head.

She returned with a bowl of ice cream, chocolate syrup, nuts and a cherry, and said, *"I* would." Placing the bowl on the coffee table, she knelt before me and began to undo my belt.

I was paralyzed, I imagined my mother's horror should she walk in and find me. I remembered Pastor Helmond's recent sermon in which he declared, "Sex is a sweet-tasting poison which will surely *kill* your *soul!"* I remembered my Bible teacher at school telling the class, "Sex is such a dangerous, unhealthy diversion that, when faced with sexual desires, even married couples should take a cold shower or run around the block instead of having intercourse unless, of course, it's done only to reproduce." Long before I even knew what it was, I was told sex was a moral crime, the most treacherous curve on the road to heaven. But when Jayne took me in her hand, I lost all fear of the Lake of Fire that I had so long been warned about. Placing the bowl on the floor between my legs, she turned off the lamp, spooned ice cream and chocolate onto my cock, sprinkled nuts over it, placed the cherry on the head, and hungrily, lovingly, and oh so deliciously devoured her sundae.

Her sofa converted into a bed, which we put to great use that afternoon. I was clumsy at first, but soon lost my self-consciousness as she covered my body with nibbles and kisses. I wanted to see her, touch her, *taste* her, but when I tugged at her robe, she refused to remove it. I rolled on top of her, but she pushed me away and gasped, "No, no, like *this,"* and rolled onto her knees and elbows. I knelt behind her, she guided me in, and immediately began to groan. It wasn't a sound of pleasure, it was a *groan,* and I feared I was hurting her somehow. When I started to pull out, she snapped, "No, *do* it! Hard!"

My thrusts were uncertain at first, but I soon lost myself in waves of new sensations. The robe's hem gathered between us, but when I tried to slide it up so I could stroke her back, she quickly pulled it back down again and began uttering garbled words between her gasps.

I leaned forward and whispered, "What? What'd you say?" but she spoke into her pillow after that. It would be weeks before those words became clear to me.

I went home on weak knees, saying little to my parents on

the way to my room. I remained in a stunned silence until the following afternoon when, at her request, I returned to Jayne's trailer like a somnambulist returning to bed. Once again she was wearing that robe; once again she seated me on the sofa. There she stripped me and licked every inch of my body except my cock until I put her hand on it myself and breathed, "Please . . . please . . ." She opened the bed and, as before, left her robe on and cried out as we writhed together, her sobbed words buried in her pillow.

There was only silence afterward; although we exchanged small talk before, we never spoke after. We *never* spoke of what we did. As we lay side by side that second time, I tried to stroke her hair, her neck, but she pulled away and curled into a trembling ball. Finally she whispered hoarsely, "Come back at three tomorrow."

Her strange behavior was lost on me at first; I was too overwhelmed by the fact that I was HAVING SEX. On top of that, it was with an OLDER WOMAN. And I suppose I got a charge from the fact that my lover was timid Miss Potter. Church became a new experience altogether; each time I saw Jayne mount the organ bench after carefully putting her cushion in place, I immediately grew hard—right there with Mom and Dad in our usual pew. I covered my erection with my leather-bound monogrammed Revised Standard Version Bible. I watched her throughout the sermon; sometimes her hips squirmed on that cushion, and I wondered if she was thinking of me.

She wasn't.

In the middle of our third week together, Jayne went into the kitchen to make lemonade when I arrived. I spotted her cushion on a chair against the wall and, knowing that her firm ass squirmed over that cushion during church services each week, I couldn't resist sitting on it myself. I gulped the cry of pain that came from what felt like hundreds of tiny needles puncturing my behind. I shot to my feet, grabbed my ass, then picked up the cushion. It was made of heavy brown corduroy and was flat and hard on the bottom. But it was not cushiony.

It was stuffed with tacks.

When I heard her coming, I dropped the cushion, spun around, and tried to return her smile. She leaned forward to put the tray of lemonade on the coffee table, and I stared at her ass, thinking of how she always kept it covered when we fucked, realizing that perhaps it wasn't as smooth and touchable as I'd thought . . .

For a while my thoughts were on that cushion and the questions it raised. But as we began to fuck—and that's what we did; I preferred to think at the time, in a naive sort of first-love way, that we were MAKING LOVE, but that simply wasn't the case—she started calling out again and I listened carefully to her words.

"I'm sorry . . . punish me . . . I'm so sorry I made you hard . . . p-punish me, Daddy, *punish* me!"

I stopped when the words registered, but she reached back and gripped my thigh, dug her nails in, and cried, "Don't . . . *stop!*"

I think she tried to hide her words after that, but I knew what she was saying. I know now—and probably knew then, to some extent—that I should have realized something was very wrong with quiet, timid Miss Potter and I should have stopped seeing her immediately. But she was my first lover and my first addiction. I never allowed myself to consider ending our relationship; I knew I couldn't. But her cries for punishment—from her *father!*—stayed with me and echoed in my dreams.

Jayne told me to return on Sunday, three days later. It was our longest separation yet and made me realize how attached I'd become to our visits.

I fidgeted a lot as I watched her in church that Saturday. After services there was a potluck lunch and I went to the car to help Mom carry in the food she'd brought. I asked her what she knew about Miss Potter, but she obviously didn't want to talk about her, so I dropped it. After lunch, as Dad and I were bringing the freshly washed dishes back to the car, he said, "Your mother said you asked about Miss Potter. How come? You hear something?"

I got a little nervous. "No. I just wondered . . . well, she's so involved in the church but has no friends, no family. Just wondered, that's all."

"Well, I'll tell you. Get in." We got in the front seat and he chewed on a toothpick as he spoke. "Miss Potter's a good woman. She's devoted to the church but gets no thanks for it. Your mom doesn't like talking about her because . . . well, she just doesn't think it's right. There's a lot of people in this church could take a lesson from her. Anyway, when Miss Potter was a little girl, her father, Hudson Potter, was pastor of this church. One night when she was nine or ten, Jayne left her house, walked to the St. Helena police station, and said her daddy was . . . molesting her. Sexually." He cocked a brow. "Know what I mean?"

I nodded, feeling a chill coming on.

"There was a big scandal. Pastor Potter was suspended for nearly a year. Stopped coming to church and just stayed in their little house by the grammar school. Nothing was done, really. It was all hushed up. One Sabbath about eighteen months later, Jayne asked to speak before the congregation. Said she made it all up after having an argument with her daddy. The devil had taken hold of her, but now the Holy Spirit was moving her to make amends. Everyone nodded and clicked their tongues like they'd suspected as much and offered to return Potter to the pulpit. But by then he'd become a recluse. Most said his daughter had broken him. Ruined him with her cruel lies. He died at home about a year later. Jayne's never been forgiven even though most of the people here don't even know what happened."

"Do . . . do you think she was telling the truth?"

He chewed on his toothpick a moment. "That's between her and God, son."

It was another warning I should have heeded but didn't. Five deadly words occurred to me after Dad's story: *Maybe I can help her.*

After sex the next day, when Jayne once again refused to let me touch her, I said, "But I want to. You . . . you do things to me that feel so *good,* but . . . you won't let me touch you . . . make *you* feel good."

"Is that what you want?" she whispered, smiling.

"Yes."

"You'll do anything I want?"

I smiled. "Of *course.*"

God, I was such a babe in the woods.

"Then come back on Tuesday at three and you can."

My next warning came Tuesday morning when I went grocery shopping for Mom. As I left the store hugging two brown bags, I saw Gary Sigman leaning against the car. He looked horribly pale and thin in the bright sunlight. Before I could greet him, Gary said, "I saw you leaving her place, Paul. Twice."

"What're you—"

"You know. Stay away from her. She's sick." He stared at me silently for a moment, whispered, "She'll make you do bad things," then hurried away, leaving me with my groceries.

It bothered me, yes. I gave it careful thought, yes. But did I do what he said?

No.

Jayne had the bed open when I arrived, and she immediately began to undress me, whispering, "You promised . . . anything I ask . . . anything that will make me feel good . . ." She had me lie on my back, reached under the bed for something, then put it on the bed beside me. Hiking the robe up only slightly, she turned her back to me, straddled me, and sighed as I entered. She moved on me slowly for a moment, then pointed to the object on the bed, rasping, "Take that."

I did. It was a three-foot-long whip with three strips of braided leather sprouting from the handle, each knotted at the end.

"Now *whip* me!" she hissed.

When I stuttered for a moment, she repeated the order firmly. My first strike was weak and uncertain, and she cried, "Harder!" I brought the whip down again— *"Harder!"*—and again— *"Har*-derrr!"—until it was smacking loudly against the taut terrycloth on her back. "Yes!" she cried, bucking furiously on me. "Punish me! I'm sorry I made you hard, Daddy, sorry I told, sorry, *sorry, sorry*sorry*sorry*! *Punish* me!" Her laughter was breathy and high, void of humor but so full of *joy*. I think that's what did it to me, what shattered my initial fear of and disdain for the act: her joy. She loved it.

We were both out of breath afterward and neither of us spoke. As she lay panting on the bed, moaning with each exhalation, I slowly dressed, then left.

At home I went to my bed in a daze, thinking of everything—my household chores, a phone call I had to make, maybe driving down to Napa tomorrow—except what I'd just done. . . .

My visits to Jayne's became a blur after that. The whip always awaited me on the bed. She never removed her robe. We fucked in various positions, and with each blow of the whip she cried out with delight. After a while so did I. Although I never admitted it to myself then, I came to enjoy those whippings. Part of it was the pleasure she derived from her pain. But there was something else, something I couldn't have identified back then if I'd tried or wanted to, something within me that remained hidden and dormant until I took the whip in my hand; then it crawled from its lair, suddenly in command, and swelled with pleasure at each strike. While most of those visits are hazy memories, even after only ten years, I vividly remember the day she finally took me to her bedroom.

It was a small trailer, so I assumed she slept on the sofa bed. Not so. Jayne had simply been *preparing* me for her bedroom.

In the living room she opened my pants, knelt down, and began licking my cock. "This is our secret," she whispered, attacking my erection voraciously with lips, tongue, and hands. "I'm sharing it with you because you're . . . so . . . good to me." She brought me to the edge quickly and when she saw my trembling she mumbled, "Come. Come in my face." I did and she laughed, rubbing my semen over her face and neck. She stood and kissed me tenderly. I was startled to realize it was our first kiss. Staring intensely into my eyes, she breathed, "I . . . *know* . . . you'll be so . . . *good* . . . to me." Then she led me to the back of the trailer.

Just as a church is a house of God, Jayne's little bedroom was a house of pain. The window was blackened and dim light bled through the red shade of the room's single tiny lamp. It was a garden of chains and straps and pullies all tediously connected and threaded through eyelets in the walls and ceiling. Visually, it made no sense. One wall was covered with whips of various lengths and designs. Paddles and manacles and small insectlike clamps hung from hooks. Mounted above them was a long, barbed, harpoonlike object. I wanted to be horrified by it all, and perhaps I pretended to be at first; but as that creature inside me began to awaken, teasingly flicking its black tongue, I shivered with anticipation.

Then I saw the oddest, most incongruous thing of all hanging on the wall above the bed: a large framed photograph of a man with thick black and silver hair, narrow glistening eyes that seemed to bore into my head, and a craggy face as cold as steel. Pastor Hudson Potter, I was certain.

As I began to undress, Jayne dropped her robe and quickly turned off the light. But in that instant I saw the scars and calluses on her body. All *over* her body.

She lit a candle and took some of the accoutrements from the wall: a short whip, manacles, clamps, spherical weights on thin chains . . . and the barbed rod. She attached the clamps to flaps of skin between her legs, then the weights to the clamps, groaning through clenched teeth. The tender flesh of her pussy hung impossibly low, like the flabby sinking skin of a very old woman. Climbing onto the bed, she put the manacles on her wrists and ankles and had me attach them to the chains hanging from the ceiling. At her request, I turned a crank on the wall, and she slowly rose a few feet above the bed, weights dangling from her rubbery labia. I was trembling as I flipped the latch that locked the crank.

"Now," she whispered, "whip me. Punish me."

I started slowly, like the first time, whipping her legs and sides as I knelt on the bed.

"No, *no!* My cunt! Whip my filthy, sinful, evil *cunt!*"

"Juh-Jayne, I can't—"

"Do it!"

I did.

She writhed and laughed and cried obscene apologies, her head hanging back so she could look at her father's icy face. The weights bobbed and she began to bleed as the teeth of the clamps bit into her flesh.

That was when *I* began to laugh and whip her harder. My cock stood at attention, and I began to stroke it with my free hand, breathing faster.

"Now, Paul, *now!* Put it in me!"

I stopped, confused. "What—"

"The *rod!*" she growled. "Drive it in! All the way in! *Fuck* me with it! Punish me!"

I hesitantly lifted the pointed rod from the bed; the barbs curved like small evil grins. Something happened to me then. A clean bright light inside me went out and a ragged hot flame spat up in its place. I think I smiled as I eased the rod into Jayne—

"Fuck me with it Daddy Daddy I'm sorry—"

—a bit deeper—

"—Daddy sorry I told sorry I made you hard sorry Daddy punish meee!"

—until the first barb was touching her vagina. I think it was the blood that stopped me. One of the weights plopped onto the bed taking a piece of flesh with it and I caught some blood on my face. I realized what I was about to do and gasped, pulled out the rod, dropped it, and ran to the bathroom to vomit. It wasn't because I was horrified or disgusted by what I was doing, but because I wanted— wanted *so badly*—to do it.

Jayne screamed obscenities at me as I lowered her to the bed, unhooked the manacles, and dressed. As I left her for the last time, I heard her crying, "I'm sorry, Daddy, so sorry . . . I need to be punished . . . punished . . ."

Gary Sigman committed suicide two years later. Had Jayne done that long before, things would have been very different for us all—especially for the boy who finally did what she wanted. But suicide is a sin.

Despite my parents' disapproval, I drifted away from the church; instead of attending an Adventist college, I went to UCLA. There I met Roz, a beautiful business major. One night while we were making love, I began to pound the mattress with my fist, lost in passion. When I finally heard her screams, I realized it wasn't the mattress I was pounding. I expected her to press charges, but she didn't. I paid her dental bill and never saw her again.

I tried prostitutes for a while, but they weren't safe. One night I left a motel room in Hollywood and met the girl's pimp in the parking lot. When he saw the blood on my hands and shirt, he beat me senseless. He hurried in to check on his girl, and I limped to my car and left, certain he would kill me if I didn't.

I remained parked before the boy's house for two hours, watching the reporters surrounding the front yard.

I considered visiting my parents, but they would want me to stay a while and I couldn't. I had to get back to my pet, Clarissa. Sometimes, if left alone, she stops eating, just out of spite. Sometimes I have to force her.

I found her on Sunset Boulevard. In the right light she even looks a bit like Jayne. She's about seventeen or so and says she has no family. I keep her in a box in the spare bedroom.

I guess I forgot what I was waiting for; I started the car, drove away from the house, and left Manning.

RED LIGHT

David J. Schow

*T*abloid headlines always make me laugh. You know: *I Aborted Bigfoot's Quints,* or *See Elvis' Rotting Nude Corpse,* or *Exclusive on Jack the Ripper's Grandson!* Earlier today, while passing one of those Market Street newsvendors, I saw similar hyperbolic screamers, and I laughed. I did not want to laugh; it came out as a sick coughing sound.

TASHA VODE STILL MISSING
Terrorist Kidnapping of International Cover Girl
Not Ruled Out

What the hell did they know about her? Not what I knew. They were like vampires; they sucked. Ethically. Morally.

But what did that make *me?*

At the top of the dungheap was the good old *National Perspirer,* loudly thumping the tub. A four-color cover claimed all the hot, steaming poop on Tasha's disappearance, enumerating each of her three juicy, potential fates. One: She had pulled a Marilyn Monroe. Two: She had had a Dorothy Stratten pulled *on* her by some gonzo fruitbag lover. Three: She was tucked away in the Frances Farmer suite at some remote, tastefully isolated lunatic asylum.

Or maybe she was forking over richly to manufacture all

this furious controversy in order to boost her asking price into the troposphere—in a word, hoax time.

It was pathetic. It made my gut throb with hurt and loss, and downtown San Francisco defused behind a hot saltwash of welling tears. I blamed the emissions of the Cal Trans buses lumbering up and down the street, knowing full well I couldn't cop such a rationalization, because the buses ran off electricity, like the mostly defunct streetcars. Once, I'd nearly been decapitated by a rooftop conductor pole when it broke free of the overhead webwork of wires and came swinging past, boom-low, alongside the moving bus, sparking viciously and banging off a potted sidewalk tree a foot above my head, zizzing and snapping. Welcome to the Bay Area.

I had no real excuse for tears now, and wiped my eyes with the heel of my hand. My left hand; my *good* hand. I was still getting used to the weight of the new cast on my other one.

One of the street denizens for which Union Square is infamous had stopped to stare at me. I stared back, head to toe, from the clouds of gnats around his matted hair to the solid-carbon crustiness of his bare, black feet. He caught me crying with his mad prophet eyes, and the grin that snaked his face lewdly open suggested that yes, I *should* howl with grief, I *should* pull out a Mauser and start plugging pedestrians. I put my legs in gear instead. I left him behind with the news kiosk, the scungy, sensationalist headlines, and all those horrifyingly flawless pictures of her. The bum and I ceased to exist for each other the moment we parted.

I know what happened to Tasha. Like a recurring dream, she showed up unannounced on my doorstep just four days ago. Like a ghost then, like a ghost now.

People read *People*. The truth, they never really want to know, and for good reason.

Her real name was Claudia Katz. In 1975, nobody important knew my name, or either of hers, and I'd already shot thousands of pictures of her. When I replaced my el cheapo scoop lamps with electronically synchronized umbrella shades so new that their glitter hurt your eyes even when they *weren't* flashing, I comemmorated the event by photographing her. New Year's Eve, 1974—five seconds before midnight, I let a whole roll rip past on autowind, catching her as she passed from one year into the next. Edited down, that sequence won me a plaque. Today, it's noteworthy only because Tasha is the subject.

"Claudia Katz is too spiky and dykey," she explained later, as she pulled off her workout shirt and aired a chest that would never need the assistance of the Maidenform Corporation, breasts that would soon have the sub-scribership of *Playboy* eating their fingernails. *"Claudia Katz* is somebody who does chain mail and leather doggie-collar spreads for Bitch Records. *Claudia Katz* is not somebody you'll find on the staple page in *Sports Illustrat-ed's* Swimsuit Issue."

I pushed back an f-stop and refocused. "Part your lips. Stop. Give me the tip of your tongue, just inside your teeth." Her mouth was invitingly moist; the star-filters would trap some nice little highlights. *Click-whirr click-whirr.* "Tilt your head back. Not so much . . . stop." I got a magnified closeup of the muscles beneath her skin, moving through the slow, programmed dance of positions. My big fan was on, making her amber hair float. "Hands together, arms back over your head. Turn, turn, turn . . . whoa, right there, stop!" *Click-whirr*—another thousandth of a second, immo-bilized. *"Sports Illustrated?* Why bother aiming it at a bunch of beer-swilling beat-offs in baseball caps, anyway?"

"You don't understand the way the world works, do you?" She spoke to the camera lens, because she knew I was in there, watching. "You've got to make people look at your picture and either want you, or want to *be* you. When they anticipate your next picture, that means they're fantasizing about you. Saying to themselves, 'Geez, I wonder what she looks like in bed, without that damned bathing suit on?'"

It was my privilege to know the answer to that one already. Grinning, I baited her: "The women say that, do they?"

"No, not the women, you dork." The warm, come-hither expression on her face was entirely contrary to her tone. She was, after all, very good at her job. *Click-whirr.* "The men.

When all the men in the country, in the world, lust for you, then you can say no to the lot of them. If all the men want you, then all the women lust to *be* you. Voila."

"Excluding lesbians, Tibetian lamas and some Kalahari bushmen." Her reply begged my sarcasm. She expected it. "Not that, um, lust and envy aren't *admirable* goals . . ."

If I had not been shooting, her brow would have rearranged and a familiar crease would appear between her eyes, indicating her annoyance at my childish, defeatist, irrelevant, smartass remark. And then she'd say—

"You just don't understand." Right on cue. "But I'll be on top someday. You'll see."

"I'd like to see you on top after you finish your shower." It flew out of my mouth before I could stop it. File a lawsuit if you want. "It's your turn."

She decided not to blow up, and rolled her eyes to keep from giggling. *Click-whirr.* My heart fumbled a beat. I'd just netted a shot of an honest-to-U.S.-Grant human being, peeking out from behind a cover-girl facade of plastic. Nude from the waist up, sensual not from flaunted sexuality, but because her expression let you in on the secret that the whole sham was strictly for laughs and wages. A real woman, not a fantasy image. I wanted that photo. It reduced the rest of the roll to an exhausted, mundane repertoire of tit shots—pretty billboard face, pasted-on bedroom eyes of that inhuman chromium color, the "ideal," a dime per double dozen from one shining sea to the next, from the four-star hookers at the Beverly Hills Hotel to the smartly attired, totally paranoid corporate ladies who took their Manhattan business lunches in neat quartets.

"To hell with the shower," she had said then, lunging at me with mischief in her eyes.

I still have that photo. Not framed, not displayed. I don't make the effort to look at it anymore. I can't.

Claudia—Tasha—got precisely what she wanted. That part you know, unless you've spent the last decade eating wallaby-burgers in the Australian outback. The tiny differences in the way we perceived the world and its opportunities finally grew large enough to wedge between us. Her astronomical income had little to do with it. It was me. I made the classic mistake of trying to keep her by blurting out proclamations of love before my career, my life, was fully mobilized. When you're clawing through the riptide of your twenties, it's like a cosmic rule that you cannot be totally satisfied by your emotional life and your professional life simultaneously. We had been climbing partners, until I put everything on hold to fall in love with her. So she left, and became famous. Not many people know my name even today. They don't have to; I pull down a plush enough income. But it did come to pass that everybody wanted Tasha. Everybody still does.

I was halfway through my third mug of coffee at the Hostel Restaurant when I admitted to myself that I was consciously avoiding going home. Bad stuff waited for me out there. A Latino busboy had made off with my plate. Past the smoky front windows, Geary Street was acruise with the bun-boys that gave the Tenderloin its rep. In New York, where things are less euphemistic, they're called fudge-packers. I wondered what gays made of all the media fuss over Tasha.

Nicole was giving me the eye. She's my favorite combat-hardened coffeeshop waitress in the charted universe, an elegant willowsprout of West Indies mocha black, with a heaving bosom and a lilting, exotic way of speaking the English language. When I watch her move about her chores at the Hostel, I think she'd probably jump my bones on the spot if she thought I could *click-whirr* her into the Tasha Vode saddle—worldwide model, budding cinema star, headliner. And still missing. When I try to formulate some logical nonsense for what happened to her, I fail just like I did with the street bum. Nothing comes out. Instead, I watch Nicole as she strolls over to recharge my cup. She watches me watching her.

"How'd you know I wanted more, Nicole?"

She narrows her panther eyes and blesses me with an evil smile. "Because you white boys *always* want more, hon."

My house *cum* studio hangs off the north end of the Fieldings' Point Pier, which is owned by a white-maned, sea-salt type named Dickie Barnhardt, whom no mortal dares address as "Richard." He sold me my home and plays caretaker to his pier. I live in a fabulous, indifferently-planned spill-together of rooms, like building blocks dumped haphazardly into a corner. Spiderwebbing it together are twelve crooked little stairways, inside and out. At first I called it my Dr. Seuss House. On the very top is a lighthouse tower that still works. Dickie showed me how to operate it, and from time to time I play keeper of the maritime flame because the notion is so irresistibly romantic. In return for spiffing up the place, I got another plaque—this one from the U.S. Lighthouse Society in San Francisco. Lighthouses have long been outmoded by navigational technology, and the Society is devoted to a program of historical preservation. There's no use for my little beacon. But there are nights when I cannot bear to keep it dark.

After ten years without a postcard, Tasha knew exactly where to find me. Maybe she followed the light. I answered my downstairs door with the alkaline smell of developer clinging to my hands; the doorknob was greened from all the times I'd done it. And there she was.

Was I surprised? I knew instantly it was her, knew it from the way the ocean tilted and tried to slide off the edge of the world, knew it because all the organs in my body tried to rush together and clog up my throat.

"You look like you just swallowed a starfish," she said. She was burrowed into a minky-lush fur that hid everything but the tips of her boots. The chill sea breeze pushed wisps of her hair around. I don't have to describe what her face looked like. If you want to know, just haul your ass down to Slater's Periodicals and check out the covers of any half-dozen current glamour and pop-fashion magazines. *That's* what she looked like, brother.

Her eyes seemed backed up with tears, but maybe tears alone were insufficient to breach the Tasha forcefield, or maybe she used some brand of eyeliner so expensive that it was tear-resistant. I asked her why she was crying, invited her in, and then did not give her room to answer me. I was too busy babbling, trying to race past ten years in ten minutes and disguise my nervousness with light banter. She sensed my disorientation and rode it out, patiently, the way she used to. I fixed coffee and brandy. She sipped hers with picture-perfect lips, sitting at the breakfast overlook I'd glassed-in last summer. I needed the drink. She needed contact, and hinted at it by letting her leg brush mine beneath the booth-style table. My need for chitchat and my awareness of the past hung around, dumbing things up like a stubborn chaperone. Beyond the booth's half-turret of windowpanes, green breakers crashed onto the rocks and foamed violently away.

Her eyes cleared, marking time between me and the ocean outside. They grew darkly stormy, registering the thunderheads that were rolling in with the dusk to lash the beach with an evening sweep of rain.

At last, I ran out of stupid questions.

She closed my hand up in both of hers. My heartbeat meddled with my breathing. She had already guessed which of my odd little Caligari staircases led to the bedroom loft.

The night sky was embossed by tines of lightning somewhere between us and Japan. Fat drops splatted against the seaward hurricane glass and skidded to the right as a strong offshore wind caught and blew them. I had opened the shutters on the shore side, and the wooden blades of the ceiling fan cast down cool air to prickle our flesh, sweat-speckled from fervent but honest lovemaking.

A lot of women had drifted through my viewfinder after Tasha had left me. Except for two or three mental timebombs and outright snow queens, I coupled enthusiastically with all of them. I forgot how to say no. Sometimes I was artificially nice; most of the time I was making the entire sex pay because one of their number had dumped me. The right people found out my name, yes. My studio filled up with eager young lovelies. No brag, just a living. I settled into a pattern of rejecting them about the time they tried to form any sort of lasting attachment, or tried to storm my meticulously erected walls. Some of them were annoyingly persistent, but I got good at predicting when they would turn sloppy and pleading . . . and that made snuffing their flames oddly fulfilling. I was consistent, if not happy. I took a perverse pleasure in booting cover girls out of my bed on a regular basis, and hoped that Joe Normal was envious as hell.

Lust. Envy. Admirable goals, I thought, as she lay with her hair covering my face, both of her legs hugging one of mine. We had turned out to be pretty much alike after all.

When I mumbled, she stirred from her doze. "What . . . ?"

"I said, I want a picture of you, just like you are, right this moment."

Her eyes snapped open, gleaming in the faint light. "No." She spoke into the hollow of my neck, her voice distant, the sound of it barely impressing the air. "No pictures. No more pictures. Ever."

The businessman part of my brain perked up: *What neurosis could this be?* Was Tasha Vode abandoning her career? Would it be as successful as her abandonment of me? And what was the difference? For what she earned in a month, I could buy the beach frontage below for several miles in both directions. What difference? I'd gotten her back, against all the rules of reality, and here I was looking for the loophole. Her career had cleaved us apart, and now it was making us cleave back together. Funny how a word can have opposing definitions.

After five minutes of tossing and turning, she decided not to make me work for it. "Got anything warm?" She cracked a helpless smile. "Down in the kitchen, I mean."

"Real cocoa. Loaded with crap that's bad for you. Not from an envelope. Topped with marshmallows, also real, packed with whatever carcinogens the cocoa doesn't have."

"Sounds luscious. Bring a whole pot."

"You can help."

"No. I want to watch the storm." Water pelted the glass. Now and then lightning would suggest how turbulent the ocean had gotten, and I thought of firing up my beacon. Perhaps there was a seafarer out there who was as romantic about boats as I was about lighthouses, and had gotten caught in the squall without the latest in high-tech directional doodads.

I did it. Then I dusted off an old TV tray for use as a

serving platter, and brought the cocoa pot and accoutrements up the narrow stairs, clanking and rattling all the way.

My carbon-arc beam scanned the surface of the water in long, lazy turns. She was facing her diaphanous reflection in the glass, looking through her own image into the dark void beyond.

I had pulled on canvas pants to make the kitchen run, but Tasha was still perfectly naked and nakedly perfect, a siren contemplating shipwrecks. She drifted back from the window. I pitied my imaginary seafarer, stuck out in the cold, away from the warmth of her.

"You know those natives in Africa?" she said as I served. "The ones who wouldn't let missionaries take their pictures because they thought the camera would trap their souls?"

"It's a common belief. West Indians still hold to the voodoo value of snapshots. *Mucho* mojo. Even bad snapshots." I couldn't help that last remark. What a pro I am.

"You remember April McClanahan?" She spoke toward the sea. To my reflection.

"You mean Crystal Climax, right?"

She nodded. "Also of wide renown as Cherry Whipp."

All three were a lady with whom Tasha had shared a garret during her flirtation with the hardcore film industry in the early 1970s. Don't swallow the negative hype for a second—every woman who is anyone in film or modeling has made similar contacts. Tasha never moved beyond a couple of relatively innocuous missionary-position features, respectable porn for slumming yip-yups, a one-week run at the Pussycat Theatre, max. April, on the other hand, moved into the hardcore mainstream—*Hustler* covers, videocassette toplines, "fully erect" notices in the film ratings. And no, she didn't get strangled or blow her brains all over a motel room with a Saturday Night Special. Last I heard, she was doing TV commercials for bleach and fabric softener as "Valerie Winston," a sort of Marilyn Chambers in reverse.

"April once told me she'd figured out, with a calculator, that she was responsible for more orgasms in one year than anybody else." Tasha held the big porcelain mug in both hands, to warm her palms. "She averaged out how many moviehouses were showing her films, how many times per day, multiplied by howevermany guys she figured were getting their jollies in the audience per show. Plus whoever was doing likewise to her pictures in god knows how many stroke magazines. Or gratifying themselves to the sex advice column she did for *Leather Life*. I remember her looking at me and saying, 'Think of all the energy that must produce. All those orgasms were born because of me. Me.'"

"I'm sure there are legions of guys jollying to your photos, too," I said. "No doubt, somebody out there is yanking his crank to Christie Brinkley's smile, right now."

"It's not the same thing. April was tough. She got something back." She sat on the bed facing me, legs tucked. She reminded me of Edvard Eriksen's famous sculpture of the Little Mermaid, rendered not in bronze but coaxed from milk-white moonstone, heated by living yellow electricity called down from a black sky, and warmed by warm Arctic eyes—the warmest blue that exists in our world.

"You mean April didn't mind getting that porn star rap laid on her . . . literally?"

I could see her sadness being blotted away by acid bitterness. "The people in porn have it easier. The thuds out there in Bozo-land *know* in their tiny little hearts that porn queens fuck for jobs. Whereas cover girls or legit models who rarely do buff or full-frontal are suspect."

"You can't deny the public their imaginary intrigues."

"What it always boils down to is, 'Climb off it, bitch—who did you *really* blow to get that last *Vogue* cover?' They feed off you. They achieve gratification in a far dirtier way, by wanting you and resenting you at the same time. By hating your success enough to keep all the tabloids in business. It's a draining thing, all taking and no giving, like . . ."

"Psychic vampirism?" It was so easy for someone in her position to sense that her public loved her only in the way a tumor loves its host. But a blacker part of my mind tasted a subtle tang of revenge. She'd left me to go chase what she wanted . . . and when she'd finally sunk in her teeth, she'd gotten the flavor of bile and chalk and ashes. I suppose I should have been ashamed of myself for embracing that hateful satisfaction so readily. And from the hurt neutrality on her face, she might have been reading the thoughts in my head. She watched her cocoa instead of drinking it—always a bad sign.

Just as much as I never said no, I never apologized. Not for anything.

After a cool silence, she said, "You're saying to yourself, 'She's got it made, for christsake. What right does she have to be dissatisfied with anything?' Right?"

"Maybe a tiny bit, yeah." She let me take her hand regardless. She needed the contact. The missing ten years settled between us to fog the issue. I was resentful, yes. Did I want to help her? Same answer. When I guiltily tried to pull back my hand she kept ahold of it. It made me feel forgiven; absolved, almost.

"In science class, in eighth grade, they taught us that when you smell something, your nose is actually drawing in tiny molecular bits of whatever it is you're smelling. Particles."

"Which means you clamped both hands over your mouth and nose whenever you passed a dog turd on the sidewalk after school, am I right?" My prescription for sticky emotional situations is rigid: Always—*always* joke your way out.

Her smile came and went. "The idea stuck in my head. If you smelled something long enough, it would run out of molecules and poof—it wouldn't exist anymore."

"Uh-huh, if you stood around sniffing for a couple of eons." Fortunately, I'd forgotten most of the junk with which school had tried to clog my head. About hard science I knew squat, like math. But I did know that there were billions or trillions of molecules in any given object.

"My point is that each one of us only has so much to give." She cleared her throat, almost as though it hurt her, and pressed valiantly onward. "What if you were to run out of pieces all of a sudden?"

"Happens all the time," I said airily. "That's what a nervous breakdown is. Entertainers who can't give their audiences an ounce more collapse onstage. Corporate guys get physically ill and can't go near a meeting room. People exceed their operational limits . . . and you're in one of the most high-pressure professions there is."

"No." She was shaking her head to prevent me from

clouding her train of thought. "I mean run out of pieces literally. Suppose every photo of me ever taken was an infinitesimal piece? Every magazine ad, every negative, every frame of motion picture film—another tiny molecule of me, stolen away to feed an audience that is *never* satiated. And when someone is fully consumed—vampirized—they move on, still hungry, to pick their next victim by making him or her a star. That's why they're called consumers."

I looked up from the muddy lees in my cup just in time to see the passing lighthouse beam blank the ghost of her reflection from the windowpanes. Just like her smile, it came and went.

Her voice had downshifted into the husky and quavering register of confession. Now I was really uncomfortable. "I know there are celebrities who've had their picture taken two million more times than I have. But maybe they can afford it." She stretched across the bed to place her head on my thigh and hug my waist, connecting herself. "Maybe some of us don't have so many pieces . . ."

I held her while the storm rallied for a renewed assault. My modest but brave beam of lamplight chopped through it. She did not grimace, or redden, or sob; her tears just began spilling out, coursing down in perfect wet lines to darken my pantleg.

Did I want to help her?

She feared that consumers wanted so much of her that pretty soon there would be nothing left to consume. And Claudia Katz no longer existed, except in my head. I'd fallen in love with her, become addicted to her . . . and now she was clinging to me because Tasha Vode was almost used up, and after that, if there was not Claudia, there was nothing. She had not brought her exhaustion home to my stoop to prove she could still jerk my leash after ten years. She had done it because the so-called friends who had gorged themselves on her personality were now nodding and clucking about celebrity lifestyles and answering their machines and juggling in new appointments to replace her as the undertow dragged her away to oblivion.

I stroked her hair until it was all out of her face. The tears dried while the seastorm churned. She snoozed, curled up, her face at peace, and I gently disengaged. Then, with a zealot's devotion toward proving her fears were all in her imagination, I went downstairs to load up one of my Nikons.

I asked her how she felt the next morning. When she said terrific, I spilled the beans.

"You *what*—?"

"I repeat for clarity: I took pictures of you while you were asleep. Over a hundred exposures of you wound up in my dark blue sheets, sleeping through a gale. And guess what— you're still among the living this morning." I refilled her coffee cup and used my tongs to pluck croissants out of the warmer.

She cut loose a capacious sigh, but put her protests on hold. "Don't do that again. Or you'll lose me."

I wasn't sure whether she meant she'd fade to nothingness on the spot, or stomp out if I defied her superstitions a second time. "You slept like a stone, love. Barely changed position all night." My ego was begging to be told that our mattress gymnastics had put her under, but when I saw the care she took to lift her coffee cup with both hands, I knew better.

"Look at this shit," she said with disgust. "I can barely hold up my head, let alone my coffee. I'm slouching. Models aren't supposed to *slouch*, for christsake." She forced her sitting posture straight and smiled weakly. Her voice was a bit hoarse this morning, almost clogged.

"Hey lady—slouch away." Worry stabbed at my insides while I tried to sound expansive and confident. "Do what thou wilt. Sleep all day if that's your pleasure. Just wait till you discover what I've learned to cook in the last ten years. Real salads. Stuff you have to saute. Food with *wine* in it. I can artistically dish up all the squares you require. Loaf on the beach. Read my library. I have said it; it is good." I watched a glint of caution try to burn away the happiness in her eyes. She did so want to believe me. "And no more photographs. Promise. Anybody who tries has gotta shoot through yours truly."

She brightened at that. I'd gotten the reaction I wanted from her. It was the challenge-and-reward game. And goddamned if that tiny acid-drop of doubt didn't settle into my brain, sizzling—*what if what if what if.*

What if I was playing it safe because she might be right?

"I don't want to see those pictures," she said. "Don't even develop them."

"I'll toss 'em in the woodstove right now, if that's what you'd like." I'd made my point.

She gave a theatrical shudder. "Don't burn them. That's too much like a horror story I read once. I might shuffle off the coil along with my own pictures."

The rolls of film were lined up on my miscellaneous shelf downstairs, in the darkroom, the room with the red lightbulbs. Expose the film to anything but that mellow, crimson glow and it blanked into silver nitrate nothingness. The rolls could stay down there, sealed into their little black plastic vials. Forever, if that's what she wanted.

She kept watch on the sea while we destroyed our Continental breakfast. "I thought maybe we could brave the overcast later, and drive down past Point Pitt for dinner," I said. "Steaks, salads and a bottle or two of Cabernet. If anybody asks whether you're Tasha Vode, just blink and say, 'Who?'"

The life had surged back into her expression. "Maybe. Or maybe seafood. But I want you to do something for me, first."

"Your wish . . ."

"Don't you have any work to do today?"

Who were we kidding; I think we both knew I'd do almost anything she asked. "Nothing that can't wait."

"Then carry me back up to the bedroom."

My narrow little stairway was a tight shot, but we negotiated it successfully after a mild bump or two. Our robes got in the way, so we left them crumpled on the stairs about halfway up.

Her need for contact was vital.

Outside the bedroom window it got dark. I did not notice. All I could see was her.

Her eyes were capable of a breathtaking syllabary of expressions, and I felt my own eyes become lenses, trying to record them all. I stopped being friend or lover to be a camera, to trap what it was about her that made total strangers hear those jungle drums. There were thousands, maybe millions of men out there in the darkness, who fantasized about being inside her the way I was now, who played my role and spoke my half of the dialogue whenever they passed a newsstand. Their wanting never ceased.

Her eyes told me they knew what I was up to. They did not approve.

Her calling was one of the few that made you a veteran before puberty was done. If you lucked out, you'd become wealthy while still legally a child; if you weren't so lucky, you'd be left a burned-out has-been before you graduated high school. The attrition rate was worse than that for professional athletes, who could at least fall back on commercials for razors and lite beer when middle age called them out. But she did not seem the sort of human being who could relish the living death of celebrity game shows. Staying beautiful had been an unending war; each touchup a skirmish that stole away another irreclaimable chunk of time. Doing it for ten years, and staying the best, had been draining. Her outside was being used up. Her hipbones felt like flint arrowheads beneath soft tissue paper.

Her hand slid down and felt the cingulum cinched drawstring-tight above my balls. Comprehension dawned in her eyes, followed by that strange tolerance of hers for my various idiocies. I can't relate the exact sequence (to come was, for me, a necessary agony by now), but I was almost certain that her rapidfire contractions began the instant she slipped the knot of the cingulum. Unbound, I offloaded lavishly. Her fingers whitened with pressure on my shoulders, then relaxed, reddening with blood. I watched the pupils of those warm Arctic eyes expand hotly in the dimness as she took what was mine. Until that moment, her own orgasms had seemed insubstantial somehow. Disconnected from her. Spasms of her equipment more than sparky showers in her brain. Her breath had barely raised condensation on my skin. Now she came into focus, filled, flushed, and radiating heat.

After holding me for a lapse of time impossible to measure, she said, "Don't try to impress. You're not performing with a capital *P."* Her eyes saw that I had been intimidated by the imagined skills of her past decade of lovers, and thus the girdle cord trick. Stupid. "Don't you see? You're the only one who ever gave anything back."

"Tasha, you don't really believe that—"

"Try Claudia." It was not a command but a gentle urging. But it, too, was vital. "You're the only one who can give me back some of myself; replace what the others have taken. Give me more." Her reverent tone bordered on love—that word I could rarely force myself to speak, even frivolously.

Who better to give her back some of herself? I was a goddamn repository of her identity. With other women I had never bothered worrying, and so had never been befuddled as I was now. I'd made love to Claudia, not the exterior self that the rest of the world was busy eating. And now she was steering.

I gave her back to herself; her eyes said so, her voice said so, and I tried to hush the voice in my head that said I was not being compensated for this drain. I tried to ignore the numberless black canisters of film that beckoned me from the room with the red light. And later, past midnight, when the storm thundered in, I carefully took twice what I had given her. No matter how much we have, as Nicole the waitress would say, we always want more.

"Skull full of sparrow shit," she said the following day, as we bumped knees and elbows trying to dress for dinner. "Gorgeous but ditzy. Vacuous. Vapid. Pampered. Transient values. A real spoiled-rotten—"

"I think I get the stereotype," I said. "You're just not stupid enough to be happy as a model anymore, right?"

"Ex-model." She watched the sea bounce back the glare of late afternoon. "You don't believe me, do you?"

"What I believe scares the crap out of me." I tried to veneer what I said with good humor, to defang my fears. "I believe, for example, that you might be a ghost. And ghosts never stay."

She waggled her eyebrows. "I could haunt your lighthouse. Or maybe I'm just your wish-fulfillment."

"Don't laugh. I've often thought that I'm not really

earning a living as a photographer." Merely speaking that last word caused the slightest hesitation in the natural flow of her movements; she was *that* sensitized to it. "I'm not really sleeping with Tas . . . uh, Claudia Katz." She caught that slip, too, but forgave it. "Actually, I'm really a dirtbag litter basket picker up in the Mission. And all of this is a hallucinatory fantasy I invented while loitering near a magazine rack with Tasha Vode's picture at hand, hm?"

"Ack," she said with mock horror. "You're one of *them*. The pod-folk."

"Are we gone, or what?"

She stepped back from the mirror, inside of a bulky, deep-blue ski sweater with maroon patterning, soft boots of grey suede, and black slacks so tight they made my groin ache. Her eyes filled up with me, and they were the aquamarine color of the sunlit ocean outside. "We're gone," she said, and led the way down the stairs.

I followed, thinking that when she left me again I'd at least have those hundreds of photographs of her in my bed. Ghosts never stay.

Outside there was a son of a bitch, and an asshole.

The son of a bitch was crouched in ambush right next to my front door. His partner, the asshole, was leaning on my XLS, getting cloudy fingerprints all over the front fender. I had backed out the front door, to lock it, and heard his voice talking, before anything else.

"Miss Vode, do you have any comment on your abrupt—"

Tasha—*Claudia*—started to scream.

I turned as she recoiled and grabbed my hand. I saw the asshole. Any humanity he might have claimed was obliterated by the vision of a huge, green check for an exclusive article that lit up his eyes. A pod man. Someone had recognized us in the restaurant last night, and sent him to ambush us in the name of the public's right to know. He brandished a huge audio microphone at us as though it was a scepter of power. It had a red foam windscreen and looked like a phallic lollipop.

Her scream sliced his question neatly off. She scrambled

backward, hair flying, trying to interpose me between herself and the enemy, clawing at her head, crushing her eyes shut and *screaming*. That sound filled my veins with liquid nitrogen.

The son of a bitch was behind us. From the instant we had stepped into the sunlight, he'd had us nailed in his viewfinder. The video rig into which he was harnessed ground silently away; the red bubble light over the lens hood was on.

And Tasha screamed.

Maybe she jerked her hand away, maybe I let it go, but her grip went foggy in mine as I launched myself at the cameraman, eating up the distance between us like a barracuda. Only once in my whole life had I ever hit a man in anger, and now I doubled my own personal best by delivering a roundhouse punch right into the black glass maw of his lens, filling his face up with his own camera, breaking his nose, two front teeth, and the three middle fingers of my fist. He faded to black and went down like a medieval knight trapped by the weight of his own armor. I swarmed over him and used my good hand to rip out his electronic heart, wresting away porta-cam, tape and all. Cables shredded like torn ligaments and shiny tape viscera trailed as I heaved it, spinning, over the pier rail and into a sea the same color as Tasha's eyes. The red light expired.

Her scream . . . wasn't. There was a sound of pain as translucent as rice paper, thin as a flake of mica, drowned out by the roar of water meeting beach.

By the time I cranked my head around—two dozen slow-motion shots, easy—neither of her was there anymore. I thought I saw her eyes, in Arctic-cold afterburn, winking out last.

"Did you *see*—?"

"You're trespassing!" bellowed Dickie Barnhardt, wobbling toward the asshole with his side-to-side Popeye gait, pressed flat and pissed off. The asshole's face was flash-frozen into a bloodless bas-relief of shock and disbelief. His mouth hung slack, showing off a lot of expensive fillings. His mike lay forgotten at his feet.

"Did you see . . . did . . . she just . . ."

Dickie bounced his ashwood walking stick off the

asshole's forehead. He joined his fallen mike in a boneless tumble to the planks of the pier. Dickie's face was alight with a bizarre expression that said it had been too long since he'd found a good excuse to raise physical mayhem, and he was proud of his forthright defense of tenant and territory. "You okay?" he said, squinting at me and spying the fresh blood on my hand.

"Dickie . . . did you see what happened to Tasha?" My voice switched in and out. My throat constricted. My unbroken hand closed on empty space. Too late.

He grinned a seaworthy grin and nudged the unconscious idiot at his feet. "Who's Tasha, son?"

I drink my coffee left-handed, and the cast mummifying my right hand gives me something to stare at contemplatively.

I think most often of that videotape, decomposing down there among the sand sharks and the jellyfish that sometimes bob to the surface near Dickie's pier. I think that the tiny bit of footage recorded by that poor, busted-up son of a bitch cameraman would not have mattered one damn, if I hadn't shot so much film of Tasha to prove she had nothing to fear. So many pieces. I pushed her right to the edge, cannibalizing her in the name of love.

The black plastic cans of film are still on the shelf down in my darkroom, lined up like inquisitors already convinced of my guilt. The thought of dunking that film in developer makes me want to stick a gun in my ear and pull the trigger, twice if I had the time.

Then I consider another way out, and wonder how long it would take me to catch up with her; how many pieces I have.

I never cried much before. Now the tears unload at the least provocation. It's sloppy, and messy, and unprofessional, and I hate it. It makes Nicole stare at me the way the street bum did, like I've tipped over into psycholand.

When she makes her rounds to fill my cup, she watches me. The wariness in her eyes is new. She sees my notice dip from her eyes to her sumptuous chest and back, in a guilty but unalterable ritual. I force a smile for her, gamely, but it stays pasted across my face a beat too long, insisting too urgently that everything is okay. She doesn't ask. I wave my unbroken hand over my cup to indicate *no more,* and Nicole tilts her head with a queer, new expression—as though this white boy is trying to trick her. But she knows better. She always has.

AUTHOR BIOGRAPHIES

Graham Masterton

Graham Masterton is the author of fifteen horror novels, including the filmed *The Manitou,* and has won awards from the Mystery Writers of America and the West Coast Review of Books. He is highly qualified to appear in a collection of erotic horror, having served four years as executive editor of the British edition of *Penthouse* and having authored four how-to sex manuals.

Richard Matheson

Regarded as a seminal author of modern horror since the early '50s, Matheson has sold more than ninety short stories, fourteen "Twilight Zone" scripts, eleven novels, and six short story collections, and has written close to twenty produced screenplays. Matheson is currently preparing two screenplays and is over eight hundred pages into the manuscript for his latest novel.

Robert R. McCammon

McCammon burst on the horror scene in the early '70s and has already left his mark, with nine novels to his credit, including *Swan Song* and *Stinger.* His most recent novel is *The Wolf's Hour.*

F. Paul Wilson

Wilson, who grew up in New Jersey glued to Zacherley TV reruns, is the author of three science fiction novels, two horror novels (including the filmed *The Keep)*, a supernatural medical thriller, and his latest novel, *Black Wind*. When not writing, Wilson practices medicine. "Ménage à Trois" has been significantly revised for this collection and has never before appeared in this form.

Richard Christian Matheson

Born in 1953, Matheson, who readily cites his father as his mentor, cut his fiction teeth on short stories and then moved on to screenplays for TV and film production companies including Universal, Columbia, Warner Bros., MGM, and UA. In 1988 he began his own production company for development and production of features.

Chet Williamson

Williamson is the author of four novels and short fiction that has appeared in magazines such as *The New Yorker*, *Playboy*, *Twilight Zone* and *Fantasy & Science Fiction*. "Blood Night" is his attempt at "the ultimate wet dream story—this is the one my wife is embarrassed about."

Mick Garris

Garris rose to prominence as a story editor for Steven Spielberg's "Amazing Stories" TV series, for which he wrote several teleplays and directed an episode. His film screenplay work includes *Fly 2* and *batteries not included*, and he rewrote and directed *Critters 2*.

Ramsey Campbell

The president of the British Fantasy Society and a full-time writer since 1973, Campbell has won two World Fantasy awards and three British Fantasy awards. He is also author of a collection of his own erotic horror fiction, *Scared Stiff*.

Lisa Tuttle

Tuttle is an expatriate Texan, currently residing in London. More than sixty of her fiction efforts have been published since her first short story appeared in 1972. She is the author of three novels and several nonfiction works, including the *Encyclopedia of Feminism*.

Theodore Sturgeon

Sturgeon's long and distinguished writing career produced more than two hundred stories, some legendary "Star Trek" episodes, a batch of influential novels, and a multitude of admirers and friends among his writing peers.

J. N. Williamson

A man with a colorful past as everything from a Pinkerton detective to an astrologer, Williamson is a prolific author who has penned over thirty novels and ninety short stories. He is the editor of the *Masques* anthology series.

Michael Garrett

Garrett is past president of Birmingham's Magic City Writers. His work has appeared in *Twilight Zone, Dun's Review,* and others, and his first novel, *Keeper,* is due shortly. "Reunion" is a substantially reworked version of a tale originally published in *Chic*.

Harlan Ellison

During Ellison's forty-year career, which has produced forty-four books, more than fifteen hundred stories, essays, articles, and newspaper columns, two dozen teleplays, and twelve screenplays, he has won more awards than any other living fantasist. These include eight and a half Hugos, three Nebulas, the Edgar Allen Poe award, and four Writers Guild of America awards for outstanding teleplay.

Mike Newton

Mike Newton is a chief scribe of the Mack Bolan series, having penned over thirty Bolans as well as over thirty other fiction and nonfiction titles. "Pretty Is . . ." is his first piece of published short horror fiction.

Gary Brandner

Brandner has been writing full-time since 1969, and is the author of the popular *Howling* series, among others. "Aunt Edith" is a substantially rewritten version of an earlier published work called "Her Aunt the Witch."

Dennis Etchison

The author of three short story collections of his own work, Etchison is also a master of the horror anthology as editor of *Cutting Edge* and the *Masters of Darkness* series. A Los Angeles resident, he is currently at work on a screenplay for John Carpenter.

John Skipp and Craig Spector

Skipp and Spector's initial co-writing efforts were rock songs for their high school bands. A mutual interest in horror films and fiction led them to write several popular horror novels in tandem, including *The Light at the End* and *The Scream*.

Rex Miller

Miller's first-ever novel *Slob* was hailed by people like Stephen King and Harlan Ellison. "The Voice," Miller's first published piece of short fiction, is, he claims, based on a true-life incident from his days as a top-rated DJ.

Robert Bloch

Best known for his novel *Psycho,* which became a classic Hitchcock film, Bloch has authored nineteen novels, more than thirty short story collections, and several produced screenplays.

Steve Rasnic Tem

The prolific and diverse Tem has sold over a hundred pieces of short fiction in the fantasy, horror, science fiction, and mystery fields. "What I'm interested in is disturbing the reader," Tem says, a goal achieved—and then some—in "Carnal House."

Les Daniels

Daniels's work includes the popular Don Sebastian vampire series, plus nonfiction works in the horror and comics fields. "They're Coming for You," Daniels's first short story, was nominated for a World Fantasy Award in 1987.

Jeff Gelb

Gelb is a former FM rock DJ and columnist for the music industry trade journal *Radio & Records.* His first novel, *Specters,* saw print in 1988. Gelb is currently working on a second in collaboration with Michael Garrett.

Ray Garton

Garton is the author of five horror novels, many of which include strong erotic elements. Garton teaches creative writing at a California university.

David J. Schow

Schow has a double life. As an accomplished horror writer, he has had fiction published in *Twilight Zone, Night Cry,* and others, has authored two novels, and has written *The Outer Limits: The Official Companion.* Under a number of pseudonyms, Schow has penned sixteen TV/film tie-ins and series books. "Red Light" won the 1987 World Fantasy Award for Short Story.

Innocent
People Caught
In The Grip Of
TERROR!

These thrilling novels—where deranged minds create sinister schemes, placing victims in mortal danger and striking horror in their hearts—will keep you in white-knuckled suspense!

____ **TAPPING AT THE WINDOW** by Linda Lane McCall
65846/$3.95

____ **SPIRIT WARRIORS** by Devin O'Branagan 66774/$4.50

____ **LIVE GIRLS** by Ray Garton 62628/$3.95

____ **GHOST STORY** by Peter Straub 64889/$4.95

____ **HOT BLOOD: AN ANTHOLOGY OF
PROVOCATIVE HORROR** by Edited by Jeff Gelb &
Lonn Friend 66424/$3.95

____ **DEATHBELL** by Guy Smith 67434/$3.50

____ **VIDEO KILL**
by Joanne Fluke 66663/$3.95

____ **THE NIGHTMARE BLONDE**
by Morton Wolson 64522/$3.50

____ **UNHOLY COMMUNION**
by Adrian Savage 64743/$3.50

____ **BEAST RISING** by Greg Almquist 63497/$3.50

____ **CRUCIFAX**
by Ray Garton 62629/$3.95

____ **THE TROUPE**
by Gordon Linzner 66354/$3.50

POCKET
BOOKS

**Simon & Schuster, Mail Order Dept. TER
200 Old Tappan Rd., Old Tappan, N.J. 07675**

Please send me the books I have checked above. I am enclosing $_____ (please add 75¢ to cover postage and handling for each order. N.Y.S. and N.Y.C. residents please add appropriate sales tax). Send check or money order—no cash or C.O.D.'s please. Allow up to six weeks for delivery. For purchases over $10.00 you may use VISA: card number, expiration date and customer signature must be included.

Name _____

Address _____

City _____ State/Zip _____

VISA Card No. _____ Exp. Date _____

Signature _____
                                                    351-07